Job-Boj

Jorge Guzmán

JOB-BOJ

Translated from the Spanish by Monica Ruiz Anderson

DALKEY ARCHIVE PRESS

Originally published in Spanish by Seix Barral as *Job-Boj* in 1968.
Copyright © Jorge Guzmán
Translation copyright © 2017 by Monica Ruiz Anderson
First Dalkey Archive edition, 2017

Libary of Congress Cataloging-in-Publication Data
Identifiers: ISBN 978-1-62897-1-651
LC record available at https://catalog.loc.gov/

Partially funded by a grant by the Illinois Arts Council, a state agency.
Traducción financiada por el Consejo Nacional de la Cultura y las Artes, Fondo para el Fomento del Libro y la Lectura, convocatoria 2016.

www.dalkeyarchive.com
Victoria, TX / Mclean, IL / Dublin

Dalkey Archive Press publications are, in part, made possible through the support of the University of Houston-Victoria and its programs in creative writing, publishing, and translation.

Printed on permanent/durable acid-free paper

Introduction

FIRST PUBLISHED IN 1967, *Job-Boj* is Jorge Guzmán's first work of fiction. The story takes place in Bolivia, the US, and Chile, territories that the narrator describes through the dominant emotions of the two main characters: enthusiasm, pleasure, intense pain, perverse fear, and hope. These feelings are so often entangled with one another that it becomes unclear whether they belong to two distinct personalities, or to one person. A bold and gifted writer, Guzmán's innovative storytelling will keep the reader guessing and captivated from beginning to end.

As Michael Doudoroff put it, Guzmán is "one of the best-kept secrets in recent Spanish American fiction." This statement calls to mind Umberto Eco's position that there are, in the history of literature, gems that may never be valued as such. Dalkey Archive Press believes this to be so. After its many years out of the spotlight, *Job-Boj* will finally have its day. The narrative of *Job-Boj* not only crosses regional borders; it also transcends time by remaining current even today, fifty years after its first release. *Job-Boj* was among the first works of postmodern fiction in Chile. The book's cosmopolitan and urban themes focus on the effects of modernization and class mobility in the 1950s and 1960s. Beyond its postmodern style—and in fact an intricate part of it—the book also makes many intertextual references to works from the Spanish Golden Age, Heidegger, Shakespeare, the Bible, mythology, and Latin American poetry. This relationship with masterpieces of Western culture feels natural and lends the novel—perhaps counterintuitively—a welcome contemporaneity.

While Guzmán's writing often takes on the assembled form of postmodern experimentation, the fragmentary aspects of such form are often drawn together in his work by a more fundamental principle of complementary polarity. This can be identified in his two historical novels based on significant periods and characters of Chilean history. Both *Ay Mamá Inés* (1993) and *La ley del gallinero* (1999) emphasize the power struggles of two antagonistic social factions. The competing ideological perspectives of the narratives affirm the existence of a widespread regional *mestizaje*—the mixing of languages, cultures, histories, and ethnicities—of which no character on either side is excluded. As highly conceptualized as Guzmán's novels can be, his narrative craft is to make his theoretical vision a naturalized element of the narration. Consequently, he must not fear what Stendhal did: that political events do not belong in a literary text. In Guzmán's *oeuvre*, the polarities of politics instead map out the terrain on which the novels progress.

Guzmán's historical novels garnered great recognition in Chile and *Ay Mamá Inés* won all the awards that Chile bestows upon narrative works. *Con ojos de niño* received the 2008 Critics Choice Award in Chile. It is a tale of two poor children and their distinct roads to finding happiness in the midst of their extreme poverty. *Cuando florece la higuera* received the Jaén Literary Award for Fiction in 2003. Its fragmented and decentered narrative further confirms Guzmán as a bold and skillful novelist. Yet polarity drives this narrative forward as well, with the contradictions among those who support Pinochet's repressive regime and those who oppose it. Similarly, *Deus Machi*, Guzmán's latest novel, has two opposing cultures, the Mapuche and the Spanish, and although the latter enslave and mistreat the former and rob them of their territory, the Mapuche's presence remains in the souls of the victors, especially the main characters.

Job-Boj does not escape Guzmán's polar logic: the character Job faces his opposite and mirror image, Boj. Boj is concerned only with his egocentric and hedonistic desires, be it food, drink, merriment, or sex. He is single, a co-owner of a successful business, has many friends, and spends all his time enjoying his work during the day and partying at night. He dares to do all, and fears nothing. His future is rife with possibilities as he contemplates either married life or a prospecting adventure into the Bolivian jungle. In contrast, Job fears everything: women, failure, and even himself. In spite of these evident differences, however, the reader might see them as two sides of the same coin. These two characters, with very different expectations, will find a type of rare union at the conclusion of the novel.

As its name suggests, *Job-Boj*, a palindrome, has two story lines representing two distinct periods in the narrator's life, one the mirror image of the other. It is structured with no explicit clarification about the relationship between the two. The reader might gather from clues dropped throughout, however, that the two stories represent distinct periods in the life of one man. As an older man, the protagonist-narrator remembers his past life of self-indulgence, his carousing friends, and his young lover. The narratives he weaves are composed primarily of interior monologue where the reader can sense the humor, lunacy, lust, impotence, self-adulation, and nostalgia he feels about his former life. It can be said that *Job-Boj* has two souls, two consciousnesses, two bodies, two worldviews, antithetical, but not mutually exclusive. One can think about affirmation, happiness, and animalistic pleasure while at the same time meditating on life and death, fear of what the future may hold, or fear of solitude, depression, and abandonment.

Guzmán's novel demands an active, vigilant reader, who will be attentive to the subtle changes in setting and mental state of the narrator as the storyline progresses. After a while one finds oneself feeling an enormous amount of pleasure in going from the self-satisfied, narcissistic, and hedonistic worldview of Boj to the depressed and complaining Job. What unites the two is the temperament of the novel that balances one against the other with a light and intelligent irony.

The initial and alternating chapters, indicated by Arabic numerals, depict the narrator's life as a young man, living as an expatriate Chilean in Cochabamba, Bolivia as he feverishly prepares for his lover's arrival. In the chapters with Roman numerals, the character's life is depicted approximately a decade later as a married thirty-something academic living in Texas and the several years as a graduate student leading up to that point. He now has a wife, but no friends, and his time is spent complaining and being unhappy. The narrative traces his mental state from periods of feeling paranoia, humiliation, failure, irritation, and uncertainty through a deterioration that culminates in complete mental breakdown.

Job-Boj received a prestigious second place prize from Biblioteca Breve de Seix Barral in 1966. For some 20 years, Guzmán did not write fiction, but dedicated his time to literary research and publications. He has written several research papers for various Latin American journals and has published a number of scholarly books such as: *Una constante didáctico-moral del Libro de Buen Amor* (1963), *Diferencias latinoamericanas* (1984), and *Contra el secreto professional: lectura mestiza de César Vallejo* (1991).

His latest published work of fiction, a series of erotic short stories, *Cuerpos*, was published in 2014.

A translator's goal is to convey the spirit and effect of the original while maintaining its style. I have endeavored to respect the author's writing style and not oversimplify the novel in favor of readability. Where the author has opted to forego the use of punctuation, I have done the same. To preserve the authenticity of the Spanish text, I have left some words in Spanish, most of which, if not all, will be understood by the reader. In doing this translation my goal was not to translate Jorge Guzmán, but rather to rewrite the novel as he might have if English were his first language.

I would like to thank Dr. Jorge Guzmán for allowing me to translate his book, for his clear explanations, and for his great suggestions. I would like to thank my husband for his unwavering support and encouragement, my parents for never allowing me to forget my heritage, and my four sons for being my *raison d'être*.

"Here knights eat and sleep, and die in their beds, and make their wills before dying . . ."

—*Don Quixote*, Part I, chapter 6

"This insult is the penalty of my sin; and it is the righteous chastisement of heaven that jackals should devour a vanquished knight, and wasps sting him and pigs trample him under foot."

—*Don Quixote*, Part II, chapter 68

Job-Boj

1

As HUNGRY FOR pleasure as a dying beast, and for money as a gambler, she was traveling on the international train trailing after her long and unexpected telegram letting me know that love and the agonies of love were bringing her to me. I smiled, certain that by now my beloved must be showing off for someone, probably the hotel maid, the battery of her chaste and expensive looks. At the same time, the silent tooth of desire was undoubtedly gnawing at her lower belly, for her covetousness would always demand more funds than she could bring with her. Like a leopard that cannot change its spots. The long months we'd been apart were not enough to have changed her figure or her temperament. Luckily for me, I was ready to revel in both. The news filled me with joy, making me even happier than I usually was. Her presence was the only thing I could ask for to fulfill the pleasure that made my heart swell endlessly. Nothing else could so enhance the beauty of the city, the loveliness of the sweet summer, and the joy that I derived from my work.

With the exception of the grocer woman, I had been perfectly celibate this entire time. By the time I went to bed every night in my clean, quiet, and lonely apartment, I very often realized that for many hours I hadn't uttered a single word. My romantic tryst had not lasted long. I now desperately avoided the woman. Her breath was foul with a peculiar type of halitosis that proliferated in the city. I likened it to curdled milk with honey, plus the smell of someone's gullet. I was never able to find out her marital status or any other worthwhile information. Ultimately, it was simply a failed attempt at pleasure in the midst of hard work and carnal yearnings. Whenever Leroy recalled the episode, he never failed to give me well-deserved praise for my sense of morality. I had to be very strong to reject the attentions of the lady while we went hungry and her store was bursting with cheeses, breads, and American preserves. The truth was that the shortage was serious and the appeals of a hungry Leroy were valid and did not fall on deaf ears. Yet there was also the issue of the bad breath and the exasperating desperate squash-shaped tits. To top it all off, along with her keys she left me a little note with a picture of a heart with an arrow through it and dripping blood that spelled out: "I desperately want to spend a night of pleasure with you. I'll be waiting for you at the store." The heart made Leroy laugh until he cried. It made me sad. What bothered me was the whole store thing. But neither sadness nor a potent temptation to eat regularly could make me forget what I already knew from very few and bitter past experiences. I returned the keys to their owner and went back to work.

Now, free from the woman's dispiriting company, I found that I was either kind of perplexed or tired. When I had the time and felt like being amused, I looked for entertainment far from the bedroom. I was happy to go on innocent dates with girls whose voices were sweet and demure, like all the girls from Cochabamba. I took them either swimming or to the movies. Also, I had developed a passion for dancing. I had learned to dance recently and from the moment I could take my first dance step I could think of no better way to truly enjoy myself. At the slightest provocation I would find myself praising dancing and was very public about my intention to make up for all the years in which ignorance had made me prefer other nonsense to this wondrous activity. Nothing could make me refuse an invitation. However, after a few months of deep enjoyment, I had begun to notice that friends and acquaintances were quietly organizing dances behind my back. I had to keep my eyes open for the slightest signs and even put on a poker face when I was able to guess a time and place so that I would be able to crash the party and dance all night until my partners withered on me. I was saddened when Leroy told me that two or three phenomenal brawls that had ensued on different occasions were blamed solely on me. It was said that they all came about because of my habit of showing up alone; and it was true that I did, but only so I could choose a good dance partner. I didn't mean to offend anyone.

The telegram gladdened me. It was almost jumping in my pocket while I was having breakfast at Bar Ayacucho. As always, it was nearly half past seven and I had a strong cup of Yungas coffee and four soft-boiled eggs in front of me, my eyes glued to the waist or calves of the young waitress. Odd girl. She was an extraordinary beauty, but had an expressionless face. I never got more than a sentence out of her and she was never friendly or pleasant. She worked like a machine. At one in the morning, she was still taking orders from the pool hall at the back and at seven I would invariably find her serving breakfast without moving one facial muscle. Noticing the ruffian-like appearance of the owners of the bar, I imagined that she was their shared lover and that they'd threatened her with atrocious punishments if she didn't show customers an iron exterior. She did, however, get upset once. I had just settled in for lunch at my usual table, and as soon as she saw me, she came over, swiftly and efficiently, with a bowl of soup in hand, and spilled it all over my jacket and pants. Although the liquid was hot enough to burn and I felt I had the right to feel offended, the energy with which I jumped to my feet was over-the-top; so was the look of rage on my face. Nevertheless, I was touched when I saw the startled expression that paralyzed her. Her beautiful, almond-shaped eyes had widened to the point of being scary; a barely visible tremor rattled her chest and shoulders. All her muscles had stiffened from the intensity of her emotions. She swallowed with difficulty, as if her mouth were dry, and then burst out laughing. If I'd been able to discern even the slightest bit of remorse in her irresistible laughter, if her delight hadn't been so free and relished, things probably would have been less painful for me, but I had the impression that she was earnestly looking for pieces of potato or noodles on me so that she could laugh even harder. And with each new discovery, her laughter intensified. Since then, whenever she served me, her face expressionless, it somehow reminded me of my own perplexed and dirty appearance as I held the front of my pants with my thumb and index finger to keep away the sweltering clothes. Only when her back was turned was I able to discreetly enjoy her beauty. Now, I remembered that Blanca would be in the city, near this very place tomorrow; that she was now having breakfast hundreds of miles away, staring at the sea, suitcases packed. I felt my face burning up as I looked at the waist of the little waitress while she was walking away.

What sounded like a sleepy elephant walked up the stairs. Over the steps came Leroy's head, his hair still wet from the shower, searching for me in the empty room. On his face was the expression he wore when he was about to tell a lie. He dropped onto the chair, frowning, and with just a hint of his usual booming voice, ordered a tea with lemon and aspirin. Then, as the girl walked away, he corrected, "No, two aspirin," but he had to repeat it a little louder to be heard. He began to move his eyes and head toward me heavily. And since I didn't feel like hearing his story, I put an affectionate hand on his forearm, instead of on his mouth.

"Ssssshhhhhhh. Quiet, old man! Don't get excited. I'm going to tell you what's going on. Everything hurts right now, even your hair. The only reason you are not crying is because you are a man. Isn't that right? The wisest thing you could do would be to call in sick today. It's Saturday and you need to see a doctor and you won't be able to tomorrow. Right?"

"No . . . don't be . . . don't be . . . stop screwing with . . . people," he responded, his voice tired and full of loathing.

"Wait, Leroy old man, wait. I think all this has to do with last night's carousing. I don't know why I think that, you know, I just have a hunch, a sixth sense. Listen, you bloody moron, don't you think it's getting a little wearisome that every single weekend Tu Padre, Osvaldo and that animal Musarana, beat the crap out of you at poker and then drag you to Perla Azul to buy liters of counterfeit whisky with the money they just won from you and then dance with the beauties there that don't have ten healthy teeth among them?"

"Ah, no. No, man. That's where you're wrong. There were

three new ones that looked like goddesses. Osvaldo fell head over heels in love with Clarita, and we couldn't even get near the other two."

"Fine, fine. I get it. The flesh is weak and all of that, but at least forget about poker."

Leroy stared at me, nodding, as if my words had finally revealed to him the error of his ways. However, he did so very deliberately, to demonstrate the seriousness of his ailment. All of this showed me how determined he was to call in sick, and to get me to support him on that.

"True. You are absolutely right. It's stupid. You are absolutely right. These bastards have taken me for a fool. Last night I had to lend Osvaldo money to pay for Clarita because he forgot the money he'd won off me at the house. That's the last straw. But, you know something, bro? This is it. It's over. No more. Hey, but now I'm dying. Everything hurts. I'm serious. Just thinking about the sound of a saw, it's like it's going right through my brain. Man, that chick is gorgeous. Why does she have to walk around all day like she's PMSing? Don't you agree?"

"Look, Leroy, I'm going to make a list again of all the things we have to do today," I said quickly, because the girl was approaching with my friend's order and I feared she might have overheard the comment. Also, I had to find a way to keep from laughing, because it was true that the poor girl looked like she was PMSing. "I already made you one yesterday, remember? The machines are in miserable condition. We have to solder a couple of new saws, lock them, and sharpen them. We have to sharpen the blades of the edger. We have to grease and clean all the others. Shall I list them? The band saw, the jigsaw . . ."

"OK, OK, OK."

"And we have two sick workers. And don't suggest the Pamani brothers, they have a specific contract. So have a man's breakfast, not tea with lemon, and grin and bear it."

That last part was for the benefit of the girl as much as for Leroy, who had a stoic expression on his face as he stared in despair at the cup she'd just placed before him with two packets of aspirin artistically positioned on the plate. If she had noticed my manly speech, no one could say by looking at her stony expression as she removed the cutlery I was no longer using. Leroy suddenly perked up.

"That's it! You've got it! What I am is terribly hungry. That's what I am, bro. But there's no time; the truck comes at seven thirty; there's five minutes left. What do you say? I'll order a steak and eggs, a few hot peppers and I'll come in half an hour . . ."

I cursed at him some more, rather unenthusiastically, because I was running out of resolve. He had to decide whether to wait for lunch or gorge on bananas when we drove by the La Cancha marketplace. He painfully swallowed his tea and aspirin and stood up immediately to showcase his determination and bad mood. When we passed by the counter, I took the opportunity to remind the owner that as of the next day I would not be eating breakfast or lunch at his establishment. My reminder was casual and the man rewarded me with a bland smile. I had paid for all my meals until Sunday, so he probably couldn't have cared less if I dropped dead right then and there.

We went down the dirt-covered stairs and upon exiting the building Leroy's eyes narrowed at the glorious brightness of the morning. The gesture seemed almost blasphemous to me because I found the cleanness of the air and the greenness of the trees of the town square so refreshing. We sat on a bench to wait for the truck. Without looking, Leroy refused the cigarette I offered him. As I lit mine and filled my lungs with luminous air and smoke, he stretched out his legs and let his head hang back as if to sleep and took a deep breath.

In the middle of the deserted square I removed some snot from my nose to get more airflow, and while I hurried to unstick it from my finger before Leroy opened his eyes, I checked out the windows of the buildings. For a few minutes I didn't notice anything; then someone opened the shutters of one that was almost right in front of us, on the second floor of the Paris Hotel, at the arches of the town square. I wondered whether it had been a woman's head that I'd seen. Almost immediately, the neighbor's window opened just as I had gotten rid of the snot and was rubbing my fingers against the slightly dusty bench. It was a woman who had surely just left the bed or maybe stayed up all night with a man, as Blanca would do with me tomorrow: wrapped in transparent clothes, naked, perfumed, smooth, warm, accommodating, satisfied, and asleep. The windows of the hotel remained open and deserted, shedding light on who-knows-what scene; she had retired inside. It occurred to me that perhaps she'd gotten up at that hour to breastfeed her eighth child.

A small figure hobbled down the sidewalk alongside the arches. The hurried animal-like quality of his movements made me smile. He stumbled on the last of the three steps leading to the street, almost bumped into a sleepy police officer and waved at me with kindness. Before leaning in to take the padlocks off the metal security gates, he waited until I had removed the cigarette from my mouth and returned his greeting. The affable Jew thought me very rich or at least I assumed he did because every once in a while I shopped at his store for pieces of bad ivory or good crystal at the request of any one of my friends who thought himself less refined. The metal gates shook the empty street with the clatter of tin. It had always intrigued me that he arrived so early at his shop. Before slipping inside, he gave me another friendly wave. Like a small, gentle mouse, quick despite the limp that he had from the concentration camp; I almost thought I had imagined him where he'd been just seconds before.

A gentle little breeze carried the scent of magnolias like the morning itself, fresh and new. An unperturbed black cat crossed the street, very deliberately, observing everything with caution. He even found a quiet place to lift one of his paws and lick it with long and careful tongue strokes before moving onto the sidewalk. On the other side of the portals, the truck showed up moving quicker than usual. Leroy was still sprawled on the bench, his face turned toward the foliage, his eyes closed. I raised my hand and quietly let it fall on one of his shoulders with as much heaviness as I could muster.

"Get up, you nitwit, Flammini's here."

"Oww! Miserable bastard!" he moaned, stiffening. One could almost see the waves of pain crashing against the walls of his skull. "Ouch! Bastard, how could you even think to do that? I feel like my eyeballs are going to pop out if I open my eyes." For a while, he remained with his head sunken between his shoulders and then slowly separated his eyelids, looking very determined.

"Listen, I can't go to work today. I'm serious, man. Why go if I can't even stand up? Right?"

The truck parked at the corner and Flammini urgently stuck his head out to see what was going on. When he saw me approaching, he stuck it back in, but I could see the fingers of his left hand tapping impatiently on the steering wheel.

"Don't forget we're getting paid for the dining tables today," I yelled at Leroy from beside the truck.

Of course, I had no intention of paying him one red cent. He'd already spent his portion in advances. But I was sure that the mere mention of money, the simple scent of a bill, would make him feel better. He dragged himself onto the truck.

"So what's up with him?" Flammini asked me, his voice full of understanding.

"He's seriously ill," I replied, as Leroy was painfully scrunching his body to fit into the cab. He finally sat down, acting as if his bones were made of glass or as if there were tacks on the seat. He greeted Flammini by agonizingly pushing a few syllables out of his mouth.

"So it was true then," Flammini commented as he put the truck in first; Leroy looked at him. "That he was dying, I mean. If Leroy continues like this, he'll for sure die on us any day now, che," he added, as if asking for my opinion. I decided to ignore him.

He drove as always, carefully and slowly. But despite his restraint, it seemed to me that with his half smile of distant concern he had wanted to imply that we were somehow to blame for the slight delay. I was hoping he would keep up his tradition and provoke Leroy into a technical discussion, and forget his penchant for always blaming us.

"Dammit! When are they going to understand that streets are for cars?" he said. And he was right. We were going past the La Cancha market and there were countless indigenous men with slanted eyes and *cholas* in their *polleras* walking in front of the truck or suddenly running across the road or just standing there chatting, so he had to slow down. After yelling "shit" several times, he must have gotten bored because he hung on to the horn, hit the gas and we sped past like a flash amid an avenue of frantic leaps and swearing in Quechua that none of us understood. Leroy's dying demeanor had been improving as we moved away from the city center and he was now beginning to look very awake. He was getting annoyed at what Flammini was doing and asked him innocently:

"How about if we run over a few little puppies, don Esteban?"

Flammini loved dogs. I glanced at him to see if his expression changed and looked like it had that time they almost got into a serious altercation. Leroy found barking annoying when he was driving, so if the miserable dog started running next to the front tire, he would veer slightly and catch him with the back one. The worst part was that Flammini was also driving that day, and the little animal overdid it. This gave Leroy enough time to gently nudge the steering wheel while Flammini's guard was down. Several weeks later, when the poor foreman could finally discuss the matter, he said that he'd had several sleepless nights because just as he was on the brink of falling asleep he would again hear the crunching sounds of the dog's bones. Whenever he remembered that sound and the insomnia, his face would grimace as if he'd swallowed something disgusting.

"Don't be a savage," he said dryly. But it didn't take him long to recover. His vindictive intentions were a little distracted while he concentrated on dodging deep potholes as the pavement came to an end. The urban district ended there, but the only part of the dirt road that needed attention was at the beginning. Having weathered the potholes, he asked absent-mindedly:

"So what are you going to do today?"

"The same as always: work."

"How? And didn't you already finish the patio furniture that you were making to send to Santa Cruz?"

"No, not even close. We haven't even started it yet. What we did finish were the dining room sets for Koké."

"I see. So then today you'll be starting on the patio sets? They are patio sets, right?"

"To be honest, don Esteban, I don't know."

"What do you mean you don't know?"

"I don't know if we'll get to them today or not. Why do you ask?"

"No reason. I thought you would spend the morning just doing maintenance."

"That's what I wanted, but I don't know if we'll be able to. I think we're going to be pretty busy. I think Pablo rented out the machines to the Pamanis who have an urgent contract."

The foreman did not respond. I turned to look at the road ahead full of satisfaction because the only goal of all that intrusive questioning had been to piss me off. As if saying: Of course I remember that dog, and I also know don Pablo gave his permission to lend the machines out, and you two don't. And of course you're not going to clean or fix any fucking machine, because you may very well be partners and dog killers and defenders of *cholos*, but don Pablo is the owner and the Pamani brothers will be using everything and will delay you by at least one day, ha, ha, ha." But as the wise saying goes: "The best laid plans of mice and men often go awry" and the same goes for the intentions of my friend Flammini, whose taunting had backfired because the Pamanis were excellent individuals and would probably even end up helping us, if they were able to.

As it always happened in cases like this, Flammini tried to show off his European education and started whistling *A Hero's Life*. I kicked Leroy in the shin, he was a talented musician, after all, and they performed a duet. After a few beats, Flammini was teaching my friend how to whistle it right. There you go! In the midst of the dispute, we arrived at the factory. Ramón had just opened the second side of the gate; he was holding a piece of bread and a lit cigarette in his left hand, finishing breakfast. We were greeted with a wave and that engaging smile of his that showed the stumps of blackened front teeth. Behind us, in a cloud of dust, came a truck full of workers, also late. They began slowly getting off, laughing and teasing, and dispersed into the empty storehouses, as if swallowed by the peace and the morning light and the environs of the silent machines.

"Good morning, Ramón. The aluminum is coming today," said Flammini. Ramón was facing the other way and shaking his head at someone asking him something from the truck shed. "Ramón, Ramón, the aluminum is coming today."

"Good morning. What aluminum?"

"From the aircraft coolers; to make the floor tile molds. We'll see if your idea works."

"Finally! Did you get them from Lloyd Aereo? What time are they bringing them?"

"Don Pablo and I picked them out last night. I think they're bringing them this morning," Flammini stated, looking at his watch. Then he started walking quickly toward the warehouses.

After three tries, the motor of one of the dump trucks started. Then the others followed. Their cabs shook with their tiny drivers inside, warming up. Nearby, the compressors of the tile section huffed and puffed. As I walked toward the warehouses to change, I became aware again of my contentment. The workday had begun. Tonight I would play poker, or go to the movies, or dancing; anything to keep me from waiting impatiently; and tomorrow, Blanca.

I

IT'S ELEVEN AT night. My confident and self-assured dance partners either smile at me amicably or look over my shoulder at other men they like better. Nevertheless, they are so exquisitely polite that they converse with me interestedly and enthusiastically between numbers. It's true that my current partner, for example, indulges me right now by paying me close attention, and even seems to have a real desire to stay by my side while at the same time making sure that I don't get bored. I feel good with her, and a little less alienated from these people; she has a snub, hesitant and welcoming nose. She does not dance very well, but does so with ease and abandonment, meekly letting me lead her, but without paying much attention to the music. She helps me tolerate the bits and pieces of conversations that I hear as I pass by and the gestures I see as we move around the room. Nonetheless, I am still waiting for Victoria's arrival. It isn't an intense desire, but if I decided to come tonight it was more than anything so that I could see her. And now I'm missing her golden hair, her strong body, and her somewhat weary voice.

Carlos, the head of the *Instituto Autonomo de Investigación* at which I've ended up, is trying to be wittingly festive over at one of the corners of the room. He routinely bores me to tears or to total distraction so I believe he dislikes me very much. We voted him in and his power is mostly symbolic, so it astonishes me to see him so regularly surrounded by some of us, creating a forum for worn-out and trivial discourse where they discuss and quote public readings. They are "*Dasein*" for the moment, smiling and posturing. Others, who know him well, say that he's an excellent

15

man. Now, as my dance partner distractedly pushes her belly into my hip, they are selecting records and joking about their *Verlässlichkeit*. As I pass by the group, one of them questions the metaphysical character of the recordness of records in general, somewhat jokingly, and a bit because he obviously doesn't know what he's talking about. He also started recently, like me, and perhaps for that reason nobody bothers to give him much information; they limit themselves to looking at him with a hint of malice and a dose of bonhomie. To change the subject, Carlos announces that he would like to dance a tango. One of the men from the group suddenly feigns grief and asks loudly, frowning from the effort, whether or not electronic gramophones meet that ideal that objects have, *kalokagathia*. How shameful and discouraging to think that Victoria is also corrupted by these affable and pleasant semi-scholars, sorry excuses for men who put in one or two hours of hard work per week, irresponsible bastardizers of culture. She must now be lowering her splendid body into a modest desk chair, lost in those little booklets where she polishes her classical languages or her German and then back to Greek Lyric or Rilke in the original only to have these demigods of masturbation and laziness disgrace them. She must be sitting as she always does with her shoulders thrown back, her neck bent, her hands lying listlessly on her lap or on the table. She does not look up if she's interrupted; she simply turns her head a little and responds with a combination of harshness and affection.

"Hey, don't you think they could talk about something else, especially when they are at a party?" I ask my partner, as I point to Carlos's group.

She makes a gesture of annoyance without looking at me, and we separate because the song we were dancing to has come to an end.

"Let's rest a bit," she says, turning her back to me.

While she searches for a place for us to sit, I look her over from behind and note that under the extremely light dress, she has a very straight back, and a slim waist of which my right hand retains a steady and warm impression. From her torso up, she is very slim, but below the waist her figure spreads out somewhat too much. I wonder if my rude comment about her friends has earned me her anger or her approval.

The only things to sit on are a few mattresses that someone has arranged against the wall bent in half so that the bottom half can be used as the seat and the other half as a backrest. There is a huge nail, tied with a red ribbon, hanging from the lintel of the front door with a cardboard sign on each side that reads: "El Clavo Nightclub." I sit before my partner does to avoid an inevitable reflex: if her dress were to get tangled up as she was about to sit I would be right across from her, and without a doubt would stare at her legs until she blushed. She is in love with Carlos, so I have reason to believe that she probably didn't appreciate my observation very much.

"And Pablo is not even here yet," she says.

"Pablo who?"

"The secretary of the institute, Victoria's fiancé."

"Ah, right. Why? Is he a drag?"

"Why do you feign ignorance? Haven't you heard him at the Friday sessions?"

"Of course I have, but I never understand what he's saying."

"Lucky you. I get so exasperated that I can't even begin to think about anything else. I don't know if it's *what* he's saying or *how* he's saying it, but when he starts talking, I get chills."

"I think it's both," I say, pleased. "Because he doesn't know much about what he's talking about, but he says it with such obstinacy . . ."

"I'm so happy to hear someone say that," she interrupts me. "I have been mulling that over for the last two years, but I wasn't that convinced. Do you really think he doesn't know much?"

"Listen," I say, giving more weight to my reflections by using a restrained and modest tone. "I don't know if he's ignorant about everything, but the times I've heard him giving a lecture about things that I know about, he has seemed very illiterate to me. And since he is forever teaching literature to critics, history to historians, and medicine to doctors . . ."

"Hey, what do you do?"

"What do you mean, what do I do?"

"Sure. What do you do for a living? Where do you work?"

"Well, here and at the university."

"At the university too? At the Universidad de Chile?"

"Yes."

"And how did they manage to convince you to work here?"

"Why? You don't think I should work here?"

"I don't know," she replies. "It seems odd. I . . . Is it true that you were in the jungle?"

But as I am about to respond to her, she shifts around and as she leans on her hand to do so, there's a crunching sound and she says: "Oh, I broke it." She picks up a fountain pen that neither of us had noticed before and it is bent in half.

"How stupid to leave it there!" I say, truly annoyed, because the conversation was starting to be about me and now, by the time we find the owner and explain what happened, the mood will be gone. "Let me see it; maybe it's not as damaged as it looks."

But it's even more damaged than it appears on the surface. The cap, when it twisted, took the tip of the pen with it and part of the body and left it looking like a flattened crab. As I am unable to repair it, or get back to our lost conversation, or to cheer up the look of dismay on my partner's face, I am thankful that at least it didn't have any ink in it.

"Can it be repaired?"

"I'd say no. The body's broken and the nib is splayed. Do you have any idea whose it might be?"

"It looks like Carlos's," she says and turns away, signaling to Carlos who is still in the middle of his original group at the other end of the room.

Carlos looks at her. After a number of her attempts to get his attention, he points to himself with his index finger and lifts his head interrogatively. She nods and he motions to us to wait a minute. He finishes the sentence she interrupted, and the group bursts out laughing. I feel slightly ridiculous with the remains of the pen in my hand, and the crowd's laughter makes me feel even worse. It makes me look at myself suddenly from the outside, at the possibility that others have noticed the long time I have spent with my partner, because in truth we have been in a rather long and familiar conversation. Well, perhaps everyone has noticed and has criticized me for being so ridiculous. Carlos comes up to her and says, smiling:

"Yes? Did you want something?"

"Is this your pen?"

Before taking it from my outstretched hand, Carlos hurriedly feels his jacket pockets. Then he reaches for the remains that I am offering and holds them up to his eyes because the room is blanketed in a pleasant darkness.

"Of course it's mine," he says indignantly. "The only thing that's left to do now to is throw the piece of garbage away," he adds while glancing around the room as if looking for a waste paper basket.

My partner's repentant expression annoys me. But mostly I find Carlos's rudeness intolerable; I was almost starting to fall in love with this woman who is so sweet-smelling and with such a docile waist and, incidentally, is so interested and caring, when the pen came to be under her hand and ruined everything. Because she's now crushed by Carlos's wrath and she looks up at him.

"Where did you find it?"

"I broke it," she says. "I leaned on it with my hand without realizing that it was there."

"Didn't you see it?"

"Well, no. No, I didn't, Carlos. It's very dark in here . . ."

"Fine, it doesn't matter, don't worry about it," states Carlos as he turns his back to us and leaves.

I feel nauseated. The ignorant brute left just as I was about to take matters into my own hands, I tell myself. But that's not true. I know that I've become pale and that I can barely control my breathing. The truth is that I was scared and I don't know why. The fact is that from the first moment I have been choking on the words I would have uttered if I dared. She looks at me quickly and a cold, embarrassed tingle travels down my spine. There is still time to stand, walk toward the group that Carlos has rejoined, and say to him: "Listen, old man, I didn't at all like the way you treated her, and if you don't go over there right now and apologize I am going to have to teach you how to treat women." But I also know that I won't dare and that is what is humiliating for me. How would the group look at me if I did that? She herself might even consider that I am intruding in her relationship with Carlos. Additionally, the scandal of a physical fight would force me to leave the institute. I look at her again and notice the womanly heaviness of her thighs, the gently curved belly, the fineness of the waistline just below the small breasts . . . The complexity of her gesture could be understood as angry, or embarrassed, or understanding, or even simply jovial. I sit back down again, sick with humiliation, and again know that I will not do what I need to do to get rid of it. A lot of time will have to pass before she will get over the impression she now has of me. A wave of anger ravages my ribs from the inside, but I fear looking even more ridiculous, having to give up all the plans and projects that I have for myself at the institute. I don't know if I am afraid or not that Carlos could beat me if I had to fight him, but I internally consider the possibility and it horrifies me.

"Hey, can you do me a favor?"

"Sure," she answers, almost eagerly.

"Can you get me a drink?"

She gets up immediately, smiling as if everything were normal, and lists the types of liquor available. I ask her to bring me the strongest one she can find, then I watch her as she moves away toward the kitchen.

I am very relieved at her quiet kindness but do not rejoice; I would like to have a thousand hours to talk to her and see if we can reestablish a healthy relationship that is free and characterized by sexual desires, even if we ultimately remain as indifferent as we have always been. I would like for her to meet my frolicking and cavorting friends of the past so that they can tell her who I am, or at least who I used to be. It is, however, absurd to imagine them in the midst of these people.

Victoria comes in. She ducks slightly as she walks under the nail and the posters. My dance partner returns with a drink of pure Pisco on the rocks and leaves immediately. I am grateful, because I've suddenly realized that I urgently need to urinate. I make my way across the room, walk by Victoria, who doesn't see me, engrossed in the enthusiastic welcomes she is getting from everyone. After passing through the hallway, I get to the bathroom. I manage to make out the figure of a woman adjusting something under her dress and I leave, apologizing incoherently. It's my dance partner. She walks out of the restroom unconcerned and relaxed and returns to the room without looking at me.

Inside the bathroom, I cannot find a safe place to put down my glass. Everything has been taken out of its original location and placed in full view on account of the move. I urinate at length while listening to the sound of the music in the distance and taking small sips of cold alcohol with true delight. I remember that I also forgot to lock the door and let my bladder keep emptying almost by itself as I try to decide if I should stop the operation. I hear a few footsteps down the hall and I rush to the door feeling the cold liquid and air. When I start again, trying to keep whoever is outside from hearing me, my eyes fill with tears.

Back in the room, I discover Victoria dancing with Carlos. She looks much happier than I've ever seen her, but I feel certain displeasure when I notice that she's laughing too much. Carlos flirts with her; it's apparent that at intervals he considers that what he's about to say deserves a moment's pause. He moves away a little from Victoria and complements what he is about to say with his right hand raised, palm forward, like a cop jokingly directing traffic.

Carlos's group has disintegrated and poor Dagoberto is standing alone beside the turntable not knowing what to do with himself. He insistently tries to catch my eye as I move to observe Victoria better. The miserable individual cannot dance, but instead, believes that he dominates modern philosophy and that I need to be instructed in it. He looks determined to find an audience. My partner is nowhere in sight. Anyway, after the pen incident and especially after the bathroom fiasco, it would seem to me a little unseemly to ask her to dance. The groups have dispersed; almost everyone is now dancing and Dagoberto could not find the courage to approach anyone, not even to move away from the turntable where Carlos's group left him when it split up. He puts one hand in his pocket, sticks out his chest and glances around at the couples dancing. Now, since he cannot stay there moving his head from side to side like a beacon, he starts to despair, his heart sinks and he ends up pretending to examine the record jackets. I feel almost duty bound to yield to the pity I feel for him and let him give me a small lecture on something, but I feel like dancing.

There's a good rhythmic broken tango playing and I am dancing with Victoria. Even now that I am embracing this woman that I barely know, I keep mentally repeating to myself: "Will you risk dancing with me, Victoria?" It seems to me a truly sophisticated way to ask, and I am still reveling that she limited herself to smiling and opening her arms to allow me to hold her, because she couldn't think of what to say. I find her body surprising at first. It amazes me that she has a solid but perceptible layer of fat around her waist. I also never expected the firmness and abandonment with which she puts her hand in mine. Is this the same girl who is preparing a paper on the theme of death in Rilke? Because it's not only this new tactile sense of her body that's amazing; the pleasure she made me feel when she first agreed to dance with me has now turned into the bliss of dancing with her. This woman reveals the essence of the dance; she follows my lead like a slave drunken with joy and enthusiasm who can guess my intention at the slightest hint. As soon as we complete a move or change steps, I feel like she already knows the direction and rhythm and speed that I was going to impose and follows me even before I know what I want. I don't know if she feels the same way, but I think she cannot be oblivious to what she does and what she creates, that, she too, like me, is being rocked by a true miracle. She keeps her gaze fixed on the floor, so I cannot see her expression. There is a misstep for a second and she immediately looks up at me as if accusing me while at the same time asking me to not let it happen again. I'm not holding her firmly enough. We are too far apart. When she feels the tension of my arm around her waist, she tilts her head back again and lets herself be absorbed by the music. Her dancing is becoming more and more adaptable, submissive, and enthusiastic. It seems as though we are finding each other endlessly, over and over again, wherever my body goes, we are moving together in space, to my renewed surprise and delight. And each time, as she passes through these rhythmic avenues in the air, the beginning of a new step is there for me to lead her into and she will launch herself into it with a profoundly animalistic, violent, yet sweet force. We finish the dance.

"Wait," she says to me, without looking up.

She breaks my hold, leans heavily on my arm and throws her shoes aside, shaking her feet, without caring where the shoes might land.

Wonderful woman, wonderful, strong, and beautiful animal, wonderful wonder. Fill my heart again and again and again with your presence. Because it would be awful if I were to suddenly open my arms to hold you and you were not there; this dirty lie of institutes and scholars, this filthy hall of mirrors where men and women take the form of sheets of newsprint, would again become reality. Do not forget that Carlos is waiting, right over there in the world next door with a broken pen in the heart; that Dagoberto has countless lectures written in some folder. If you return to me every time, perhaps I can still keep seeing what you allow me to discover simply by holding you: the meaning of being a man or a woman, the possibility of finding happiness in the truth.

The dance has finished and has left us orphaned. We walk alone through the silent streets as if searching for something.

"Do you want to take me somewhere?" she asks, quietly.

"No. Just home, Victoria. These things don't last, you know?" I say, and feel as if I've just crushed every bone in my body.

2

THINGS WERE NOT looking good for me at all. It's impossible to play a good poker game when one's stomach is so distended after eating a full lunch and then fifteen empanadas. The fact that Leroy had put away another fifteen didn't matter to me. At any rate, he was a fish at poker and therefore insignificant. What did concern me was my frame of mind. My eyes were darting up and down the sun-shimmering walls and along the asphalted streets, as if looking for a sheltered place to rest. From my bloated stomach a talkative and stupid happiness rushed to my head. My armpits were damp and I was experiencing a carefree camaraderie with my friends as we chatted up the street satiated with food and laughter, none of us very alert, and our feet dragging. I personally would have been able to pinpoint the swampy region of my brain, way in the back, where my spirit had weakened, debilitated by food and heat, and that was now napping in a dark and heavy haze. Leroy still had some energy left and talked and talked making a hornet-like buzzing sound. The only one that seemed to be following his story with some interest was Cacho. Apparently Osvaldo didn't give a rat's ass about an old man he didn't know or the machine that had impaled him and I had been a witness to the accident. After going around in circles in his exasperatingly slow narrative, Leroy finally got to the part about the machine attacking the old man.

"Do you know what a wood shaper is?"

"No, shithead," replied Osvaldo, without looking up from the pavement.

"Listen, it's like a wood lathe that works vertically, but in the place where lathes have a tool rest, the shaper has a spindle and where the lathe has a spindle . . ."

"The shaper has a tool rest," Osvaldo interrupted.

"No, the shaper doesn't have a tool rest. And if you don't let me finish I'm going to throttle you, shithead."

"It's just that you never get to the point, idiot. I stopped listening to you four blocks ago and you're still going on about the same thing. Who cares about the shaper or the shitter or whatever the hell it is? Just tell us what happened to the old man. We're falling asleep."

"What happened is that he started the machine with two cutters that were much too big and one of them broke off and pierced him in the gut. I'd warned him. The machine moves at thirty-three hundred rpm."

"And where had he put the knife? In the spindle, or the tool rest, or the rpm?" asked Osvaldo

"If you don't stop screwing around, I'm going to stick a shoe up your rpm, Osvaldo, my dear," warned Leroy.

"OK, Osvaldo, stop messing around. Think of all the blood!"

Cacho and Osvaldo started arguing about old man Pamani's possibilities of survival. Cacho figured he was dead by now; the other one was betting that he was going to kick the bucket by Sunday morning.

"Old men are tough," he concluded. "The only thing that can do them in is early mornings and spring time. It's true, don't laugh."

I couldn't resist interrupting.

"And do you know what the heartless Leroy did? They laid the old man down in one of the offices and while they waited for the ambulance to arrive one of the secretaries squatted down beside him to console him. While she wiped away her tears with one hand, she rubbed the old man's forehead with the other. And this asshole sat down on a chair across from her so that he could look at her panties while the old man was bleeding to death."

"And what was the secretary like?" Osvaldo asked.

"Yolita," replied Leroy, excited. "You know her, the one with the freckles."

"Yolita! I totally agree. Totally agree. Even if he'd had to kill an old man, two old men, a whole squadron of old men. What color were they, Leroy, old buddy?"

"White and tiny."

"How fitting: the virginal color," said Osvaldo as he rubbed his hands together and rolled his eyes. Nobody laughed at his joke.

I had started sweating profusely from too much food and heat. In addition, a garrulous demon relentlessly prompted me to talk. And he who does not concentrate before playing is better off not playing; it's like asking for trouble. Now, if a wretched player is paying attention to each one of the hairs dripping sweat under his shirt, and chit-chat threatens to overflow from within him at any moment, playing is out of the question. To top it all off, almost all of my opponents had just received a month's pay, and it's not easy to clean out a rich man. When we arrived at the house, I was about to keep walking toward my place a mere two blocks away, but I stuck to the group out of sheer inertia. For the millionth time, Cacho was telling of the adventure of the dead woman's arm. He had stolen it from the cemetery one night after spying on the burial from behind a tree. He had no other choice but to steal it because she was the only one that was buried that day and he had to prepare for a class and corpses were scarce at school.

"Don't lie," Osvaldo interrupted, as always. "It was one of the only times that we were swimming in corpses. You just wanted to show off how macho you were, you philistine; that's all. You'd had a fight with Anita Jordan too and were feeling very romantic. Admit it."

"You're always talking nonsense and making people look bad," Cacho accused him, his eyes widening from resentment and rage.

Luckily, before Osvaldo could finish opening the gate and turn toward Cacho who was staring him in the back of the neck like a tiger ready to pounce, Landivar, Tu Padre, and Eugenio came around the corner. They were laughing their heads off and when they saw us yelled out an energetic "BRAVO!" that distracted Cacho. They were happy to see us; they were afraid they might have missed the weekly game. My lack of interest increased: there would be seven of us at the table. Landivar was the defining one. El Camba played like an angel. Necessity had made him a true professional; he sort of had to pay for his law studies by trapping fools at pool or poker, because with his salary he wouldn't have had enough to graduate as a cockroach.

"Musarana's not coming?"

"No. He had a bet with Mínima," said Tu Padre.

"Huh?"

"Zóxima; that pretty, skinny girl; the one that looks like a cat. Haven't you ever seen her? You must've seen her. She chases Musarana around like a foal chasing its mare. Her parents left this morning for La Paz and she locked herself in with Musa to see who could stay in bed the longest. Lucky son-of-a-bitch! Minima's so yummy and soft. That dirty old man must be having a blast," Osvaldo conjectured, glassy-eyed. "She's so yu-u-ummy!" he added, spellbound.

Musarana's absence allowed me to smile pleasantly at the new arrivals. I was glad that his recreational activities were keeping him away, because he was also a shark at poker. And I would need money by the bucketful if I was going to woo Blanca. I had to shower her with gifts. I had to take her dancing to Pascana, and to restaurants and swimming. If there was time, maybe we'd be able to fly to Santa Cruz for a few hot days. In the tropical summer, a woman's natural tendency toward wearing as little clothing as possible, which was so delightfully accentuated and enthusiastic in Blanquita, would find its home there, in the scorching heat.

A small dog that had been sleeping next to Osvaldo's door, jumped up, stretched out his back and legs in a sort of contented shudder, and, while Osvaldo looked for his key, sniffed us timidly one by one, stretching his neck out to reach our knees. He quickly lost interest and went to pee over by a garden stake.

"Careful! That one there, well, that's the dangerous one, che," laughed Landivar. "How can you be such a prick, che? Look at the little doggy . . . you almost can't see it."

"Quiet, Mediterranean," replied Eugenio, who was the one who'd climbed the tree that one time.

Leroy was quiet and helpful. The rest of us spread out across the room. He helped prepare the square plank that we used as a games table. When Osvaldo discovered that he'd misplaced the poker chips, Leroy immediately volunteered suggestions of possible hiding places and helped him check them. They started off by messing up a dresser, drawer by drawer. Inside the room, the heat was much more oppressive than outdoors. I thought I could feel the onslaught of the sun on the tin roof above our heads, creating a kind of heavy silence where the noise of others became sluggish and one felt drowsy. Tu Padre was perceptibly unraveling when they couldn't find the chips in any of the furniture. He ended up lying on the floor, his head on the pillow that he'd at first been sitting on. He seemed to be smoking only so that the smoke would come out of his mouth and he could stare at it through half-closed eyelids as it dissolved.

Eugenio had fashioned a stool for himself by placing various books atop one another. He looked pitiful sitting on it, leafing through a magazine. He was the epitome of someone who is not really looking at anything and tries to assume a certain posture so that no one will notice his inner misery. He must have been feeling the abyss of vice opening at his feet, the devouring vortex that leads to drugs, brothels, and the gallows. The first time Tu Padre invited him to a poker game, months ago, he almost wet himself from horror and surprise. Those things were immoral. Only greed had helped him overcome it, but now he felt like an elephant balancing on a high wire. "It's so hot," he said, looking out at the window. No one answered. He remained in the same spot, motionless. Then he asked my opinion directly: "Don't you agree that it's much too hot?"

He was within a hair's breadth of noticing that I was laughing at him. I was enjoying looking at his overall flabby shape and mainly, when he directed the question to me, I had just realized that his cheeks looked like buttocks; it was as if there was an ass gazing meditatively out the window. Luckily Tu Padre interrupted. He turned his eyes toward Eugenio, tucked his head into his pillow; pulled the saliva soaked, brown-stained cigarette out from between his lips and said, as if asking for strength:

"Sonny, Eugenio, my sweet Eugenito. I'll bet you one of my nuts, whichever one you prefer, that you'd rather be going swimming."

We laughed a little bit and Eugenio turned his facial butt cheeks to the magazine making a sulking sound. From the other side of the room, Leroy raised his voice to curse Osvaldo's mess. He had just piled all the books from a shelf in the middle of the floor and, standing next to the pile, was questioning Osvaldo about places that had perhaps escaped the search in the chaos of all the useless junk and garbage in the shithole that was his place. Osvaldo answered no, with much restraint, as if he hadn't heard the atrocities the other had just hurled at him. They'd looked everywhere, perhaps not well, but there was nowhere else to look. Leroy started up again. The only thing I wanted was for them to be quiet, because I was about to fall asleep. Finally, just as he was about to restart on the drawers, Leroy asked whether someone had borrowed them. Osvaldo turned to us furiously, yelling:

"Bastard!" He was screaming at Tu Padre, "Bastard!"

Tu Padre opened his eyes with deliberate leisureliness.

"Are you talking to me, Osvaldo? Are my ears deceiving me? Have I lived long enough for you to speak that way to your best friend in the world? To 'your father'? And all because of a few sad and worn poker chips? No. No. Oh, no. There's no friendship left in this world. No wonder we live with wars and revolutions and rape and assaults in abandoned . . ."

Osvaldo kicked him gently on the ribs.

"Stop this nonsense and go and get them. Look how we turned everything upside down, half-wit, and the bastard knew this whole time."

"Me go look for them, Osvaldo? Oh, no, son. No way. First insults, now orders? Never. Before getting up off here, I'd rather the world come to an end. Here are the keys to the prince's private bedchamber. If anyone wants poker chips and poker, let him move his ass and get them. You won't move me with a tow truck."

Osvaldo became pig-headed and wouldn't go. It was a great opportunity for him to go and prepare for a psychiatry test he had on Monday. Eugenio closed his magazine and got up off the books, somewhat hopeful and scared. Cacho, who'd been motionless in a corner, turned surprised at the ones arguing; but he immediately immersed himself in contemplation, staring at something that was walking up the wall that must have been very small; he was probably hoping that someone would finally ask him what had caught his eye. Tu Padre's hand was still raised, balancing his keychain in the air. Leroy walked toward him, took the keys, stepped on his stomach, and left the room.

"They are on my nightstand, my loyal servant," Tu Padre informed him.

After some time in which we all kept doing what we were doing, which was a sort of suspense-filled and boring existence, we could see the tip of Leroy's shoe hooking the bottom of the door to let its owner pass, carrying a box of poker chips in one hand, and in the other, a triumphant fruit bowl full of peaches. Tu Padre got up right away, dismayed and screaming bloody murder. He declared, almost in tears, that these were the most expensive peaches in all of Cochabamba and its surroundings; that they'd cost him more than a lover. All was in vain. As far as Leroy was concerned, the gigantic yellow drupes were payment for his sacrifice. Inspired by the spirit of Robin Hood, he wanted to share them with his friends. He gave us half a fruit each and kept two whole ones for himself. He put one aside for later and sank his teeth into the other making slurping sounds. The peach juice served as a pretext for me to ask Osvaldo for a towel and soap. I'd decided that I needed to run through a meticulous, almost ritualistic washing of those hands of mine if they were going to win. Leroy followed me to the bathroom. He looked like he had something important to discuss. I immersed myself in finding a place on the bathroom sink that was sufficiently neat for me to dirty with soap. While he pissed, Leroy was concentrating more than was necessary; I would have guessed that he was holding it in so that the process would last longer. Then he stood next to me with the obvious pretext of waiting for me to finish using the sink. I was massaging and scratching each playing finger without rushing, waiting to feel that inner signal that they were clean enough. Suddenly he said: "Hey, bro, I don't think I'm going to be able to play." Since I didn't reply he continued, "I'm flat broke. I got soaked last night . . . Hey, that bill; did they pay it this morning?"

"Hmmmm," I said. My left index-finger nail was not as perfect as I would have liked. It occurred to me that if I was going to keep playing poker, I would have to wear gloves each time I touched a stick of wood or worked on a motor.

"Hey, bro, could you spot me a little from the patio sets? Even if it's just a bit?"

"Listen, old man, truthfully, no. You know that the patio sets won't be ready for at least another two weeks, right? You know that Blanca is arriving tomorrow and that I need money. I'm sorry, but I can't."

Everything was in order. I returned the soap to the soap dish and proceeded to dry my hands.

"Fine, then I just won't play, that's all. What can I do about it?"

He looked offended and sounded as if I were to blame. It bothered me. I was hoping that the hand washing would refresh my thinking, would help me prepare for the game. If Leroy hadn't shown up with this excessive whining, by now I'd be concentrating on the only thing I cared about at the moment: beating the others. Instead, after his crap, I was almost ready to start washing my hands again. The worst part of it was that I couldn't get over the anger I felt over being angry.

"That's it, old man," I answered. "That's the best solution you could have come up with. And if you'd had the same idea these last three months, twice a week, on average, you'd be swimming in cash."

He did not respond and we left the bathroom in silence. Me, congratulating myself for my exemplary behavior; Leroy overwhelmed by the lesson and by the strength of my resolve. Or at least that's what I thought until I saw him settling in squarely across from me, between Tu Padre and Cacho, take out his wallet and get as many poker chips as the rest of us. Even though I knew him quite well, his nerve didn't fail to surprise me. I congratulated myself inwardly.

". . . and all because . . ." Cacho was saying, "Do you know what happened to the arm I was telling you about?"

"Of course: you forgot to inject it with formaldehyde, you left it in the can, went to sleep, and by the next morning it was completely rotten," recited Osvaldo, in a tired tone. Then he warned us, simulating alarm: "Don't ask him what he did with the arm. If you're still interested, I can make you a map even so that we can continue the game."

If Leroy hadn't intervened, things could have gotten much worse, because when Cacho ended up losing his patience you had to knock him unconscious to calm him down. He would have ruined the game for all of us and possibly Osvaldo's teeth. His tone, and Osvaldo's defiant and terrorized expression, bothered all of us when he declared that he couldn't take another word, and then insisted on asking over and over again:

"And, what are you going to do about it? Huh? What are you going to do? Huh? What are you going to do?"

"Kick the shit out of you, you fucking bastard," the other exploded.

"OK, OK, stop it," Leroy mediated with great control. "You're both going too far, especially you, Osvaldo."

As soon as Cacho felt supported, he calmed down immediately. He even apologized to us.

"It's just that Osvaldo tries one's patience; that's enough mocking. He's always interrupting and making people look stupid."

Osvaldo stayed quiet, endlessly shuffling a deck of cards. We all noticed, however, that his hands were shaking a bit. Landivar, who was quietly shuffling the other deck, rushed to start the game by dealing out our cards. Nevertheless, the altercation made the air tense and detrimental to the game.

Eugenio was sitting to El Camba's right. I thought the seating arrangement was disastrous for a fledgling little bird like him, and the poor guy was so keen too. It saddened me, moreover, seeing how his habitual puritan remorse had been transformed into a smile full of greed and faith in the future. I felt like grabbing him and literally kicking him off the table. Yet I was swayed by the possibility of him learning his lesson from the callous hand of experience. The sad thing was that his haughtiness was justified; in a previous game that we'd dragged him to, he had such an appalling run of good luck that he even managed to snatch a big pot from Landivar and me. By the time he got up off the table he was rolling in it. Since then he'd been convinced that all he has to do is sit down and ask for cards.

The whole thing started out quite apathetically. The unending search for the poker chips; Osvaldo and Cacho's argument; Leroy's victim-like expression; all of it contributed to cooling off the game. Even the hands were played with indifference. Only Eugenio seemed to take pleasure in everyone's lack of enthusiasm. He scrutinized our gestures as if looking for our fear at his presence. The expression on his face seemed to be saying "you asked for it" or "now you're going to get it." When it was his turn to shuffle he couldn't restrain himself and asked Landivar and me:

"So, turkeys, did you bring me my allowance? I hope you don't start up again like last time saying you don't have any more money."

"No need to worry, che. You know that playing with me is like playing with the Federal Reserve. And if you win too much off of us, I'll just sic the puppy on you," El Camba answered affectionately. Some laughed. The air was lighter. I ignored Eugenio. The one that was annoying me was Leroy, and I intended to leave him penniless. The game progressed without incident. Someone would win a little at a time and then someone else would win almost immediately. The light from the window stretched across the floor as the afternoon went on and grew hotter. After a while I started to feel the sun on my knees. At somewhat regular intervals, I was forced to buy chips from either Leroy or Eugenio, in front of whom a small little pile of winnings was starting to grow. But the growth was extremely slow; so slow, in fact, that Eugenio's nerves were starting to fray. Landivar and I were the sources of the money, but I was the one hurting the most. The rest were pretty much the same as at the beginning. The drawn out game was shifting small winnings from here to there and then back again, trying our patience. When Leroy asked us to pause the game so that he could eat his second peach, we disagreed for no reason. He decided to eat it regardless, without withdrawing from playing. He was a bit more excited than at the beginning.

"Osvaldo, buddy, lend me some cutlery so that I don't get the cards dirty."

"Stop being a pest. Stick the peach up your . . . somewhere," said Osvaldo absent-mindedly without looking away from what seemed to be an unlikely hand.

Leroy went ahead and sank his teeth into the peach. Osvaldo's naturalness helped dissipate the bad air from earlier. Cacho was the only one who didn't smile. The sun was now beating on my torso and I discovered that I just couldn't take it for a moment longer.

"Do you mind if I close the window?" I asked.

"Leave it, I will close it," said Osvaldo, getting up, still hypnotized by his cards. "It really is too hot."

The cool shade completely transformed the room. With my pupils still constricted I scanned the seated shadows of the other players. I told myself that I was experiencing intense comfort in the cool and light semi-darkness. Perhaps it was the change in the lighting that made Leroy lose control over what he had left of the peach. It flew out of his hands and landed on Landivar's pants.

"Nothing gets rid of peach juice stains," Tu Padre declared.

A tragedy for the poor Camba, we all realized, because the suit he was wearing was the only one he had in the world. The "twenty-oneliest" he called it. Even Leroy was worried, but Landivar behaved like the gentleman that he was and he even refused to interrupt the game to wash out the stain. I couldn't

care less about El Camba's nudity. I was saying to myself that
what had happened while I was washing my hands was happening once more; again I was on the verge of definitively concentrating on the game and again Leroy, the moron, had interfered.
It was just that this time, what annoyed me was the delay and
nothing else. Because in the shade, the sweat from my forehead
had dried and my body was now cool and refreshed. At the same
time, my inner self had become cheerful, predatory and ruthless.
The cards, my friends, every detail, were there as simple contrib-
utors for me to win the game. I felt the skin of my temples go
tense out of absolute anticipation and alacrity. Out of every fiber
of my being there was confirmation of the power that I'd found
within me to win the game. In this state, it's impossible to lose.
Just as it sounds: it cannot be done. How could it not annoy
me then, when Tu Padre, to my right, interrupted the dealing
of the cards and left everyone's hand there, lying on the table?
And all because that idiot Leroy had decided to leave Landivar
naked with his peach and get everyone's attention on his damaged pants instead of on greed, where I needed it to be. Because
luck is faster than time and I needed speed. I felt like I couldn't
lose. Not even Landivar's good playing, or Eugenio's ridiculously
good luck, even at its best moments, could take this power that
allowed me to so very easily dominate the game and the players. In an entirely natural way, it just so happened that the laws
governing this particular constellation that we'd neared a while
ago, that looked like chaos and disorder, had actually revealed
themselves to me. Moreover, what was happening was that the
Id, until then dominated and restricted by the sphere of hope,
of foolish temporariness, had suddenly exceeded its own limits,
reaching its true dimension and now covered the entire constellation, dominating it. And it was not, furthermore, anything dramatic. Sitting there in front of an incomplete game that awaited
me face down on the table, I could wait quietly for the peach
disturbance to end and then it would be my time, my time to
beat them. I was even sure that as soon as they fixated their eyes
again on their respective hands, they would respond immediately, for the first time that afternoon, to the rules of the game.

I simply set upon myself, as I directed a sympathetic smile to myself, the obligation of not speaking another word that did not have to do directly with the game, as the price of preserving my certainty. In the mood called luck, I was able to clearly perceive and determine at once: Leroy's awkwardness, Eugenio's keenness, Landivar's precise calculations and everyone else's vague hunger for victory. I was right, as soon as the hype over the pants was over, I won with bad cards, bluffing effortlessly. Now, if I could give myself an excellent hand and the others a good hand, the day would be assured. I dealt the cards as if I were pushing time on with the movements of my hands.

"And to think that, statistically at this moment there is an infinite array of possibilities in the hands that we are about to receive," stated Cacho, gloomily, as he watched his cards fall onto the table. He used his "important things" voice. He always used it when he was instructing someone. I supposed that what he meant was that statistically, the card combinations that we were about to receive, were difficult to predict exactly, as per the so-called laws of probability. As I was just about finished dealing out the cards, it amused me to realize that Cacho was mistaken on the last point. When probability does not exist or rather, if we make our own luck, the statistic becomes laughable.

"I don't get it," said Osvaldo. I suppose we all noted with relief that it was the first time they acknowledged each other that afternoon. It was also noticeable that Osvaldo effectively wanted to know what the other meant and not dis him.

He listened very attentively to the mind-numbing explanation, to the chagrin of the rest of us, who didn't interrupt him so as to solidify their reconciliation. When I picked up my cards, I found four queens and an ace. I felt like rubbing my cards in Cacho's face, but showing them to him and saying "take that" would not make any sense to him. After offering everyone cards, I threw out my ace and got a ten instead. Cacho had begged Osvaldo to wait until the end of the game, because the book he was reading had a lot more interesting information about luck. With relief, I turned all my attention to the game. Landivar and Eugenio had also asked for a card;

Leroy, two; the others were out. I asked for bets. Leroy very prudently upped the ante. I got the impression that his two cards had worked out well and he was getting the lay of the land. Eugenio was much too eager and upped the ante a few times; or perhaps he was too dumb. The only thing that was clear was that Eugenio thought he had a very good hand. Leroy was an unknown quantity; he always played with decorum at the beginning. It was almost to be expected that Landivar, if he had a good hand, would accept the bet without upping anything. All I wanted to do was to double the bet on poor Eugenio. I did so. Leroy doubled mine. Seeing the pile of chips reminded me of the story of the grains of wheat; double for each dummy. Eugenio started guessing out loud at what the rest of us had. When I asked him to speak up, he said:

"Let's see, you asked for one, right? You might have gotten four good ones in your hand and asked for a new one just to throw us off. Let's see," he smiled ingeniously, "look me in the eye, did you get a good one?"

"Alright, say what you have to say already."

"It seems to me," he turned toward Leroy. "It seems to me that he's bluffing, because he never ups so much when he has a good hand. What should I do: should I stay, or not?"

"Do whatever you want, but get on with it," said Osvaldo, annoyed.

"Butt out; it's none of your business," replied Eugenio, his voice somewhat shrill. "Anyway, it's my money I'm playing."

"Well, if you're afraid of losing it, just fold then."

"I'm staying," said Eugenio. The edges of his eyelids were red. I could understand him; he had just bet half of his monthly wages. Of course there was still no reason for him to be such a dick and so unpleasant, but that was another matter.

"You?" I asked Landivar.

"You figure, che? That's way too much money," said El Camba, folding.

If there ever was a time when I would be able to avenge Leroy's dirty trick without remorse, this was it, so I doubled the bet without mercy. What unsettled me was that he folded immediately, because all he had done was to throw away his money more than his cards. Eugenio's eyes scanned his cards and the chips, back and forth, as if it were a tennis game. He finally decided and folded, leaving me the win without a fight and risk free. Instead, he started to beg me to show him my cards anyway. He seemed to despair at the thought that he had relinquished a few weeks of living like a prince out of sheer cowardice. If I'd answered anything I would have said something to remind him of his mother, so I limited myself to putting my five winning cards back into the deck. Before the next round started, he even commented that I had taken much more than his winnings of the entire afternoon.

"More even," he corrected, "more than today's winnings and my winnings from the other day. Just so you know."

It seemed to me that he was looking for an excuse to leave the table, and it pleased me; things were heating up and Eugenio was going to lose his hide if he continued. He played one more hand, lost again and regretted it again.

"Look, Eugenio," Landivar said to him, "stop playing, che, even if it's just for a while. When there's a bad streak, there's nothing you can do about it. I know what I'm talking about."

Eugenio followed his advice, but stayed where he was, watching us play. After a while, when I'd forgotten he even existed, because I was focusing on my own winnings, it seemed to me that he was getting bored. He offered to arrange Landivar's chips for him; El Camba didn't let him. Then he started circling around us, comparing our hands.

"What do you think," he suddenly asked, "should I return to the game or should I go to the movies?"

"Do whatever you want, as long as you don't pester us," answered Cacho, grumpily.

"It's just that I can't leave when I'm losing," he reflected, returning to his seat.

"OK, do you want cards or not?" asked Osvaldo who was about to deal and it annoyed him to have to add the cards we had removed when he stopped playing.

"OK, gimme," the other replied.

The cards were added and the speed of the game seemed to increase. Just back in, Eugenio won twice. Perhaps it would have been better if he'd lost right at the beginning. As soon as the chips started to go, he started to utter regrets. No one bothered to answer him anymore. Everyone was probably trying to not hear him, as I was doing. In half an hour he had nothing left of his monthly wages. The greater part of it had ended up in my pockets and the rest in Landivar's. In spare moments, I couldn't help but admire the excellence of El Camba's game; it was a real pleasure to see the ease with which he played and the promptness with which he leveraged every minor advantage and slowly accrued his chips even though luck was on my side. Leroy had lost heavily, as always, and was indebted to Tu Padre, who, upon seeing things get serious, played with great restraint and forced himself to abstain whenever the cards were not entirely satisfactory. He had managed to keep his losses to a very decent standard. The others must have been doing silent calculations of reductions to their monthly budget.

The game completely lost its course because Eugenio tried to borrow money from each one of us and everyone turned him down. I suppose we refused him more out of charity than the shocking disgust we felt at his behavior. I was certain that any amount we would give him would last him no more than a quarter of an hour. He resorted to begging and completely ruined the game, because no one can play calmly when a grown man is about to burst into tears uttering a mendicant speech that cannot be addressed. Finally, completely hysterical, he began to enumerate all the favors he'd done for Osvaldo, to make clear how immoral it would be if he did not lend him money. His voice was hoarse because of the tears; he spoke in short phrases that seemed a little threatening, as if invoking some evil power against the person who kept refusing. Tu Padre proposed stopping the game. We all agreed, embarrassed and enraged by the scene. Only Leroy insisted that we keep playing; but he wanted to play Chinese poker and Landivar and I refused. It was a good break even for our eyes, because the sun had set and it was hard to see the suits on the cards. We quickly left the room and stood in the garden, waiting for our turn to use the bathroom and pretending not to see Eugenio's overwhelmed silhouette. Osvaldo peeked out the door of his room and said, "Hey, do you want to borrow a towel and soap."

"I'd appreciate that, yes, thank you very much."

The air was cool and quiet in the garden, and the twilight, blue as a jewel; the trees in the garden looked like compact shadows. From down the street, we could hear women's soft and cheerful voices.

II

EVER SINCE WE arrived at the bus station and Doctor Hemstrong asked us if we were the guests she was expecting, I've gotten one surprise after another. I like that she is not overly friendly, that she doesn't say, like everyone else does, that every silly thing my wife and I tell her is interesting.

I almost like her old face crowned by those stray hairs that she seems to have forgotten up there. I'm astonished at the excellent car that keeps us cool in the awful Houston heat, where the houses quietly march by in the twilight through the closed windows. But the old woman makes me uncomfortable; the two or three times that I've spoken, she has taken her eyes off the road to give me a weird look, somewhat forceful, polite and disapproving. Perhaps I have awakened in her a spontaneous and irresistible dislike. As I'm sitting in the back, while the two women chat up front, I endeavor to guess what she feels or thinks about us by observing what she says and what her fat cheek and the corner of her right eye can reveal to me, since they are the only things I can see.

"This university is for black students," she informs us while pointing to a somewhat sad looking cluster of buildings to our left. "It's a good thing that they built them. All who want to be educated should be educated. There is segregation in this state, unfortunately, as you probably know."

"And what is it like?" I want to know, hoping that she will answer that it is very good, so that I have something to politely praise.

"Not great, as you can imagine. In general, universities are not having much luck getting good professors, true scientists.

The ones that aren't snatched away by industry are fought over by good universities."

"The same thing is happening with the humanities," I comment with the objective gravity of someone who knows what he's talking about. "Not only in the exact sciences. Although in our field there's no competition from industry."

"Funny, I didn't know that. I didn't think humanists were so scarce. Of course it's not my field; I don't know anything about that."

"What's happening is that registration has increased significantly in the so-called social sciences. There is greater interest in philosophy and letters among students, after the war."

"Yes, that's true," she agrees. "Even *I* dabble in the languages. Now we are entering my neighborhood," she informs my wife. "It's old; the former wealthy area of the city. Luckily it hasn't deteriorated. The original owners still own and live in the homes."

"It's very pretty," my wife responds, looking through the car window at a park-like area with huge trees on well-manicured lawns with great big houses randomly located very distant from each other.

Our hostess turns right and we drive along a paved road that winds around the trees. The afternoon twilight is pleasantly thickening. It's as if we were fifty miles from the city, in some storybook forest. However, the change in lighting suddenly depresses me. It seems to remind me of some vague childhood event, some happy afternoon of years past that must also have ended abruptly. I look almost in horror at the shapes of the two women. Dr. Hemstrong is now driving slowly; she turns on the lights and we start going through a green tunnel. In the dimness of the interior of the car my attention is drawn to my own hands that have, stupidly and lengthily, been resting on my knees; I lift my hands up in front of my face and turn them palm up and then palm down again. They strike me as a link between this gloomy forest that I never planned to come to on those evenings long ago when my future was being forged, and some other undefinable entity that is not at all related to this forest, nor to the dynamic old woman, nor to my mesmerized wife. The road suddenly widens onto a huge driveway with a three-car garage and all the doors are closed.

"We're here," the old woman informs us, unnecessarily, after stopping the car. "Jacques has not arrived," she adds immediately. "He has a prehistoric car that almost always runs. Jacques is a French scholarship student that lives with me. He studies at Rice. Excellent young man; he'll be happy to meet you. When he's here, he leaves the car outdoors. He says the car will get spoiled if he leaves it in the garage."

As she's speaking, she walks toward the rear of the car and opens the trunk. I smile approvingly, but blankly. I take out our luggage and follow her to the entrance, with a constant smile on my face; on the surface, it must look like I'm telling myself that I've just heard something extremely worthwhile and funny, as if I were thankful to hear the latest on Jacques and his beater. However, as I enter the carpeted hallway covered in prints and pictures, I see the indifferent expression on Dr. Hemstrong's face and my smile disappears. I stay standing there with the bags hanging from my arms, feeling uncomfortable, because I preceded my wife into the house and the old woman is stiff and motionless, waiting for her to enter. Finally, the small procession starts. The señora moves with surprising speed for her years; my wife has to pick up the pace to follow her and I can barely do so, afraid to knock something over with the suitcases and make a mess.

"You'll have to forgive me for leaving you alone for a little while," she says as she's walking away. "I still have a couple of things to do downtown before dinner. But I suppose you might even thank me for giving you time to freshen up alone after your trip. This is your bedroom. I am very glad you were able to accept my invitation. I'll leave you now. See you in a bit."

She smiles at us as she leaves the room. I put the suitcases on the floor, somewhat surprised by the woman's efficiency, but rather relieved that she has left us alone. My wife delightedly observes the room's furnishings and then, removing her shoes, jumps onto the huge bed, which must be very springy because it looks as if she had jumped on cotton.

"I wonder if this is the old woman's bedroom?" she whispers.

I shrug my shoulders, afraid that we might be heard from outside. In front of the bed, there's an enormous television set. I do not dare turn it on until I'm sure that the owner is gone. The place is delightfully cool and the refreshing feeling increases because the sound of water falling comes through one of the windows. I go near it to see what is happening; my wife continues lying on the bed joyfully.

"Do you know where that water is from?" I ask, impressed.

"No, where?"

"From a combination dehumidifier and air-conditioner. What our elegant noses are now breathing in is mountain air; not that disgusting gulf air."

"Hey," she whispers, pointing to the door through which Dr. Hemstrong disappeared, "the old woman must be filthy rich."

"She must be," I agree, checking out the room once again with great satisfaction. "After all, all sorrows are lessened with cool and dry air. Don't you agree?"

Dr. Hemstrong's footsteps swiftly approach our door. By the time she knocks on the door, Adriana has jumped off the bed and onto the floor. I don't know why, but I feel like I've been caught doing something wrong or that I'm about to be surprised and so I rush to what I believe to be the bathroom. The place smells of pure luxury; it's covered in marble and laden with perfume bottles and pots of talc; all new, untouched and expensive, waiting for guests, for us, to perfume and talc ourselves until we get nauseous. I cannot wait for the two women to stop whispering so that I can tell Adriana that I've discovered something outrageous: the shower has two regular taps, one hot, one cold, and a third with ice water. And, additionally, next to the gigantic marble bathtub there's a magazine rack full of ophthalmology publications and the latest issues of *National Geographic*. Just as the conversation is waning outside, I stumble upon a well-used Russian grammar text.

"Come see this," I call out. "Come in, look."

Adriana hurries to look at the jars that the hostess has left for her use, and says, laughing:

"See that? This is what any self-respecting woman expects to find in a bathroom; and to think that I've been looking for that nasty Bond Street perfume since Panama."

"Are these any better?" I ask, trying to show surprise.

"A thousand times better. How can you even ask? There's no comparison."

Afraid that she will start to tell me all the names and virtues of each bottle, I try to distract her by pointing out the ice water tap.

"Look, put your hand under the running water."

"Why? What is so special about it?"

"Ice water. Water like melted snow. That's what's so special about it."

"What? Artificially chilled? Outrageous!" she says, shuddering at the thought, "Who would think of such a thing?"

I don't know why, but her disdain for the chilled water, which I love and think is the greatest luxury in the house, seems to me like a personal criticism. Just as I was glad and tried to admire the variety of perfumes and pestiferous powders at her disposal, could she not at least refrain from showing displeasure at what I like?

"What did the señora want?"

"To say that she would be back soon and that we should make ourselves at home."

"Did the good señora not mention any special plethora of alcoholic beverages available for the pleasure of her guests?"

"Yes, she said there were drinks and ice in the living room. Do you want to have a bath first?"

"No, I don't think I want to bathe yet, although perhaps it may be better to have a nice shower instead. Don't you think so?"

"Well, while you decide, I'll have a bath."

She walks toward the bedroom and I'm suddenly tired of the bathroom. It's built for a different lifestyle. It satisfies other interests. It belongs to a foreign world. As far as ophthalmology, I barely know it exists. I'm not interested in *National Geographic*; if I want anything out of geography it is to travel, not to see exotic little monkeys. This woman and her money cannot buy the things that I search for, right? Which things? My own face looking back at me feverishly from the mirror surprises me.

"Could you help me move this suitcase?" Adriana calls out. "It's too heavy."

"How could it not be heavy if you filled it with every rag we own?" I complain while moving the suitcase to where she wants it. "All these clothes for just three days."

"Ah, and now you will see how foresighted your wife is. I bet you that there won't be anything left that isn't worn at least once. Señora Hemstrong invited us, along with the Frenchman, to some restaurant where she says they have the best shellfish in the state; we have to dress appropriately. Don't you agree? And tomorrow there will be something else and the next day another. You'll see. There is nothing worse than not having anything to wear. Don't you agree?"

"Fine, have your shower soon so I can have mine and change my clothes."

"Look, I have to hang up everything in the suitcases. You'd be doing me a favor if you shower first."

"Fine. Where did you put my clothes?"

"Do me a favor. Go to the bathroom right now and I will take them in to you. If you start rifling through the suitcases, you'll mess up everything."

"Fine, woman, fine."

"But hurry up . . ." she nags while I lose myself again amongst the marble, the talc, and the perfumes. I have a burning desire to get out of here without saying a word and finding some little Mexican place where they sell tortillas and chili con carne. Meanwhile, Adriana and the Frenchman and the ophthalmologist can treat themselves to shrimp a la whatever.

The shower is excellent. Just as I like it. I leave the shower refreshed and comforted by the piston-like violence with which the apparatus massages you with almost slush-like water after a hot shower. As I lazily dry myself off, Adriana shows up and whispers to me.

"Hurry, please. I think the old woman is back."

"Where are my clothes?"

"On the bed. Hurry up, don't be rude. We can't keep her waiting. It's almost eight."

I dress as if to catch the last plane to paradise. I'm enraged that I'm losing the restful and refreshing sensation of the shower. I've never been able to get used to shirts with cufflinks and, in my haste, I leave the cuffs dangling like dishrags.

"Adriana, Adriana."

Since she doesn't respond, I angrily knock on the door.

"Wait a minute," she shrieks from inside, "just a minute."

"Where did you put my ties?" I shout.

"I can't hear you."

"My ties, where are my ties?"

"What do you want, for goodness' sake?" she asks, furiously, standing at the door wrapped in a towel up to her underarms.

"I want to know here you put my ties, because you gave me green socks and a red tie."

"There is no green tie," she informs me. "But I think that one looks perfectly fine."

"How can this be fine? I'm going to look like an impressionist painting, can't you see?"

"And what do you want me to do? There is no green tie."

"But . . ."

"Stop yelling please. The best thing you could do would be to go downstairs and chat with that woman. There are only red ties."

I put the red rag around my neck, mute with indignation and fear that our argument will be heard outside. As I'm about to leave, Adriana requests:

"Tell her I'll be down in a minute, please."

"Fine."

There is no one in the living room, but it's evident that some-one is at home. I remain standing, without knowing where to look or how to stand; I would like to offer whoever walks in the image of a worldly man who is completely at ease anywhere. The footsteps moving past the walls of the living room are quiet for a few moments, but are soon audible again. Many times they seem to be about to burst in before me with their owner in tow. But a few minutes go by and the pose I had acquired begins to tire me; I feel a light numbness in my calves. Since the place looks more like a showroom because of the vast amount of paintings, prints, drawings and watercolors and God knows what else, covering the walls, I decide that it would look better if I were to observe them. If only I could relate one to a well-known author or to a school, I would be able to talk about it and make a great impression. And even though I have no idea about art—I don't even like it—I start to walk around the room with my chin in the air, pretending to be fascinated by various pieces. After having my eyes wander astonishingly over a number of them, I come across one completed in colored pencil that not even I would think deserves the honor of a frame.

"Hello," the old voice of Dr. Hemstrong, whom I didn't hear walk in, greets me. "Are you somewhat more rested from the trip?"

"Oh, we weren't tired. It's only a three-hour trip."

"Great!" she approves vehemently. "We'll have to wait for Jacques for a bit. He called to apologize. He wanted us to go ahead without him, but I don't think it will hurt us to have two drinks instead of one, right?"

"From my perspective I can tell you that, personally, I will rather benefit from the delay."

"Would you like something to drink?"

"Yes, please. Thank you."

"There is ice and a variety of spirits," she says, pointing to a table I'd already noticed, where there are about twenty different bottles.

"The delay works well for Adriana; she's running a little late."

"It's only natural. She must have been very tired. You are not used to this climate. The weather in your country is so mild. I was there with my husband . . . Can't find what you are looking for?"

"To be honest, I am looking for whisky."

"To your right," she says and sits on a chair that looks well used, "those three bottles."

"We were there the same year the war ended, in the spring

of 1945. It was very nice. I would have liked to have been able to stay longer, but I had to attend an ophthalmology conference in Buenos Aires."

"What a shame. Did you have enough time to visit the southern regions, the lakes?"

"No, just the capital. The ice is in that bucket. I'd like a whisky as well, but with soda, please."

"Oh, sorry."

From her chair, she watches me somewhat annoyed and somewhat curious, frowning slightly under her old messy hair. I hope she doesn't notice that I'm blushing. In order to excuse myself I was about to say that in my country ladies don't drink and that's why I didn't think to offer her a drink; which, on top of being completely idiotic, was also false.

"Sit down," she orders me, after taking the glass I extended. "You have received a philosophy scholarship, I believe."

"That's correct, señora."

"That surprises me," she says with the best smile of the afternoon.

"Why?"

"It seems to me that philosophy is practiced in Europe, say, France or Germany. I'm under the impression that my countrymen are not very strong on philosophical reflection. I don't know if I'm mistaken. The only thing that I've heard about is behaviorism."

"Well, there is much more. There are excellent professors. Also," I add with much cynicism, "European scholarships are much more difficult to obtain. Here they need foreign language instructors. In practice, they trade what they can offer for what they need."

She stares at me intently as I speak, showing no emotion or comprehension. After I'm done, she waits a few moments as if expecting something more. Then she takes a drink pensively and her features light up before she looks at me again.

"Traveling is always good. And, do you know what? It occurs to me that philosophy is not your most definitive interest. I think that what you want is something else."

"That is true, actually," I reply, somewhat flattered and confused. "I have spent many years on this and every time, every single time, philosophy seems less valuable to me. The thing is that my interests are of another order. Of course philosophical knowledge is always useful in any cultural, creative, or other undertaking."

"So, you have realized that philosophy doesn't interest you completely, but you'd at least like to conclude your efforts with a doctorate. Is that right?"

"Not exactly that, but rather . . ."

I hear my wife's footsteps; she must have finished getting ready.

"Here comes Adriana," Dr. Hemstrong states happily, turning her head toward the stairs. "Come and have a drink with us while we wait for Jacques to arrive, Adriana."

"Thank you, señora. How awful that I took so long! The house is so lovely that one doesn't feel like doing anything."

"Wonderful, do it. Your husband and I were discussing the weather in your country."

"Do you want a drink?" I ask.

"No, thank you. So you have also been to South America?" she says, throwing her purse on a coffee table and sitting down.

I have a feeling that the old woman's dislike of me has increased. If I wasn't certain that I haven't said anything definitely impertinent or anything like that, the old woman's personal rejection would worry me. I have to believe that she has misunderstood me. Perhaps she's taken something I said negatively. Maybe she just dislikes me and what I stand for. Why? What reason could there be? No one would say that this is a sensitive old woman.

3

I OPENED MY apartment door with a blemish on my happiness that prevented me from getting my hard-earned enjoyment out of the thick wad of poker winnings in my pocket. I introduced the key into the lock, slowly shaking my head, thinking: "that gather downward to the sea." I had just greeted the homeowner as I went past the garden. As I observed him crouching in the shadows handling the garden hose, in my mind I could almost touch the cancer that was rotting his liver and that was probably, in that position, squishing against his old ribs. The gloomy vision of this old man made me remember the other, Pamani, who had probably finished bleeding to death by now and was perhaps stretched out in his coffin or on some marble slab. I walked into the house full of metaphysical regret, remembering the countless generations who had returned to dust, and shut the door gently behind me without looking. There, I was struck motionless by deep sentiment; the infinite void of death. But my house didn't remember death at all. Even in the shadow of the last twilight, one could see that everything was shining and exuded the scent of recently applied wax, diluted by the pristine air of the rooms. I almost burst out laughing when I told myself that if I had won less money at the game, I would have also cared a lot less about the deadly fate of the two old men. And, if I had lost, perhaps my inner comment would have been: *There's that fucking old man again, dying, and ruining his family's life with the garden hose and the whimpering.* I let go of the bitter gesture and dejected shoulders. As old women say, "They were born to die." Or as the poet once conceded: "Every creature that walks the earth ends up on

the spit." Out of sentimentality and foolish guilt I had to feel
unhappy or pretend to myself that I was, simply because I was
as healthy as a horse, dripping money, drunk with the joy of living, and Blanca would soon be falling into my bed from infinite
space. To top it all off, I was personally ready to die any time it
was necessary. The seed and root of my contentment consisted
precisely in that I saw no real difference between noticing, for
example, that my apartment glistened because it was so clean
and tidy, and noticing that my poor landlord had a tumor in his
liver or that Pamani had gotten a good sized piece of steel in the
ribs; or among all these things and winning at poker or waiting
for Blanca, or having someone say to me: "Your time is up, my
friend, start preparing your little coffin and hurry up about it." It
wasn't fair to either of the two old men to smear their problems
with my cheap sentimentality. It also didn't seem fair to me, as I
prepared a bacon-and-six-egg omelet, that they were treating my
landlord so badly. They didn't want to give him the opportunity
that everyone deserves; it was preposterous that I knew about his
liver and he thought he had gallstones. The only thing he got out
of the deal was that now I was careful to not drive him up the
wall, ever since his almost-widow had informed me, her voice
muffled by her tears, about the reason for his constant bad temper. Even sometimes, without being overly sentimental, when
I would see him hunched over and silently bustling among his
plants, I felt a modicum of regret for the outbursts I'd subjected
him to before knowing that at any moment now—Poof!—he'd
be gone! Although, when you think about it, it wasn't my fault
that his agony, whose cause was unknown to him, had turned
him into a royal pain. He had even succeeded in causing the
poor old woman to have a nervous breakdown . . . I realized
that, in spite of all my reflections, the landlord was tangled up
in my thoughts even over the aroma of my coffee mug and my
bacon omelet. I also wasn't able to forget completely about the
bloodless ghost of the other old man.

Instead of dirtying a plate, I put the pan on a sheet of paper
and took it to the window with my mug. Everything was so wonderfully tidy that I didn't want to move even one single chair out

of place, so I stood there and ate while looking outside, filling my mouth and my eyes at the same time. Everything was happening as it always did. The customary spring afternoon storm was punishing the face of the Tunari and the high area of the valley, while overhead the city sky was still cloudless. There was the frustrated trajectory of black clouds over the blue sky that started from the summit of the mountain and came toward the city without reaching it. Far away, it unloaded dark, silent waterfalls made visible by the lightning. Even though I'd already seen them so many times, there was something very beautiful about these storms. I was almost looking for something unusual in them: rays that reached the ground, rare colors in the clouds— anything new. However, Blanca's proximity afforded them some newness. Indeed, they embellished the air with scents and subtleties; it was just that over there, on the other side, the jungle began; it was because I had just made money at work and at gambling. It was simply that I had this house and these storms for Blanca for tomorrow. Perhaps, in a mere twenty-four hours, she would be mine right here. I watched it all with a certain amount of devotion, because hope allowed objects and time a certain magical and dignifying anticipation.

I returned the dishes to the kitchen and washed them until they shone again. I obsessively cleaned the grease stains that had fallen on the kitchen counter; I found it a brilliant solution to use the paper from the pan. Satisfied, I looked at my work; I walked backward out of the kitchen in order to see whether I had missed any details. Now, with my belly silenced and the old men doubtlessly dying, I could spend my time counting my money, being possessed by the most delightful greed. I emptied my pockets onto the table, spreading it out as much as possible. The pile was impressive and deserved the fanfare I devoted to it as I sorted it into bundles of the same denomination; each bill smoothed out beforehand, wrinkle by wrinkle. Once the pile was organized, its visual proportions seemed much too modest. Due to my overwhelming greediness, I felt a nagging sensation because of the money that I'd loaned to Eugenio. But, what else could I have done when I went into the bathroom and the poor bastard was bawling his eyes out and wasn't even asking me for anything anymore? Besides, it was almost certain that even if he asked, no one was going to lend him a penny because he was such an idiot and a pussy. And to think that I had to insist that he take the money; his self-respect had shown up at the same time as his tears and his snot! If I had pretended to be offended, I would have been able to keep quite a tidy sum for myself. Oh well. There's nothing I can do about it now. Poor bastard. There was nothing more to be done in this clean and expectant house either. The storm over the Tunari had ended and all I could see through the window were houses. Only the pleasant fullness in my stomach still accompanied me. I suddenly realized that the world was immersed in a sweet and cozy silence. Nothing stirred or hurried in the house or in the garden or in any of the houses and gardens for many blocks around. From where I was, I was able to see a corner of the bathroom door; beyond it, the bedroom was waiting for me with a fresh set of sheets. What my body yearned for was a good shower, a rest on the bed, and some light reading. But I had begged my friends to come by and pick me up at around ten if they could find a worthwhile Saturday night destination. If I was sleeping, they would come up and whistle and shout until they got me out of bed. The idea that I would be forced to get dressed again took away from the allure of the plan. It wasn't worth it. I lit a cigarette and since I didn't want to dirty even the ashtrays, I started pacing from the living room to the bathroom where I shook off the ashes into the toilet. Besides, it's impossible to sleep when you are expecting within twenty-four hours to, as Leroy would put it, make a woman's toes curl.

The group came to pick me up half an hour late and I was not happy when they showed up. I was annoyed when I saw the four of them carelessly coming in off the street leaving footprints on the freshly waxed floor. It also irritated me that after waiting for them for so long they showed up pleased with themselves for having the sensational idea of going to La Perla Azul, where, on top of getting bored dancing with ugly and languid women, I would have to pay for the privilege. I told them so. Tu Padre stared at me and slowly took a seat on the sofa. Once he was comfortable, he said:

"If I were to tell people this, nobody would believe me. Seriously: no one. We have walked through this cemetery of a place, mausoleum by mausoleum, niche by niche, and there wasn't one dead body out of its coffin. Even poor Musarana, who is exhausted, came with us to check out all the possible places to go, get it? Just to see if we could find a worthwhile place where you could dance and drink. And you dare to complain. Hey, do me a favor: take your reputation into account, my old man. Let's see, Musa, tell him about your exploits so that he'll realize, so that he will appreciate, your sacrifice and understand his gross ingratitude. Go ahead, Musa, tell him."

"OK, asshole, stop your nonsense," Musarana was irritated, demure and almost blushing.

"So are we going to La Perla Azul, or not?" Leroy asked.

"Quiet, old man," Tu Padre said, "Understand that we are talking about moral issues and not just any shit. Let virtue and friendship shine first and then we'll decide."

"Fine," Leroy ignored him, apprehensively. "Are we going to stand around here talking all night or are we going to La Perla?"

"Let's go. It's better than a poke in the eye with a sharp stick," I replied.

God only knows what the reference to a poke in the eye reminded Musarana of in association with La Perla Azul, but he laughed until it hurt. He couldn't breathe. It was as if he'd never heard anything so funny; in this flash of acceptance, he even seemed to forget some of the formality with which he always treated me. He even went so far as to slap me on the shoulder.

We had to walk to the town square to find a cab. I was the only one who didn't mind the walk because I was in no hurry to get there. Frankly, I was not in the mood for the hustle and bustle of a brothel. Leroy and Osvaldo couldn't wait to get to La Perla. While we walked, they kept looking behind so that an oncoming cab wouldn't get past us. They were barely following the little bits of conversation because they didn't want to be distracted, and they even stood in the middle of the street so that they would be able to see the cab approaching from a distance. What surprised me most, however, was that Musarana also seemed to show excitement and a certain amount of urgency. When we arrived at the town square and calmly got into the cab, my surprise turned into shock. As soon as we told the cabbie where to take us, Musarana started a very detailed narrative of his exploits that he promised would be funny and pleasant. We found out everything from the color and size of the seduced Mínima's nipples to what she said and begged for when she was enjoying herself. Perhaps it was fool's pride combined with the darkness inside the cab that made Musarana open up so obscenely; it may have been on account of that stupendous relationship that he and I had because of the "poke in the eye" comment earlier. Perhaps he wanted to slowly get to the high point of his conquest, that almost coincided with the arrival at La Perla, and came down to the poor girl suddenly bursting into tears because she could no longer take the pain and Musarana, the big guy, had had to threaten to beat her for real if she didn't let him finish. In spite of my intense desire to choke the bastard and throw him out the window, it still seemed to me that we arrived at La Perla much too soon.

There were only a few people there. Two or three couples, appearing somewhat disheartened, and a number of women, looking fresh because it was still early, were talking more excitedly than usual, standing by the piano next to the empty orchestra stage. The music was coming from some invisible automatic device. I was trying to distinguish some of the goddesses that Leroy had mentioned, but as we walked across the huge tile dance floor, there was not even one single half-human half-goddess crossbreed. Luckily, I still had hope because of the density of the women in the group. The person I did see, to my astonishment, was don Joaquin; he was half hidden at a secluded table away from everyone, flirting with a generously proportioned mound of flesh. One could see he was complimenting and praising her by his ample and curving gestures. I was certain that the good old man had seen me before I saw him and was playing dumb.

"Look who's over there," laughed Leroy, elbowing me.

"Yeah, man, don Joaquin."

"Spring has sprung! It must be *that* time of the year," he commented, bursting into laughter.

Musarana, Tu Padre, and Leroy, as regular and single-minded customers would do, took the lead in moving toward the group of women and Osvaldo and I brought up the rear. I didn't feel like we were welcome. Without interrupting their conversation, they turned toward us, one of them said something and they closed their circle again laughing heartily and noisily. I felt a little embarrassed and looked around at others to see their expressions. The women feigned shock when our three friends butted into their group.

"Is this any way to welcome your sweetie, pretty ones?" Tu Padre greeted, opening his arms wide and smiling radiantly. "Doesn't anyone have a kiss for the best client of the house?"

Perhaps his mistake was in closing his eyes and stretching out his cheek to receive the welcoming kisses; or maybe his cheek was ill placed; much too close to a pretty woman (one of the goddesses, I presumed), but her face was somewhat sweaty and flushed. She moved her hands in a sort of spasm, as if to hit Tu Padre, then cowered without daring to and burst into tears of rage.

"And what did the fucking little doctor want? Did he maybe want us to pick him up at home with a marching band? You think that because you pay us we have to kiss your ass. Fucking shit little doc, that's what I say," she interrupted herself, her face whitewashed with fury, while her throat was burning with countless insults; they were coming out as moans of stunning impotence that were frankly impressive. She suddenly burst out: "Look, doctor shithead, here's your mommy."

And in one fell swoop she turned her back to us at the same time as she lifted her skirts from behind and bent over; exposing her naked very round and very white butt. Musarana's hand was so quick that the slap he gave her sounded like an explosion against her buttocks. This eased the situation somewhat because several of the women and one or another customer started laughing. I was having an enormous amount of fun. If someone had predicted that Tu Padre would be welcomed with an anal display at La Perla, I would have come just to see it. It was obvious that he couldn't stand the humiliation. While two friends took the girl away, he followed her with his eyes, unable to get over it.

"Don't listen to her," a somewhat older woman said gently, grabbing his arm. "She's a sloppy drunk. She's new. Every time she starts to drink the same thing happens. We don't know what to do anymore . . ."

You could tell by looking at Tu Padre's silly, smiling, and forgiving face that the explanation did nothing but confirm the insult. In the silence and stillness that followed, I could see doña Manuela popping her white head in to see what the fuss was about, but upon seeing that everything had calmed down, she exited without intervening. At that moment, just as Osvaldo was exhibiting a "let's continue the party" and "there's nothing wrong here" smile, a scrawny woman with greasy hair came up to us.

"That may very well be," she said, "but it's true that you walk around like you own the place. And you do that everywhere," she started happily, but offensively, mimicking our dominant way of walking and talking as if we were saying: "Let's see, down on all fours." "Hurry up, filthy bitch, I'm thirsty." "Lick the floor clean for me so that I can step on it."

"You don't have to lick anything if you don't want to, my beauty, and come and dance with me," replied Tu Padre, who had almost regained complete control of himself, but not quite, and seemed to want to end the matter peacefully. As he spoke he had taken the scrawny woman by the hand. She jerked it away from him violently and arrogantly and insolently said:

"I'll dance if you buy me a whisky."

Tu Padre paled intensely now. I got the impression that he was trembling. This time, he grabbed her by the arm and shaking her, howled:

"You'll dance, whore, even if I don't pay you anything, and if you don't, I'll kick the shit out of you. This is what happens when you put up with crap from these filthy bitches."

Everyone was staring at us blankly. Although the whole thing was laughable and I had not enjoyed myself quite so much in a long time, I quickly searched for a nearby chair just in case I had to fight my way to the door. Near the entrance there was a group of about six guys who must have arrived there shortly after we did who struck me as worth watching. By now, I was sure that if things hadn't escalated further it was solely due to the reputation for knife fighting that we had as Chileans. I was somewhat worried about what Leroy might do, because if he got all fired up, there would be hell to pay. Luckily, there were no warning signs that this might be the case, but he was not laughing. His neck was somewhat stiff, his head somewhat tilted and his lower lip was hanging out. I don't think he noticed the guys at the door, but he had his eye on a couple of other guys who were quietly watching us, leaning against a wall and who must have been the bouncers. Musarana looked confused and Osvaldo's eyes were bulging out of pure fear. Tu Padre jerked the girl toward him. But, when we all expected her to start screaming or to bite him or something like that, enormous tears started streaming down her cheeks. She followed him, very docile, out into the middle of the dance floor. She seemed to me to be in some sort of trance.

"And now the ruffian grabs her by the hair and drags her along the floor kicking her in the ribs as a tango plays in the background," Musarana joked. I almost burst out laughing, but the situation made me contain it. There were two other couples on the dance floor. When Tu Padre approached them, one of the guys grabbed his partner and took her back to the table looking as if he were about to vomit. The other one was indecisive; he lost his rhythm as he agonizingly looked all around him giving us and his partner meritorious glances. Fear kept him from deciding anything, so he kept dancing and stumbling.

At any rate, the danger had passed. We each chose a woman for ourselves and Musarana took his to the dance floor immediately. When the dance finished and they returned to the table, Tu Padre must have realized that, because of his precipitousness, he was stuck with one of the ugliest girls of the house. Tact or fear of the repercussions made him keep her. She had stopped crying, but from time to time she let out sighs and whimpers as if she needed air and she would give Tu Padre a look that was somewhere between submissive and wounded. Something strange must have happened to Tu Padre; in his usual style, he started pampering her; he whispered in her ear and fed her pure Pisco as if she were a child. As time went by, the pain she felt was turning into a sort of radiant devotion. I was dancing nonstop with a girl of about seventeen, more youthful than pretty, and was having a grand old time. Nevertheless, from time to time I was checking on Tu Padre, because he could very well be faking it and end up spitting on the girl or something like that. My partner was fine; she didn't show much interest. She was kind of engrossed in herself with a sort of somnambulism that was docile and lukewarm.

Leroy, who preferred his women meaty and was an awful dancer, had sat down with a fatty on his lap. The woman looked bored and often threw fleeting glances around the room timidly, as if embarrassed to be where she was and of being touched in public, but she made no attempt to move from there. Tu Padre's behavior had probably earned us a reputation as terrible macho-men. Musarana, like me, was dancing but he was arguing with his partner. Osvaldo, on the other hand, was making his partner yawn by trying to teach her something; judging by the mysterious intensity on his face, I figured it must be what he called philosophy.

As we danced, I noticed that the girl was increasingly rubbing against me. It surprised me that she would do it so cautiously, almost timidly, as if she couldn't help it and she were embarrassed by it. It made no sense; the procedure was totally normal; she would simply have to ask a question; make an invitation like any other. Suddenly I felt my partner put her head on my chest and with great tenderness say:

"Is it true that you never sleep with a woman when you come here?"

"True, I've never slept with a woman here. Who told you?"

"They all say so. Will you go to bed with me?"

"I don't know. Why?"

"Let's go to bed, do you want to? Shall we?"

"Doña Manuela will scold you, because you're not making your clients drink first and want to rush them into bed," I replied jokingly.

"What do I care? I don't give a damn. Stupid old woman," she exploded, quickly taking her face off my shoulder. "Hey, don't you like women?"

"Of course I like them, but I don't like all of them."

"And me, do you like me?"

"You? Yes."

"Let's go then, shall we? Let's go now?"

Her eyes were glassy, her breathing spasmodic and her nostrils tense and pulsating. She was extraordinarily beautiful.

"Where are you from?"

"Tocopilla. Why do you like talking so much? Please, please, let's go, take me," she pleaded with despair.

"OK, let's go. Why did you leave Tocopilla?" I asked, taking her arm so she could guide me to the bedroom.

"Because I wanted to. Because I felt like it and because this old miserable woman offered me a whole bunch of things."

We were leaving the dance floor when all hell broke loose. Out in the hallway leading to the toilets, Osvaldo and the greasy scrawny girl were shouting frantically. I couldn't understand anything that they were saying. I had to yank my girl off of me and she started yelling at me furiously: "Fucking asshole!" as I ran toward the commotion. The scrawny girl was howling so loudly and shaking so desperately that I couldn't hear what Osvaldo was trying to tell me. The only thing that was clear was that whatever was happening was happening in the bathroom.

When I walked in I discovered what was going on with Tu Padre. They had him on the floor. He had gone down with his left arm in an awkward position and was aimlessly kicking at the three guys who were in turn, kicking him much more efficiently. Somewhat confused and intimidated by the surprise and commotion, I was taking charge of things when Leroy, who was a great fighter, pounced into the middle of the situation like an earthquake. I started trying to lift Tu Padre up, but it was quite difficult. It's not easy to crouch in the middle of kicks and fists coming from everywhere. Besides, every time I managed to get Tu Padre to his feet, he fell down again. I decided to carry him, because the rage of his aggressors was mainly directed at him, and if he stayed on the floor, someone would eventually kick him somewhere where he would need surgery. Yet one more guy had slipped into the bathroom and poor Leroy was having a hell of a time keeping so many men away from Tu Padre and me. Luckily Musarana had taken up the defense at the entrance and had already bashed one of them on the head with a chair. That reassured me, but I would have liked to know what the hell Osvaldo was doing and where. He showed no signs of life apart from the screams at the beginning. With Tu Padre across my shoulders, my right hand holding him, and my left hand practically useless, I began to move toward the door. Every once in a while I could hear the comforting sound of Leroy's fist hitting something solid. Another guy approached me, obviously intending to block my way; but despite the irritating pretense, the only thing that I could think of was to kick him with Tu Padre's feet. I lost my balance and we both ended up on the floor again. Luckily, in the complex combination of kicking and screaming that we were doing, our assailant came to be underneath us. The best thing was that Tu Padre's head swerved in such a way that it landed squarely on the enemy's face. When I stood up again and pulled Tu Padre off him, the poor guy was very feebly rolling on the tiles and bleeding profusely from his mouth and nose. And with the blow, I discovered Osvaldo; he was almost sitting on a urinal, his back against the wall, terrified, watching the whole scene. Tu Padre seemed a little more alert, perhaps because of the latest blow, and even helped me get him back up on my shoulders.

"Osvaldo, Osvaldo, the dagger," Leroy cried out with a shred of femininity and affliction in his voice.

There was an immediate and paralyzing jolt within the enemy ranks. From the back of the bathroom came Osvaldo's hunched figure. One might have said that the shiny thing he had in his hand dragged him toward the group because he held it as confidently as if he had a snake by the tail. A rush of terrified men ran out of the room like a shot. In their desperation they almost swept Musarana along with them as he was still guarding the door, chair in hand, bellowing out atrocities. It's possible that the clients and women who were still in the main room assumed that something dreadful would come out chasing the forsaken men; when we left the bathroom the place was deserted. Of course, at the door, a distraught doña Manuela was waiting for us. She wanted to know who would pay for the bill and for the chair that Musarana had broken on the back of the guy who had tried to enter the bathroom. As we were pondering the issue, a taxi dropped off two drunks in front of us. The urgent desire to disappear and the providence of the taxi showing up seemed evident to us. There was still the fear that our adversaries would regain their courage or show up with a weapon. But it seemed fair to me that we should fulfil the old woman's demands before hightailing it out of there. And it seemed even more reasonable for Tu Padre to be the one to pay for both things; so while I held him, Osvaldo took out his wallet and paid doña Manuela; we added a generous tip so that the idiot would learn not to make trouble for no reason.

We were about to jump into the cab when the driver stopped us. He claimed that Tu Padre was drunk and that he would vomit all over his seats. Since it was the only cab for miles around, we didn't tell him to go to hell and instead lay Tu Padre down on the floor of the cab. Doña Manuela watched as we did so, endeavoring to rhetorically lament our misfortunes.

"Old bitch," said Osvaldo after the taxi took off. "I bet you that she's now going to charge the other group for the same chair."

He seemed to be in a pretty good mood and even seemed to expect that we would laugh at his joke, but no one paid any attention. We were somewhat worried about Tu Padre's lethargy. He had begun to complain somewhat absentmindedly and painfully. Musarana was absorbed in some extreme excitement that almost made him shiver. Leroy and I were still immersed in a deep stupor as a result of giving and receiving so many blows and kicks. As we approached the city, our friend's groans were becoming more unbearable.

"I feel like sticking my shoe in this idiot's mouth so that he'll be quiet," an angry Leroy muttered. "'*This is what happens when you put up with crap from these filthy bitches*,' and the moron doesn't even know what happened while the rest of us idiots got pummeled."

Leroy was right: we were running out of patience with all his whimpering. Besides, in the silence and darkness of the taxi, we were starting to feel the pain and the idea of the shoe in the mouth was a tempting one. Osvaldo couldn't help himself. For a while he considered how Tu Padre was flailing around at our feet and then he decided.

"We have to check his shoulder, it might be serious."

We made the cab stop. Everyone got out but me, who would help get the lump out from the inside. We put him down on the grass and gravel at the side of the road, in front of the car's lights. He seemed to become lucid for a moment and he must've been quite startled, almost terribly so to see us all standing over and surrounding him in the middle of the night, glowing like ghosts. His eyes dilated out of fear and he attempted to escape or to defend himself.

"No, no, stay still, my old man. We just want to have a look at your shoulder, that's all. It won't hurt one bit. Do you understand me? We're just going to look at your shoulder," Osvaldo soothed him. The authoritarian serenity of his voice surprised me. Tu Padre stopped moving around. He let us bare his shoulder and feel it without squirming. A couple of men walked by and kept turning their heads back to look at us as they moved away. They must have thought we were killing Tu Padre. Osvaldo stood up and whispered to me:

"It's dislocated. I'll try to reduce it. It's my specialty."

He attempted to concentrate by looking at the black sky for a moment. He slowly nodded to himself a few times. He bent over Tu Padre again. He took the damaged limb in both hands and manipulated it in an odd way. It was almost as if he were shifting gears in a car. As he did so, he counted:

"One . . . two . . . three . . ."

Even through Tu Padre's shrieking we could hear the ugly sound of human bone finding its natural location.

"It can't have hurt him. It's just a reflex," said Osvaldo, getting up. "Hey, I was forgetting, for fuck's sake: now we have to immobilize him. Where are we going to get a rag from?"

"From his shirt," replied Leroy.

It took us forever to try and finish taking his shirt off without dislocating his shoulder again. As I was holding him by the healthy arm I noticed his skin covered in a sticky sweat. Osvaldo's dagger allowed us to partially cut the shirt up into strips without making its owner shriek too much.

We decided to go to my house first and take stock of our injuries. By the time we got out of the cab, Tu Padre had already become somewhat able to move on his own. It took some work on our part, but we were able to help him go up the stairs and we slipped in through the door like a parade of deteriorated ghosts. When we turned on the lights, we were in for quite a surprise. Each one of us checked out the other four and then we all burst into laughter. Even Tu Padre was laughing; one of his eyes was monstrously swollen and one of his ears was still oozing blood. When we told him, he sank deeper into the sofa where we'd sat him and cautiously, but awkwardly, explored his ear with his index finger. Then he explained that he didn't remember a thing.

"Someone must have held me down, right?" And he smiled so modestly and joyfully that we burst into laughter again.

Leroy's nose was swollen all the way up to his hairline and was bent toward the right side of his face. My injuries were less severe: they had also hit me on the nose, but not as squarely, and they'd only made my nose bleed a little bit. My clothing, however, was more laughable; one of the sleeves of my blazer and a good part of its lapel were completely missing.

Tu Padre was trying to recline again, but he couldn't get comfortable in any position. As he tried to, he let out loud and arduous groans. I suspected he was exaggerating, but was concerned about how tightly he held on to his ribs with his right hand. And since, without a doubt, Leroy's nose required medical attention, we agreed to take them to the hospital. Osvaldo remembered that Cacho was on duty that night. Leroy completely rejected the idea of entrusting his nose to Cacho, and even Tu Padre had recovered his senses enough to say that he preferred a rib in the lung to allowing Cacho to treat him professionally. Osvaldo used his medical voice to remind them that there were efficient people at the hospital and we could use Cacho as a messenger to go and get them. Seeing as they had no other alternative, they agreed. Suddenly, when Osvaldo asked if he could use my bathroom and I was about to leave the room to look for an undamaged blazer, Leroy burst out laughing again. He seemed to want to say something. He was pointing at Osvaldo, who had turned around very surprised, but his laughter kept him from talking. He finally spit it out:

"And this . . . ha, ha, ha . . . this pussy, sitting the whole time on a . . . ha, ha, ha . . . on a pisser . . . ha, ha, ha . . . and with a dagger in his pocket. The only . . . the only time he needs it, he forgets it 'cause he's so bloody scared . . . ha, ha, ha."

III

PEPE ALBA BRIEFLY feigns an asinine interest in my target pistol, leaning over it and asking inappropriate questions while Professor Ramachiotti completely refuses to have anything to do with such horrible instruments of death. Señora Alba is conversing with Adriana as a very fat and ugly girl of about fourteen accompanies them. I don't know who she belongs to, but she seems to be related to the Albas. Professor Ramachiotti declares that my interest in such objects is only because, unlike him in his home country, I've never been politically persecuted. I feel like telling him to go to hell, since he is reproaching me for my condition of never having been persecuted, but instead I politely agree with him that it must be very unpleasant to live hand to mouth because of one's ideals. All three of us men are standing in the middle of the living-dining room because the women are sitting on three of our seats and none of us dares to take the fourth. Pepe Alba, the egghead, watches me and I get the impression that I disgust him somewhat; the fear of being judged as less than clean makes me perspire even more and I feel the sweat creeping up quietly behind my ears and crawling inside my shirt collar. I have to wipe my face often to keep the viscous river flowing off my head from running down my nose. "The heat in here is infernal," I say to relieve the tension, and then wipe my neck. "The worst is the humidity," Alba says jauntily: "It makes me feel like passing out. You're lucky you sweat. You have an excellent cooling system. If you only knew how I suffer for my inability to perspire, ugh." "Excellent, yes, but repugnant to those around you," I answer, turning into a smile my desire to plunge him into the street through the uselessly open door; there is probably not one breeze in the entire hemisphere. Alba briefly shoots a conspiratorial glance at Ramachiotti and I feel like telling them that I was also in the middle of cleaning my gun, especially since no one expects after-lunch visitors, and particularly when classes have yet to start at the university and the town is half deserted. "Could we not step outside for a bit?" asks Alba, looking at the three women who are at that moment laughing and ignoring us. From the side it looks as if he has no jaw. "OK, let's go," I agree, surprised; besides, these barracks are like ovens. They are all metal. "We'll be back," Alba explains to his wife as he walks past her. Outside, under the stifling oppression of the harsh skies, he takes my arm for a moment and then releases it; he must have noticed that my shirt was soaking wet. "Professor Ramachiotti and I wanted to warn you," he says, looking at the other man. And I ask: "What about?" "Warn is not exactly the right word, Pepe," Ramachiotti points out. He grimaces as if looking for the right word to use as his huge mouth puckers into several soft and repulsive folds. "We were thinking that we had a certain duty toward you as a compatriot. At the end of the day, we are Latinos, che, all brothers, even if we have just met." Despite the looks of the sky, out here the heat is much more bearable and as we walk the thick air makes contact with my body mimicking a breeze. I nod without understanding a thing. "The Department where you will be working, we know it better than anyone, and more importantly, from the point of view of a Latino, a descendant of the Spaniards, which is very different," Ramachiotti continues. "We had to warn you." "About what?" Alba looks as if he is about to speak, but stays quiet. "About everything, che, everything, you understand that in these cases one cannot be overly explicit. After all is said and done, we owe the Department some loyalty; although we owe more to a compatriot. All of us Latinos are compatriots at heart, believe me." There's not one soul on the streets of Blake Park; I wonder how it will all look in about ten days, when the students arrive and move into the barracks. "Thank you," I tell him, "thank you, Dr. Ramachiotti; I imagine it must have been

difficult for you to make the decision, Doctor, and I appreciate it." "Listen, we are on the same side, che, and don't call me
Doctor, that's for people who care about titles, not for me; I am
a simple man; a true Latino. I don't want you to see a professor
when you look at me, but a friend." Alba stares at the nails of his
right hand, seeming to imply that the other man is lying, that
he does not have a doctorate at all, but that vanity keeps him
from telling me outright. "Is the end of summer always like this
here?" I ask them. "No, no, it's much worse," Alba informs me
enthusiastically, "It's hotter and more humid." We have walked
around the block. The women are waiting for us at the door of
the house. "But the one you have to be most careful of is old
lady McDonald; she's the one with the most influence within
the Department, and she's a snake; she hates Latinos." Alba's face
seems to signal that he hasn't heard; that he's more interested
in something that is happening far away, next to the hospital. I
sense fear in his eyes. It occurs to me that Ramachiotti is trying
to dignify the ragged folds of his toad-like mouth. I'm sure good
old Mrs. McDonald is a very respectable person. We have arrived
where the women are. I'm sweating again. My monitors quickly
take their leave, urged by Señora Alba. All four climb aboard the
car they arrived in and wave. "What did they want?" Adriana
wants to know. "Disrespectful pigs," I spit out, "Hey, why is it
that everyone has lost respect for me, even those who don't even
know me? They came to warn me about the difficulties that I
would encounter at work; about Mrs. McDonald. Bastards."
"There you go with your bullshit again," Adriana comments,
"Maybe they meant well."

I look at my feet and as I walk on the wet ground I feel nau-
sea creeping up into my throat. I see earthworms, eviscerated
by people's shoes, lying in the middle of the moisture that is
still dripping from the gigantic chestnut trees from last night's
rain that drew out the poor critters to their crushing deaths or
to painful efforts to reach a little bit further, in the midst of
the sloping morning sun that skims the hot pavement and the
hot walls and burns my eyeballs. Several rows of early morning
students emerge from everywhere and head toward the campus

buildings. The women stir something within me with their light
blouses falling loosely over their shorts, sitting at mid-thigh, their
juvenile rear ends firm, heavy and uncontaminated, outrageously
healthy, transparent plastic raincoats hanging from their arms
also loaded with books and notebooks, wearing thick cotton
socks and tennis shoes. I just got out of the shower and I already
feel my body getting sticky under clothing that is hotter than
my skin. I look in despair at the gray building where I will have
to hole myself up to teach for three hours this morning. It waits
for me indifferently among the trees, with its doors open toward
a dark interior where I see a colorful stream of students disappear into and go up the brick staircase by the entrance gesturing
with their heads and shoulders as they converse. Three hours to
go before I can drink a couple of cold beers. By then, the morning will almost have died a slow death beneath the midday sun.

I spend many afternoons alone in the house, after lunch,
when even misfortune loses its blind meaning and continues
emitting waves of silence after every heartbeat. I place the electric fan on top of the dresser, but before I do so, I stare at all
the objects: a small tray for the family correspondence, pins and
knickknacks in a porcelain dish, a photograph of me as a condemned man, resting on the polished surface. I finally let it rest
on the wooden surface, vaguely surprised that they remembered
to put felt on the bottom of it so that the metal would not scrape
against the wood. I hear the loving and maternal voice of the
girl next door as she says goodbye to her husband. She closes
her door and, one might say, vanishes, as I no longer hear her.
I plug in the device and run it; as it swivels once from side to
side, I adjust the inclination and move it forward a bit so as to
ensure that it will blow directly on the spot on the bed where
I plan to sit. Once I verify that I have everything I need on the
nightstand—pencil, files, both books, ashtray—I lie down on
the bed. The rhythmic sound of the fan as it moves to and fro
disturbs me; as does the strong breeze that passes over me. When
it blows straight at me, I feel almost refreshed and on the verge of
relaxing, but I know it will last only for an instant and I immediately feel my ears burning on the sides of my head. I take off my

clothes and try to study, but the fan stirs the pages of the book and shoots my files in all directions as soon as I drop my guard. Nevertheless, I need to find a way to study in spite of the heat, the fear, the frayed nerves caused by the noise. I decide I need to change my outlook, to quietly allow whatever needs to happen to happen. A surge of terror rushes up my spine. The worst part of it all is that, while one is alive, one has to keep on living.

When good people make a great deal out of simply having an outdoor barbecue, when the sun has already set, but the shade is completely useless because one's sweat is still thick, then the good people laugh, walk around with cold drinks in their hands, and talk and joke. I fear that I smell of wet dog, mildew, of clothing stuck to my body, and there is not even one breeze blowing. I move close to Adriana who is helping Mrs. Cole get the meat ready for the fire, but do not dare to ask her anything in front of anyone else or to call her over. I smile at both women, who don't see my smile and I walk away, taking the foul smell with me, through the garden grass, unable to approach any of the groups talking and drinking. At the back there are several children noisily playing. Many stars have already come out in the muggy night sky.

On the Fourth of July, as we were sitting on a hillside at City Park at dusk, waiting to watch the fireworks, with Adriana and Marta and Otto and Peluda, Otto told me: "No, che, all I lost were my so-called fine motor skills, but if I were to kick you, you'd never notice the difference." As I opened another button of my shirt, I was disgustingly humiliated and felt like beating the living daylights out of him.

4

THE DAMNED DOG kept barking and barking. It had occurred to me that it would be best to go to sleep as late as possible to shorten the wait time the following day; but as far as I could see, amongst broken noses, damaged ribs and hysterical dogs, I simply wouldn't be able to sleep a wink all night. Naturally, the wretched animal had to wait for precisely the moment when my inner circuits began to settle down and my thoughts began to resemble a nighttime backdrop where many wires would come together, where a single, solitary line in a very soft, flowing voice would unfold, very, very slowly, lulling me to sleep. After returning from the hospital, where they had straightened out Leroy's nose and manufactured a ribcage for Tu Padre out of adhesive tape, I had barely been able to undress because of fatigue and lack of sleep. Now, stretched out between my sheets, my pillow started pulsating under my ear. It took me awhile to quiet it down, but when I was finally able to, I remained stiff and much too still. I started to feel hot. Additionally, a large area of my hip was sore, probably because I was kicked there. Annoyed because I couldn't find the position that so easily put me to sleep every night, I decided to smoke a cigarette. And the beastly canine? What? Nothing, silent. Sleeping in his dog house lulled to sleep by the rain, no doubt, waiting for the precise moment when I would have put out my cigarette and was well on my way to unconsciousness to start going crazy barking again. If it weren't because the situation was so messed up and because security guards were sniffing around the city, alert to any disturbance, I would have taken advantage of the dog's ruckus to fire a few rounds toward the garden. With all the trouble there was, they would have cordoned off the whole block at the first sign of a shot and sounded horns and raided houses. If the wicked dog had had any consideration for the nerves of those around him, he would have at least barked continuously. Instead, he was quiet just long enough to make one believe that he had gotten tired and one would relax and start listening to the gentle crackling of the rain, and then he would start barking again. More or less once a month he would have these attacks and nobody paid attention. It was time that someone expressed disapproval, even if that meant shooting into the air. Besides, I thought with a leap of enthusiasm that made the bed creak, what better way to broadcast Blanca's arrival! Although, what huge turmoil this would cause the poor landlord! But I remembered having heard somewhere that a good upheaval benefited the overall state of the body and even served as a visceral cleansing. According to me, it would even pay homage to what was left of the landlord: not pussyfooting around him, not treating him with kid gloves, return him to the joyous land of the living. Finally, it would be fitting that a happy coincidence should bring the sweet animal and the bullet together in the darkness. This was the night for quarrels. Why not create another one of epic proportions? *The ghostly conspirator, silent as a snake and alert as a powerful feline, quietly opened the drawer of the bedside table and put his hand right on the gun. The stifled tremor of rainfall could be heard on the roof as it fell on the barking dog, and on black leaves and on nighttime watchmen. What happens, I wonder, when a loud noise erupts amongst sleeping citizens? His infinite amount of experience, the vastness of his human knowledge, registered everything and foretold all. They would jump from sleep to wakefulness as if they had received a kick in the butt; with stale and pasty mouths, and ask their aging and decaying women: "Huh? What? What? Did you hear that?" And so they would remain for a while, with their heads in the air, until the shock wore off. And the next day the women would converse with their neighbors, but no one would know anything for certain. In the steady hand of the conspirator, the cold and heavy Walther P-38 bespoke an irrevocable decision, of the old days of heroic deeds and romance. The steely features of his face, carved in stone, weathered by the smoke of a thousand battles, barely shook the shadows when it appeared at the window, which moved so softly and so quietly that, had someone been watching, they wouldn't have believed their eyes. A few drops of rain came into the room and fell onto his bare feet, but, if they had been covered in blood a thousand times before, would he now even notice that the water had dampened them? Now this. Now, to punish evil. Then, a precise and amazing escape. They say he ran toward the plains, toward the mountain range; toward the jungle, the hills, the great rivers. He has a friend in the palm forest. The jaguar helps him. He has passed the terrible initiation rituals of the Ayoreo peoples. The breasts of the sleeping maidens tremble with longing and fantasy, because the image of the lone vigilante and his overwhelming destiny crosses their strange dreams as it goes crying into their hearts. The womb of all non-celibate insomniacs opens up toward the dreaded insemination. The dog was still barking. And the years passed. A long time passed in Santa Ana without anyone wondering who he was. He lived alone, hunted alone, and would certainly die alone. The slide of the gun closed over the bullet as an archer's right hand closes over the bowstring, while at the end of his implacable arm, the dead eye of the barrel scans the night searching, blue Erinys, rolling its tongue to whistle at death, lightly holding its fiery breath. The cold steel beats against his palm, because even the brave embrace emotions, but no one, not even the most secret of spiders in its nest, is ever aware of them.*

And what if this turned into a real madhouse? After all, the gun was not even mine, and Ramón was not going to like having me show up saying, "Here you go, bud," with who knows what story. And besides, the police would not appreciate jokes about illegal weapons imports. The whole idea was most certainly quite idiotic. I gave myself the option of quietly returning to my bedroom and putting the weapon back in its drawer. I was somewhat cold and the most tempting thing of all was the urgency with which the warm and dry sheets called out to me. I was too old to be playing with guns. It was all true, but the dog kept barking and it was unreasonable to allow one's nerves to be frayed in that manner. Blanca's imminent arrival required celebration and outrageous ritual. What was perhaps the most serious and pivotal was that I had taken the foolish game entirely too far. I suddenly realized that I had become too involved without knowing how, but committed to the end. If I were to now return to my bed because of apprehension, the matter would take on serious dimensions of fear. To hell with the old man and his liver, and the police and their conspiracies! Blanca's arrival must be celebrated for fuck's sakes! The two shots, one right after the other, almost made the gun fly out of my hand. The noise made my ears ring and the flashes blinded me for several seconds. Almost immediately came the sound of quick footsteps from somewhere. So, as it turned out, there was someone lurking in the shadows and the stupid dog had reason to bark, for once.

Without turning on the light, I searched for the box containing the tin soldiers, I made a hole in the sawdust that housed them, buried the gun, shook the box to level off the surface and jumped into bed. I immediately realized that all I had done was idiotic. I should have turned on the light; it was the natural thing to do. Besides, I had probably left the floor covered in sawdust and footprints right up to the bed. And now I could no longer turn on the light to verify anything, because then I would definitely look suspicious. Couldn't I? Of course I could. If I stayed still on the bed it would be the same as not having fired at all. I got up. I turned on all the lights of the house. Through the window I could smell the wet garden. I noticed that the floor around the box containing the soldiers was clean. None of the other houses had lights on. The clock ticked gently from its usual place. The city was still asleep.

The bedsheets welcomed me joyfully. I had a funny but pleasant taste in my mouth. While I decided that nothing would make me tell Blanca about such childishness, I felt my facial muscles smiling at the thought that she would want to know. The impression that something was missing took me away from the threshold of sleep for a moment, but I was able to go back to it without completely returning to wakefulness: the dog had stopped barking.

IV

I CAREFULLY LIFT my right foot and try to rest my heel right on
the corner of the coffee table; I do not set it down until I can
feel, through the leather of my shoe, that I have positioned it
squarely on. I sense that it is probably best somehow to wait
awhile before putting my left foot up as well. I feel as though I
could settle in and fall asleep here, sitting up. However, I fear
that as soon as I make myself comfortable and cross my hands
over my stomach and shut my eyes, she will immediately suggest going for a walk or start asking me questions. First, I make
sure that she is not looking at me, that she seems engrossed in
the book resting on her lap; then, stealthily, I make my left leg
hover in the air, and slowly stretch it out until my ankles are
lined up and then, little by little, I lower the top one over the
bottom one until it lands directly on top. Convinced that she
has not noticed me, I feel a sense of accomplishment, believing
at the same time, that I am being very clever in observing her,
because my eyes are focused well over her head, toward the triangle of blue sky peeking through the window. However, I cannot remain this way for too long, and in order to avert my eyes,
for example, down to my hands, I would have to look past her.
I could do other things, of course. I could look up toward the
left side or toward the right side of the ceiling, but that would
be idiotic. I choose to close my eyes and point them toward the
floor before opening them again, in such a way as to keep watching her. Now, on top of the green carpet, the rectangular pages
of the now expired Sunday papers, already old news before the
day is half done, surround me in a geometric pattern. Its life

span is *shorter than a rose's*, shorter than a rose's, where terror
lies within its little black letters, photographs and comic strips.
I feel my face frowning; had she been watching me, she might
have thought me to be in intense pain. She has, in fact, raised
her head and, looking at me, smiling, adjusts a lock of stray
hair and places it over her ear with her index finger. The gesture
greatly astonishes me. I have never seen her do that ever before;
she awakens my consciousness with little flashes of light, I feel
almost obliged to smile back at her. Her facial features relax into
a happy expression. A strange spirit has entered the peace of the
afternoon and illuminates it from within, but just at this very
moment a heavy vehicle from the city goes down Highway 218
making the entire house shake. It seems like it's taking forever to
drive by. My facial muscles twitch again and get stiff even after
the noise has subsided and I can hear it disappearing into the
distance. There's something surprising about finding the newspaper sections still there, on the green carpet, reinstated into the
silence, and that she is reading again. Perhaps if I don't move at
all and do not try to fall asleep, she will continue as she is without realizing that her skirt is now disheveled and the edge of her
panties is visible because she raised her knees while absorbed in
her reading to better support her book. If she were to notice
that I was staring at her legs, she would undoubtedly straighten
out her skirt; I feel a combination of embarrassment and anger
pretending to not notice. Instead, I try insistently, sweetly, over
and over again, to turn her on with my mind, to rub my psyche
against that area of her thigh next to her sex, visible behind her
calves. It infuriates me, when I look at her face, how she keeps
reading so calmly, nothing about her betrays any excitement or
interest, only the irises of her eyes move from left to right to the
rhythm of the lines of the book. Perhaps I was not concentrating
intensely enough or long enough. I prepare to insist with my
imagination turned into fingers, tongue, titillation, sexual com-
mands, but I cannot see clearly the area where the work would
need to be done. If only she would move her legs a little to the
left, easy enough for her, my remote stimulation would surely
work. A little bit. A little bit to the left. That is the first thing I

need to get her to do, to move her calves. An immense yearning
grows within me, almost like a distant memory of a paradise,
where I once lived, where all I would have had to do was to
voice my desire and it would have been immediately satisfied.
It annoys me to think about it. It annoys me to know that she
would ever so sweetly reply, but with harshness in the back of
her eyes: "Wouldn't you prefer to take a nap instead? Instead of
me showing you my legs and things of the sort?" And I know
that I don't want that, nor do I want to work, or go out and see
anything, or visit anyone, or have anyone visit me. I want to stay
here, quietly, listening to my hair fall out and my gums recede.
I also want to drink. Surprisingly, she turns exactly the way that
I want her to; but in one fluid motion, without even lifting her
eyes off the page, she holds the book in one hand while tightly
cinching her skirt around her thighs. I extend all ten fingers in
front of my eyes and observe them, making my thumbs almost
touch; I let my hands close together on their own, and then
open them up violently, my fingers like spokes on a wheel, the
skin of my knuckles wrinkled, veins and tendons thick under
my hairy skin, feeling infinitely miserable and idiotic. I get up
heavily; I know that my feet are firmly placed on the floor and
moving toward the kitchen in hard isochronic tones, very solid
and manly. Does she notice? I rest my left hand on the refrig-
erator while I bend my torso and firmly grab the handle with
my right, dry and warm against the shiny metal that becomes
misted up where my skin comes into contact with it. I let go
of the handle and for an instant, I see the imprint left by my
hand, but the moisture disappears almost immediately. I touch
the metal once more and the contact seems magical: an inner
dull and buzzing sound begins to emanate from the device. Of
course I know that the noise is made by a small compressor that
makes these machines run; but that is not enough, I stay there,
unmoving, listening attentively to the sound; listening almost
in desperation. It momentarily seems like an enormous amount
of water far away, it makes me think of spring floods; luckily it
has not rained. But it is more similar to the noise of an excited
crowd; one might say that there is a radio somewhere in the

room and that it is transmitting the indistinct roar of the village. Or as if the house, as if the air inside the house, were full of the voice of the masses.

"Are you looking for something?" she asks from her chair.

"Yes, a beer," I reply. I open the fridge and remove a can. I can feel my heart beating in my throat.

"Can't find it?" she insists.

"Yes, woman, I found it."

As I return to the room with an open can in my hand, I find her lost in her reading again. I return to my chair and try to resume the exact same position as before. It seems to me that it is important to be exactly as before, but I do not know if that is because I want to avoid something that may otherwise happen or because I was extraordinarily comfortable as I was before and want to be so again. I sense that her forehead has tensed up; I imagine that she needs for me to say something, anything, so that she can reply with something unpleasant. I do not plan to say anything. I concentrate on the marvelous coldness of the sweating can in my hand and on the cold liquid descending down my gullet. I also hope that she will again get careless with her skirt.

"Do you want to go to bed with me?" she asks, abruptly turning her heard toward me and closing her book furiously on the arm of the chair.

"No, thank you," I say, softly, surprised and somewhat fearful of her aggressiveness and strange ability to guess my thoughts. "Do you want to?" I add, in a happy and carefree voice, to exasperate her, like that of a ready and willing, and understanding friend.

"I want nothing. The only thing I want I've already told you a million times; for you to not act like a moron, sitting on that chair all day."

I sip on a continuous trickle of beer, staring at her, without pulling the can away from my mouth. She bends down to look for the shoes she'd taken off while reading. She finds only one and puts it on. I could tell her where the other one is; I'm staring right at it. With one foot inside a shoe and the other on the carpet, she feels around on the floor searching blindly under the chair and everywhere. I sit there, can still in my mouth. She gets down on all fours on the carpet and immediately finds the missing shoe almost right in front of her nose. She gets up, turns her back to me, and puts on her shoe, without looking at me at all and with her eyes full of tears as she walks by me and goes into the bedroom. I continue sipping on my beer, not knowing what to do. I look down at the book she abandoned on the arm of the chair, blue binding. I can see the labels they affixed on the spine of the book at the library. Through the window, the blue line of the sky remains unaltered. My fan of newspaper pages still surrounds me. But now there's a crease on the carpet that she left while feeling around for her shoe. The crease bothers me; it's a long indentation that messes up the whole floor. I get up without letting go of my can and I remove the dent by pulling at the fibers toward the window. She is violently moving around the room; since the moment I stood up to straighten out the carpet, I have heard the drawers of the dresser open and close about ten times. I am about to sit on my chair again, but the sounds have stopped and I am curious. I also feel a sort of affection, a tired anger.

I open the door and find her standing in her slip in front of the mirror, combing her hair. On the bed, a dress and her purse await her. She looks at me fleetingly through the mirror, without turning around, and continues fixing her hair.

"Where are you going?" I ask from the door.

"I don't know," she replies angrily, "someplace where I can get a break if even for a little while from having to watch you sit around doing nothing all day on that disgusting chair. I'm sick and tired of watching you and smiling at you and offering you things that you don't want or need."

"Well, alright then, sweetheart, then don't do it," I reply, walking slowly backward and pulling on the door handle until it closes.

I return to my chair, but do not sit down. I shake the can in my hand and turn it upside down over my open mouth to verify that it's empty; one droplet starts to accumulate on the border and finally falls, but it does not fall on my tongue as I expected, but on my teeth. I cannot bear the satisfied, round, and quiet presence of the can in my hand. I hurl it through the kitchen door against the back wall, but I miss and hit a dishcloth instead. The can ricochets gently and falls to the ground quietly; rolls a few times and comes to rest on the tiled floor. I bend over slowly and purposefully to pick it up. I hear the sound of the front door that she must have closed as she left, and I feel the empty air of the house on my entire body. After feeling confused and dejected for a while, standing in the middle of the kitchen, I decide to try and finish organizing last night's files; perhaps I can even begin writing the chapter for the critics. I deposit the empty can in the garbage, open the fridge; confirm that I have five cans left. I grab one, open it, and take a long swig. I catch myself making idiotic expressions with my cheeks.

5

I woke up late. I spent some time trying to go back to that addictive light sleep, so sweet in the silence and light of a Sunday morning. All I needed was a hearty breakfast to wholeheartedly enjoy the perfect night's sleep. I wondered if the old egg vendor woman had come by and I felt like yelling out: "*Ruuunntuuu!!*" as she did, to announce her presence. Lovesick, I wished then that I had been awakened by a woman walking quietly by my bedroom with an armful of groceries. Suddenly, I was fully awake, because I remembered that I had to pick up Blanca, and I was struck by the fear that it might be too late and that she had already arrived at the station. But as I quickly jumped out of bed, I noticed that the tranquil clock said it was a little past ten. I sat there, panting, waiting for my eyes to get used to the light and for my heart to come down from my Adam's apple and return to its rightful place after such a jolt. Then I began to wander throughout the house, not knowing what to do. I concluded that I was still half asleep because all I could think of was how pleasant the cool floorboards felt on the soles of my bare feet and I was walking about, sitting, yawning, gulping and sniffling on every chair within reach. With my head in my hands, looking at my navel hairs through the opening in my pajamas, I figured it would not be a bad idea to go back to bed and sleep for another three hours; it would save me the wait later. But of course even the slightest hint of sleepiness dissipated immediately. I started to walk around the house again, but now I was filled with uncertainty. What would I do with a whole morning ahead of me? Should I shower first or make myself something to eat? What would I use to replace the bread I didn't have? I had no cereal ready either. Or should I first make my bed and then worry about everything else? But then the bed would not have enough time to air out properly and Blanca would be sleeping on it tonight. And what about the pajamas I was wearing? Should I wear them again tonight? I smiled pitifully at my reflection in the bathroom mirror where I had ended up:

And you are going to wear pajamas tonight, asshole? What pajamas, huh? Why the pajamas, moron? Will you kiss her on the forehead and then sleep on the floor outside her door and shiver in your pajamas all night? Is that it, douchebag? Idiot.

Suddenly I realized that I, the morning, the polished floor, and the silence of the Sunday had all arisen with our mouths wide open and our ribs sparkling so that we could rub them against Blanca's skin when the train deposited her in front of us full of stupid aspirations and ambitions, tired, beautiful and dizzy with desire, into this world of ours that she didn't know.

"That's it!" I yelled at my reflection, "A piece of ass!"

In the bathroom, in the living room, in the kitchen, it seemed to me I could already see the imprint of a long cry of pleasure that we would be leaving copulation after copulation, from one piece of furniture to another, from kissing to biting. It was just that a whole year of relative celibacy was now making me feel like a volcano ready to erupt or like I had a coiled spring ready to burst out of my groin or sperm boiling over in my testicles. God, how one needed a woman for these types of mornings, to possess her, her body still limp from sleep, smiling lovingly, her features barely discernible in the semi-darkness of mid-morning, and afterward, hearing her from the bed with the happiest of ears, toiling about in the kitchen with the breakfast dishes and rustling her nightie around with her bare thighs, over her nude stomach, filling the house with those soft whooshing sounds that women's clothes make. Blanca tonight. Blanca today after lunch or whenever that damned train, that was always late, finally got here. Oh, no: that's too long a wait. A few blocks away there was a possible substitute; just far enough away to give me time to shower, dress, shave, grab my swimsuit, and leave. For sure

I would find her as always: in the sun, the strap of her swimsuit undone as she sunbathed by her pool or perhaps it was her
father's or her elderly, wholly incapable, soft, and somnolent
husband's pool. This was why the curves of her breasts rested on
the towel that was laid out on the grass, almost escaping from the
cloth, while she was all alone and lost in thought. And on top of
having that exquisite body waiting for me there in the sun, that
was the only part of town where mosquitos were abundant. It
was as if they raised them there; as if, besides providing swimming and the girl, they had purposely endeavored to provide
mosquito bites to anyone who wanted to return to the jungle
accustomed to the fierce poison. Seriously though, it was another
possibility for spending the morning: renewing the natural vac-
cine against mosquitoes, soaking in the pool, and even, perhaps,
ending up between the blonde and tanned thighs of their owner.
She would be alone, stretched out and distracted and I would
come to her side . . . probably would not have time: the train at
noon. And the bed still needed to be made, and the ashtrays that
my friends had dirtied needed cleaning. I opened the windows,
sighing in resignation, to see if the floor also needed attention.
I stepped on something hard that hurt the bottom of my foot:
a bullet capsule from the night before; the other one was a bit
further away. In the sun, they looked completely ridiculous, but
they reminded me that I would also have to deal with the gun
and clean it, because with the little pieces of wood, tannins, and
humidity inside the box, it could become moldy or break into
splinters.

My need for a woman upset me. Perhaps the solution was to
go to the Germans' pool. Perhaps she was indeed alone and she
might even be in the mood for some hanky-panky . . . But there
was also no time and I needed her now and not when Blanca was
scheduled to arrive. I suddenly became furious with my beloved:
how difficult would it have been for her to arrive one day earlier?
Regardless, I was going to touch every inch of her as soon as I
could stick a finger where it mattered. Open, open, open, open.

Under the circumstances, it would be best to do the usual: brush
your teeth, shower, and my good sir, shave very, very closely. But

*first everything had to be set up, cleaned and organized. Are you
familiar with the Entropic Principle? Are you? You are not? Well,
never mind, my friend, anyway, it rules over you. What it is to not
know. No? "He who does not know is like he who does not see," Tu
Padre. "He who pisses and does not fart is like he who goes to school
and does not read," Tu Padre as well. It would not have made any
difference to leave everything as is: "Besides, she won't stay a virgin
for long in my hands."* Those two strong and adventurous hands
that the mirror discredited by not revealing their inner strength
and the ability of their touch and that for the moment were slippery with patches of greasy skin from the night before, would
soon close around her waist, thumbs on her navel, subjugating
her, making her submit. Scented lotions releasing their dizzy-
ing fragrances, warmed by the white walls. And the quivering
twin fawns, dreaming, throbbing in their sleep, lifting their red
noses, swelling with passion when licked, then they faint, limp
with compliance and frenzy. If only Tu Padre, the stupid idiot,
had not insisted on receiving his well-deserved beating, right
when my girl's wonderful nymphomania . . . Don't set me as a
seal upon thine heart or as a seal upon thine arm, my dearest;
oh, no, because you would immediately believe that there is no
coin large enough or thick enough or hard enough to pay for
your sacrifice. Although, really and truly, I swear to Gehenna,
that your love is much, much sweeter than wine.

The best thing to do would be to immediately prepare breakfast. But what breakfast if the wicked old woman had brought
nothing? Besides, the kitchen would have gotten all messed
up. Downtown, that was the solution: being served. For this
heroic hunger, there were no conventional solutions. A few Salta
empanadas; many, many Salta *empanadas*, because this hunger
was real. A noisy dragon rumbled in my belly. It would have
been better not to have had to spend a single penny on such
an endeavor. Go out into the street, smiling, humble and trembling, and stick my hand out as people went by: "Sir, ah, kind
sir, my good sir, could you spare a few empanadas for my little
dragon? An *empanada*, for God's sake." "But you see, my kind
sir, if I pay for them, I'd have to do it with my own money. I

have two million saved up, but to be used for love and only for love, and other than that I have not a penny in the world. A little *empanada*? One *empanada*? Just one? I could almost see the tasty meat pies, positioned in threes on the plate, and feel them on my tongue and between my teeth, just hot enough, soft and filling; this was making me drool and made me decide to postpone all other ventures until after breakfast. *Time to shower then, and be quick about it.* I would have to dry myself with toilet paper, although that was very uncomfortable and I would need half a roll; but, just like there's only one mother, there was only one towel, and it couldn't be touched until Blanca had used it first. On my way to the shower, I was grateful to Pablo because the housekeeper his wife had gotten me was excellent; the only thing missing was for someone to suggest to her how important it was to deal with towels; she seemed to have an aversion to them. She would gather and leave them in unlikely places as they became dirty. Telling Pablo felt almost rude; but I could not tell his wife either; and I certainly could not tell the housekeeper, because she had her own key and because I never saw her. I couldn't leave her a note either: she didn't know how to read. I couldn't go see her at home: I didn't know where she lived. I opened the tap with baited breath; luckily water came out instead of the gargling noises that came out at other times. I turned on the electricity and held my hand under the shower waiting for it to warm up, thinking with relief that Blanca would surely bring a towel to save me. My hand advised me that the wait was over and I stood underneath with the same nagging apprehension as always; one of these days I was going to electrocute myself with the device. But I did it, right? And with just an old headlight, that's right Mr. Doubtful-son-of-a-gun Flammini, yes sir, you and your doubtful slimy face and wrinkled smiley nose and with an electric stove burner cleverly inserted into the ingenious holes. I spent that whole morning, yes, and I singed two fingers, yes. But here it is, producing its lovely plastic smell and gurgling hot water, and sucking soapy residue down the drain, between puffs of fragrant steam, where right now these hairy and wet feet could slip. "The worst accidents happen at home." "Nothing is more risky than a bathtub." "The dark-skinned girl next door broke her tailbone." Ah, how delightful that the fragrant, soapy water has an obvious gray grime! Who would ever get tired of soaping themselves up and not getting clean? Nevertheless, that sad moment when one's skin is clean always arrives. Now, for the sake of attaining the scent, which will slowly penetrate through my shirt and jacket, until it finally reaches Blanca's nose, again, I must wash from the very top of my head to my pubic bone and with lots of soft and lubricating foam like a wet suit made of snow on my face and hair. If I were to lose my sight, good heavens, I would also lose all my self-confidence. And now, blind, naked and soapy, forget about it. Now the entire world has turned into a slide, full of sharp edges lying in wait for elbows and heads to snap and make cracking sounds as they break, like boney watermelons.

"Shit!"

That's what happens when your mind wanders and you start thinking about stupid things; luckily I was able to hang on to the window frame. "Do not play like that, you might stay that way," or hurt yourself. "I once knew a boy . . ." but I did it, didn't I? One day, one day I won't be able to. My chest will be full of phlegm, my trembling legs will be all withered, and my head will be ten inches closer to my knees than it is now. My sclerotic shoulder and my skinny wrist will reach with a tentative hand toward my knees, which I can now do without even trying, but before I can reach halfway, the soap will devilishly slip and my fingers will be left clawing at the air by my unsoaped knees. Does he have balls? Yes, of course, and what balls! Anyone else in his place . . . bang! Crash! Yes, sir, yes I do. For this *and* for that. And when I finally and painfully find it, and I turn and try to pick it up, the fiery fork of my sciatica will strike me from my waist to my heels and will immobilize me under the shower like a statue miserably standing under the sun or under pigeon poop. And the same thing will happen when I try to hunch over a woman; that is, old man, assuming that one will want to. But no; oh, no; a million times and a million trillion times not. Certainly you can be forever young. But how? By eating yogurt? By standing on my head? Yes, sir, just like that. And also by smoking, and getting plastered and by simply wanting it. Yes, sir, I have and I can. Now a cold shower, like a handful of pebbles on the skin. Up we go, adrenal glands, back to it. Sh . . . Sh . . . Shit. Up, up. A long stream of water over the back of the strong neck, and down over the powerful loins. A turn and a shot to the testicles. Pchfff. Sileeeeeeeence.

V

WHEN THE YEAR ends with gifts, dances, and sometimes low-key family drink fests or a certain elegance or luxury or even misery, even if one ends up sitting in the dark at the stroke of midnight, even if one's eyes are tired from studying a subject that, ultimately, is not even directly related to what one calls one's field, I think, virtually nothing valuable or compelling can come from it, nothing that will effectively eliminate the contagious spirit of the season. However, they also belong to me; they are also our Christmas and our New Year. I remember when, in the midst of the heat of those long ago years, my brother and I would hope for a new pair of shoes, because the ones we had belonged more in the garbage than on anyone's feet, and my aunt would appear, cherished even more because of the distance, with her loving smile and those countless caramels resting in their scented boxes. I am certain that I did in fact see her in that carriage that the passage of time has added a meditative parrot standing on the lantern, and I am sure that she had a whip in her hand to whip the horse, and she only pretended she did not see me, standing there in surprise, while her wagon shook the cobblestone streets. The only thing that did not make sense was that it was autumn at the time, and not the Christmas season, which is in the middle of summer in my country. The weather and sunshine of the summer months was what best suited her and her bladder drums and the tin soldiers in her suitcases. I had spent too much time on the streets and at the public school in town to not know that Santa Claus didn't exist. And the mood of the day before was subtly like today's, when I would not expect anything worthwhile simply because the calendar said December 25th. Tonight is Christmas Eve and tomorrow, Christmas. And those icicles that I now see from this armchair where I am waiting for her to come back from Midnight Mass, lit like crystals by the light of the neighboring barracks, where sweet sounds of a house party vanish into the night, remind me of the vibration of the pavement or the cobblestones of the streets of my childhood, lulled to sleep by the sun. My mother would come in then, into the room that was all at once a dining room, a play room, and a meeting room where our infrequent and peculiar guests would gather; here, however, no one brings me sweet-smelling dainties and yet, I feel a certain tenderness when I see a snowman in a top hat next to a colorful glass ball. She left it there so she could light it when she returned, because it's not a snowman, it's a candle. Nothing is really beginning or ending. It is simply a link to other physical and emotional states; the illusion of that Christmas when Blanca and I placed the candy eggs in the copper-lined basket next to the Christmas tree, that unexpectedly fell afterward, leaving us in awe, as if it were an omen of our bad and divergent fate. Bad fate? No sir, don't complain. Maybe so for her, poor, poor greedy thing, she destroyed her very own heart; as if she could have devoured it and found happiness. I wish her well, hopefully at this very moment she is enjoying the animated company of someone that, unlike me, she would not have to cheer up by remembering that couple that she had seen or made up living in a shanty town hut; they only had one candle to light an empty table in a wretched room, but they were celebrating their Christmas by singing together and keeping time with castanets made out of two spoons held together between their fingers. Me, not me. Oberon and Titania again create for me an eternal, inexistent springtime. Puck is again dancing merrily, spreading his magic dust in the enchanted forest that I will now never, ever know.

"Come in," I reply, motionless and weary.

A head especially suited for Black Tom appears in the doorway.

"Do you know if Christmas Mass begins right at midnight? Is it true that it never starts late?" he asks.

"I suppose so. I don't know."

"And do you know what church your wife might have gone to?"

"No, I don't know that either. I think she said Saint Wenceslas, but I'm not sure."

The shithead stays quiet, but doesn't leave, in spite of my obvious rudeness. He is letting in the cold outside air and making me freeze. He stays there with half his body out the door and the other blurry half inside. I suppose he remains there so that I will ask about the reason for his questions so that he can complain about poor Jane, with her cleaning rag always in hand or taking care of someone else's kids or wiping her own kids' rear ends.

"Is something wrong?"

I have to believe he is alluding to the fact that I am sitting alone in the dark on Christmas Eve. It seems to me that he spoke with an anxious inflection, a certain greed to find out about other people's disagreements.

"No, nothing at all. I was studying for an Elizabethan theater test that I have next week and my eyes got tired. So I turned off the light."

"Well, how studious! We are at home with some friends. Would you like to join us? Or perhaps when Adriana gets back, you can both come to the party?"

"I will ask her when she arrives. Thank you very much."

I would have preferred to tell him to go to hell so that he would leave me alone. But at least, in contrast, he must have felt envy and bitterness at being the rotten deadbeat that he is. I stay quiet. I hope that he will get nervous and leave.

"I won't bother you anymore. In a little while, we will come and get you."

"You know, Tom? Thanks a million, but I have worked a lot today and I think I will go to bed as soon as I have dinner. I am very tired. Thanks a million."

"Hey, if you keep this up, you'll kill yourself. You have to enjoy yourself a little."

"If I feel up to it, I'll go," I reply despondently.

"I hope so. It would be a shame to spend the evening sleeping. OK, see you later."

He motions goodbye before closing the door. I hear the snow outside crunching under his shoes and then I am comforted by the sound of the door of his barrack closing behind him. It makes me laugh that in order to appear like an integrationist so that the other idiots of the neighborhood would learn, I am now stuck with this piece of shit's friendship. What kind of Christmas is the disgusting slacker giving you, Jane? What happened to the parties that you dreamt of as a young girl in your bombed-out English home? Then I hoped. Hopefully she, like the couple with the spoons and a wine demijohn to keep them warm, is now enjoying what she always promised herself. Nothing begins and nothing ends. Today is another day, another night, on Earth devastated by tears. "Son, who asked you?" More spoons pretending to be castanets in the teary eyes of people who are not like me, who are not on the road to triumph, and glory. Shit. Shit. Again. The afternoon was in love, summer-scented; I wanted that spruce, but today I have a better recollection of that afternoon and of the woman that was waiting for me, the first woman in my young life, sweaty and poor; the clean air; the solitary distance of the newly-formed stars. Why not confess that Christmas carols still make me emotional? "Let's all sing. Why don't you sing with your brother; with us? It's because you don't love us. You don't love your parents. That's not true, right? You love your mother, right? This boy doesn't love anyone." "Remember that the poor thing is sickly. You will have other drums; other tin soldiers much more beautiful than these ones. He may not. He doesn't love anyone, absolutely no one. Heart of stone." This radio that Elmer loaned me was perhaps already in use back then. Why not let myself become emotional? Everywhere, angelic voices, children's choirs, young women's choirs, soft voices, are singing. There is but one star in the sky. That is because tonight is Christmas Eve; and tomorrow, Christmas. Home is sweet, my friend; always forgiving. The shoe had a hole in it. The night was warm and noisy. It

was our young friends, in their new clothes, blushingly looking
at the hems of their cheap new dresses. The floors seemed to be
sprawling, and it made my steps more certain. It's always forgiving. She embarrassed me: she told everyone that I had saved
a piece of my hard-boiled egg from breakfast; I had put it in
the dresser drawer for my Christmas Aunt. This old, well-loved
radio, covered in dust, honest and dilapidated with its warm little light, came before aerodynamic chairs and nylon panties. That
will never return. Who knows, buddy, who knows. "I brought a
radio." "A radio? Really? You bought it? Does it work? Is it ours?"
No, it wasn't ours. It is sweet, my friend, it always forgives. He
had brought it home to fix it, but could not. Everything turned
on: that marvelous little light, the spark of red light sleeping
inside the tubes; the numbers of the rotating dial were clearly
visible. I, who had never been so close to a miracle, probably
didn't expect anything special to come out of those speakers and
that's probably why I still remember how beautiful that quiet
and flickering hum of the device was, magically turned on under
my father's disappointed nose. *A Midsummer Night's Dream. The
Winter's Tale.* We have never returned there. Found only within
the pages of a book, and as speech—their only true form—in
the fictional world of the stage are the imitations of what is
most concrete in the history of man: the imitation of dreams.
The Fairy Queen, with all her fairy love watching from behind
delightful trees, cradles a harmless, but ridiculous monster in her
arms. He's a good person, with an ass's head and all, a relative of
the wind and the forest, of the harmony among the "sweet tiny
bells of melodious feathers" and uneasy breast, of love all smiles
and sweetness, with dawn always imminent. Titania distant and
cherished. Fine breasts, scented skirts, snow-white and crystalline skin, golden hair, indescribable face leaning, finally, over a
joyous, pure and young beloved. Forever young. I wanted the
spruce tree; but under the warm sky, while the city lights came
on in the distance, I was unable to cut it down. I simply damaged it and then abandoned it, because it was getting late and
it was theft and I must have been (when wasn't I?) scared. And
she, infected with poetry and the sinister omen of the candy

eggs, attributed her own meaning to Christmas in her own private celebration. Later on, she wrote those long epistolary pages in which she would recreate the tradition saying, among other things: "What kind of criminal would dare to commit such a heinous crime on such a loving and peaceful night?" Hopefully, these days, with her spoons or castanets she is quietly going to hell, perhaps raising some new wretched member of the featherless race who will receive his drums and his soldiers and his new shoes without holes or bare patches tomorrow; he will clap his chubby little hands together to the delight of both his procreators and his aunt, because she will be there as well—if he is—though she will not be better than the one I had. Not better than those skates: I am still thankful that she kindly gave them to me the night before. A different aunt; without a carriage, without a piece of hardboiled egg, without an autumn parrot to embody one's dreams: "Better to do it now. Why wait until tomorrow? It is better to give joy to others as soon as one can, especially to children. And you'll be a scoundrel, but you're still a child. This is your gift. It's not much. Remember: your father is dead. We are poor; you know that." I skated halfway through the city with my dead father on my mind, dodging police, until I reached Sylvia's house; I returned at eleven at night without having seen her, and they reprimanded me until after New Year's for it. Who is Sylvia? What is she? She is no longer, she was. Poor thing. She would be happy to have me look at her reed-like waist again. Poor thing. Fuck! The scary thing is that nothing matters to me at all. I haven't even been able to listen to the faint sound of the poor old radio with any love. Why not, finally, submit to the sad call of the Christmas carols?—Of peace—Of love. It is a sweet friend. A star. It is far better than aspirin. It always knows. It is three times better. Let the sleigh bells ring, the little bells. *A donkey is going to Bethlehem, rin, rin . . . laden with chocolate . . .*

I wonder if some radio station somewhere around here is playing that old Spanish Christmas carol. Could it be? Let's take a look . . . Don't be stupid, my friend. How can you expect that some radio station in this rich, industrious, progressive, and traditional region of the Bible Belt or Corn Belt would ever dream of playing an old Spanish Christmas carol? Let them fill our ears with the sounds of bells and peace and love and reindeer and sleighs . . . Although perhaps I owe my memories to a powerful rendition of a song from back then. How did the one about the turnips go again? That's it.

If anyone could understand me, they would take it the wrong way and with good reason. My friends from back then and I would not have sung that filth either on Christmas Eve.

"Come in."

Again. Worst case, maybe someone heard me. No, not this time. This time it's a woman.

"Good evening."

"Good evening. Is Adriana in?"

"No, Betty, she went to church."

"Sorry, was that you singing?"

"Yes, it was."

I must be as red as a beet and if I don't turn on the light it will be rude of me and if I do she will see my beet-red face. Luckily she reads my body language and tries to stop me.

"Oh, no, don't trouble yourself. I will phone her in a little while."

"I was studying . . ." I start to explain.

"It's not important. Bye," she says.

I sit back down again. I notice that the radio is playing softly, old and sweet. Something has humiliated me. The one my father brought to repair never did broadcast any music. Your aunt is not coming this year. Let him have the soldiers, poor thing. What criminal would dare . . . Bye, bye. I can clearly make out the outline of my hand, the hand that will acquire everything that they always wanted; and perhaps also what none of us ever wanted. It hangs down toward the floor, over the arm of the chair. It seems to point to the book that lies there, closed, and that I really did study until my eyes hurt.

6

BLANCA ARRIVED. IT changed the course of time, it changed the city, it changed everything. Only the reassuring and loving presence of the money I'd won reminded me of a poker game that, set in other coordinates of time, had retreated from the immediate past to the absolute past.

One thing didn't change: I had to keep sleeping alone. Only a fool could have ever imagined that Blanquita would ever travel alone, especially if she were doing so in order to sleep with a man. When the international train finally crawled into the station in the darkness, six hours late, and I found my beloved looking at me through the window as if she were about to cry, a round and smiling face emerged from behind her: her sister. The sister was passionate about physical exercise, charity, hard work, and prudence. I hated her with downright schoolboy hatred. Because who would tolerate, for example, some woman inserting ads in teen magazines announcing that she's willing to help people in distress and, to add insult to injury, her name is Luisa, but she signs as María Pía? And that was not something that Blanca was making up, because several times she showed me her sister's letters from her protégés and they were so unbelievable that no one could possibly invent them, not even Blanca. She was even romantically involved with an inmate, who had been unfairly convicted, and who passed himself off as a French count. To prove his nationality, he had written her some letters in French, wink, wink. And perhaps with the same intent, in the last letters of the collection that my beloved and I reviewed, he recommended to the sister that she should stand in front of a mirror in black panties, pulled down to her thighs, and rub her breasts.

In the hustle and bustle of getting the suitcases, I asked Blanca why the hell she had brought her sister along and she shrugged as if it had been some weather phenomenon. However, once we had everything in the taxi and we got inside it, the sister shrank in her seat and said, with a dramatic and adventurous gesture:

"So, where are you taking us now?"

That's when the great idea occurred to me.

"To my house, of course. Where else?"

It's not a bad thing to live with two women. That is, if the sister didn't limit herself, as I suspected, to just epistolary pursuits. I had spent enough time without hearing from my, say, soul, for us to have a grand old time. Monday, Wednesday, and Friday with one; Tuesday, Thursday, and Saturday with the other; Sunday, laundry and ironing.

"Really?" the sister blurted out, "but won't you find it a huge hassle for you? I mean, is your home big enough for us to not get in your way? Maybe a hotel would be better," she added, lowering her lashes.

"Of course it's no bother. None at all. It's not very big, but you two can sleep in the bedroom and I can set up my air mattress and sleep in the living room. Going to a hotel makes no sense. How can you even consider that? Besides, the ones in the city are not very comfortable," I lied.

And that's when Blanca blew it. She'd been waiting for her sister to make the decision. She'd been looking alternately at her sister, at the people walking by, and at me the entire time with a vague satisfied smile that one could barely notice in the darkness of the taxi. However, when she saw that her sister was very willing, she started to find it a magnificent idea.

"Fantastic. We will go to your house. It'll be great, all waking up together. We can bring you breakfast in bed. You'll have two women. No, for God's sake, how immoral; two sisters," she corrected herself, laughing.

"That's right," I completed, my tone a little contrite to show what a good winner I was. "That's right; you'll see that we fit perfectly."

"I think," Luisa rudely interrupted, "that it would be best for us to go to a hotel."

In the midst of my bewilderment, I was starting to worry about the resignation and contempt that I could see in the driver's face as he glanced at me impatiently from time to time in the rearview mirror. It embarrassed me that he was witnessing the unfortunate position that the two women were putting me in.

"Tell me, do you know of a good hotel in the city?" I prompted, to at least include him in the conversation.

"No, I don't. I'm not a tourist guide. I just take people where they tell me to take them. There's no reason why I should know about hotels."

The sister looked at me. Perhaps if she hadn't looked at me things would have been different, because the guy's rudeness did annoy me somewhat. But, seeing the sister's stately eyebrow rise, I couldn't just ignore it: I would have completely agreed with the poor fellow even if he had told me to go to hell.

"Perhaps it's best to go to a hotel, after all, as Luisa says," my beloved conceded, completely ignoring the incident with the driver. "But we would need one that is not too expensive. It cannot be too awful either, of course, if we are going to be there by ourselves. Something good, but not ritzy . . ."

"Look, quite frankly, I don't know a lot about hotels. Unfortunately it didn't occur to me to find out."

"You could take them to the London Hotel," suggested the driver, very politely, as if someone else had been responsible for the outburst earlier.

"No way, man, what are you thinking!" I jumped, because although it was true that I knew nothing about hotels, I had stayed at that one for a few nights. "Know something? I really believe you will not be as comfortable anywhere as you would be at my place. Of course if you don't think it is suitable . . . or whatever . . ."

At this point the driver switched off the engine because Blanca sweetly took up the defense and her sister a stubborn offense; it showed that the matter was far from resolved. Of those who had arrived on the train, no one was left on the streets; I figured that by now they were probably at home recounting the vicissitudes of the journey or showering or finishing their meals or going to bed with their lovers. A railway employee came out to pick up a blackboard announcing the train schedules in front of the station door. Suddenly the sister let out a little cry of terror and ended up almost sitting on Blanca's lap, who was in the middle. A man's head had appeared out of nowhere and was protruding into the window. We couldn't make out his face.

"Sorry, dear lady, sorry sir. Forgive me for having frightened the lady. My intentions were much friendlier, but my clumsiness has spoiled it. Forgive me. I was standing over here, sir, and I allowed myself, sir, to hear your conversation. I am one of those fools who is always, if you'll allow me, looking to help, especially people like you, who, one can tell, by your mere presence, that you are respectable people. Also, I noticed by the tone of your voice that you are not from here . . ."

"No, we are Chilean," said Blanca, delighted with her condition as a foreigner.

"But what a happy coincidence, Señorita! I too am from our sweet homeland. Allow me, Adalberto Lientur Elizaguirre, at your service."

"Charmed," chirped the sister with delight, stretching an elegant hand that the kind stranger gently shook in the shadows.

The scene was rewarding me for all the recent setbacks. Had it not been because Blanca was going to become as furious as a dragon if I let them continue making fools of themselves, and because the possibilities of coupling with a female dragon are few, I would have let the charade continue; it was getting tiresome. As Adalberto Lientur Elizaguirre was about to open the door to continue his scam, I lit a cigarette so that he would be able to see my face. He winced. I had never seen don Joaquin so confused and annoyed with himself.

"Forgive me, please. I did not realize . . . It's just that with the crappy lighting here, sir, one would not recognize his own mother. How very foolish of me . . . believe me, I'm sorry. That's not funny, *patrón*. You could have saved me the embarrassment from the start."

It was obvious by his tone that, although he was confused and taken aback, don Joaquin was starting to see the funny side of the situation and was stifling his laughter. Suddenly he let it out.

"Way to go, *patrón*, way to waste people's time. I'm going to have to wear glasses. Forgive me."

I asked him to join us for dinner, while four bright and scandalized eyes full of surprise and disapproval reprimanded me, but don Joaquin politely refused. He stuck his head in and said softly, yet naturally:

"If you are missing a bag, *patrón*, don't worry; they send them to your house. Untouched. So long. So sorry ladies, I wish you the best. Take them to the Chuquisaca, *patrón*. See you soon."

"What bag was he talking about? Who is that guy?" Blanca asked, alarmed.

"To the Chuquisaca, sir?" the driver wanted to know.

"To the Chuquisaca," I replied and settled back comfortably to have a smoke.

"My black bag!" Blanca shrieked, "Where did we leave my black bag? I gave it to you when we first got off the train."

"Look, Blanca, please, don't make a scene. Be thankful that you just got back something that you had lost."

"But listen! That's where I have all my money and my jewelry."

"Don't worry. Don Joaquin is very honest. If he said your dammed suitcase would show up at the house untouched, then that's what's going to happen," I said, holding in my laughter because of the jewelry. The poor soul sounded as if she had lost the Koh-i-Noor.

"But, understand . . ."

"Shut up!"

Blanca stared at me, paralyzed with shock and horror, about to cry. The sister stared fixedly out the window, perfectly poised.

"Everything looks very poor and very dirty," she said.

It pleased me that she would say that to annoy me. As if I were the founder of the city or the municipal council chair. It was not going to be easy to get the sisters to forgive me for the don Joaquin incident. Meanwhile, the driver tried to turn on the ignition without audible result.

"That's it, damn it, it's dead, that's just great," he said, angrily, irrationally striking the instrument panel.

"Shall we push?" I proposed.

"No. What for? It's dead. And there's nowhere now to buy another one. You'll have to go in another car, then."

"True, there's no choice," I informed my exasperated travelers.

"But, there must be *something* that can be done to make this thing go?" Blanca shrieked again, as if blaming me for my inability to resuscitate dead batteries.

"Nothing. Replacing the battery would be the only option. The driver is right; there's no point in staying in here," I answered politely.

We removed the luggage from the trunk of the car, I, stifling my laughter and the driver, his fury. When we were done and came back to the defenselessness of the sidewalk, I started to provide a discouraging analysis of the situation to the travelers, as I glanced at the driver, who was still with us, out of the corner of my eye.

"It's a difficult situation; taxis don't come to the station unless there's a train. Yours was the last one."

"Never?" the sister asked. She had lost her composure. Her voice sounded sharp, as if slipping out, pushed from behind by tears.

"Well, sometimes, yes, but only by chance. And if we stay and no one comes? Huh? I could call a friend to come and get us, but where do I get a phone? There isn't one for blocks."

"How about here at the station?" groaned the sister.

"Sure there are, but they close up and leave as soon as the last train arrives. Only the baggage porters with their carts are left.

"Those ones?" Blanca asked.

"Those ones. The downside is that they are much more expensive than a car; and we have to stay close to them. The hotel is about twenty blocks away. Hopefully they won't close the reception desk in the meantime," I added wickedly.

I resented the interest that my mischief seemed to awaken in the driver. It made me uncomfortable; he was sticking to us like glue and we were beginning to cause a disturbance with all the luggage scattered on the ground, the two sisters listening in dismay to my ramblings on, the driver with his curious expectations and the plentiful baggage porters with their carts repeatedly offering their services.

"Well, I think we have no choice but to hire a cart," I added.

"Will you not pay the fare then?" the driver asked, very alarmed.

"And why should I pay you if you have not taken us anywhere?"

"But, I would have taken you . . . and if you hadn't discussed it so much, the car wouldn't have died and I would have taken you. So you have to pay up, that's all, and right now. If not, we'll go to the police."

"Ah, very good, excellent. Let's go to the police station right away. While you file the complaint, I'm going to call my friend Soruco and I'm going to tell him how you are charging for services that you haven't provided and that you have been complaining about the government's economic policy, that it doesn't care about car batteries and is ruining the country and that you are saying we'd be better off with a different government. OK, let's go."

The driver took a few hesitant steps behind me. He probably hadn't understood much of my little speech, but he'd caught the name of the police chief who was my friend, and he stopped me in a whiny and conciliatory voice.

"Now, now, no need to get mad, *tatay*. Instead, help me out, then. If you pay me the fare, you'll be helping me to buy a battery, even if it's a used one. If you don't, I'll have to stay like this, unable to work. Help me out."

He asked for an exorbitant amount, but after haggling for a while and perhaps because Blanca approached us and the poor man looked at both sisters suspiciously, we agreed on a quarter of the original fee. Blanca watched indignantly as I counted the bills in the semi-darkness. As the driver returned to his car, she was starting to criticize how I'd dealt with the issue. But I almost completely agreed with the driver; if they hadn't been talking so much and had simply gone to my apartment, what happened wouldn't have happened; so . . . shut up. I was about to join the group where the sister was half-heartedly fighting against the offers of the luggage handlers, when Blanca took my arm and said, touching my ear with her lips:

"Don't be silly. If we go to your house, we'll be stuck with her there all the time and it will be a drag."

So I walked pensively across the city. I marveled at the erotic foresight and intelligence of my beloved so much that I wasn't paying attention to our luggage porter, who was pulling on his cart and acting as if he were moving an overwhelming weight. We were greeted by a somewhat distant concierge and a porter who took our luggage from the cart almost in disgust and carried them up the stairs trying not to rub them against his clothes. And he had good reason: the luggage porter had the occasional fat and shiny cockroach-like louse.

My role as protector of defenseless travelers was beginning to weigh on me. The dire predictions I had made with regard to transportation had momentarily returned them to a childhood state. I had to register them at reception, pointing to the document that the clerk was asking for; then I had to accompany them to their room, tip the porter who brought the luggage, and finally, fail at getting them some dinner, because the dining room and the kitchens were closed for the night. But, since bad luck comes in threes, at the moment when I was about to leave them to freshen up, Blanca infuriated me by informing me that the sister was menstruating and that it made her prone to tears. I couldn't figure out why she told me. To bug me; to make things even worse. Could be. Family folklore said that sister Luisa couldn't eat on trains because of ghastly motion sickness, but she felt better as soon as her feet touched solid ground and then she would get hungry. I figured that motion sickness and her period were a dreadful combination somehow for her appetite . . . that Blanca meant that it didn't matter that I was unable to get them any food . . . that it mattered painfully . . . that Blanca was being stupid.

I did, however, have a chance to admire the sister's level-headedness. Even when they appeared at the top of the stairs, refreshed and smiling, even when they ended up at my house, eating stale bread (revived by Blanca's skillfulness), with bacon and cheese left overs, I didn't notice any anguish. She had great control over her emotions. She turned out to be the perfect guest, really. Frightened by the foreignness of the place, she'd forgotten the issue with the accommodations and with don Joaquin. Before I'd finished opening the door she was praising the merits of my house. She smiled charmingly when she noticed the stack of boxes full of sawdust that I kept in my dining room; her face lit up with fraternal tenderness. Single men were like that: beloved, helpless, inefficient.

"I had nowhere to put them," I apologized, "and there are several thousand tin soldiers."

"Tin soldiers? Show me! Let's see them!" the sister blurted out, as if that were her sole reason for making the trip.

I had to take out several models of each figurine, moving the very heavy boxes, to reciprocate their courtesy. For every one I took out, they asked in wonder what each of them was.

"And this, what is this?"

"Those are troops."

"And these others?"

"Soldiers firing a gun."

"And this other one, so odd."

"That's barbed wire, you know, they put it on the battlefield so that the enemy can't advance."

"And how do they advance?" the sister asked.

"The other is an infantry soldier," I answered, "and this one is wounded; there's not much demand for him."

"Because if one side can't move ahead, neither can the other side," the sister continued, relentlessly.

"Hey, you know, the best thing would be for me to fin-ish showing you the apartment and we can try to eat the few scrapings that I have left. I guess I was so excited with your arrival that I forgot to do the shopping."

They answered in unison that it didn't matter at all, how could I even think of it; I should show them the kitchen and I would see what Blanca could whip up with a crust of bread and whatever was available. Their four loving hands took me by the arms and cried together:

"To the kitchen!"

Once inside, Blanca took complete control of the extreme poverty of the kitchen that was evident in the shiny pots and pans and, turning toward the two of us, banished us to the living room with a flamboyant finger, without allowing me to even guide her first attempts. The sister had momentarily forgotten the barbed wire and sank into a chair, smiling. I sat across from her. She explored the room with an approving look that she then fixated on me tenderly. I observed her hips, midriff, waist, and tits. Then there was a somewhat uncomfortable silence, and we occasionally shot each other friendly smiles across the room.

She seemed to realize that I wasn't paying the slightest attention to her and that my heart was in the kitchen; I was torn between the desire to conceal that I was dying to leave her alone and the desire to tell her so. So I was happy to smile at her, but I was also happy that she seemed to realize that she was the third wheel. Luckily, Blanca called me because she could not find the salt. I had the impression that I had heard her with my stomach. I closed the kitchen door behind me and, after picking up the salt that had fallen under the cupboard days ago, stayed and watched her work. Actually, the only thing we were able to do that night was have a quickie.

The sister pretended not to have noticed anything or perhaps hunger had distracted her entirely. When we came out of the kitchen, the sister joyfully and, perfectly naturally, accompanied us to the dining room. We concluded the evening drinking the remains of a bottle of whiskey that I almost consumed by myself, listening to them narrate the ups and downs of their journey and the news from home. As I dreamily wondered if it was possible to convince Blanca to return to the kitchen, I smiled or looked amazed, as required by their stories, while they kept interrupting each other excited that they were entertaining me. Intermittently, thoughts of the succulence and warmth of Blanca's midriff filled my thoughts to the point of returning me to a fetal state.

I was unable to drag Blanca back into the kitchen. The sister was anxious to get some rest and as soon as she could, my beloved took the dirty dishes to the kitchen sink, where they stayed, smelling of cold food and waiting until the next day. Then we unenthusiastically hurried out onto the street. The sister had thrown in the towel; the exhaustion caused by the dizziness and the menstruation had hit her like a ton of bricks; she leaned on my arm, smiling, but with her entire body weight; of course she repeatedly protested that it was unnecessary, that she could move perfectly well by herself, but she let herself be persuaded easily that it was more fun to continue like this. And indeed it was; if she hadn't allowed me to hide in the kitchen with Blanca, at least she was rubbing her beautiful tit on my forearm like a caress, while righteous fate gave her the fierce malaise that seemed to possess her now; and yet with all that and hanging from my arm, Luisa now barely seemed like a woman to me. She was radically different from the other one who was walking on her own and supple and who had just left me a visual image of her hands, and also other much more intimate images of her skin and muscles, the tight tendons of her legs, her underclothes, and her hair. I now saw in the poor sister no more than an overwhelmed female-shaped lump, quite palatable, but also quite remote.

I decided that the only thing that could cheer me up would be to walk naturally, telling myself things to pretend that I was walking down the street, herding my women back to the hotel where I stabled them after rendering them helpless with fits of pleasure. Like the one dangling from my arm; just out of bed, the unfortunate wretch. She still had much to learn, but she will soon enough become an expert; blunders of women from foreign places that I imported and provided for. Perhaps once back at the hotel it would be good to let her know who's the boss again, so that she doesn't get used to . . .

"What are we doing tomorrow?" Blanca asked.

"I work."

"Of course. How silly of me," Blanca said, looking at me, lovingly, over her sister's head. "At what time do you leave?"

"Quarter to seven."

"Do you make your own breakfast?"

"No. I have breakfast at a bar at the square. It's the only thing open at that hour."

"Tomorrow, we will make your breakfast," Blanca said, beaming with joy. I felt the sister tense up apprehensively.

"Don't be silly. It's quite late now and you're tired from the trip, tomorrow you won't wake up until lunchtime. Besides, let's just say you're not an early riser. And look at Luisa."

"No, nevertheless, tomorrow we will prepare your breakfast or I'll do it myself, if Luisa can't make it," Blanca insisted, with a childlike stubbornness. My heart skipped a beat at the thought of spending all morning alone with her. I observed the sister's face searching for a hint of possible irritation; if she decided to be stubborn, as sick as she was, she was capable of getting up and smiling and being courageous and not letting anyone go to bed in peace. I noted with pleasure that she seemed immersed in her discomfort.

The night was clear and beautiful. Suddenly I got tired of leading the sister. I would gladly have hung her from any passerby going in our direction; or in any direction. I was glad when we arrived at the hotel door.

"This is it, Blanca. Where are you going?"

"What? We are here already? It can't be. We haven't gone by the square yet," she said, stopping to check out the ugly building from top to bottom. All the lights were turned off, even the ones by the door.

"Of course we haven't. The town square is further up and two blocks to the right."

"Are you sure?"

"Come on, Blanca, yes. Look: behind us, during the day, you

can see a mountain with three peaks; that's the Tunari; my house is that way. This hotel is between my apartment and the town square, but a little to the left; two blocks to the left. See?" I asked as I held the door open and pushed the sister into the darkness of the hallway. A bellhop that was dozing off on a bench was startled when he heard us; his face seemed to want an explanation, but he got lost in thought again and said nothing.

The sister made up her mind as hastily as one at the threshold of death and climbed up the stairs in a graceless wave of petticoats and skirts. Blanca stayed for just a moment, she cast a nervous glance at the bellhop, pressed against me, looked deeply into my eyes, as one would imagine a lover would to make up for all those months of sad separation, and probably finding nothing else to say, asked anxiously and with intensity.

"How are you? Tell me, how are you really?"

"Horny," I answered. She slapped my face noisily and shot up the stairs.

She stopped at the landing, holding on to the railing, she peeked out from under her arm, nodding and said, whistling the words in the empty darkness:

"Me too."

VI

IF THE STREETS weren't deserted, I'd be embarrassed to accompany her. Her hips are not very wide, but one can tell they are very shapely and she sways back and forth as she walks. She moves them a lot. God only knows where she lives, and I'm tired, and now that it's no longer snowing, it will start getting extremely cold.

"Why do they call you Ros?"

"Because my name is Rosalynd. Do you know what time it is?"

Her chin is tucked into her chest as she answers me. Her humped back amuses me.

"The clock at the corner says 12:17. No, it changed: and 18."

"I was just asking to have something to say. The crunching sound of the snow beneath our feet scared me a little."

"Hmmm."

"Not much of an imagination, right?"

What is unfortunate is the girdle-like tightness of her pants compared to the wideness of the jacket that only reaches her waist. From a distance, it probably looks like she is naked from the waist down and has turned blue from the cold. I don't want to accompany this woman anywhere; and I don't want to leave her. I don't want to go home because I can no longer stand opening the door quietly so that other woman can say hello and stay in bed, rigid, for whatever unknown reason, for example out of fear that I will make her remove her nightgown and open her legs and she takes longer and longer each time and then it's "be careful," "it hurts a little," "slow down please," "stay still for a minute, just for a minute," and it's useless to try to turn her on with caresses or anything and get off almost without any pleasure it seems more like pissing than anything else and leaves me with the impression of a tiresome and repeated gesture and that she's done me a huge favor and knowing full well that those closed doors are always there on the sleepy walls and my body hurts from trying to hold that sleepless position on that shitty bed that, come summer or winter, is always hotter than I would like and that it is a chaos of sheets and mattress and nightmarish softness . . . What the hell? What is that? Fucking car! It was the chains on the tires that sounded so weird. Hopefully she didn't notice. She keeps walking with her head down so that the cold doesn't hit her squarely in the face. She didn't notice anything. The car drives very slowly to the corner and stops there to wait for the red light to turn green so he can take off again in the middle of the deserted city. I reached him just a moment before the light changed. Or did I? Or had it changed a split second before my foot was in line with the rear bumper? I cannot keep doing this shit and have everyone realize that something must be happening to me like now this poor soul with her tight pants and two books under her arm rushing as fast as she can to keep up with me because of my stupid desire to not let the car get away as if I could prevent from happening whatever is going to happen whether I get to the car or not because I left her behind and she is simply trying to coexist for a moment with a jerk and to keep her balance with her two hands in her pants pockets as the tight and cheap fabric visibly displays her knuckles over her flat belly.

"Sorry I made you wait for me. I can't walk at the same pace as you. The ground is very slippery, you know," she says, sweetly, submissively.

I notice her shoes for the first time and I feel badly that she has to wear them at this time of the year. Inadequate shoes and tight and cheap pants and her body hunched over to better withstand the cold.

"Forgive me. I didn't realize that I was leaving you behind. If you want to, hold on to my arm."

She links her arm in mine and squeezes without intimacy,

with the sole intention of putting her fist back in her pocket. When we try to walk, we are too close together and almost lose our balance when her hip collides against mine. We take a few more steps, but we walk at different speeds and get in each other's way.

"If you don't mind, I will hold you."

"Better."

She lets go of my arm, puts her hand back in her pocket and moves her elbow away from her side, and stays there, hunched over, her feet apart and wedged into the snow on the sidewalk, waiting for me to hold her. The feel of her arm in my hand surprises me, it is slim and muscular, not at all inviting. Surely she now feels a tremendous stabilizing force reliable like steel guiding her through the night to her home on the dangerous ice-encrusted pavement that makes her beautiful narrow hips sway and invite me to electrifying and noisy delights even though I have to work tomorrow and they are there those hypocritical smiling faces as the bastards wait huddled in their bitterness for me to make a mistake and one day go too far and tell someone to go to hell and they hope it is someone important so that I will be screwed and nevertheless when she is nude she must be quite warm firm and quiet and entering her will be like tearing a thin web that I will have to start to separate with my fingers before hearing her cry of pain and surprise the wonderful thing is that I'm starting to respond but as far as desire real desire I don't feel it not one little bit oh God there is nothing but terror there is nothing but death death lodging itself on this new prey on my old and worn-out bones who could without desire without love forsaken by himself sit and mourn at that very door jamb with his head between his knees. I am also a perfect idiot in all other things; she must not have even imagined anything of the sort.

"It hurts. You're holding my arm too tightly."

"Oh, sorry. Forgive me, please; I didn't realize. My hands are very rough. I'm always breaking things; sticks, eggs, cups. Hey, it would be good to find a place where we could have a hot drink. I'm freezing."

"Yes, that's a good idea."

"Do you know of a place we could go? Everything closes here. Even the jazz club is closed by now."

"My house."

"It's not too late?"

"You can come in for a minute and then leave right away. I would feel guilty if I let you go like this, freezing because you walked me home."

"Excellent. I was thinking of you. Where is your house?"

"Right here; at the end of the block, next to the flower shop. Do you see it? Why were you thinking of me?"

"Pardon?"

"You said that you were saying something because of me. Not because of you, I suppose."

"Oh, that it's getting late."

Our steps are now in sync. We are walking together toward her house. It seems that we were moving at random earlier. She swipes her pockets by the front door. Her brow is doubly furrowed because of the cold temperature and because she is worried. She finally hears the distinct sound of the keys and looks at me as if we had triumphed together. She puts a finger to her lips motioning for me to be silent and carefully opens the door. Before she silently closes it, I catch a glimpse of the steep stairs and then stop in the darkness, her hand holding mine as she leads me up the stairs. And if right now all the lights were to suddenly turn on and a vociferous father who stayed up just to surprise her or brothers armed with stakes or simply one of those furious meddlesome puritans started to accuse her of being a whore or accused me of being immoral and it would not be unusual for an entire regiment to appear because there is no place to put one's foot down without the stairs cracking as if they were in pain even though both my jaws are in pain from tightening them so much out of caution why did I have to come here to this lion's den when I barely have enough energy to crawl through these endless and senseless days what a relief that I can finally make out a light up there that hopefully will not belong to someone who is furious who is waiting for her to be accountable to them or waiting for me to answer to them to stir up a hornet's nest and shriek out obscenities don't react that way we just met and she was nice enough to invite me in to have something hot there was nowhere to go in town by the time that we finished studying and I was helping the whole group sir but I realize that this is not a good time and if she was holding my hand it was only to guide me up the stairs and nothing else although perhaps she is already counting on being savagely possessed or maybe not and I am only alert from the waist up so hopefully she doesn't live here alone finally we are in the light but nothing is clear and there is no other sound but that of our steps and also Ros I can make out your silhouette above the light and passing under that door waist hips and the start of your legs until I can see that triangle of air that thin women have below their sex that is why classical sculptors never have them with straight legs as it would interrupt the shape but seeing it is very intimate and its all the same to me you know that the only thing I really want from you is your company and your conversation to find shelter for my fatigue in your presence although perhaps that which is born of the depths of my soul is to sob in despair while beating my chest with my fists expelling the fetid and pulsating bubble of premature aging of impotence of fear full or a purulent pulsating clot occupying that place that should be splendidly occupied by the nude image of this silent young woman and instead leaves me bewildered and gives me chills my body with its world lost yesterday only yesterday I was another someone whom I never knew explicitly whom I never met as a human being because if I had I never would have become lost and I cannot find the road back and one day as soon as tomorrow I will die without love without courage without youth.

She doesn't turn on the light. She takes my coat and hangs it up on an invisible knob that she has to reach by climbing with one knee on what looks like a gigantic trunk. She then takes off her shoes and gestures for my boots. When she moves her legs, the sound of the coarse fabric of her pants seems strange as thigh rubs against thigh.

"Sit down. I'll put the kettle on."

Despite it being a whisper, her voice sounds somewhat false. I docilely look for a chair in the darkness.

"I much prefer being in the dark, with just the streetlight. People in this building are very nosy and . . . and . . . they fall asleep early."

I stay there thinking that she'd been smiling at me before turning away. I sit down awkwardly; I am surprised to discover that my legs and arms are trembling a bit. Through the galleon-stern-shaped window, I see the amazing, soft and clean image of a snowy street. I wait for her to reveal what she wants to reveal. I hear the sound of her feet; clad only in wool stockings. She moves with ease, but as if considering every move. She walks by me and looks for another chair across the table; she sits wearily and stares into the street with her face in her hands.

"The snow is so beautiful. I often sit here for hours watching it fall. Don't you like it?"

"I don't know. Winter bothers me less than summer. I don't care for this city snow. Tomorrow, when the traffic starts, it will become filthy: they cover it with salt and sand; it gets mixed with mud . . ."

She is perfectly still, exactly as she would be in a public place, waiting for the waiter to appear with our order. Not I. I am worldly. I dominate the situation. She must believe me to be a descendant of countless Spanish nobles who even today continue to dine next to the fireplace with its smoke covered coat of arms above it, attended to by mute swarm of servants. She must imagine that she is boring me or perhaps she is grief-stricken because she cannot think of another topic of conversation besides the time and the weather.

"But it is still beautiful. When it first falls it leaves everything soft and clean. Besides, it is so nice to awaken surrounded by that beautiful shimmering silence left by the snow. Before opening your eyes, you already know how everything looks outside."

"Of course: the streets are full of old men who died trying to push cars that wouldn't start, the roads are blocked, a few poor old women flabbergasted by the cold are cleaning the sidewalk in front of their houses, an army of workers risking their hide to repair cut cables . . . A thousand interesting things."

"So, tell me: you don't like nature. Do you?"

"Do I like nature? I don't know. Tell me one thing first, innocent and charming girl: what is nature? Because if I answer you and then it turns out that we aren't speaking of the same thing, we aren't going to understand each other."

"Oh," she exclaims, annoyed, "you know what I mean by 'nature.' The same thing everyone else means. I like all seasons; I like dawn, midday and dusk; I like the smell of fried bacon mixed with the smell of burnt firewood; I like rivers and mountains. I like to go hunting and swimming and ice-skating."

"Let's see. Slow down, slow down. See how it was not so easy? Going hunting has nothing to do with nature; neither does ice-skating; fried bacon, even less. And we'd have to see if dawn in the city is different from dawn in the mountains or on the coast or in the desert. Don't you agree?"

"I don't know. I don't care. That has nothing to do with anything. You don't want to understand me. I'm talking about something else."

"What do you mean something else?"

"Well . . ."

"Pardon me. That sound. Do you hear it?"

"Yes, it appears that the water is boiling."

"Wouldn't it be a good idea to go see it?"

In the darkness her haunches seem more powerful. She stands up half smiling and half angry. She left the light on in the kitchen, and now, when she gets to the door, it flashes on her, overpoweringly. She disappears inside without looking at me. And now it's almost one in the morning and I am getting incredibly bored playing this game poor thing trying to give me access to her soul with the only hackneyed key that she is familiar with that she has been taught but also disappointed with what I'm showing her because there doesn't seem to be in me anything but a certain capacity to suddenly worry about abstract issues, explanations that are difficult for her subtle distinctions of concepts a brain that operates with magnitudes as free and as commonplace and as banal as the conversation we're having and that should lead us to bed, but that is already too long for foreplay and seems more like rejection and utter stupidity that would try anyone's patience and who knows what time I will finally get home to be on time tomorrow, today, good morning sir I'm always bothering you I now have a piece from a nineteenth-century novelist and I would like for you to do me a favor and take a look when you have the time at a translation that is in this book but it is better to be here waiting for her wool stockings to touch the floor I will not be able to sleep anyway talk play I'd rather not have to swallow my insomnia in my horrible bedroom feeling on top of everything else guilty this awful oppression in my stomach has begun again if only I could take a sip of something strong perhaps she has something.

"I must apologize. I have run out of everything. All I found was some leftover tea: I prepared it in case you wanted some. Do you mind?"

She says it with a certain degree of affection, as if she were truly afraid that I wouldn't like what she has prepared for me and wanted or needed my approval. She sets the cups on the table. Her movements are very cautious.

"I have some crackers. Do you want some?"

"No, thank you, but bring some for yourself."

"I don't want any either. Sorry," she states as she sits down and fixes something on her pants, "tomorrow is my shopping day and I have nothing left."

"Don't worry. I'm happy with tea. I like it a lot."

She smiles briefly and stares at me intently and distractedly at the same time. I make out the solid contours of her face that create a very attractive oval; beneath her neck, small breasts expand and contract with her breathing under the loose knit of her woolen cardigan. "Is it wool?" She parts her lips to speak; they remain silent as her gaze follows the movement of my hand that ends up caressing the weave on her forearm.

"Sorry. It is wool. What were you about to say?"

"It's not wool, it's acrylic. I was going to say that you Latin men are infuriating."

"Really? Why?"

"See? Exactly because of that."

"I don't understand a word you're saying. What are you talking about?"

"If I had said to a man, a boy from here, that he was infuriating, he would have been upset; he would have taken me seriously. You, however, don't fret, you almost yawn. The only thing that occurs to you is to ask: 'Really? And why?' Do you understand?"

"Less than before."

"You despise women. You think of them as possessions. You don't answer them. You almost don't hear them."

"Why are you looking at me like that and not answering? Say something. Oh, indeed, I was forgetting; Latinos probably don't bother giving explanations to women."

"No. Only to foolish women. Those who are happy when they can wrap a guy around their little finger. Those who have allowed for their womanhood to become corrupted and want to dress like men to see if they can ruin the human race even more than it's already ruined."

"You think I dress like a man?"

"No, child, I don't mean you. Luckily the difference between you and a man is extremely obvious. If it weren't so, I wouldn't be here talking to you, believe me. Tell me the truth; would you not find it excruciatingly boring if I had thrown myself to the floor in despair and had scratched my forehead in pain and had made tearful arguments when you found me infuriating?"

"Yeah, true," she laughs.

And how sweet and submissive and astonishingly you say it golden girl through barely parted lips no wonder I spent the whole afternoon distracted secretly looking at you and I lent myself to accompany you here but come, come close because it's time to make your body shudder and put your head on my shoulder and for you to look at me with those cowering eyes and then close them while you wait.

"Come."

"Yes, in a minute. I'll turn off the stove first. We could suffocate."

I shouldn't have let her go because standing here like an idiot in the middle of the room I am a living contradiction of the Latin lover *vive la différence* letting the female go to reduce the risk of fatal suffocation when she would expect that dying during an orgasm would be a small price to pay sad tribute to a delirious embrace to passion what passion if the little bit that had awakened in me was smothered by that stupid woman with her idea of walking around turning off stoves before allowing me to turn her on this is ridiculous this is idiotic irritating but also her silhouette there against the light of the kitchen waits for me perfectly still because she perhaps wants to show demureness she is almost beautiful and what are you going to do back we go to restart the games and ruses.

"Did you turn off the gas, cautious girl?"

"Yes," she replies, her voice empty.

"Come."

I wonder what time it is now and what time it will be when we are done too bad we can no longer use carcinogenic glow in the dark watches it might start snowing again despite the cold and then I'm screwed because I refused to leave the house wearing my coat's tacky hood and now my neck will get covered in icicles and my ears frostbitten and where do I get a crappy taxi at this hour to keep me warm to trust that he will get me home to sequester myself from the cold outdoors while this one will be in here falling asleep all nice and cozy and the other one over there ready to jump at the slightest noise Ros dear you are the essence of disappointment first there was the possibility of suffocation and now your silence and docility the warm darkness the caressing sound of your socks on the polished floor you had to have this hard lump of a body you had to have a rigid mouth or maybe I have bad breath and a tongue that is downright elusive pointy, and uninviting and it had to happen that our bodies don't fit well together and have become tangled up and we are unable to rest hand or mouth or knee against one another or hold each other so as not to lose our balance or be uncomfortable fine fine we have to hasten this my hand to the small of your back damned cardigan covering your bare skin that unfortunately covers admittedly smooth but noticeable muscles leading to your ribs toward your back it must be pleasurable to look at your soft back and spinal canal where the clasp of your bra must be while with my other hand I firmly hold you your belly and your hips glued to my body but what belly all I can feel is your pubic bone it would be so wonderful and glorious to feel desire by now and not have to waste time let's go to bed calmly and without further delay and you can take your bra off yourself because it looks like the clasp is stuck let's see I can keep holding you and applying pressure with one hand while with the other I can manipulate your clothing smiling like an international expert at undressing women.

She throws back her torso, looking at me with mocking and loving eyes. She brings her hand up to her back under her cardigan and I immediately hear the sound of the unbound breasts. The only thing that remains is to hold her in my arms and carry her off to bed. But something makes her move away from me in fear. She looks toward the window. I turn and see nothing. It seems, however, that there was a sound.

"Wait. Be quiet. Please," she whispers in my ear.

She quickly disappears into where I suppose the bathroom and bedroom are located. Before she comes back I now clearly hear what I previously only thought I heard. Someone is throwing snowballs at the window from the street. They burst and remain adhered to the glass. Now for sure this will turn into a madhouse for sure recriminations will fly the one throwing the snowballs is probably a man probably her boyfriend he will probably come upstairs and I don't know if I will be able to face the idiot's righteous anger and maybe she doesn't like to be defended because they say it's the same everywhere that they like to be beaten especially when they are caught with someone else's hands in the cookie jar but that would be humiliating for me and I am extremely sure that I would not dare defend her oh sweet smell oh wonderful deception and wiles of women oh prudent and surprising female and poor wretch when he sees you from below where he is pissing himself from the cold and desire and all he will see is his modest beloved huddled up to her neck in her chaste and harsh robe and will notice through her angry gestures how offended and upset she is because the shameless man dares to arrive at this hour at her rigid threshold.

"Who was it?"

"People . . . friends . . ."

"Your boyfriend?"

"Yes."

"Do you want me to go?"

She looks at me briefly. On her face, an expression that seems like disgust or surprise.

"Do whatever you want," she finally says. "Yes, you'd better go," she adds, absolving herself of the situation.

"Fine. Do me a favor and bring me my boots."

"They're here on the heating vent. If you want them, get them yourself."

She feigns utter indifference sitting at the table again rapt in contemplation of her teacup I would like to give her a good beating or slap her ass a couple of hundred times and leave my fingers imprinted on it because her attitude is way too inconsistent as she sits two steps away from me in that absurd half-open robe that reveals her street clothes underneath and in particular the disheveled bra that is probably ill positioned on her breasts while I am standing like an idiot in the middle of some strange woman's living room who is now thinking of something else and who wanted to be mine.

"We could call your boyfriend to hand them to me."

"Idiot," she replies.

She gets up and walks past me without looking at me, leaving me alone in the living room.

I have no doubt that if I follow her and lightly force her she would take me back again and that would satisfy me more and it would give her an excuse if I forced her to want to anyway ah my friend ah you truly believe you are capable of forcing her to accept you no and a thousand times no I could also turn on the lights and start dancing and singing loudly and unleash a huge all out scandal but it's extremely late and there would be too much explaining to do in the middle of all this cold and all this snow that stretches out in long blocks toward my house what I have to do now miserably is find a somewhere to sit and put my boots on take my hoodless coat off the hook take out the things I had brought with me and put them on and perhaps the cold air and the walk will help me relax so that I can work tomorrow.

7

TRUTH BE TOLD, the two damned women pissed me off so much
that I was seeing red when they showed up as they had promised, together and sisterly and smilingly, at almost dawn, on the
first day after their arrival in town. I had woken up much earlier, feverish with desire, but certain that I wouldn't hear from
either of them until noon. I mean, certain, but hopeful; so much
so that it took me awhile to decide to go into the bathroom,
because I figured that Blanca might arrive and I would not hear
the bell or that I might be in the shower just when it rang. And
so, driven by delirious desire, I walked halfway down the stairs
in my pajamas with the intention of leaving a paper at the gate
letting her know to just come right in. But then I remembered
how fearful she was and, although the dog was not going to
do anything to her, it would be enough for him to look at her
to prevent her from setting a foot in the door. I thought about
looking for the dog and locking him up in his doghouse, but I
couldn't find him anywhere in the garden and as I checked for
him on tiptoe, suddenly the landlords' housekeeper appeared
and stood there smiling mockingly at my back as I returned back
inside with what I believed to be very sneaky nonchalance, but
it must have seemed like affable madness to the *cholita*. When
I reached the top of the stairs, I spotted her among the plants,
still watching, slyly, pretending that she was looking for something in the bushes. It made me laugh a little and gave me great
joy seeing the figure of the woman down there in the still sleepy
green garden, as if she'd stopped to play in the middle of dawn.
I felt a widespread love for humankind in general and a tender

acceptance of the absence of my beloved who would at this time be relaxing in the warmth of the morning sleep.

Consequently, I was furious when a casual glance toward the gate met with the two figures motioning for my attention. The normal thing would have been for them not to come; what would have been abnormally wonderful, if Blanca had arrived alone; the weird and idiotic thing was that they both came to prepare breakfast. Nevertheless, I went downstairs with great tenderness and hypocrisy and when I got there they both greeted me with a kiss on the cheek, smelling of toothpaste. I smiled at them, masking my face with a warm and poised demeanor, while thinking that despite having their clothes a little wrinkled by the suitcases, they were so clean and scrubbed and dressed that they almost seemed like two ideas dressed up as women and sprinkled with several antibacterials. Ushering them upstairs, with their two pairs of hips swaying in front of me, I wanted to burst out in praise, saying something like: "I assure you that you two have the best pair of rear-ends for several miles around." Instead, I expressed my amazement that they'd been able to locate the house on their own before dawn. They looked at each other, laughing, radiant.

"That was the least of it. Isn't that right, Lu?" said Blanca, bubbling with mystery and raising a package in the air that she had tucked into a shopping bag.

"Don't call me Lu," the other replied coyly, swelling with joy at the sound of her childhood nickname. "And don't talk so loud; Remember that we didn't even want to ring the doorbell."

"Why did you not want to ring the bell?"

"We didn't want to make noise and bother that poor sick man. We'll do what we did today every morning when we come by to make you breakfast," Blanca informed me lovingly.

But no sooner were they inside the house than, by the single-mindedness of their actions, and their insistence that I continue doing what I was doing before they arrived, they made me understand that I had lost all control over my place. Blanca let me accompany her to the kitchen, but after she'd shown me what items they'd been able to get that early in the morning (freshly baked bread, fresh butter, jam, a can of cereal, eggs, powdered milk), she placed a playful hand on my back and pushed me out of her domain saying:

"Go shave now. You almost cut my lips with your stubble."

I left without looking back, partly so she wouldn't see my stupid contented face. I had forgiven her for showing up with her sister. Not even deodorants seemed to me worthy of consideration as I grinned stupidly at my face in the mirror, I shaved with a new blade, careful as always to make sure that the gray foam didn't get on my shirt while listening as the two women moved around my house. Through the crescent of the skylight I could see a piece of crystalline sky. It made me want to sing. As I was washing and drying the blade and making the rest of the razor sparkle, Blanca's head popped in the door.

"Your breakfast is ready, my lord and master," she whispered, after looking at me for an instant as a cow looks at her calf.

The table was lavish and joyful. They'd managed to give my dining room an almost British appearance, despite the boxes full of soldiers, with only a few touches of jam and poached eggs and neatly organized pieces of toast. I'd had vague hopes that the setup of the room would allow me to get my hands under the skirts of either one. But of course I couldn't, and besides, it wasn't likely that either of them would let me in the presence of the other. I was so angry at the elegance of the situation that it was really difficult to not pinch the sister's butt when I moved the chair for her. Instead, I promised myself joyfully that someday I would commit such an atrocity that would start a truly wild party that would end up with me throwing one of the sisters on top of all the nicely organized saucers and undressing her on top of the butter and all kinds of sticky foods, along with a healthy dose of screaming and shattering of dishes.

"Tell me," said the sister, spreading jam on her bread, "is there a swimming pool in Cochabamba?"

"Of course there is. Several. Why?" I asked, distractedly, disappointed by the small mass of the two soft boiled eggs I had just eaten.

"And are they open at this time?"

"No doubt. There's even one that never closes. Seriously: this is the best climate in the world. Are you a swimmer?"

"Yes, I swim a little. When you left I had just started taking lessons. Don't you remember?" she answered quietly, very modestly. "How beautiful this all is! In the light of day it all looks truly wonderful. Everything is wonderful. All wonderful. What is this street called?"

"Ballivián. The best in the city. Beautiful, isn't it?"

"What are you looking for?" Blanca asked me, my beloved was anxious about the well-being of her master.

"Nothing. I was just looking. Don't mind me."

"Do you know what surprises me the most?" the sister continued. "How clean your house is. And you don't even have servants."

"Oh, how great that you reminded me! I have a woman who comes every day. Do you mind if we let her keep coming?"

"Look," admonished Blanca, "if that woman so much as pokes her nose in the hallway while we're here, we'll go home immediately. Do you want more coffee?"

"Please."

"For the two or three weeks that we're here, we will absolutely do everything for you. How much sugar do you take?"

"What do you mean two or three weeks? Why two or three weeks?" I asked with a heavy heart, thinking that as soon as two Mondays from now I would be alone again, when it was clear that a year of bed and Blanca would not have sufficed to satisfy my desire and the desperate need of her presence that arose in me at precisely that moment.

"Of course," she answered with tears in her eyes. "Don't forget that we both work. At best, they said they would write to us if we could take an extra week off. How much sugar do you take?"

"Three, please."

We fell silent. The sisters feigned or felt the same inner sorrow as I. I decided to lighten the mood, but couldn't think of how. The sister gave me material, asking:

"You thought we wouldn't be able to find the house on our own, didn't you?"

I immediately came up with stimulating praise to discuss their achievement. I told several anecdotes of foreigners, some of my own, which tended to highlight how unfit we ordinary mortals were at getting used to unfamiliar geography.

"And don't think a sense of direction is anything to sneeze at," I added, frowning slightly to make my musings appear more noteworthy. "It really is important. It has to do with the use of time that appears to be one of the objective manifestations of real intelligence. And there's no doubt; no one doubts that there must be a relationship between intelligence and spatiality."

"What's that? How?" the sister asked.

I was annoyed because I couldn't make my praise more convincing. What I said sounded hollow and convoluted even to me. I had to provide concrete evidence of fools lost in the living room of their houses and of different geniuses found in labyrinthine places. It was not easy to make them up, but I was rewarded by my audience's keen interest. Blanca became voracious; it always happened when she received praise. Without waiting for the other one to settle down, she said to no one in particular:

"What do you think about this butter? The saleswoman was right: it's very good."

"Excellent," I added. "Really great. Tastes like farm butter. Where did you get it?"

"Shhhhh. It's a secret, a secret," she responded and grimaced calling for a new dissertation and this time not on spatiality in general, but on the spatiality of grocery stores in unfamiliar time zones in order to drive home the value of my assessment. Fortunately a gentle beeping from Flammini's truck sounded below. I signaled to him that I would come downstairs immediately and rushed to the door with my jacket in my hand. Blanca was right at the exit, full of love, the image of the woman in love who sees her husband off, full of affection. She kissed me as I passed by and asked:

"What time will you be here for lunch?"

"At five after one. Bye. Oh, the cleaning woman will come by, I suppose. Tell her, please, that I won't need her for the next two weeks. Be nice to her," I added from the stairs, half-jokingly,

half-seriously because I feared that Blanquita would act snootily
and scare the girl away forever.

"Bye. We'll have some surprises for you."

"Bye, thanks," I smiled, with a heavy heart and true gratitude.

From that day on, they never missed their loving morning
commitment. They kept coming at the light of dawn to dispense
the female care that I'd been devoid of for so long. They kept
calling me from below, without ringing the bell "so as not to
bother that poor fellow." They continued bringing fresh provisions of mysterious origin that were meant to fill me with awe.
They never ceased asking to be praised for the intelligence with
which they were gifted, the love they showed me, the lovely
feminine qualities that they had learned in their distant home.

They got used to it all quite quickly, perhaps simply because
this would only last them three weeks at most. They used the
words "always" and "never" with irritating frequency. "I love that
you are never late for lunch," Blanca commented once, filling
me with joy, because I could see in her face that she lovingly
approved of my punctuality. "One thing I admire about you is
that you never complain of fatigue despite how hard you work,"
she said at another time and I thought she could also take into
account all the times that I mounted her, and I felt fantastic.
When I arrived at noon, she would hurriedly blush and comment: "You always surprise me in my slip; but it doesn't matter,
right? It's just that it's a little hot," she would add coquettishly
and accompany me while reminding me: "Your beer is in the living room, as always." And indeed there it would be, on the coffee
table, the cold perspiring bottle, with a glass and a bottle opener.
Lunch itself was abundant, delightful, rewarding and the sisters
always took turns serving it. They also always stayed at the table,
sipping their coffee while I brushed my teeth cursing again at the
beer, because it made me sleepy. In the afternoons, after work,
I always found my beloved again fully covered, and the light
tension that had contorted the modest sister's face hours before,
because Blanca showed me her underwear so naturally, had disappeared. The truth is that I did not like that very much either.
I would have preferred that she wear clothing more appropriate

to the heat she felt or had stayed in the nude; what she was doing indicated disarray more than the need to cool down.

So, the two or three times that I took Leroy to lunch, I felt a bit of malignant joy not only at spoiling Blanca's daily ritual, but also that the visit forced her to cover up. But these little bits of joy didn't even begin to pay the price of Leroy's lunch. No sooner would Blanca disappear in search of her clothing than Luisa would pop into the room, smiling from ear to ear and offering our guest a beer on top of it all; then she would settle in immediately and start flirting with Leroy, shamelessly declaring that there was something about him that she'd never seen before, something about him substantiating the wonderful effects that travel and adventure had upon men. I could see on the adventurer a hint of bashfulness, but the overall effect was great satisfaction; even if the sister had told him how beautiful he looked, it seemed to me that he would have simply smiled modestly. Personally, I didn't like it one bit. While Leroy received all the praise, I might as well have been swallowed up by the earth; and besides, I could see that the girl would end up underneath Leroy and I already had her pegged as a member of my own harem just waiting for the right opportunity to come along. Moreover, when Blanca reappeared, the spirit that reigned at home took its usual soft and sultry course. It was true that the sisters had become experts in the geography of the city stores in an amazingly short time. However, when Leroy saw the two women cheerfully and affectionately question me as soon as I entered the room about where I had acquired my provisions previously, he couldn't help but look at me askance, and that was downright humiliating. The worst part was that, after obtaining my confession, ("I used to buy the pork chops at that butcher shop on General Achá Street") spontaneous self-criticism and grateful praise were expected, because those chops that I was now devouring like a hungry wild animal (sometimes they were hams, or steaks, or cheese, etc.) were certainly the most delicate, meaty secret that the market had to offer. The worst part was that Leroy, the moron, was not in the game so if they asked him he could afford to respond very mannishly and carelessly.

"Look, I don't know. I eat anything anywhere. I care more about quantity than quality. These chops of yours though, are excellent."

And that left me looking like a pussy worried about gourmet delicacies, Blanca with an empty smile, Luisa beaming with pride and Leroy, the asshole, much closer to her bed. The gentle sister immediately began an homage to men with good digestion. She enthusiastically laughed at those effeminate men who ate cooked rice and avoided coffee and butter. The shameless Leroy calmly accepted the compliments and the implied accusation against me in the vibrating voice of the sister. I ate in silence, pondering in amusement at the blindness of love or lust, because my poor friend was suffering from liver failure that hit him under the ribs like a grenade at least once a month, while I could have easily feasted on nails in the absence of something softer. But it was not for me to stand in the way of my good friend by reminding him of his gastric woes, so I focused on cramming succulent fried foods swimming in sauce down my gullet, as I listened to Luisa's distant droning on Leroy's behalf.

And so, nothing could spare me from observing that my caregivers were going overboard to compensate me for so many months of well spent solitude. And I don't mean in a general distracted sense where I happily noticed that I was now better fed, sleeping better, and better taken care of than before their arrival. No, the benefits included a complete detail by detail breakdown of the household tasks of each one of the twenty-four blessed hours of the infernal day. Had I ever seen my home cleaner and tidier? No, no, certainly not. Was there mayhem here anymore as was once the norm? No, no, no. Did this home lack any staple foods anymore (fresh bread, rice, spaghetti noodles, etc.)? No, not anymore, not now, certainly not now. Were perfectly useful items (pork skins, sugar covered in ants) wasted anymore? Of course not, oh, no, no, no, no, oh, no.

It is, therefore, not surprising that although I was extremely happy to have the two women with me, despite returning happily to my house because they were waiting for me, I often delayed my return as much as I could. I went so far as to invent very serious hardships that threatened my huge profits or bonuses for imaginary deliveries, all to stay at the factory until dinnertime. After the workers' truck and the employee van and Flammini's pickup left the place and Ramón dismissed them with a vague gesture and closed the gate, the two of us and Leroy went into the repair shop and spent a quiet afternoon. The three of us got busy tinkering around with our submarplane, our *Crawling Pig*, and drinking coffee. We did not talk very much lately, despite Ramón dying of curiosity since Blanca's arrival; he wanted to know why she was here, what she was like, how long she would be staying; and I suppose he would also have liked to know about my sex life with her; but in general he was too discreet to ask anything directly. If I knew of his intrusiveness, I owed it all to Leroy, to whom he spoke more freely. He almost made me laugh when he asked me one day:

"I saw you with a young lady on the street the other day, maestro. Is she your girlfriend?"

"She is," I answered distractedly.

I was adjusting the valves of the submarplane's engine and pretended to be immersed in knocking the valve into its hole so that he would not see my face.

"Forgive my saying so, maestro, but she is beautiful."

"Yes, she's very pretty," I admitted, without changing my tone. "Hey, Ramón, is this valve OK?"

"It still needs a lot of work," he ruled, after looking at it quickly. "Hey maestro, tell me one thing; don't you feel remorse at going to the jungle and leaving that gorgeous creature here alone?"

"No. Why?"

"And what does she say?"

"Nothing. I haven't told her yet. But as soon as I tell her she will be happy. She's like that: she wants what I want," I lied.

We kept working in silence. Leroy was next to one of the windows of the workshop, waiting for the water to boil for coffee. We were surrounded by the guard dogs that Ramón had released after the staff left. After having roamed around their nocturnal kingdom and barked and ran till they dropped, they started to settle down as always and quietly returned to observe and sniff us distractedly and then lied down near us and started falling asleep to the sounds of us working. The silence was such that when we momentarily stopped pounding on the valves, the workshop filled up with a barely audible murmur that seemed to come from everywhere, as if the workshop itself were breathing, and it had the rhythm of the slow and skinny ribs of the four dogs.

"Let's see, maestro," Ramón interrupted, leaving the valve in its hole, "does she want what you want or does she resign herself to what you want?"

"Man, she wants what I want. If I want to go to the jungle, she wants me to go to the jungle," I kept lying.

Ramón returned to his valve. There was no more than a sliver of sun still visible through the tops of the windows. While I was thinking that I would have given anything for Blanca to have been like that, I tried to remember that the valve I was holding between my fingers was part of the engine that I needed to take me to the jungle, because I was afraid I'd be distracted or get bored with the work and botch it up. I looked disgustingly at lazy Leroy, his ass was on a crate, his elbows on his knees, and his jaws between his hands as he sloppily stared at the water that was just now starting to create wisps of steam barely distinguishable in the sudden darkness of the workshop as the sun disappeared. Ramón stood up and went to turn on the light.

"It can't be. No way," he uttered as he walked back, almost as if he were talking to himself. "Do you really think that she, knowing what the jungle is like, would want you to risk your neck, maestro?"

"And what's so weird about that? Have you never met a woman who always wants what you want, Ramón?" I continued with my lie.

"No, maestro. A woman who always wants what I want, no, never, and maybe I wouldn't even like it. Now, a woman who says she wants the same thing that I want, yes, but that just makes me angry. And besides, I don't think it's fair."

"What isn't fair?"

"You have to choose, maestro: the woman or the jungle."

"No, Ramón. No, Ramón," I said slowly, "in order to get the woman you have to have the jungle. That is it."

"But how can that be, maestro?" Ramón said, somewhat exasperated, "either I have to not be in the jungle or she can't be with me. There's no solution."

I knew why Ramón was taking this so much to heart, and did not blame him. He had told us long ago that he had decided not to marry a woman he was in love with because he knew that he would never give up the jungle and he didn't want to make her suffer. At first it had seemed like a serious thing; now it felt like what it was; a more or less romantic story. But how was I going to make Ramón understand that he was thinking nonsense if he thought he could challenge me with his experiences? I decided to change the subject. After all, if women were on this side, then gold was on the other.

"It could be," I said. "Maybe I'm wrong. Do you know what I think, Ramón? That when it comes to women, only the wearer knows where the shoe pinches."

"True enough," Ramón agreed, returning to his valve.

"Do you know what I've been thinking about all day? About Werner, El Gringo."

"Look at that, how funny; me too," Ramón jumped with a somewhat dimwitted enthusiasm. He turned toward Leroy who looked like a chicken hypnotized by the water. "Isn't it true that I told you, maestro? Since yesterday."

Leroy looked at us slowly, nodded, as if it were difficult to remember, and turned to look at the water again. I was grateful, as it served my purposes, because I wanted to talk about gold and Leroy was unpredictable in his topics—as well as pushy. If he started to describe, let's say, an elephant, he would take longer to do so then it would take the mother elephant to give birth to her calf.

"And to think, damn it, that right now the dumbass is sitting there like a king, and we're here fixing junk," Ramón reflected, putting one hand on his waist and with a look of disgust on his face. "I sometimes think, maestros, that that is nothing but crap.

Every time you want in there, the bullshit starts: backpacks, hammocks, canned meats, vitamins . . ."

"And shoes, salt, guns, and a machete . . ." I added, "But I think, Ramón, that without all that stuff the only thing you become is a stark-naked dead man. You'd have to be a barbarian . . ."

"No way. Look at El Gringo Werner," said Ramón completely forgetting the valves and standing up on his crate. Leroy stared at us as if he were hearing a Chinese dialogue and not wanting to; honestly, his face looked weird. "Let's see, maestros; he had no weapons with him."

"Right: El Gringo," I agreed, "but El Gringo is almost a savage. Remember that he told us he'd been living there for about fifteen years. Who knows what he had with him when he first arrived."

"No way. It's not necessary. It's incredible how little a man needs to live. Do you want to know, maestro? In 1947 I was right here in Cochabamba and I had to leave like a shot . . . I left for Santa Cruz. You won't believe me, maestro, but I did the entire journey on foot and the only things I had with me were a mattress and a gun. And take into account that I couldn't walk on the road. What's up with that crappy stove, che? That water should have boiled years ago. It must be broken."

"It's beginning to," said Leroy, startled, as if he'd been woken up.

Ramón got off the crate he was on, stepping backward. His face radiant, as if the apparatus had done him a personal favor by getting the water ready so that he could preside over the making of the coffee. One of the dogs raised his ears, watched as Ramón walked over him, thrashed the floor lovingly with his calm tail and went back to sleep.

"Anyways, it must be broken," he insisted, bending over the water, "otherwise we would have the coffee in our bladders by now."

He lined up the blackened pot, the sugar bowl, the can of coffee (that had once held soldering paste) and a teaspoon on the bench. He looked around as if missing something, violently kicked away another one of the dogs that had come to rub up against his pant leg, and then started to generously ration out the fragrant powder into the upper compartment of the coffee maker.

"This is real aroma, che," he burst out, carried away by enthusiasm, putting his nose inside the can.

"And what a great guy El Gringo was," I insisted, fearing that Leroy would want to know what troubles Ramón had gotten into in 1947 and why the hell he was traveling with a mattress. "Would you live by yourself in that wasteland, Ramón?"

"I would really like it, maestro," he answered with admirable naturalness. "But it must not be, I think, at all easy. To think that it is kilometers and kilometers without anyone to talk to, and then the dry season, and then the summer floods, and the food, and who knows what else . . . and he had even become friendly with the Yanaigua, the dumbass, hell. They've put arrows through tons of missionaries, che. It's not easy, no way."

He'd put water inside the lower compartment of the coffee maker and was fixedly looking at the process, waiting for it to boil again and the steam to expand the powder and release its aroma. In his opinion, that was the most delicate part of the whole thing. So I banged around some more with my valve and waited for him to quickly remove the blackened container away from the top of the stove. Only after he had started to pour the boiling water over the vaporized coffee after many concentrated operations did I burst out pretending I had an unexpected enlightenment.

"Hey, Ramón, tell me something: what if we accepted his invitation, how great would that be?

"What invitation?"

"Remember that he told us spontaneously that if we wanted to share his washing station we could stay?"

"Yes, maestro, I remember."

"Look, we would have the submarplane to carry the soil. In a few days we can dig a canal to wash the gold; Leroy and I will do it; you can go pig hunting if you want to. We will get a little water pump from Pablo . . . and bring on the gold. Hey? What do you say? Don't you think it's a great idea?" I stopped talking, trying to appeal to Leroy's greed.

"I don't know. It might be a good idea," Leroy answered resentfully. He had been listening to me with half an ear. He really ticked me off. In my imagination I was manipulating extremely heavy goldbricks from El Gringo's washing site and there was good old Leroy indifferently admitting that it could be a good idea. I felt like kicking him in the teeth for being such an idiot. It made me furious whenever Leroy was in a black mood; normally I was able to infuriate him too by saying things like: "Oh, right, forgive me; I hadn't noticed your monthly visitor had arrived." To which he would answer: "Shut up asshole." But now, if I started hurling obscenities at him, it would degrade the conversation and I had worked too hard to get it to this point. I decided to not pay any attention to him. Luckily Ramón was paying much more attention to the coffee maker than to El Gringo. He must have thought that Leroy was also enthused and hungry for gold.

"Let's not behave like children," he said, lifting his head "Let's see: El Gringo said that production was very slow, remember?"

"Of course I remember. But take into account that he was pan washing and in his spare time," I jumped in.

"Yes, maestro, that's true, but let me continue. Let's say it yields ten . . . let's say even fifteen grams. Remember how hot it is out there. Remember how little water El Gringo's well yields. We could never wash more than two tons per day. How much is that? Twenty, maybe thirty grams, per day *for three* of us. It's not worth the bother maestros, breaking your back, seeing a woman once a year and living in fear because of the Yanaiguas, all that for a pittance. Pass me the cups, please, maestro," he begged as if he were asking Leroy to cut his veins.

"Listen, Ramón, you're speaking in bad faith. El Gringo has never tested his washing site. We can't know if it's fifteen grams or two hundred. Besides, being near the Yanaiguas would be more pleasant than unpleasant for you," I teased him while Leroy walked toward the back of the workshop, where we kept the three mugs on the tool shelf.

"Well, we can't know. We would have to go again and test it ourselves," Ramón agreed in a merely descriptive tone as he took the mugs. "Thank you, maestro. You can add our own sugar. For me: one, two, three, four, five, and . . . six."

It annoyed me when Leroy did not laugh. He always did whenever he would see Ramón thicken his coffee with sugar. He was more affected now by PMS than other times. Ramón climbed on top of the mechanics' bench and squatted there, sitting on his heels, like an ape, placed the full mug next to his right foot, slapped at his body looking for his smoking paraphernalia, took out a cigarette and holding it between fingers without lighting it, picked up the mug and began to sip his syrup with noise and delight.

"We could do that if you want to; go by El Gringo's place and grab some samples. We'd have to take him some of those seeds he wanted. Then we'd have to follow along the palm trees and see if we find the cliff. It's no wonder they say it's the best in the world, che," he stated cheerfully, leaving the almost licked mug on the bench. Then he dried off his whiskers for no reason, combing them with the back of his hand. And without changing positions he lit the cigarette and exhaled the smoke through his mouth and nose. Leroy was now paying us malicious and spiteful attention; drinking coffee in short spurts and staring at us. Through the windows we could see the twilight becoming denser in the empty and silent warehouses.

"Let's see, maestro, do me a favor; look outside and tell me if the lights are on."

"Nope. Everything's off," I said.

"Hell, what could have happened to the night watchman that he's not here?" worried Ramón, looking at his watch, "I will have to go turn them on, che."

"It's not necessary, maestro; they just went on," I informed him.

"That's good, che. I didn't feel like moving . . ."

"Hey, Ramón, I like the idea of the sampling. But, what if we stayed there for a few days? We could even finance the trip with a few grams . . ."

"Look, maestro, how should I put this?" Ramón started, putting his clenched hands over his ears in what made him definitely look like a meditating chimpanzee, "let's see, well, think about it. What would be our purpose in going to the jungle? To annoy the poor gringo or to look for gold? If I were El Gringo, hell, if you were El Gringo, how would you like it if three assholes just showed up at your place, maestro, with a bloody noisy vehicle, and stayed all day long, asking you a bunch of bullshit and went into your home and you couldn't even fart in peace for fear of them smelling it?"

I couldn't stop laughing imagining the succession of scenes that Ramón was conjuring up and especially imagining poor Werner worried, constricting his ass and shooting toward the jungle to vent out his intestines. But when I stopped laughing I decided to insist on the human kindness factor.

"He might even like having visitors. He probably gets lonely sometimes. Remember that he invited us."

"Sure he was probably glad that we went. And he did invite us, che, but only for a little while. If he wanted to travel in packs, he would come back here or he would go rub elbows with his Swiss compatriots. Besides, we shouldn't be . . . well," he blurted out, lighting another cigarette. "OK, suppose that after all that preparation, we arrive at the same place again, suppose we find gold (and it won't be much anyway) suppose we go there and go, go, go, carrying soil, and loading up the channel, and pouring water on it and ruining El Gringo's life: What would be the point, maestros?"

"The gold, of course, Ramón, the gold. What else?"

"What gold, maestro? If things were good, and we didn't have to fuck over some nice guy to exploit it and we had discovered it ourselves, you know what I would do? I would bring in other guys, I would set up a business and with the profit I would go somewhere else to look for something else that was worthwhile. Have you heard talk about the Jesuit treasure or of the cave full of gold for Atahualpa's ransom? That shit is worthwhile and it ain't no chicken feed, as the maestro here says. Che, I'm becoming so foulmouthed, thanks to you!"

As far as I was concerned, the poor gringo's gold had awakened in me a selfish greed and above all a pretty gluttonous, but basically sordid one, and my good wings began to shiver again, the same wings that I discovered in myself with an almost religious joy when, sometimes, little old man Salamanca spoke of almost unimaginable treasures while asking for more tea for his leftover bread and then more bread for his leftover tea, and kept overlapping, because he was so dead hungry; or Rengifo the Goth, swimming in gold and presumed dead in those days (we had planned to have a phenomenal celebration bender in his honor when the presumption was confirmed), because he hadn't shown up for our annual banquet, despite the fact that we were far into the rainy season; the magnificent Goth who acknowledged that gold perverted him, but that if it had run out in the sands where he was washing, he would still have kept going into the jungle, by himself as always; It seemed to us proof of his assertions that he'd never saved a penny in his entire wonderful life.

When Leroy and I left the factory, the road was already quite dark. I realized in the light of the last lightbulb that Leroy's depression hadn't diminished. I decided to continue ignoring him and as we walked toward the bus stop in the darkness, I withdrew into my inner joy, fearful that he would open up and reveal secrets that would draw me into some ridiculous problem that was overwhelming him. I wanted to talk about our next trip. But I couldn't do that with Leroy and despite my enthusiasm, the serene contemplation of the nature of things and the shudder of the abyss did not forsake me and I promised myself that I would not say even a peep about it to Blanca. Because I knew that, if I gave in to the temptation of talking, she would skin me alive with a mere glance. I wanted so much to talk about my trip that I wanted to invite Leroy to dinner, even at the risk of having to lift his spirits; I even felt a hypocritical sympathy for his likely misfortunes. But suddenly a truly oppressive desire for Blanca came over me; all the desire for the jungle and for talking turned into desire for Blanca. When the old jalopy of a bus began to move, I was about to jump off of it and take off running, because it seemed that nothing would be as fast as my feet for the urgency that I felt. It was enough that I had taken him over for lunch so many times. I had no reason to ruin my evening plans simply because the miserable wretch was manic-depressive.

Since the night after the arrival of the sisters, that part of the day had been set. After dinner, Lu, the understanding and excellent one, would clear the table; she didn't drink coffee, so she would leave Blanca and me alone in the dining room and retire to the kitchen from where she would emit spiritual waves of resigned disapproval along with the noise of the dishes, cutlery, and running water. In my desperation, I'd invited Blanca out for a walk along the city on the first day and it had worked out so well that we continued doing it. At first, before leaving I used to poke my head in the kitchen to ask Luisa if she needed anything and then, without much ado, I informed her that her sister and I were going for a short stroll; now, we simply yelled out to her as we left and that was it. When we left the house, Blanca was normally rather pale and I could sense a certain degree of clumsiness in her when she went up or down the stairs. We took the same path every night, toward the park first and then along the shoreline of the Rocha River. Sometimes we were distracted for a bit by the night air or the moon or a conversation. However, at that time of night the respectable people and the rest were already inside and we often noticed that we had the entire city at our disposal like a huge bedroom. We had the occasional interruption and got through it by laughing and by straightening out Blanca's clothes, but there were also several comfortable and shady areas throughout our route. There was that tree with a hole in it, and a rock in the river that she especially liked, and lastly the sand and the wide and spacious grounds covered by the blackness of the night. We were never out that long, but were almost always relieved to see from the street that there was no light in the living room, a sign that the discreet sister was no longer at the apartment and we could hasten up the stairs flooded by happiness and sometimes covered in adobe powder or river sand or even mud when it rained. It would not do to show up with someone to talk about the jungle.

VII

HE IS SCRAPING the decay off my teeth with a small steel instrument. Outside I hear the sounds of airplanes flying overhead in the clear and hot sky; and there is no way to leave all this behind. Where would I go if I were to leave it behind? With his hand inside my mouth, the poor cripple stares at the blonde's legs. She almost always has her appointments at about the same time I do and she lets her dress quietly ride up her legs under the watchful eye of the cripple as he scrapes my teeth by feel and under the loving smile of the dentistry student who almost kisses her to reassure her every time she uses her appealingly girlish voice to declare that she is scared of those horrible machines that they introduce near the pearls of her mouth, beyond her ruby red lips, inside her fragrant and colored cheeks; her color so mingled, and of so singular a temper, as if she had chosen it for herself. And the rising roundness of her small breasts, who is able to figure forth unto thee? So distracted is the eye of man when he does behold them. And how, I wonder, does that miserable jerk feel when he inconspicuously touches them, in a flurry of drill bits and cotton balls, with his elbows, wrists, forearms, and what have you? The ill-fated aircraft roll across the sky and the cripple has released me for a bit while he goes to the counter to get more sterilized scrapers. I take the opportunity to turn toward the patient behind me, just as they remove his upper teeth. And instead of what I desperately wanted to see, because sitting behind me, the woman that I searched for through all the corners of the precarious world is always there, beautiful and smiling, refined and buxom, mysterious and newly born to the universe of entities; rather than she, I clearly see huge dentures gleaming with saliva, abandoning a bare oral cavity. And all around me, there are seated bodies with dental problems, gingiva-osseous issues, and gum disease, each of them attended to by a spiritual doppelgänger of my cripple, uniformed in white, in several rows. All these things keep my furry tongue company in the darkness, and have a name that surely the cripple knows and I do not, however, gingiva-osseous would be an excellent word that in its plural form should be gingivas-osseous and not gingiva-ossa as so many fools would call it the tranquil tuberous tenders taking so titillatingly their tragic tartarstrophe to transform your tender non triumphant ticking, my beloved. Hide your smile before the cripple comes back and immobilizes me, take away your breast; keep the flower of your silence for me alone, because it is snowing in Moscow and wolves are howling from hunger and the same thing is happening to the Kodiak bears on their border island, but it is quite possible that all they will get will be sizeable rations of atomic ashes on their famished snouts, and then, instead of me going hunting across mountains and plains, instead of keeping that beautiful smile for me, that yesterday would have saved you from a tragic destiny, doll made of flesh, looking in store windows decorated with dolls made of plastic and wetting your rosy cheeks with tears because of the motherhood that the cabaret denied you, it is best for each of us to continue on our journey as if today had not happened. In other words, there's no need to take away anything, and there's no point in my letting my teeth be scraped by the wretched cripple who is planning his future with a drill bit in hand, little metal tool in hand, dragging his leg toward an opulent tomorrow. Because, how do we, sweetheart, get out of this shithole?

"Did I work on the right side already?"

"I don't know. I think so."

"With the scraper?"

"Man, I have no idea."

Allow me to keep talking to you without looking at you. The cripple won't let me. See? Don't laugh, beautiful, you might soon be crying. Bitter you will turn tomorrow. True you will turn tomorrow. To a brothel you will turn tomorrow. Alone you will be tomorrow. Tomorrow? Do you see my helpless little one? Do you see that we barely know each other and we are already no longer interesting to each other and have nothing to say to one another? Do you see how our passion now wilts? It is the lack of communication, the incurable isolation of contemporary men and women. All will end; perhaps I will return to my tiny country and you will lose yourself in a ladies' wear store; and it will be better that way. Sweet captured sheep, I will forget you; it is almost not abandonment my leaving you here with the lecherous and smiling mouth repairer. It's you who didn't know how to love me; my tears searched for your eyes to cry together over the hunger in your heart, but you didn't know how to see it. I will tell you nothing of the poor neighborhoods where I grew up and that I then abandoned along with all those other joys to throw myself into the quest for success and happiness in your birthplace and where I did not find a sweet well or a perennial fountain. And nevertheless, while I was speaking with you, I was fearless. The truth, my dear, is that I would like to stay with you forever. There is nothing beyond these doors for me.

"We will have to finish today's appointment with this molar; we're almost out of time."

Oh, beloved, do not leave. Do not rise. Do not smile, because your smile means farewell. Wicked cripple, if you'd left my mouth alone two minutes ago, when I expected that the premolar scratching would calm your thirst for cleaning and earning praise, she and I would at this very moment be leaving the room together. In your professional ethics classes, if you have them, they should have a seminar on the undeniable superiority of love over dental plaque. Instead, I have to be content with only guessing at how she sashays toward the door with her beautiful mouth finally closed and her dress finally covering her lingerie. Let go of my molar, crippled shepherd. There will also be a need to meditate on the subtle and seamless fabric of a society that no longer binds one at the ankles (no? and what about the Jews who were burned to the bone with white phosphorous? and political prisoners? and delinquent women whimpering, "No, for the love of God, not there, I'll say and do whatever you want me to, sir, not there, not there, for the love of God"?) but instead binds us with whatever, with a small aseptic metal tool that scratches at the small shadow of my open mouth. Even when one has much more important things to think about, because what is in play is no small thing, it's nothing less than a wonderful unknown woman who is leaving me. It would be so, so stupidly simple to say: "OK, my friend, that's enough; moderation is the mother of satisfaction; two and a half hours of dental work is enough for any mortal. And for next time, try not to let that damned ortho-pedic shoe squeak so much, alright?" Someday I will say that to him; in the end it's nothing more than turning over a coin and showing the other side. Or throwing chickpeas and pissing while lost in thought at opening night speeches. Sure they have given me plenty of beatings, but you should see what fun I've had . . . But I didn't do that earlier and I'm not interested in doing it now. Because, let's suppose that I tell the cripple to cut it out and then I rush out hastily down the stairs. What's most likely to hap-pen is that there will be some simpleton waiting for her, or that even without that, I would not dare approach her. What assur-ance would I have of anything? Another woman, another bed, another set of mutual recriminations. Officer, this filthy South American has made indecent proposals to me. Oh, a university instructor! A candidate for the highest grades granted by our institution! Oh, what scandal. Who would have said it?! Oh the grief! Perhaps the proper thing to do would be to approach her in the shadows, in the warm silence of the autumn night. "Do you live here alone?" "No, she lives here too, but she is now visiting her parents. She will not be back until the day after tomorrow."

"Alright, that'll be it for today. See you next Thursday at the same time?"

"Perfect. See you Thursday."

"See you Thursday."

And the only way to separate myself from this situation would be to do so. The locus of any narrative as I see it, at least, "in my world," is this buzzing beehive where they all savagely tear each other apart, screaming, when they could be dispersed through a .38-caliber hole. To avoid disgorging brain matter everywhere, I could use a towel, as one does when one has a toothache. Oh, cherished one, why have you gone? Come back, come back and I promise you there will be no insanity or beauty that we won't have, pleasures that we shall not enjoy, freedoms that are kept from us. Oh well, it's not that big a deal anyway; there's an unrefined quality about her that is surely enough to crush anyone, and plus I have sore gums; next time I have to remember to ask him if it's OK to smoke immediately afterward.

8

BLANCA REMAINED STILL for a long while, resting, sitting on the rock. I could barely make her out by the light of the stars, the shrunken figure by my side, hugging her knees, as if she were contemplating the water of the river that we could barely see and only because it reflected the starry sky.

"Give me a cigarette, please," she asked, raising her voice just above the murmur of the river.

I lit two at once, trying to distinguish her expression by the light of the match, but the flame blinded me and I was unable to see anything. Something was happening with her. Whatever it was, it seemed awful, because this was not the time for problems; it was the time for bed.

"Shall we go?" I proposed sweetly.

"Alright," she answered without moving. She inhaled the smoke at length. With her hand, she wiped something off her lip and stayed sitting there, watching the darkness. After a while and just as I was thinking about starting to caress her again, she came to life. "Hey, tell me something: does Pocho have a girl-friend or fiancée or something?"

"Who? Leroy?" I jumped, trying to guess where the question was headed. "I don't know. I don't suppose so."

"Don't lie. How can you not know if he has someone or not?"

"It's true: I don't know. He had a girlfriend, but I think they broke up not too long ago. Why does it surprise you that I don't know? We men don't talk about such things. If they tell you, they tell you; if they don't, they don't."

"And what was her name?"

"Eugenia."

"What did you think of her?"

"Pretty, but a bit fat, a bit dumb too. Has lots of money."

"And that matters?" she replied, offended, and turned sharply toward me.

At that moment I would have drowned her without hesitation. What the hell did it matter to me what she thought, for the millionth time, about money in relation to love? Or if the damned girl's name was Eugenia or Iphigenia or Assenia? Or anything else that kept us from immediately returning home in the sweet night full of air and silence and flowers?

"I don't know if it matters to Leroy, but since you wanted to know, I told you. Why do you ask? Are you interested in Leroy as a suitor?"

"Don't be an idiot. I think his face looks like a sausage. Do you think Lu would have a chance with him?"

"I don't know. How would I know if she has a chance? I haven't the slightest idea. It does look like he wants her though, that's for sure. Hey, let's get going, OK?"

"Wait a minute. Do you think Leroy has given much thought to getting married or anything like that?"

"I don't know, woman, stop asking nonsense. I suppose sometimes he thinks he will and other times he thinks there's no way he will, just like any normal man. Get up and let's get going," she held out an obedient hand so that I could help her get up, but she pulled it away as soon as she was on her feet.

She tossed the cigarette toward the water with a gesture that even in the darkness seemed annoyed and violent. The red ember's miniscule trajectory, like a domestic meteorite, filled me with infinite happiness and sexual excitement. I also shot mine as far as I could. I almost started singing out of pleasure and surprise when I noticed that the same thing was happening, the ember seemed to blaze a red trail in the air. If I'd had a thousand lit cigarettes I would have tossed them all and I would have burst with so much happiness and surprise. When I turned toward Blanca I was sure I would be met with the open arms, ready to dance on the sand or sing a duet or take off our clothes and begin a dinosaur mating ritual. But she'd begun to walk away up river, toward the road, with a gloomy and upright gait that filled me with bewilderment and rage; although the situation also made me laugh a little, because after all is said and done, the unpredictable Blanca was walking toward my bed at that very moment and that was exactly what I wanted. Of course appearances had to be maintained. I abstained from touching her or saying anything for a long while. It was only when we were approaching the first street lights that I took her by the arm with a delicate caress and asked her:

"Why don't you tell me what's bothering you? Did I say something that upset you?"

"No, nothing. Nothing's bothering me."

"Let's see," I said, smiling understandingly, "why don't you tell your lord and master what's the matter?"

"I won't tell my lord and master what's the matter with me, because there is nothing the matter with me. I already told you once."

We walked along Ballivián Avenue, and as if the devil himself had bestowed passersby everywhere, whenever I was about to begin fiercely reprimanding her, someone would walk by and leave me with my ribs full of wind and a hand in the air, without being able to say anything. I decided to wait until we were inside the house. I was remembering similar situations in the past and could see with dismay the immediate unlikelihood of our climbing into bed. What could really be happening to Blanca? Nothing new; exactly the same as many other times in the past. As we climbed up the stairs of my house and as I ran my hands down her buttocks, looking for the end of the curve where the legs begin, she shot me an unexpected look of hatred from above, the threatening stare of an obstinately unapproachable animal, the same as years before. What could have provoked the attack? Whatever it was, it could be fixed. Her voice, body language, and movements had that certain stiff quality through which I'd maneuvered successfully many times before and spent countless hours being annoyed at but covering up with a hypocritical smile of concern and caring. For the moment, all my advances would be condemned to be immediate and enraging failures. For quite a while, whenever I would ask her what was happening she would reply to me with stupid, hurtful and distant answers. I would also not be able to place my supplicant hands on any part of her body where normally she would accept my caresses relaxing with expectant passivity. However, out of a certain playful perversity, I forced her to stop by pushing her roughly against the cement railing and explored her hips, belly, pubis, thighs as she remained stiff and indifferent under my hand in a type of offended surprise, while at the same time the face of my beloved turned upward toward the sky, enraged. I felt a vehement desire to possess her right then and there in a rabid sexual domination that would then continue inside the house. Previous experience had shown that it always worked out well, at least as far as she was concerned. After a while of resisting or ill will, of feigning indignation or pain, she would give in entirely and would even be soft as silk for two or three days. It was I who didn't have such a great time. What ruined it for me was the fear of her discovering violence as a new source of pleasure. I had to content myself with letting her move again and pushing her inside the dark house with a caress along the length of her back. She hastened to turn on the light as if urged by the desire to show me the hard and evasive stare of her alarmingly huge eyes, her face pale from tightening her jaws.

I definitively opted to take the hypocritical road. If I showed the ire she had awakened in me, she would immediately return to the hotel. She locked herself in the bathroom and remained there for a long time; when she finally reappeared she found me engrossed in reading a magazine, from where I raised my head and sweetly asked her how she was feeling.

"Not very well, thanks," she replied.

Only after endlessly reiterating that I was interested in knowing what was the matter did she finally answer me with something more explicit. But in the meantime, we went around and around the place, stopped, I tried to put my hand in her cleavage, she pushed me away defensively without taking the hint, I would put my hands in my pockets, thinking it would be a good thing if an earthquake would start or a small mouse would show up or some other catastrophe would occur that could open a door for us.

"I don't plan to tell you anything," she declared apocalyptically from an armchair she'd sat on to show me her absence of love. Now I would get nothing out of her.

"But, why are you saying that, woman? Try and we'll see."

"No way, no way am I going to be the same idiot again that I've always been. You have never given a damn about what might happen to me. And you don't care now either. If you say you care, you are lying."

Her body was leaning forward, both her hands were hanging onto the arms of the chair, by her knees, gathering momentum so that she could throw her words at me with more ferocity through her eyes, mouth, and nostrils. I chose to move closer and respond with all the hypocrisy and love I had left.

"Of course I care, Blanca. How could I not care? Think about it, if I've spent all this time asking you what's the matter, there must be a reason. Why else would it be?"

"You know why? Do you want me to tell you why you keep asking me and using that sweet tone and innocent face? Because you want to take me to bed. That's why. All you want is for this argument to be over once and for all so you can calmly take me to bed."

I was dumbfounded and almost burst out with rage. It was completely true, but at the same time one of those huge falsehoods that are not worth discussing. I remained in the offended and proud silence of the innocent man wrongly accused. I wanted very much to pursue the matter and ask her what other damn thing she had to offer besides her ass, and let her know that, in my opinion, it was the only thing she had in the right place, and not even entirely so; it was difficult not to remind her that she was being ungrateful, because if I had a good time, so did she. But I did not dare say so. Like the other thing, it was very true and very false at the same time.

"Look," I began, with the most irritating, objective and cold tone I could muster, "I'm going to tell you something. I think that the best thing we can do is for you to grab your things and we'll go. When we get to the hotel, you get into a warm bath or have a cold shower or do whatever it is you want to do and then go to bed. Quite frankly, I am much too tired to spend all night long fighting with a hysterical woman."

Her eyes started cascading tears. It seemed that her chest was going to burst from indignation, pain, insults, spasms, and terrible surprises. She choked on the words she wanted to overwhelm me with as she communicated that not only was she going to go immediately to her hotel, but to her country the next day or that very night if she could get a flight. I seethed with delight and mocking dislike.

"Love of mine," I informed her, "it cannot be done. In order to get all your papers in order you need at least a week. So stop making scenes and ridiculous declarations. You are not a child."

She grabbed the arms of the chair with both hands because her sobs threatened to make her lose her balance. She looked at me first through the waterfall of tears and then shrank down to hold her head in her hands. She began to whimper with honesty, despair, explosions, and nasal noises. I was moved slightly as I looked at the top of her head. Her black silky hair curved over her ears and ran down gracefully into a tie at the nape of her neck. I began to notice that her thin and stunned shoulders were within reach of my fingertips, almost asking me to lean over and shelter them in a conciliatory hug. But that would have been a fatal mistake. If I had committed it, she would have left the city immediately, even if she had to walk to do so. A sudden enlightenment made me shout with amazing strength:

"Stop crying immediately! Immediately, woman!"

And astonishingly that resulted in her trembling shoulders instantly quieting down. Then she sat there, unmoving, until her torso relaxed, and she held her forehead in her loosely clasped hands in front of her, like a very tiny and sad little girl. From time to time she softly whimpered, almost sighing. In that position, her waist looked incredibly small.

She stood up slowly, without looking up. I was undecided as to whether to leave her alone and go outside in the street or insult her or pretend to be offended and distant. The success of making her be quiet had stupefied me; I had no idea what to do next. She reached out and when she found me, purely by touch, she held onto me, submissively, lovingly, and calm.

"I don't want to leave," she whispered, pleadingly. "Let me stay, please. Do you want me to stay?"

So we ended up in bed, with a little less enthusiasm than other days, but with a little more tenderness. If Blanca had better control over herself and over the circumstances, she would have ruined both. At precisely the wrong moment, perhaps because it seemed most suitable to her, she couldn't stand the urge to call to my attention the magnitude of her love and to make me see that I had at hand evidence of her love and devotion. In order to handle her more violently, I had supported myself on the bed and had lifted my torso over her; since she had decided to be tender, she kept her eyes open, looking at me sweetly. It was beautiful to see her smile framed by her black hair spread out across the bedsheet. But if she insisted on holding a dialogue with me intending to prove things to me, she would ruin everything.

When the storm was over, I noticed that she was crying. She told me it was out of pleasure and happiness. Huge tears were gently streaming down her face, out of the corners of her eyes toward her ears; both her ears were wet. I would have liked for the night to have been just beginning, for the party not to be ending because we had spent the beginning of the evening on nonsense. It was extremely late and even if we had gotten up immediately, we would have had to make a huge fuss to awaken the hotel doorman to let us in.

Additionally, the explanation for her anger was still pending. Naturally I didn't want to hear it now; however, she was not going to spare me her explanation so easily. I could already tell in the gradual hardening of her face, where there was only a faint trace of tears and joy, that she was eager to explain and round out the evening. The night would have been incomplete for her had she not found a gap through which to fit in a full confession. I decided to make a sacrifice for love, and I began to stroke her hair and wait for the explanation. I consoled myself by remembering that there was not much left of the night, so it almost didn't matter that I was losing a bit of the pleasure I needed or losing it all. And indeed, together with her arguments, the light of dawn snuck in through the window. I didn't understand a thing, but as a new day was beginning, I felt free from having to exert further efforts. She'd been desperate, aching, crazed with grief, fears, and inner loneliness. It had all started when we decided not to continue our walk (I almost asked which walk), more precisely when I had said, "Get up and let's get going"; but what really had precipitated the horror was when she discovered that she'd gotten river sand in her mouth. She asked me if I realized what that meant. "River sand in my mouth," I nodded slowly and frowned. It was then that, hysterical because every time she put her teeth together the grains of sand made her teeth gnash, she would have preferred death or jumping in the river or returning home.

The sun was shining. I waited for it to completely cover the bed. Blanca was very still, her eyes round with so much meaning, looking up toward the ceiling. She seemed to be listening to the sounds of the center of the Earth.

"Do you know what I'm thinking?" she asked slyly.

"No, what is it?"

"About Luisa's face when she sees the untouched bed next to hers. I would pay to see it. Hopefully she'll stop her nonsense and quit annoying me."

"Has she said anything?"

"No, nothing. You know what she's like; she acts like a martyr; asks questions. 'Are we going to be able to go to the movies tomorrow?' 'Or do you have something to do?' things like that."

"Maybe she'll be even worse now that she has a reason to be," I conjectured. "Do you know something? I think that what she needs is a man; Leroy could be our salvation. I have a feeling she would be soft as silk afterward."

"That is what angers me most," she jumped, sitting up on her elbow. "It's not Leroy that Luisa wants. It's you . . . and don't pretend you didn't know, because you see it clearly."

"What do you think of the idea?"

"I'd scratch your eyes out."

"Sweetheart, what do my eyes have to do with it?"

"Cheeky," she said, laughing and lying back down on the bed, her fears allayed. "I mean it. I'll scratch out whatever I have to. With my fingernails."

"Hey, don't you want to leave now?"

"What for? I wouldn't think of it. Let's shower and I'll make you some breakfast. What a beautiful day! I adore you. It would be so beautiful to wake up like this every day," she sighed, in a saddened voice.

"Hmmm. Let's see. Be quiet. Do you hear that? There are sounds coming from somewhere, but they're not annoying. That screeching of metal is the *cholita* from next door going to get milk and bread. Do you hear it? Do you hear that other one?"

"Yes, now I do. Sounds like an alarm clock. Where could it be coming from?"

"It reminds me of when I was a child. Don't you find that this city is wonderfully peaceful and beautiful? Hey, if you like it, why don't you stay?"

She didn't reply. She squeezed her body against mine, distracted and happy, as if she were thinking of something else. She seemed to be drunk with happy sensations; a kind of suffocation of consciousness in the brightness, freshness, and peace in which her body floated.

"It would be like a dream," she articulated, sleepily. "I would do nothing but take care of you. It must be good to take care of you, in spite of how uncouth you are," she reasoned, fully opening her eyes. "It would be good to be able to make my lord and master's life as sweet as he allowed me to."

"OK, OK, enough with plans for the future and more breakfasts in the present, my beloved lady. Time's a wasting. Up we go, into the kitchen."

She looked at me with theatrical and charming disapproval and put on my pajama top, but added the pants when I told her a woman is more alluring fully clothed than half naked. She looked adorably ugly among all the folds of extra fabric.

VIII

As soon as the voice inside says, "Come in," and I grip the door handle, it occurs to me that I shouldn't have come. However, it doesn't occur to me to turn around and head out the way I came in, because being here somehow gives me relief or hope or perhaps because I'm a prisoner of the long hallway that I had to walk down to get here, or of the old receptionist who took down my information, or of all these buildings designed to provide medical care to the university and the city. The man looks at me threateningly without getting up from behind the desk, greets me, and points to a chair. Fortunately this place looks like something else; it looks as if it were destined to be a laboratory or perhaps a huge kitchen because of its wall tile. I get the impression that this man could easily be a complete idiot. Has he ever considered anything even remotely like what I'm about to tell him? And what is it that I'm about to tell him? I have nothing to say; it is just a few insignificant aches and pains. I am about to stand up and politely excuse myself and add: "I had a small problem, but I feel better now; sorry for bothering you. See you later."

"So," he says to me, "how can I help you?"

"I need for you to give me a few pills or something, because I want to eat and sleep again. I have to prepare for my comprehensive exams for my doctorate and I also have to work."

"How long has it been since you last ate?"

"Hmmm, almost three weeks."

"Nothing?"

"Liquids. They are the only thing I can swallow."

"Oh, then don't worry; one can live for a long time on just fluids. Have you lost weight?" he asks with irritating calmness

163

and lights a burnt old pipe while he waits for my response.

"I don't believe so, I haven't weighed myself."

"And you don't sleep?" he adds unintelligibly.

"Pardon?"

"How long has it been since you last slept?"

"I sleep, but two or three hours, no more than that, and not well . . . with nightmares and things. They don't sell anything without a prescription at the drugstore."

"Alright, relax. I will give you some pills. But first let me warn you: different drugs called sedatives have a limited effect both in time and results. Pills alone won't get you anywhere. They're not magic. Would you like to describe to me in detail what it is that you're feeling?"

"No. I'm frightened."

"Of what?" he asks, with the match still in his hand. While I try to figure out what it is that frightens me, he folds the match into several pieces, and lifting his elbow and letting his hand hang over his shoulder, flicks it into the ashtray with a circular movement.

"Of everything."

He moves away from the desk and then his head disappears as if he were looking for something in a bottom drawer. It sounds like he's rummaging through papers. Outside, the awful humid heat falls on everything; I imagine, with insane terror, the vast amount of space that hospital buildings occupy, spread out on the soft grass-covered hills, where, beneath the sun, sick patients and health care workers dressed in white move about. I'm sure that I will not succeed if I try to light a cigarette, the ache in my stomach has kept my muscles constricted all day and my hands tremble much too much. I would like to smoke; it would help me to think about what he said, that they are not magic. They are not magical, I understand perfectly and it fills me with despair as well as contempt for myself. I'm disgusted and humiliated at being so tired that it would occur to me that they could possibly sell magical things in the drugstores. At this point, I could get up and tell him that I have understood, to excuse me for both-ering him, thank him. He gets up suddenly and violently throws a magazine at my face. I grab it easily in the air.

"Did that scare you?"

"No."

He extends out his hands, palms up, at shoulder height to indicate that the incident has proven me wrong, that the contradiction of my universal fear is staring me in the face. I find the whole thing a trifle childish.

"Very well, but you do understand that there was no reason for me to be frightened. Magazines aren't weapons; I have no reason to suspect that you would have aggressive intentions toward me. In addition, I have never implied that there are not others in worse shape than me. What I fear are things like the atomic bomb, as well as the unpredictable nature of everything."

"OK," he responds very calmly. "That is very natural. After all you and I are living a few kilometers away from Strategic Air Command. What you would have to do would be to communicate your fear to all those fools who think there's nothing to worry about."

"Very well, but I'm the one who can't eat or sleep."

"Do you want us to see if there are other options? Would you like that?" he asks. He had let his pipe go out and was about to light it again. Meanwhile he observes me over the pipe, his hand and match burning.

"Fine."

"Do you have financial difficulties? I mean debt, low wages, you understand."

"No, rather the opposite. I don't think I've ever had so much disposable income in my life."

"Does that bother you?"

"Look, in and of itself, no. Although sometimes it bothers me. Not always, though."

"Hmmm. Not enough news of your country?"

"No."

"Too much?"

"No."

"What is the atmosphere like with your superiors at the university?"

"Very good."

"Would you say, that, let's say, they go out of their way to solve your problems or help you?"

"No."

"Are you here alone?"

"No."

"What about your family life?"

The summer outside continues oppressively. I am doubly thankful for the air-conditioning unit that keeps everything cool and is so quiet. The questions have annoyed me to no end. There is something rotten about all of this. I know that if I tell him he will think that he has hit the nail on the head, and it might be true, but that is not what matters. It is true that I'm shattered, it's true that I'm barely thirty and a decrepit old fogy; that unless I'm half drunk, the fear of death is so gut-wrenching and ear-splitting that I hear voices in the murmur of the fridge, that I curse the day that I was born to die, that the little bit of sleep that I am able to get unleashes, through nightmarish images, how repulsive and hideous my life must be. This is all so true that out of sheer terror of death I am tempted to take my own life. But my coming here, this interrogation, the whole thing, is false and disgusting, and above all, useless and harmful. Bad magic. The pipe has gone out again, but he keeps sucking on it producing an irritating sound of saliva in the cylinder. It is very difficult to speak, because what I would like to say is entirely something else, but I finally say no, that I have never seen my mother naked, that perhaps I wanted to go to bed with everyone and torture and kill everyone when I still didn't know what those three things were; that I'm no more and no less of a pussy than any quiet boy next door; that that's not it. He interrupts me seemingly interested.

"And what do you mean by all that?"

He was not as much of a fool as he seemed. When you speak to him seriously, he understands. Far away, there's a sound of a siren and I cannot express something that I was thinking about, that I'd almost thought of when he asked about that . . . Because that was the crux of the matter. But none of this helps at all. I'm scared, damn it, and that's all, and I cannot continue like this, because I will burst. What is happening outside, in the vast and empty open space? Why is the siren going at this hour? What is everyone else thinking or doing? Perhaps leaning over instrument panels, sending orders over the radio, flying in airplanes at enormous altitudes. The siren gets nearer and nearer; they must be bringing an accident victim to the hospital.

"Can you give me some pills?"

9

I'D BEEN SUFFERING from a violent attack of compassionate love since lunch. Perhaps it was due to Blanca's inefficient grief that invariably made us end up in bed. Perhaps on some level it made me sad to subdue her, remove her clothes, make her laugh, ignore her. I was working out an estimate for some bar furniture that had just been ordered and my eyes often strayed out the window to the warehouses and my imagination would stab me with unfortunate images of my beloved. From the secretary's offices I could hear the voices of Yolita and her two friends, all I heard were simply feminine sounding noises, because I couldn't make out the words. Despite the difference in tone and timbre and everything, I would suddenly almost jump out of my chair with the certainty that Blanca had just come in and was saying something. And there I was again, haunted by a repulsive yet loving compassion. It was because at lunch, determined as she always was to make my life more affordable and organized and domestic, she'd suddenly asked me why I used store bought wax when the floors would shine if I used a homemade product. Then she proceeded to describe in detail how the paste was made; it consisted of melting candles in paraffin and adding a little raw wax; she knew the proportions and all she needed were the ingredients and some containers and if I brought them to her, she would be able to make as many liters as I wanted that very same afternoon. I laughed, caressed her hair, and told her there was no need and a heartbreaking pity settled in my stomach. I had made my way to work without saying a word, overwhelmed by the memory of her graceful figure, smiling and submissive, that disgustingly wrenched at my gut with the sharp claw of pity. I was experiencing an almost excruciating desire to leave work for the afternoon and rush out to the stores in search of countless gifts that I imagined would compensate because neglect, loneliness, and old age threatened her. As if the horror that besieged her could be exorcised when surrounded by material proof of my thoughtfulness. But the quotes required did not allow for delays and besides, it was much too early and the stores would be closed. Instead I decided I would pay attention to even the smallest of her desires and satisfy them. When I had to go down to the first floor to check on some information with the foreman, the ravaged and bitter figure of an old woman who was very humbly asking Yolita something almost exploded in my eyes; my heart stopped for an instant with the fear that perhaps, in the years to come, she too would have to find out something, in some office, and she would look like Pamani's widow with a little bundle between her gnarled hands.

At about five o'clock in the afternoon, I had to seriously focus on the quote, because if I kept going like this, I wouldn't finish. I inwardly cursed Leroy's laziness. He hadn't shown up since the day before. Had he been at work, we would have finished earlier and I wouldn't have been forced to distract myself from my absurd and savory sorrow in favor of the price of nails. Additionally, I also wanted to run to Blanca as soon as the day was done, and I would not be able to.

I sighed with resignation when I started to hear chairs being moved and the more lively conversation of the three women as they prepared to leave for the day; I imagined with rabid delight the pleasure that I would have gotten from being with Blanca while it was still light out. At that moment I heard Leroy's voice from the secretaries' office, discernible even through the wall, greeting the women.

"Hello, my beauties. Is the lion in his den?"

I prepared a string of insults to hurl at him as soon as he came in, but he rushed into the office bursting with glee:

"Brother, punch me, but listen. I am happy. I'm getting married."

"Are you serious?" I asked, honestly surprised.

"Serious, completely serious."

"And who's the unlucky girl?"

"Who else would it be but with my Chica, my beautiful Eugenita, the most beautiful of women, brother." As he praised Chica's attributes, he raised his arms and danced around the office, "How can you be working right now, slave?" he suddenly accused me, leaning on the desk.

"Hey, are you seriously getting married?" I insisted, still not convinced.

"Seriously, seriously," he assured me, changing his tone and letting himself fall onto the chair. "I'm marrying Chica in two months. What do you think about that?"

"Awful."

"What?"

I could see that he was very annoyed by my verdict. I had no choice but to explain.

"The thing is old man, that I had other plans for you. It had occurred to me that you could 'take care' of Luisita and calm her down for a little while. She won't leave Blanca and me alone. Let me ask you a personal question. How is it that you didn't seduce her before? Because she did all she could: she complimented you, she batted her eyelashes, swayed her hips, her behind."

"I didn't notice, brother. I didn't notice," Leroy groaned. "Hey, but there's still time. Better late than never."

"Don't be immoral. Besides, you're screwed now, because Lu is a young woman with high principles and will prefer to keep working out and swimming and ruining it for the rest of us."

Leroy was quiet, as if thinking. He was making some ape-like gestures with his mouth and eyebrows that made him look somewhat worried, somewhat ridiculous. He stared at his hand, and a stupid smile crossed his face.

"Look, look, moron," he got up bursting with pride and extended the sleeves of his shirt in front of my nose. "What do you think of the gold cufflinks that my baby gave me, huh?"

"Nice. A little gaudy, but nice."

"As if, you loser. Hey man, be honest with me. What do you think of the whole thing?" he said, thickening his voice and looking at me carefully as he sat down again.

"I already told you, nice, but a little gaudy."

"Don't be an idiot. I'm being serious. Do you think that if I get married I'll be making the mistake of my life?"

"How should I know? What matters is how you see it."

"I don't see a thing, brother. The only thing I know is that I'm happy and in love with Chica. I also think that at some point one has to settle down; don't you agree? You know what I'm like. If I don't get married, I will keep screwing up and wasting my time all my life. As for seeing, I see nothing, but my mind is made up."

"That's what I was going to ask you; where did you get the nerve to take such a huge leap?"

I just wanted to annoy him. It made me somewhat uncomfortable that Leroy, famous for his indecisiveness and indifference would have made such a serious decision. All was silent; the staff had already left in their cars while we were talking. Leroy made himself comfortable on the chair, took out some weird looking cigarettes, and offered me one.

"Do you want one? They're Turkish, brother; my future mother-in-law gave them to me."

"Throw me one."

"Do you remember that night that they beat the crap out of us at the Perla Azul?"

I nodded and lit the cigarette. It was disgusting.

"When I left you guys, something came over me; one of those weird feelings; and I couldn't sleep with my nose in such a sorry state. If the light had been off at Chica's window, nothing would have happened. But bad things always come in threes; she was up reading and let me in."

"And how did she know you were there?"

"We had a system: I would throw little stones at her window. Well, first she cried because of my nose and then we made out. I was in so much pain and it was so late that I fell asleep like a rock. I woke up who knows how much later with that feeling that one gets when someone is watching."

"Oh, shit! The old woman!"

"The fucking old woman was standing at the door of the bedroom, doorknob in hand, watching over her daughter sleeping with a naked idiot."

"And what did the poor old woman do?"

"Poor old woman, poor old woman my foot . . . conniving old woman, brother. A shark of a woman. She didn't say a thing. We stared at each other for a while; I didn't even have a chance to cover myself up; she closed the door quietly and then left. What do you think? Crafty old woman."

"And what did you do?"

"I almost shit myself I was so angry. I felt like going after her and cursing up a storm at her so that she would learn . . . despicable old woman. The only thing I could think of was to wake up Chica again and screw her again. Then I got up and got the hell out of there. You should have seen poor Chica's face when I put my shoes on and started striding across the room looking for my things and talking out loud. Even the chair where I had left my pants fell over; I left it lying there; I left and almost took out the door frame when I slammed the door shut. I stayed away for about ten days."

"And you are realizing just now that you're in love up to your eyeballs and that the girl has her charms?"

"Exactly. And she does. She is as affectionate with me as a cat. The only thing the old woman has is money. She will give Eugenia the old man's money right away and more. I'll get married, buy a little truck, do deliveries for a year or two out east until I'm rolling in it and then go back to Chile and finish my studies. What do you think?"

"Great," I replied. "Throw me another one of those awful Turkish cigarettes, please. Thanks. And then what happened?"

"This is the worst part. We ran into each other by chance the other day. I'll be honest, when I saw her, all I wanted to do was to bed her. And Eugenia tells me that her mom told her everything, that the only thing is that she's a little grim-faced, but that she doesn't even forbid her from seeing me or from my visiting her, although she prefers not to have to see me. Doesn't that take the cake? I almost dropped dead."

"Shit, what a woman. If I were you I'd marry the mother. And?"

"And nothing. We're getting married. This morning we went to the airport cheek-to-cheek to drop off the old woman, she is flying to La Paz. Hey, by the way, Pablo was on the same plane and he said that they had told him about some replacement parts that were about to arrive at Importadora; he told me to let you know. So, what do you think about the whole story?"

"Great. What should I think?"

To be honest, it sounded good to me, but I wasn't in the mood to offer congratulations. Everything was rose-colored. I burdened him with a truly beautiful sermon on the duties and virtues of the state of matrimony. I elaborated on the countless advantages that a man determined to improve himself can get out of the warmth and solidity of a home that he has forged. Because in effect, if the girl, the old woman, me, and even Leroy realized that all the sad, surprising, and understanding behaviors had been calculated with a watchmaker's rigor, wisdom, and expert knowledge of the human spirit and the surprising power of the young vagina, and all of this with the crystal clear design of grabbing a hold of Leroy and nobody minded; if it was also true that there was a truck waiting for my friend in the fat family checkbook; and if, finally, the young woman's pelvis promised abundant, although somewhat stocky, descendants, and I knew that the new bridegroom was crazy about the idea of being a father, why then wouldn't Leroy's enthusiasm to stick his head or whatever it may be in the trap they were setting for him be unrestrained? And why shouldn't I satisfy the natural tendency of man to speak and provide wholesome advice?

Leroy wanted Ramón to be the second person to hear his splendid news and left me to my calculations. But first he gave me a huge hug, shook my hand, and thanked me very emotionally; I wasn't exactly sure what for. I went back to my papers happy because of Leroy's happiness and surprised myself wishing him good luck even though it seemed to me very probable that he would not have it.

I was interrupted by the racket that my two friends were making as they hastily walked through the secretaries' office when I was finishing up my work. They were bringing over a beautiful bottle of Peruvian Pisco shaped like a potbellied little Indian.

"No more numbers, maestro," Ramón roared, "not even a half number. This must be celebrated."

"Did you bastards leave any for me?"

"We haven't even opened it, maestro. We were waiting for you."

"Well done. Like a man," I approved, "and where did you get this beauty from?" I asked, grabbing the bottle.

Ramón put a hand on his chest and humbly bent over, self-consciously acknowledging the generosity of his gift. Leroy snatched the bottle away from me and said:

"Let's go to the shop. The Pisco will make me choke in this shithole of an office."

Ramón opened the bottle and we started drinking it in the coffee mugs, our joy increasing accordingly. We weren't talking very much, but whatever any one of us said, we burst out laughing. We only discussed anything actively when we were dividing the successive portions. When there was about one-third of the little Indian left, Ramón tried to create a drink out of coffee and Pisco, but after many machinations and delays, the product turned out to be repulsive; even Ramón took a shot and then spit it out of his mouth, immediately declaring that it tasted like the Balsam of Fierabras. However, in order to make it up to us, he brought out a second little Indian that seemed much more beautiful than the previous.

Before saying goodbye, by the door of the factory, we enthusiastically burst into song. We kicked the dogs that insisted on coming out to the road and offered to beat all passersby who looked at us, or stopped doing so, without leaving out two *cholitas* who stopped at a certain distance and started throwing stones at us in the dark. Ramón declared that we'd failed the rules of chivalry by threatening the women and that our punishment would be to continue singing without stopping, without taking refuge, and if either of us so much as blinked, he would forever be regarded as a blackguard and a bastard of a knight. So there we were, the knights Amadís, Tristan and Tirante singing "*Naranjitayyyyy, pinta, pintiiita*" and also once in a while staying mute when one of the avenging stones found its way to our ribs. The enemy witches, encouraged by our passivity, were shooting at us as fast as a machine gun. And there we would have remained, in the dark, putting up with the humiliating stoning if Ramón's head hadn't abruptly and violently reverberated with a powerful THWACK! He didn't even blink; he just exclaimed when he saw the light of the truth on his ill-treated head:

"Oh, no, che, the punishment doesn't fit the crime. These women are not, well, ladies, but rather Valkyries or Amazons."

And unleashing his battle cry, he charged against a fleeing storm of shrieks. He returned with his hand up in the air in a sign of victory. Ramón was a serene type of guy and sensitive in his own way. He never bothered anyone and was extremely considerate with everyone. But he cared a lot about Leroy and liked to let his hair down from time to time. His spirit lifted and he offered to treat us to dinner downtown. In unison we asked him if he had the means.

"Don't you worry, maestros, I do," he replied, without being offended.

"Hey, Ramón," Leroy objected, "and what if someone sees you?"

"That depends, maestros, on how many there are. We either beat them or we end up at the police station or in the jungle, but without our submarplane."

"But we will walk or take a bus," I stated, feeling strong and virtuous, "because if anything happens to us in one of the company trucks, Pablo will be screwed."

"I'm going to clean up, maestros; I'll just be a minute. You go ahead to the bus stop and if there's a bus, hold it so that it won't leave until I'm ready."

The bus was there and was about to leave. In fact, it had already started to move and when the driver saw us he stopped.

"Sir," Leroy said, very politely, "could you do us a favor and not leave yet? Could you wait a bit? Our friend is on his way."

"I can't. I'm running late."

And without another word he put it in first and started to take his foot off the clutch. The guy was very offended by the way that the tactless Leroy had spoken to him. In a couple of seconds, Ramón would reappear only to see the bus's rear lights and the foolish faces of his two guests, standing in the middle of the lonely dark road. So I had to take the guy's keys away in order to be able to talk more freely and more leisurely. He didn't like that one bit, but there were two of us and Leroy alone would have given him reason to think twice. He took into account the obvious feebleness of his assistant, the ticket collector, and decided to parley with us.

"It's just that I'm already late. People will be crowded waiting along the whole route. They will be angry. And I also have to eat. Just look at what time it is."

"Better if people are waiting en route," jumped Leroy, "the more people waiting, the more money you make. And it will only be for two minutes. If we were asking you to wait for an hour, then you would be right. But we are not leaving our friend stranded because you say so. How much do you make per trip? A thousand bolivianos?"

"Well, no, more like two thousand."

"See? And your bus is always half empty. Instead, if you wait, the route fills up with people, your bus fills up with people, and your pockets fill up with money. I figure you will at least pocket five thousand, as long as we wait for my friend, that is. Let's see, what junk can you buy with only two thousand, huh? However, five thousand, now that's something else. Don't you agree?"

Leroy was about to make a list of all the things one could acquire with five thousand bolivianos in spite of the look of despair on the driver's face. At that moment another passenger got on the bus, looked around in surprise, and sat down stiffly. The driver saw that as support for his argument, left

Leroy with the fingers of his left hand ready to start counting, turned toward the newcomer, and started to tell him something. The only thing I understood was the agitation of the driver. The other one listened with a look of shock on his face, but with no sympathy. From his gestures and expressions we figured that he answered something like keep-me-out-of-this-business-of-other-people's-buses. And that's when the poor man really became furious. If our wickedness had seemed reprehensible to him, the other's indifference reached him to the core. He started yelling at him things that sounded like blames and threats. Leroy and I were having the time of our lives. We lamented a bit when Ramón stepped on the bus (sparkling in his clean shirt and crowned with an impressive hat) and that there would no longer be a reason to keep the ill-tempered driver's key from him.

"See how there's no point in getting angry over inane things?" Leroy told him. "If you keep losing your damned temper you're going to get ulcers," he added admonishingly before taking a seat.

We started to roll slowly down the road. The moment had something dishearteningly anticlimactic about it. It seemed to me that for Ramón with his change of clothes and for us with the aborted incident with the driver, our enthusiasm had dampened. Watching the lit adobe houses disinterestedly and indifferently because I had seen them hundreds of times four times a day, I felt surprised and discouraged. I came to the conclusion that I felt a certain amount of envy over Leroy's decision, even if it was foolish. Was it foolish?

I could almost feel my body along the long, cold, and dark winter roads, returning to a warm and quiet home. Every evening, every sunset, my beard full of frost and my shirt covered in snow, returning to the beautiful village home, always beautiful, always good, always a glimmer of light and color over the rigid fields. The huge fireplace would emit the soft scent of burnt firewood and of country cooking that Blanca would remove from the huge village pots and would put in my bowl. Our many children would already be asleep under the secure beams of the house, warm among the soft furs. And we would chat quietly, very few times, very simple things. All would be well. How foolish!

Of course it was. And not because "those things don't happen." Besides, they don't happen. Yet somehow they could happen. But what mattered was something else. How could I not be aware, as the bus rattled wearily down the dark road, that our ride right now was moving in the direction of the Tunari? How could I forget that the jungle began beyond that point, that I could not think of anywhere else to go when, after many nights of love and many days of love, a man gets up from the bed, trembling with happiness and fulfillment and with the seductive, hard light of the horizon moored to his thoughts? Wasn't it the jungle then where I had to go?

Because if absolutely no one knows what love truly is; if it is all at once the memory of the childhood sweetheart waiting under the quiet neighborhood streetlight as well as the sad stabbing that splits apart the heart of the infidel and the set of little jars that she left behind when she went away; if love is no stranger to the most crippling joy, nor to death; if sex and God are neighbors; if indeed those who look upon Beatrice become more perfect for having done so; if the service of one's beloved, and domination of one's beloved, and the rose twice as brief, and the home, and the pearls of your mouth, and hold the mirror up to Venus, and do a striptease for me, it's not hard . . . So then, who forced me to turn this universal turmoil that is love into a sort of sociological and somewhat muddy trap where almost without fail the spirit was left motionless and rotting? As long as love was not a creation of the spirit, but rather a series of insignificant actions that either killed love or made one live hopping from loving nook to loving cranny, from the most conventional and foolish indulgence to the more conventional and foolish respectability, it was better to trust one's sense of smell, the crunch of one's joints and the medieval codes, because they were good guides, because they sounded strong and because they were strangely beautiful. And all this was true even with my desire for a simple and domestic life, and also with the envy that I felt over Leroy's impending nuptials and the little white house with a garden that he surely would have. Good smell, hard sound, beauty. That was it. My envy was foolish. Just as I couldn't lose my money at poker, I also couldn't be wrong about anything that mattered. I was standing—however precariously, so what?—at the very heart of the universe.

"Man, this thing is barely moving," Ramón said. He crossed his arms over his chest and stayed quiet for a few minutes, as if calculating the speed of the bus. Then he spoke out loudly and asked the driver something in Quechua. The poor man was having bad luck. He replied in a sort of shriek, modulating and emphasizing what he was saying with offensive gestures. Ramón looked at us flabbergasted, "Do you know what he said, *caray*? That he doesn't feel like going any faster, che. We can't let him make the customers uncomfortable with this bad temper, *caray*. We will have to let him know, che." And without another word, he stood up, walked to the front of the bus and said: "Let's see, maestro, you're going to let me drive now."

The slow offensive and defensive gestures of the poor man made him look like a snail compared to the tiger-like speed with which Ramón grabbed him by both ears, lifted him off his seat howling in pain, left him on the floor, and seated himself at the wheel. The poor devil looked at Ramón in fear and at the two of us and didn't dare say anything to anyone.

I proposed to Ramón that in order to really enjoy the drive we both should work together. I worked the accelerator and he was in charge of the rest. Of course in order to make things more interesting he had to agree to not use the brake or the clutch unless there was serious danger of killing someone. At that moment, two hurried shapes hastened off the bus: the passenger and the driver's assistant. Ramón smiled as he did when he added sugar to his coffee, turned his head in all directions as if looking for something, threw his hat back onto the seat behind him, and we took off.

IX

"What time is it?" she asks from the bathroom.

"It's eleven."

Why does she ask such stupid questions I wonder? What the hell does it matter if it's two minutes after eleven or any other time? It's late and it's nighttime and the watch on my wrist is moving with an absurd amount of effort, as if it were pushing time in circles with the second hand; as if a foreign monster, a parasite, had glued itself to my body and there it was, just sitting there, engaged in an enterprise whose sinister character consists of being useless and impossible to stop. It's completely useless, but it marks the hours in which things might occur. Not even that; it marks only the hours in which nothing occurred; as proof that nothing occurred, that it was all just a stupid nightmare, as if we were all already dead and we kept looking at timepieces measuring the nonexistent revolutions of the Earth. Dear students, have you meditated upon, and really thought about, I'm not saying merely suspected, but pondered the possibility that it's all indeed a dream? What implications would such a thing have on a world that is no longer in the seventeenth century, but rather this exact one of ours? I urge you to meditate, to ponder, I mean, within the boundaries that a simple action would acquire; let's say for example, having a dental cavity. But that isn't an action; let's say then, that of wiping your behind or cutting a small portion of steak. Someone make that fucking old man shut up. It's three twenty . . . twenty-five . . . thirty . . . thirty-five . . . and forty . . . and if I hold my breath until the clock strikes six . . .

"How was your trip?"

Always, every time, every single time, she has to ask me that when I cannot answer her. Besides, she's brushing her teeth, if I say anything, she will not hear me over the din of the brush inside her mouth. Shfffff, finally. I could swear that right now her head is leaning out the bathroom door. I will let her ask me again, to repeat herself, because I cannot tell her anything about how the damned trip was. Suddenly, amid the clear night air, we reached the little town, while the strange and powerful search-lights were the same distance away to the right, and seemed to be looking for something in the Starry Sky Tumbling Club. There was the delightful group of three blonde girls that came from inside, very serious. It occurred to me that if they reached the hot-dog stand before the bus passed in front of them, I might be able to see their faces and maybe nothing would happen; but one of them tripped or twisted an ankle or something and they stayed put and I wasn't able to see them and a jolt of ter-ror gripped my brain. Or maybe it was the old woman with her dyed hair smoking absentmindedly in the shadows of the bus. But above all, it was the searchlights. But above all it was the horrific bridge, with its traffic jam, cars driven by ghosts under the light of mercury bulbs. Everyone, each and every one, every lamppost, every nickel, every effort made by the engine, all were driven by the clock of death.

"Sweetheart, why are you not answering me? Are you asleep? How was your trip, sweetheart?"

"Very good; very comfortable. I'm a little upset right now."

It was not fair to make her witness the sight of a useless sloth lying snout down on the bed. And I'm not comfortable in this position. I will be better off on my side and this way I can see what she is doing. I feel a little better on my side, really; it's eas-ier to breathe.

"Did you take your pill?"

"No, I'd forgotten. Did you bring them? Give me one please."

They're not much help. But they must be doing me some good. The sound of the soft slipper skirts the edge of the other bed toward the suitcases, with all its weight in the room, in the trapped air, thick with moisture and heat. Under my shirt, on my chest hair, on the flaccid and loose folds of the skin of my armpits, sweat accumulates. Her presence is now more distant. It lies behind the reddish curtain of my eyelids, my eyeballs flooded in warm blood, beating, how do I know that? Could it be the noise? She is now turning on the faucet to fill the glass and that's different, her closeness makes something vibrate, something move and I notice it. The water will probably be cold and it will refresh the same throat that some twenty years ago joyfully swallowed cold and pure liquids. One can simply not stay in the same position in this dreadful heat. More than this, in the bright interrogation-like lights, there is no shade or relief, not even behind one's hands. It's better to lie on one's back. Oh God, if only I didn't have to be here, if only I didn't have to hear the sounds that come from the ground to make me tremble from twenty-one stories below.

"Adriana, what is that?"

"What? What's the matter?"

"Nothing. Forgive my screeching. It must be an ambulance or police car. Don't you think so?"

At ground level, throughout the huge city that the night is suffocating with heat, there is something going on. If I dared to go to the window, I would see it like a cockroach, if I could even see it. They are hard to spot. Once again, I know that what I think is making a sound right after the siren is mere illusion, even if it sounds like words. They cannot be words; I'm just imagining them.

"Oh my God, why does that fucking sound not stop? There's nowhere to hide in this fucking world. Everything wails— fridges, sirens, clocks."

She looks at me with her eyes huge. What did I say all that for? But it's true: the home air-conditioning unit says things from the window that hide other things; clocks are ticking on their own, completely oblivious to everything. But there's no point in whining if I cannot make it stop. And I cannot. If I try to drink that glass of shimmering water, cool and silent like a snake, with just one hand . . . It seems as if evil on Earth ends when one of those crappy things finally shuts up. But in two minutes, right away, suddenly, something will start shrieking again . . .

Leaning over me, she offers me a pill on the palm of her left hand, and, the water, like a tame viper, between the thumb and index finger of her other hand.

"Can't you hold the glass with just one hand?"

"Yes, of course I can. It's just that I'm very thirsty."

"Do you want me to order you a drink?"

She has turned away, trying to make me believe that she's doing it naturally, to take away the empty glass. But in a minute she will start up with the same old thing as usual; why do I go out; that I need to rest and not traverse the entire unknown city in this heat that I cannot bear. I will go walking downtown. There must be a bar open somewhere still. That's it: a couple of cold doubles with ice clinking in the glass to help me go to sleep. Of course I will not be able to anyway. This is much too high up, and I had to get the damned room right in the corner of the building, where my stomach is always in my throat, thinking that twenty centimeters from my head the dirty, wet, and hot concrete walls will come tumbling down twenty stories and rush toward the ground.

"Can you do me a favor and turn off the lights? This looks like a stage."

"I can't hear you. What was that, sweetheart?"

"I said that if you know how much the heat bothers me and that with these lights that look like voltaic arc lamps I feel even worse, what the hell makes you turn on all the bloody lights in the building?"

"Do you want me to turn them all off?"

"No, please leave the bathroom light on. Do you know something? I think I will spend the night walking or sitting at the edge of the lake or something. I can't bear this. How could these heathens have fathomed having a sky train in the center of the city? And it constantly goes by!"

"Do you want me to go with you?"

"No, thanks."

No, no, thank you, because I also do not dare to spend the night at any park. And because even if I did dare, even if I were not thinking about the vagrant, delinquent, morphine-addicted ghosts of gang members like shadows blending in with the shadows of the trees that take over public parks as soon as night falls; even if I were not imagining how uncomfortable the park bench that I would have to sleep on would be nor thinking of the possible police officer who would impede me from doing so, at any rate, I wouldn't want to be there with you. There is a place, there must be a place, where birds sing like they used to, where it's still possible to find the sun and love, where I could lie on the soft, white sand and the sounds of nature would lull me to sleep and not drive me to fear. But the seas of the south no longer exist; they've been devastated by the dollar and by cancer and by the vast hips of whiny, stinking rich septuagenarians. And the Greek islands are crammed with bearded men with fat bellies and foolishly naked women. And besides, what plane, what ship could take me to an amazing place where I wouldn't be me?

I have to try and relax. My head or my heart will burst if I stay this tense. How was this done in the past? You begin with the feet, over there at the extremities of the body, eyes closed; first of all the muscles of the soles of the feet, the flexor muscles. Then the tangle of tendons and muscles like little cockroaches underneath the skin. It doesn't work entirely, but the foot seems to be a little better. Then that other one, the one that allows one to lift the tip of one's foot to be able to take a step, on the outside of both tibias; that's it. It would become stiff when we climbed the hills of the mountain range, when the spring had filled the pine trees of the mountainside with shoots and sprung aromatic plants and poppies in the ravines above the tree line. Shadows of Alicia, Sylvia, and Blanca climbing the narrow and steep trails, almost too happy and loquacious, because they knew that, up above, among the sunny rocks, underneath the thin, burning sky, the amazing adventure of being possessed awaited them. Ghosts once more that descend into the fragrant evening twilight, startling sleepy birds, almost too quiet, by shady pine trees, while below, the lights of the city are beginning to come on, to the horizon of the distant hills of the coast. This must be old age; remembering that there were things that took one's breath away out of pure lust, that I also had those distant afternoons of sweet summers where I would follow, at a distance, a delicate figure cutting through the warm air, waving slightly like a flag in the wind, and that I was drunk with wanting her. I needed the touch of her skin, her scent, her deep, loving smile. I used to tell myself that in order to acquire the promise of her future and her beauty, it would have been enough to be, for example, enormously rich. And now what do I do? Now I'm lying face down in a hotel room, thousands of kilometers away from any dream, without even daring to go down to the street, where everything should be accessible, and obtainable, and easy and shitty. I'll try to relax; seriously this time. Feet first, muscle by muscle, under the skin . . . She's at the foot of the bed, standing, putting on her nightgown; it's true that one can, without opening one's eyes. You can even sense when someone moves silently and stealthily approaches you and bends over to observe you.

"Please don't cover me. Don't you feel the heat in this crappy bedroom? I can barely breathe."

"I thought you were sleeping. Don't you want to get undressed and try to sleep?"

"I don't think so. I would prefer to go for a walk. I already told you."

"Alright, go soon, then, so that you don't come back too late. You must be tired from the trip."

"Hey, if we ever come back to this city, I'm not stepping one foot in this hotel. This is ridiculous. Can you tell me how the hell we ended up here? It's not cheaper than the others, and if it were, it wouldn't matter. The only thing it has is a dirty cafeteria and people from underdeveloped countries spitting and the damned noise of the building. Moreover, it looks like a jail: 'Do not enter this floor without a pass.' Hell, we're not monkeys."

"If you want to we can move tonight. We don't have to be here if we don't want to be."

"Naturally, and we can leave your aunt and uncle here, all alone and abandoned, after you were the one who brought them."

"That doesn't matter. They won't get lost. They know this place better than we do. We will leave because we feel like it and that's that. We wouldn't even have to explain anything tomorrow."

"No, beautiful, thank you very much. It's much too late. If you'd listened to me a month ago when I told you we should go elsewhere, things would have worked out better."

"What do you mean, a month ago?"

"Sure, when we were first planning on meeting them here."

How can she not understand that I don't want to leave or to stay here or do absolutely anything? How do I get it into her head that it's not about being here or there, but rather that I was wrong about everything, that I have failed at everything despite how it may look and that it's all the same to me if she approves or disapproves, if she agrees or disagrees. But something must be done. Let's pretend that everything is at ground level. Not up there, but down here. This bed is resting on a floor that is sitting on solid ground. The cars from the neighboring parking lot are here, next to my head, separated only by a wall, which is nevertheless thick enough so as not to hear the footsteps of the sweaty passersby as they walk along loud street covered with beetles and cockroaches. The sidewalk is right in front of my nose. Across the street, the front door of the other building is dark and I can distinguish the shadow of the night watchman dozing behind the glass.

"I'm going to the bathroom to brush my teeth. I'm going to bed. Close the curtains, please. Even the bed is noisy in this hell-hole. Don't close them please, don't get up, leave them as they are; it's all the same to me, it would almost be worse."

Is this all really so bad that I cannot keep it to myself and I have to disrupt her peace of mind and ruin everything that we do? Surely not. The only appropriate gesture to not express anything or not startle anyone foolishly and to end this pain throughout my body from being so tense would be to shoot myself in the head. You hold the gun upside down with the barrel lower than the grip, you introduce it into the mouth, it rests on the soft palate and you stain a good part of the wall with brains and blood. I should have brought a gun. One should never be anywhere without a weapon. What would she do if I decided right now to put an end to all this nonsense? They don't sell weapons to foreigners in this state.

"Why are you hanging on to things as you walk?"

"I'm not hanging on to anything. It's just that I'm too tired and I had almost fallen asleep on the bed."

And it's also because the building sways in the open air with me imprisoned within it. And also because I feel the meters of emptiness sinking beneath the soles of my feet until they reach the ground right beneath me. And the fire escape stairway that hangs with its skeletal structure leading more to vertigo than to human freedom, and the four dirty concrete cliffs around me. And the elevators are much too far away and much too slow.

"Where did you put my toothbrush?" I ask, almost suffocating in the hot and diminutive bathroom.

"I don't know. I haven't seen it. Didn't you bring it?"

"No. You always forget my things. I bet none of yours are missing. But since my gums are rotting and since the only thing I really need is a toothbrush, of course you didn't bring it."

"Do you want to brush with mine?"

"It's like brushing with a cat's tail. It's useless."

"Don't exaggerate. Nothing will happen if you use it once."

I could continue complaining about her carelessness. I can tell by her voice that she feels guilty. If I went out to buy one, then she would certainly have reason to lament, despite the fact that we traveled separately and that I know perfectly well that I was the one who forgot it. But I would have to put my shoes back on, and cover the entire distance of the unending hallway to the elevator and wait for it for who knows how long. And the bags under my eyes and the fat that my skin has excreted through my nose and forehead and cheeks and even my ears are not meant for anything but rest.

"Shit!"

"What happened?" she asks from the bed.

"The water is coming out too hard and I got my pants wet. Even the bathrooms are crappy at this hotel. You don't mind if I use your toothbrush?"

"No, of course not," she says, relieved.

The toothpaste comes out of its tube like white diarrhea and soaks the bristles of the toothbrush. Quickly, but rhythmically, seven strokes per surface. Seven to the back, right side. One, two, three, four, five, six, seven. Good, good. I have to concentrate, if I start thinking about how well I'm doing it, I'll get distracted. Seven more. Now twenty-one strokes over my molars; but with the complicated formula; six, seven, eight. Now to get the fur off my tongue.

"Are you vomiting?"

"No. I was brushing my tongue."

I hear her laughing contentedly. When I return to the bedroom she tries to hold back her laughter, but I look at her and she bursts out laughing.

"What's the matter?"

"Do you always . . . always brush . . . your . . . tongue?"

"Everybody brushes their tongue," I reply, somewhat annoyed, but somewhat infected by her laughter. "Don't you brush your tongue?"

She shook her head and hid under the sheets to laugh freely. I feel my face stretched out in a smile and I keep smiling stupidly while I put on my pajamas. My skin is wet with sweat. However, I climb inside the sheets, because it seems to me that it will be even hotter to sleep on top of them. She has stopped laughing and looks at me as I get in bed.

"How do you feel?"

"Fine," I say and I stretch out on the bed. "These mattresses are much too soft. Hey, do you remember when we were children, in the summers, during the holidays? When we would play all afternoon and then be tired, and after supper we would get into bed between clean sheets? How happy those times were, weren't they? Were they really?"

10

I PARKED THE truck at the curb and although I misjudged the distance and scraped the tires, and although Chica's house was very nearby and it was almost laughable that I had borrowed a vehicle to take Blanca there for dinner and then back to her hotel in splendor and luxury, I felt unusually wealthy and refined and, after locking the car door, crossing the garden, and climbing up the stairs, I entered the house whistling softly. I was greeted by a strange air, like an empty building where someone has forgotten to turn off the lights when leaving. It seemed as if they had just carried out a dying man. Blanca completed the picture of silence. Her immobility frightened me. She was sitting on an armchair with a helpless and pitiful expression, and she even looked so absorbed in her pain that she had actually not noticed my arrival nor my proximity, and her shock, when she received my kiss on the crown of her head, was real. After the initial thrill, she raised her face toward me, very slowly; her eyes fixed and glassy, her eyebrows motionless, her lips closed and dry. She stared at me as if she couldn't see me or had never met me. There was a hellish silence throughout the house. Surreptitiously I realized that, despite her condition, my cold beer was ready on the table.

"Blanquita, what is it?" I asked, starting to get really alarmed. She didn't even move, nor reply, nor stop staring at me. To rule out the possibility that scared me, I said very sweetly: "Hey, you're not going to tell me that you're angry because I was celebrating Leroy's engagement last night, are you?"

"Whaaat?" she said, making an unpleasant gesture. "What are you talking about? What do I care if you were celebrating Pocho's engagement or whatever?"

"Then what's the matter with you?" I asked, somewhat relieved. She stayed speechless, observing me. "What is it now?" I repeated, exasperated, but with authority.

Before replying, she remained still for an eternity of seconds in her statue-like pose then laced her fingers with great deliberation and moved her feet against the fringes of the armchair. She began to speak without intonation; from time to time a vaguely disgusted smile crossed her face.

"You know something? What is happening to me now is no reason for you to worry. For the first time in my life it's a relief to not have to worry anyone or to have to depend on anyone. You know? This is the last thing that is happening in my whole life; this is it. I feel such a great relief, so great that I feel like singing. I had never noticed how tired I was. If you knew the calm happiness that I feel, you wouldn't pity me."

I had been walking backward, with my rear-end projected in that direction searching for something to sit down on and ended up plumb in front of my beer, not quite understanding what the hell Blanca was talking about. For a moment I thought she had gone nuts. I took a big gulp of cold beer with my left hand so that I could check the time without looking like I didn't care about my beloved. She had been waiting it seems, for me to say something. I was concerned about the time.

"Look, Blanca, forgive me, but quite frankly, I don't understand a word you're saying. Could you make a little bit more sense?"

"More sense? How can I possibly make more sense? How much clearer do you want me to be? This is over, that's all."

"Blanca," I asked, in the most neutral of my tones, "Blanca, are you saying the nonsense that I think you are saying? Are you saying that you are going to commit suicide?"

"Isn't death the end of it all?" she said, with a glassy stare.

My first reaction was one of intense fear. One doesn't talk about death in such a personal way without a chill going down one's spine. However, after another drink, the many years that we'd known each other prevailed and I calmed down. I could have sworn that Blanca would not cut a single fingernail if it would hurt her. Conversational routine now demanded that I should want to know the why of her atrocious decision; all of a sudden a light bulb went on in my head and I almost choked on my beer.

"Blanca! Are you . . . do you think you're pregnant?"

I didn't dare ask her if she was, only if she thought so, for fear of her response. Without noticing that I had stood up, I found myself next to Blanca who hadn't changed her expression one bit because she must have known that this way she was making her soul transparent and forever unattainable, placed by death beyond all possibility of laceration, beyond the irreversible limits of darkness, in the icy territory where neither good nor evil, neither detriment nor benefit, neither absorption nor detachment reign. Her voice didn't change either, at least not at first.

"I don't think anything. I am sure I'm expecting a child."

"But, how can you be so sure? Did you get tested? Have you seen a doctor?"

"You and your stupid last minute ideas all the time. I don't need any tests. I'm sure. But that's not what matters, you know?"

"What do you mean that's not what matters? What is it that matters then? Hey, is there any more beer?"

"Yes, there are several bottles in the fridge."

"Well, tell me then, what is it that matters?" I insisted as I backed up toward the kitchen with a foam tainted glass in my hand. Her gaze followed me until I reached the dining room door.

While I hurriedly picked up my bottle, I was reviewing somewhat feverishly the changes that this new issue would mean for me. For example, Chica's invitation. Who was going to eat the *civet de lièvre* that Leroy had threatened me with? And the wonderful wines he had promised? And what was I going to do with my joke about rabbits and their aphrodisiac and beautifying qualities that I had prepared for Blanca? With bottle in hand, I was astonished when I realized that I was taking Blanca's scene seriously. To give her the benefit of the doubt, I resigned myself to missing the banquet that would surely end up being terribly boring anyway.

"Tell me, then, what is it that matters?"

"Nothing matters. You mattered. Nothing matters any longer. If you only knew how tiring it is to have to talk when one is at peace . . . It's not because of the child, you know? Perhaps if this hadn't happened I never would have made up my mind, I never would have seen things as clearly as I do now. I thought about you, yesterday, all day long. I waited for you, sitting here until midnight. I left at midnight on the dot."

"And what does that matter?" I interrupted her, suddenly furious.

Again she stayed there, staring at me, unmoving, from the other side of the Styx, the whole universe clear in the back of her eyes, with a sort of pity for those of us on this side, especially for me.

"It matters, because I was walking down Ballivián, crying and I was scared and I needed you. And I started to remember things. Do you know what I remembered?" she interrogated me, leaning toward me, enraged. "All the times that I had to bite my lips so that I wouldn't cry from the pain you were causing me because you couldn't 'get pleasure superficially' and you laughed as you said it."

At that moment I would have given her a huge hug full of grief and affection; I almost felt the pain that she was now revealing to me and that I now realized she didn't let me see before. Only, somehow, she was lying.

"But, woman, you were the one who wanted it. How dare you complain now? Remember how angry you would get at me . . ."

"Of course I also remember, but your duty was to worry about me. The thing is that you are an inconsiderate pig. Look where we are now. Look, look at us."

By this time I didn't understand a thing. I was famished and so tired that I was wishing for the prompt arrival of the sister to save me. Despair overwhelmed me. I wanted to talk about something else, have a warm shower, and meet some other woman at Chica's dinner. But if I tried to speak of anything else that was not suicide, she would rake me over the coals. Her eyes had remained staring for a long while at a sad place on the floor by her feet; where they bore into the wood with the weight of death. But suddenly they wavered electrically in their beautiful sockets, and didn't look at me, but toward her wristwatch. She made a gesture of ghastly annoyance and said:

"If you don't change quickly, we'll be late to Pocho's fiancée's house."

The surprise left my mind blank. A flock of gray ideas scattered crazed through my consciousness before disappearing. While I recovered my inner balance, I stared at her; she didn't move a muscle. I suddenly felt possessed by a manic contentment; it was all a lie; a pure fabrication whose real reasons didn't interest me. No pregnancy, no suicide, no anything. And then I discovered, almost with tears in my eyes, that in the years that I had known her, her face had aged. I was about to lift my body off the seat; my muscles went lax and again got lost in the couch. I watched her slowly and it was true. Her body was still splendid, strong, and very agile, but it had begun its ignoble decline from the roof of the glorious temple. Time existed. Time had also begun, at some point, subtly pecking at the touchable quality that the skin of her cheeks had for my eyes.

There were too many things. Blanca was going to commit suicide, she was pregnant, age was creeping up on her. I was somewhat stunned. For the moment, the only thing I asked for was for her mood to change, that she stop suffering. If I ran to get changed it was for that purpose. I knew that, at least for me, the cure would be worse than the disease. My only nice suit had frayed sleeves and was blindingly shiny. But if I didn't change, I risked hastening her suicide, or her old age, or her pregnancy, or everything all at once. And I wanted to saturate her in happiness. I needed to be refreshed with apples and slathered with balsam, for I was faint with love.

We walked out silently. I didn't warn her about the truck to see if the surprise lightened her heart. And I noticed with joy that the rigor mortis started lessening by several degrees when, rather than taking off down the street, I opened the door and invited her to climb into it. But she said nothing about it. She simply asked me to take her to the hotel to get ready and then fell silent, watching the street. As soon as we arrived, she jumped to the curb and disappeared. My tender, in love, and slightly whiny disposition made me not care at all if I had to wait half an hour and I even thought that if we arrived when Chica's guests were already eating dessert, I wouldn't give a damn. When Blanca returned, I rushed out of the truck to chivalrously open the door for her. I so feared her sadness that I didn't even command her, as I would have preferred and decorum would have dictated, to change into more modest attire than that shocking blouse she was wearing that with its shocking décolletage and wild crinolines looked more like a nightgown. I even smiled fondly at the garment in order to ensure her inner balance. Without my asking her anything, she informed me that Lu would not be able to join us due to a migraine that was killing her. It seemed to me like a good excuse. Her voice sounded almost normal. She added that she was concerned about the violent nature of the ailment. I gave her a look of dismay and felt that my semblance reached heroic proportions. However, knowing her villainy, I wondered if it might have been better for her frame of mind to vilify her sister and say what she was thinking: that it wasn't a migraine that was consuming her, but rather Leroy's engagement. Perhaps that would have made her talk animatedly. But there was no time to find out, because we had arrived.

There must have been something impressive about Chica's house. Blanca lost her genuineness as soon as she stepped through the door. I also felt somewhat uneasy. I became flustered at the efforts of the maid who let us in to not laugh at the sight of Blanca in her breastfeeding attire. In the darkness of the street and the truck I hadn't realized the full extent of the display, but now it seemed overwhelming. Moreover, the offending fabric was a hellish purple color. But there was no choice now except to deal with the consequences whatever they might be. The maid informed us that the señorita was expecting us.

Eugenia herself came almost running to greet us, leaving behind the muted and grave sounds of the conversation of her other guests. The blouse also gave her a shock, but she didn't lose her composure as hostess. She greeted Blanca affectionately, smiling, with a kiss on the cheek. She took her by the arm to walk her over to where the others were while she informed her that they would have to become best friends, because Leroy and I were inseparable. I appreciated her warm hypocrisy seeing how Blanca's tense muscles were relaxing into a smile. I felt like a fifth wheel, an incongruent guest in the world of financial designs that Eugenia had for poor Leroy and that consisted of making him close friends with the wealthy, probably to awaken noble ambitions in him and bring him closer to those who could prop him up. My only purpose in going there was to eat, and drink, and accompany the victim and speak as little as possible. In sum, to silently say goodbye to Leroy without sorrow. The man was giving up a lot of things here, but that's what he wanted. If he'd really wanted to keep traveling to the jungle and living each day as it comes, he would have chosen a different woman and not Eugenia; with other friends, relatives, and projects. Some awesome woman who wouldn't have dreamt of hosting dinners, but with a great talent for throwing parties where individuals like Ramón and some of the poker guys (who, most certainly were not there that night) would have felt at home and where Juan Carlos Cánepa, Felipe Ovejería, and their respective wives (who were certainly all there and looking very well) would have found nothing better to do with themselves except chew their fingernails.

I made myself comfortable on a large *bergère* chair and lovingly checked the alcohol supplies, ice cubes, *canapés* that someone had distributed on different little tables within arm's reach. When I realized that I was sitting on the most comfortable and authoritarian piece of furniture in the room, probably the same one that Chica's father had sat on for years, I felt my body settle there in its rightful place.

I enjoyed my preeminence over the excellent assembly more intensely when I thought I saw Ovejería with a shadow of displeasure on his face and interpreted it as spite because I had taken his seat. I did, however, make a point of not offending him in any other way for the rest of the evening. He was a friend of the bride's family and much older than I. And most of all, I wanted to relax, drink in peace, eat, and get a glimpse at Cánepa's wife's legs every once in a while; she was spontaneously showing them off. I wanted to be Blanca's quiet support system so that she would get unpregnant, be rejuvenated, resuscitate, and show her tits. I felt extremely wise.

"Has Santiago changed much these years, Blanca?" asked Señora Ovejería.

"Very much so. There's demolition and construction everywhere you look. It's awful. Three of my siblings and I live with our mother in Providencia, near the canal. Ten years ago the house was on the outskirts of the city and now they are building an apartment block on each side. It's terrible. How long has it been since you were last there?"

The woman removed the glass of Pisco sour that she was sipping on from her mouth and held it up as she tried to remember.

"Well . . . let's see . . . about ten years. I am dying to go visit, but something or other always comes up. At first, Felipe had too much work to do here, and then (you know how men are) he took me to Europe for the first long holidays we took and . . . we keep doing the same thing . . . we always end up in Buenos Aires or in Rio or in places like that. I say Viña del Mar is the most beautiful place in the Americas, don't you agree? Felipe, how many years has it been since we were last in Chile?"

"Eleven, exactly," responded Ovejería without hesitation. "But this year you are not getting out of it, Marta. Do you know, Señorita?" he continued, turning toward Blanca, "what I want to do is not see cities or remember my past life or anything like that. What I want to do is to eat sea urchins and mussels."

"I love them too," Blanca swooned, "there is nothing I like more. My eldest brother, who is a doctor, lives in Osorno and every month when he's able he sends us huge parcels by air freight.

"Ah, Señorita," said Ovejería, rolling his eyes, "count on us at your table if we happen to be in Santiago when the package arrives."

"My pleasure."

"Kenita, give me some more of that scotch reserved for friends. It is stupendous," Ovejería continued, lifting his glass enthusiastically.

And it truly was very good. I, with my wise tiger eyes and my wet glass in my hand, approved of the joy that had just invaded Ovejería. Señora Cánepa had crossed and uncrossed her legs twice; she was observing Ovejería's face and copying his gestures, as if she were watching a movie; I concluded that she must be extremely stupid. However, I also approved of Juan Carlos the Good, when he walked half way across the room to his wife, took her hand and caressed it. He remained sitting on the arm of the sofa with the fingers of his left hand interlaced with her right. The get together was livening up.

"What are sea urchins?" the woman asked. Her voice sweet and not at all stupid.

"They are . . ." the señora began.

"They are echinoderms about this size that have five tongues inside," Blanca informed her. "Some of them also have a crustaceous parasite. Some people eat it . . . live," she added, shuddering.

"You know a lot about zoology, Señorita," Ovejería praised her as he received another serving of alcohol and ice from Chica.

"Please, don't call me Señorita. My name is Blanca."

Ovejería bowed his head in appreciation. I would say that the drink was going to his head. Leroy, with his back to the picture window at the end of the room, was whispering to Eugenia sporadically.

"Tell me something, Blanca," Marta asked seriously, "don't you find that we Chilean women are more liberal, braver than Bolivian women? For example, I don't believe that any girl here who lived with her mother would be allowed to go to another country, alone, to see her boyfriend."

"But I'm here with one of my sisters," Blanca replied, shocked.

"Oh, then you can't help me prove my theory. I was going to provide you as an example to Inés and Kena. They don't dare do anything. Why did she not come for dinner tonight?"

"Because she was ill," Eugenia responded. "She had one of those migraines . . . and don't think I didn't hear you say that we don't dare do anything. That's not true. You know about the things my mother has done . . ."

"Has she written to you, or let you know how she's doing?" Juan Carlos politely interrupted.

"Yes, she called this morning, thanks. They are both very well, Miguelito had tonsillitis, but he's better now. She says that the weather is abysmal in La Paz. We could barely hear each other."

"That boy is sickly," Ovejería pointed out, his voice lower, as if to show that he, instead, was robustly healthy. "He's always been a little bit weak, hasn't he?"

"Not so much, believe it or not. He has childhood illnesses, like everyone. But he's very tough for his age and also very intelligent."

"How old is he?" Blanca chirped.

"Twelve."

"At that age almost all children are sickly," Blanca added, in support. "My second brother, who is now an engineer and has a construction company, was very weak until he was about fourteen, then he turned out to be champion runner, javelin thrower, and I don't know what else in university. He's a giant . . ."

"Your family must be so nice, Blanca," Marta slithered, sweetly.

I noticed a slightly mocking undertone that I didn't care for at all. Juan Carlos still held his wife's hand in his and caressed her with his eyes and smiles.

"Yes," conceded Blanca, making an ugly, illogical gesture. "I remember my childhood as a very joyous time. We had one of those childhoods where one wants for nothing. My dad used to say that children should be pampered, because that is the only happy time in our lives."

"Very true," Marta agreed woefully; Ovejería looked at her.

"So they gave us whatever we wanted, as long as it was whole-some, of course, because my dad was very strict. But he adored us. He even bought us El Paico, which was a large tree farm, splendid, in Maule, so that we could spend our holidays . . ."

One of the maids showed up just in the nick of time and informed Chica that dinner was ready. Blanca felt welcome: I was noticing that she considered the time right to improve her own image in everyone's eyes, to embark on a great panegyric of her family. Perhaps she wasn't seeing the hints of mockery and impatience that escaped from between the other women's eyelashes. I'd stood up and was leaving my glass on the cocktail table and almost fell over when I realized that I regretted that Blanca was unable to continue. Stories of former family great-ness usually unleashed in me fits of indignation. On our way to the dining room, I found myself right behind the round and pillowy back of Señora Ovejería; she reminded me of a sheep walking on two legs. What did it matter to that ostentatious old woman if Blanca wanted to put on airs? Did not the poor, dumb, and innocent girl have a right to make up a dynasty of intelligence and money, and make believe that prestige followed her, compensated for her lack of education, and gave her status as an elegant and perfumed lady? Certainly the shameless dis-play of her family's greatness was not very pretty, but it allowed her to live many experiences in her life, for example, the near-tears bewilderment that befell her briefly when Eugenia invited us to sit where we wanted and she didn't know what to do. The others were laughing like old friends and somewhat charmingly competed to sit next to the women. Blanca stood there, with her huge décolletage, for an instant, with a sad hand half supported by the back of a chair and smiling vacantly, like a moron. A kind of evil started awakening within me, mixed in with a generous amount of sound mind that seemed to require that I fulfill some poetic and liberating deed. Something akin to telling all of the universe's Ovejerías and Juan Carloses to go to hell, making the most of the fact that they were right in front of me.

During dinner, Leroy actively participated in the conversa-tion and made it serious, manly. My pleasant mood returned. My

good friend was exuding a rich and triumphant air that transformed our little factory into an enviable enterprise. In fact, he
wasn't lying; simply selective. And he did it humbly, recognizing
our errors.

"But in general, things have been going well, right?" Ovejería
interrupted.

"Yes, but we have had to pay for our lack of experience. For
several months we were earning just enough to pay the workers.
In several large orders we calculated our costs wrong due to our
ignorance; we had to sacrifice our profits to maintain our good
name," Leroy stated in his coarser, more mature and relaxed
voice. When he was done, he stared affably at Ovejería, seemingly implying that his combative nature longed a bit for the
vicissitudes of his harsh beginnings.

I was genuinely amazed; I was thinking "Just look at you
now!" The idea of Leroy transformed into a daring businessman
captivated me to the extreme of forgetting to drink a delicious
creamy beverage that the others were almost done drinking.
The problem was that Leroy took this role much too seriously.
Judging that his speech had ended and having noticed that my
two neighbors, Marta and Ines' cups were empty, I gulped mine
down carelessly. And Leroy, the moron, had to turn his face full
of nostalgia toward me at exactly that moment and say:

"Remember, old man, what we went through?"

The terrible thing was that I did remember, and much too
vividly. I remembered Leroy's despair at the check that we
couldn't cover; I remembered the street where we were walking
and talking, half-jokingly and half-seriously about the possibility
of mugging someone; I remembered the innocent looking can
that had been abandoned by some mutt on the sidewalk full of
hardened cement, and I saw Leroy rolling on the ground with his
right foot in his hand bellowing: "Oh shit; oh fucking shit, oh
dammit." And he had reason to do so because he had dislocated
two of his toes when he kicked the can. I saw it all in one instant,
unfortunately coinciding with the moment that a mouthful of
cream started to go down my throat. Some vindictive deity made
me turn my head toward Señora Ovejería, and even through my

outstretched hand as I tried to stop the shower of cream, I soaked her in it. The dinner didn't manage to regain control even after Chica and Blanca rubbed the old woman down with napkins. What seemed to dismay most of the guests was that even in the midst of my coughing, I could not stop laughing; as soon as my spasms stopped, the laughter returned.

On the way back to the hotel, Blanca remained rigid and quiet. She was again pregnant, aging, and moribund.

X

"HELLO," WILSON GREETS me, as he turns away from some boys who are examining an air gun. "How can we help you?"

"By letting me look around a bit," I reply.

"Excuse me," he exclaims, startled, "has something happened to you?"

"Oh no. Why do you ask? Because of my face? I've just come from the dentist's office and this whole side of my face is numb."

"Ah," Wilson says, relieved. "Come in, come in. Make yourself at home."

As I look outside, the light of the afternoon sun seems very bright, but it's cold and windy. I could buy no gun and go into the movie theater and stay there all afternoon. Or I could phone her and ask her if she wants to go out somewhere. If I don't call her, she won't know where I am and she might make a scene later, with good reason to, by the way. Imagine the look on her face if I show up with a new revolver! Let's first look at the long weapons. No one has taken that beautiful Marlin carbine yet. All pieces machined just right, heavy and accurate. Nothing new on this shelf.

"Anything catch your eye?" Wilson asks, by my side now that he's gotten rid of the boys.

"No, nothing, thanks, just that Marlin."

"Would you like to see it?"

"No, thank you. I would prefer to see short weapons. Anything new?"

"Certainly! We have a Colt Buntline, beautiful, as well as a Python .357 Magnum. Are you familiar with them?"

"A Python! Could you show me both of them, please?"

"Of course."

He walks behind the counter, lays out one of those silicone treated suede mats and deposits the weapon on top of it. A customer I didn't see come in approaches and joins me in silent contemplation of the blue-black revolver. It's heavy and shiny, like a jewel.

"The best handgun ever made, they say," adds Wilson.

"The manufacturers say," I add and look the stranger straight in the eye, to impress him with my knowledge of weapons; he smiles.

"Believe it or not, several city marksmen say the same thing. It's very powerful. It can pierce through a car cylinder block and is very accurate."

"It's also just plain advertising," the stranger participates; Wilson looks at me as if he's trying to tell me something and stares at the revolver furiously, showing that he does not hear what the other man is saying. "I was a Texas Ranger for twenty-five years. I should know something about weapons. Don't you think so?" he asks me.

"No doubt."

"I always preferred Smith & Wesson. Great weapons. Well-made. Easy to examine. For twenty-five years I was a Ranger. Twenty-five years with a Smith & Wesson right by my hand. Do I know or don't I?"

"Of course you do."

"What do you think?" Wilson asks me, ignoring the stranger.

"May I?" says the ex-Ranger gesturing for the weapon.

I place it in his hands and he turns his back to Wilson and me. He quickly examines the cylinder closing mechanism first and then the chamber alignment against the afternoon light coming in from the street through the huge glass and aluminum door.

"Do you have a white card or a piece of paper?" he asks Wilson, without looking at him.

"No," replies Wilson. "May I please have the revolver back?"

"Yes, of course. I had never held one of these in my hand

before. It seems good. American manufacturing is first class, after all. It seems like a great weapon. I'd buy it. Of course the alignment . . . who knows . . . I'd need a piece of paper."

"Thank you for the advice," I say.

"Additionally, it's very versatile in terms of ammunition. You can use the .38 Special for entertainment or for target practice, and lots of different .357 Magnums for other purposes," Wilson adds, implying by his tone that the other does not exist, that no one has at any point interrupted our transaction.

"When I was a Ranger . . ."

"Would you like to take it?" Wilson interrupts.

"Excuse me, sir," says the stranger, firmly and with decorum, "I was telling this gentleman about things that happened when I was a Ranger. I'm not trying to bother anyone, sir. Everything I'm saying is relevant."

"Of course it is," I reply before Wilson can. "Of course. Your advice is sound in my opinion. And I think I will take the Python right now. Could you please also give me two boxes of bullets, Mr. Wilson, one of each?"

"Yes, sir, yes," Wilson replies happily.

The ex-Ranger remains by my side and observes as attentively as I do Wilson's movements as he carefully places the weapon in the box, puts the cover on it, turns away, and returns momentarily with the bullets and then packages everything together. It's only when I'm paying that he pretends to be absorbed contemplating some fishing gear hanging on a revolving rack.

"Good fishing around here?" he interrogates me jovially as I am signing the check.

"So-so. Nothing out of this world . . . they say. I've never fished here."

Once I finally receive the heavy package I say goodbye to Wilson. I want to rush back home to examine and contemplate my acquisition until I've had my fill of it, until I feel again the weariness of having spent hours wasting time with a new toy that, eventually, I will get fed up with, because it will reveal its stupid mindlessness and senselessness. The ex-Ranger leaves the store with me and starts walking next to me without hesitation.

"Very nice revolver you've got there. Very nice. Are you going to try it out right away?"

"No, I don't have anywhere to do so."

"We could go to the police shooting range. I know them all."

"That would be great, thank you. But it's late. I have to go back home."

"Are you married?"

"Yes."

"You're very lucky. Very lucky. The warmth of a home is priceless, one's wife's tenderness. You are right. You should not waste your afternoon shooting guns when you have a home to go to, a wife that is waiting for you. Which way are you going?"

"North Dubuque."

"Me too," he says happily.

We're walking by the university campus. I notice that my companion is poorly dressed. Also, I figure he is about 6'6" and talks like a megaphone. Luckily the subject of home has made him somewhat meditative. The weight of the package heightens my pace; but I also wish I hadn't made this useless purchase.

"When I was a Ranger, I often wished I had a wife and home waiting for me. At that time there was a huge influx of illegal Mexicans. We had to prevent them from coming in, and every time the border police started to get swamped with work, they called us. We had to stop them one way or another, don't you agree? In the end, it was for their own good; they were exploited as farm laborers."

"That's what I've heard. That lots of unfortunate things happened."

"That's right; many unfortunate things. Are you Mexican?"

"No. I'm not Mexican."

"Good people the Mexicans. Very backward though. The thing is that in this country we've forgotten about nature. And something happens to people when they are away from nature. They turn bad. They become indifferent. Do you like nature?"

"Yes, very much."

"I can tell. These things are noticeable right away. I would like to show you a place near here, next to the river, that I discovered.

You know? There are lots of river rats around here; they come out around this time. Would you like to see them? I'd like to show you that place."

"I too would like to see it, but it's a bit late. I have to go home."

"It's very close to here, right where Highway 218 and the river meet. A few steps away. What do you say?"

The cold wind keeps blowing and dusk is setting in. I imagine the wide body of water beneath the twilight and the trucks going down Highway 218 northbound, next to the narrow stream where there are hardly any houses and rats move about swimming with their prickly mustaches sticking out of the water. I wish I'd never bought the revolver; I wish there were no rivers, no fresh air, no highways, and no nightfall, and at the same time I am horrified at the thought of there not being any. But I will see if I dare to go all the way there. Perhaps the walk will do me good; besides, it's not time for nightcaps yet.

"Let's go see the rats."

"I've seen many things. After I left the service, you know, I started seeing things in a different light. Who knows if it was better that they laid me off after the illness. Everywhere, at any time, one sees horrible things. You know New York, right?"

"No. I've never been."

"You have to visit the Bowery; it's the drunkards' area of town. What harm do drunks do? Can you tell me? Nothing, nothing at all, of course. They are there, that's all, lying on the streets, waiting for someone to throw them a dime or for the bell to ring at the Salvation Army where they get free food. And do you know what people do to them? Tourist buses go by with their radios right at that same time to see how they run to get their food. Do you see? Hopefully the rats have come out to look for their stuff by the river. I really want you to see them. And the idiot bus driver stops the bus so that everyone gets a good view: 'The men that you see sprawled on the ground along these sidewalks are ex-millionaires, ex-judges, ex-movie stars. Today they don't even have names.' So you see any?"

"Any what?"

"Rats, any rats."

"No, it looks like none have come out yet."

We carefully checked the waxy surface of the river under the evening sky. We can hear the sound of a chainsaw in the distance. It seems to be coming from City Park along with the cold wind that makes ripples appear on the bluish and slow surface of the water. In the hills of the other riverbank there is still a little autumn sunlight that must be disappearing into the horizon behind us. I wish I hadn't come. None of the active and sympathetic rats are swimming in the river.

"Have you ever seen a skinny and blonde little girl, with two miserable pigtails, get on a suburban bus carrying a huge ceramic milk jug? Have you ever seen a man crazy with horror?"

"Well, I suppose so. Lots of folks are scared; almost everyone is scared."

"No. Now we are not understanding each other. I am not talking about fear, I'm talking about horror. The kind that leaves you with nothing but a smile-like grimace; as if they wanted to guess at their master's whims so that he won't beat them, so that they won't starve them to death; things like that. It's because man has moved away from nature."

"Perhaps he's never been a part of nature. Perhaps being a man is a need to be apart from nature."

"That could be," he says, restless and bored, avoiding making eye contact. "Maybe no one understands anything either. It looks like the rats don't want to come out so early. They probably don't want to be seen. Maybe they saw us first and are afraid we'll hurt them. But we'll wait for them so that they can see that there are people who will not hurt them . . . animals are very wise."

"Yes, it would be good to stay and show them . . . but I have to get home at some point. They're waiting for me. And besides, it's getting pretty cold."

"True," he agrees, somewhat discouraged. "It is a little. But we could wait for them for a few minutes at least."

"Frankly, I have to go back. I'm very sorry. I also would have liked to have seen them, but it's late."

The rat lover reluctantly gives up; he shows his pride with an almost undetectable shrug of his shoulders, and we begin walking back. As we turn our backs on the river, something happens to the little bit of twilight. The water shines with the last traces of light from the sky; it holds what remains of the day glued to the landscape. On the ground near the banks, however, the eye can hardly distinguish the shape of objects. I'm putting my foot on the dusty trail without any assurances. We approach a house with lit windows.

"We could come back another day," my companion suggests.

The sound of his voice elicits short, gruff, and furious barking. I stay still trying to locate the animal. The ex-Ranger keeps walking. I cannot determine where the critter is, but the sound seems to be coming from near the house. Suddenly, I'm paralyzed by the sound of running and almost immediately I make out a yellowish blob rushing toward us from my side. I am about to run, but the rat lover quickly puts himself between the dog and me; he wraps his jacket over his left forearm and tells me in an even tone:

"Don't worry, my friend, I will defend you."

"Don't be an idiot," I bellow. "It's a boxer."

But there's no time. The dog has rushed toward him without decreasing his speed. I think I see my friend smile as he leans toward the animal with his padded arm in front of him. Suddenly he unleashes a horrible scream that paralyzes the dog and me; the dog stops cold and barks spinning far out of reach of the ex-Ranger. My friend spins too, tempting the dog to seize the protected arm. But the devilish creature has either received combat training or is very intelligent. He backs away spinning and suddenly jumps up toward the man's face. The guy's speed almost makes me applaud him. Before the dog can touch him, he shoots him backward with a formidable kick. But he doesn't expect the next move; with just a howl of pain, the dog gets up and lunges with lightning speed, ignoring the padded arm, against his opponent's ankle. The pain of the dog's teeth against his bones makes my protector scream a little. This would be a good time for me to give the animal a good swift kick, as he dodges the man's hands and violently jerks at his foot; but I fear that if I attack him, the dog will turn on me. The dog pulls so violently with his muzzle that, despite his size, the victim can hardly keep his balance. I fear that if he falls, the boxer will probably aim for his neck; I decide to wait until he falls so that I can kick the dog off him. If he falls that is. Moreover, I tell myself that there is very little light and if I try to hit the dog, with so much moving around, I might kick the ex-Ranger instead. I finally feel that I can wait no longer and as I look for the appropriate angle, the rat lover yells out:

"No. Stay out of it. This animal is dangerous."

I stay still, half relieved, half confused and embarrassed, telling myself that maybe I offended my friend by intruding in the matter. A Ranger, as he says he was, probably has encountered much worse things and perhaps he's not strictly in any serious danger. However, I cannot forget that I am dealing with, no doubt, a half-demented man, a poor mentally unstable fellow; and while in the increasingly dense darkness of dusk the fighting continues, the details of which I can scarcely see, I must also remember that in the haze that his schizophrenia has probably left him, the rat lover is defending me. For that reason, when the dog finally manages to knock him over, I move toward the pair, my limbs clumsy from fear, almost ready to intervene. But then, in the semidarkness I make out one of my friend's hands reaching toward the dog and manages to do something, undoubtedly effective, because the animal lets go of his prey and utters an almost agonizing howl, and then starts rolling around, his snout toward his tail, but out of control because of the pain. At that same time the door of the house opens and a shadow yells from the lit opening:

"Fuuuull, Fuuuuull, here, Fuull, here boy."

The animal does not obey. He continues wallowing and moaning in a storm of dust and despair. My friend has laboriously managed to stand up. Ignoring both the dog and me, he moves back and forth, almost crippled by a limp, and seems to be looking for something in the grass that borders the trail. I come to help, but he has already found it and is lifting it off the ground. His jacket. After putting it on, aided by me, he rests one hand on my shoulder and says, with his throat oppressed by pain:

"Let's get out of here. Quickly; help me, please."

"But we have rights. Let's go to that house. That animal's owner has to pay for damages to your person," I object, morally outraged. "They can't have such a vicious wild animal loose like that. Imagine if this had happened to a child or to a woman."

"No, better not. Us crazy folk have no rights. Boxers never attack children. Besides, that one won't attack anyone ever again."

The animal finally sky-rockets toward the house.

"Elisa, Elisa," the voice calls from the door, "the shotgun, quick, the shotgun."

"No, for God's sake, are you crazy!? Call the police."

My friend, despite the pain he's in, moves fairly quickly, while I support most of his weight. Every time he puts down his injured foot, I hear a splashing sound; I believe it must be the blood inside his shoe. We arrive back at the corner of Ronald's sooner than I expected and turn left. Another five blocks or so and we will be at my house. Quite frankly, I wish we would go straight to the police or that the guy would go away by himself wherever, but I'm ashamed to propose anything or to just take off on him, as it's entirely possible that he may be gravely wounded.

"Let's go this way," I say, trying to turn toward Dubuque.

"Where?"

"Dude, to my house of course."

"No way. How in the world am I going to show up at your house looking like this? Think about your wife and how scared your children would be."

"That doesn't matter," I say, but I don't tell him that I have no children. "You need medical attention."

"Nonsense. It's just a scratch that's all."

"No, man, let's go to my house. We'll take a look at your foot, and if it's nothing more than a scratch, you can do whatever you want, but if it's something more serious, I will take you to a doctor myself. You might have a torn artery or something. It's no joke."

The rat lover stares at me sternly. For a moment I fear he will attack me. He finally says:

"You know nothing about wounds, my dear sir. If this were an artery, I would have fainted a long time ago. I am not going anywhere to make a scene because of a scratch. Don't push. Now, you go to your home, and I'll go to mine. Understand?"

I watch him limp down the street. Under my arm, I hold the package with the new revolver and bullets. I notice, under the streetlight that I have dog and crazy person bloodstains all over me. When I raise my head, I can no longer see the figure of my friend. I'm relieved when he's gone elsewhere with his problem, and also disgusted that I'm so relieved. But maybe it was nothing more than a slightly painful scratch after all.

11

LUISA LEFT AS soon as we were done eating. She had been in a good mood. She wanted to buy some souvenirs. Before leaving, she asked if I would accompany her at some point to pick out a tiger pelt; they sold them at the bottle shops and she didn't want to go into such a place by herself. She then gathered her things and smilingly left at a languid, lively, and attractive pace. She was busting with pride and well-being because she told us she had managed to swim nonstop for three kilometers that afternoon. As soon as I heard her steps going down the stairs, I asked Blanca:

"And? Did you have your period?"

"No," she replied, quietly.

"Any hope?"

"I don't know. My belly and my lower back hurt; same as before."

"Do your breasts hurt?"

"No, they stopped."

"Are your nipples irritated?"

"I don't know. They are very sensitive. Do you want to have a look at them?"

"Good idea," I said, moving closer.

She moved the chair away from the table a little bit to make some room; she unbuttoned her dress down the front and put her left hand down her cleavage. Without loosening or removing anything else, she forced her poor right nipple out, all deformed, almost at sternum height, over the clothing that squeezed it; it looked very ugly but entirely normal. Then she repeated the

215

same operation with the other. And although my examination tended to confirm my conviction that she was lying, her manner of speaking, her momentarily helpless appearance, the scared and interrogative gesture with which she requested my opinion while she reorganized her clothes, had me once more on the brink of believing her. Maybe it was not all lies. Maybe the outburst she would undoubtedly unleash upon me in an instant was due to her really being in despair.

Perhaps there was no reason for the annoyance I felt seeing her fasten the top button and then stay slowly feeling her left hand with the forefinger of her right, her hair on her forehead, lost in her pain.

"I don't think you have anything. They look like always . . ."

"Why am I not getting my period then?" she complained, rubbing her hands now, as if she were cold, still staring at them.

"How should I know . . . maybe you're late . . . something . . ."

She shook her head over and over. It seemed to me that the storm was brewing. I started to make noises with my mouth, blowing on my fingers and clicking my tongue, to the rhythm, a somewhat ritualistic rattle, like when the bushrangers want to make it rain. Isochronous sounds upset Blanca. But nothing happened. She again lost herself exploring the skin on the back of her hand. I asked her to make me a tea; it was more like a suggestion than an order, owing to my unbearable sweetness. She obeyed at once; she stood up without a word and went into the kitchen. She frightened me. Apprehension created frantic elaborate images in my mind where she slaughtered herself in my presence, or she returned, hair disheveled, and frantically dug the bread knife into her stomach or hurled herself down through the glass window; hopefully the dog or the *cholita* would be directly in her way down to the ground; these things happen. When she returned with the cup of tea in her hand, two small lakes of tears were being held by her eyelids. She put the cup quite beyond my reach and as she bent down, her tears spilled down her face. She spread them out even more with her fingers and said:

"What are we going to do, sweetheart? Why don't you tell me what you want me to do? We can't continue this way; we can't;

I don't let you live in peace. I make scenes every day. Please tell me what to do."

As she spoke, she shrank more and more until she was sitting on her heels in front of me. It seemed to me that she wanted to imply that she didn't dare touch me out of respect, or that my wisdom was so eminent and overwhelming that it was risky to hear it proclaimed while standing.

"Listen, dear, there is something that I'd like to ask you before anything else, OK?"

"Yes, my love?"

"If you could do me a favor and leave the drama for the movies," I said; her eyes started dilating. "You want to know what it is that we can do, right? Let's see, let's ponder deeply, let's concentrate infinitely, what can two miserable beings do who enjoy each other in bed, who get along famously, who don't need anyone else, and who discover that she is pregnant? What, oh, bewilderment, alas, pain, what? Don't you think that it's best to stop with all this drama and just get married?"

I was unable to interpret the gesture or the twitch that followed my proposal. It could have meant anything serious. However, the disarray of her disheveled hair, the stumbling noise of her feet, something cold and refined in her eyes, a sort of feminine lightning bolt that was suspended in the air, staring at me, sounded like a victory cry. But what she enunciated was:

"What did you say?"

"What you heard, woman, what you just heard me say; if things are as you say they are, let's stop wringing our hands and making scenes and let's get married. It's not such a huge deal. We've all been born in the exact same way, with slight variations, of course."

"What do you mean 'if things are as I say they are'?" she asked, her throat seething with rage, "what the hell are you thinking, you pig? What do you take me for that you could think I could be lying to you? I can't believe it, this takes the cake!"

I didn't like it one bit that she called me a pig. She paced around the room, her head held high, without looking at me, indicating that she was reflecting behind the impenetrable wall that had just gone up between her and me. I thought it was a good time to go brush my teeth while she reasoned. I left her alone. I even took time to make some funny faces in the bathroom mirror and check that my teeth gleamed and my tongue looked clean and healthy. After I returned Blanca continued her pacing. She looked like she was about to come to a conclusion; she showed a stately composure in her almost smiling face. She stopped and looked down in what appeared to be a last ditch effort; then she decided, with a slight liberating shudder.

"No," she said, confronting me. "I don't want to marry you. I also never want to see you again in my life. I would be embarrassed to see you again. I never imagined you could be so filthy to think such despicable rubbish. It never occurred to me. Tell me: How can you even touch me or look at me if you think I'm capable of lying about something like this? Be honest: Aren't you ashamed of yourself and me and this poor child that you left in my womb? Tell me, aren't you ashamed?"

She said those last words with rage. She had forgotten her decision. I thought that if her dignity had truly been wounded by the insult, she would have turned her back and would have left without a word. Instead, she was asking questions. I walked toward my cup of tea and slowly took a sip that was hard to swallow because Blanca had forgotten to put sugar in it; then I sat down sternly.

"No. No, I'm not ashamed. And besides, what I'm saying is different. Stop playacting and repeating nonsense. What I'm saying is that we should get married. Get it? Let's get married. If you don't want to, say so and that's that. But I won't put up with one more scene. Get it? Not even half a scene. I don't know what better way for a man to show his true self to a woman; everything you are saying is insulting and stupid."

"But don't you realize what you said?" her voice was now a little whiny and somewhat submissive. She found it appropriate to hide her face in her hands for a moment.

"I'll say it again. I don't want arguments, or interpretations, or anything. I want you to either say 'I want to get married' or 'I don't want get married.' That's all."

"But how do you want me to answer such a question when you ask me that way? Don't you see?"

"With your mouth."

"Dear God, don't be so cruel and callous. I want everything you want. You know what? I thought I would die of happiness when you said we should get married . . ."

"For God's sake, woman, why the hell do you keep making assumptions? Just answer the question. It's not that difficult."

"I'd like to ask you something too," she said, her eyes sad and fixated on the corner of the room. Suddenly she turned hastily toward me and wrinkled her brow, "And you? Do you really want to marry me?"

"Look," I started, after hesitating a bit, "yes, I want to. Of course I want to, but know one thing; I also want you to realize whom you would be marrying. I don't want to deceive you. I simply will not change my life for any reason. You never tire of disapproving of the things that I do, but married, single, or widowed, I plan to keep doing exactly as I'm doing. Wait, let me finish. For example, as soon as the rainy season is over, I'm leaving for the jungle, married or not. I know that the jungle is dangerous, that you would be very worried and that there would be no way to decrease your concern, because there is no mail where I'm going. I know that I will come back and that I will come back in one piece, but I don't think that'll be enough for you. If you want to marry me you will have to get used to . . ."

She interrupted me with head movements threatening to erupt into hysterics; each time her head swayed from one side to the other she let out an extremely sarcastic short laugh.

"What is wrong with you? Why are you laughing?"

Her rage reappeared, but now it was dotted with scathing laughter. She started a discouraged and final monologue. To think that just hours ago she and Luisa had been discussing how much I had changed . . . to think that they believed in how seriously I took my job . . . to think that Luisa had said she finally understood her love for me and envied her . . . ha, ha . . . but I really was much worse than anyone could imagine. For daring to declare that not only did I plan to continue my life as a savage, but to increase my savagery despite having a wife and children, she couldn't get that through her head. Because she had given me the loving gift of herself unconditionally . . . ha, ha . . . but it was one thing for an adult, self-sufficient woman in the hands of a ne'er-do-well, but it was quite another to allow a child . . . oh, no, no, it wasn't even worth the bother to try and make me understand; these things were beyond my reach; I would never understand the language.

By then I was no longer listening to her accusations. I was about to beg her not to praise my hard work, because it offended me, and to advise her that I worked only because it gave me a tremendous amount of pleasure and that if I felt like it, I would lie on my bed or on the floor until lice came out my window and I might just feel like it. But why add anything? The knot that I had in my stomach since she'd announced her pregnancy turned into inner satisfaction. At that moment I would have bet my trip to the jungle against cheap candy that there wasn't a hint of certainty about her pregnancy. She must have noticed, because as I tried to put on the hermetic face of the misunderstood, of the man who's offered everything and has been rejected, she was spacing out her sentences in increasingly long and painful silences. She then left me alone with my happiness for a long time, after which she returned composed, her hair combed, eyes lowered and confused, knelt beside me without letting me see her face and leaning her head on my knees, she kissed my hands between murmurs of appreciation. I suddenly felt strangely alone and also happy and disgusted with her and with myself. Was she really completely false and completely shallow? Or did she understand me, rather, perfectly, as I believed I understood her, but that was why she loved me and hated me at the same time, but it was beyond her strength to endure, except when it was imposed by violence? Her gently perfumed hair scattered on my knees and the subtle touch of her hands caressing the hair on my shins moved me. She stood still for a long time; I shook her gently and she seemed startled.

"I had almost fallen asleep loving you. Forgive me for everything," she said and kissed me.

I sweetly invited her into bed with me, but she refused, between hugs and kisses, saying that she preferred to take a walk with her happiness before returning to her hotel. I found it strange because it seemed natural to end up in bed after coming to our curious understanding. I pointed out that we just had five more days together if she didn't want to stay with me. She moved closer to me and whispered:

"It doesn't matter. I'll make it up to you later."

The city was lit by a waning moon. We silently took the same road as always. Blanca grabbed my arm, but did not lean on it. With some surprise I realized I was very tired, but curiously, too clearheaded; I thought it would be good to walk for a while in order to sleep peacefully.

"What did you do this afternoon?" I asked.

"Eugenia and I went shopping. We went to see an underwear smuggler after lunch. You should see the things she bought for her trousseau!"

"Nice?"

"Disgusting. Pure filth. I would die of shame if you saw me dressed like that . . ."

"Why? What was so ugly about them?"

"Can you imagine a bride picking out flesh colored underwear with a black bottom? You should have seen the two nighties. The colors! And the style! As if she wanted to seduce a dirty old man. She must not have very much respect for Pocho to dare . . ."

I felt my mouth agape in amazement. It was already quite incredible that she would almost despicably criticize the poor girl when all she had done since they'd met was to talk about her, call her, ask her out, and visit her. It just seemed monstrous to me that she would found her rejection of her on moral grounds. She didn't let me pull myself together. She declared that Eugenita was becoming intolerable to her; not so much for things that anyone would forgive, such as the ridiculousness of preparing a formal wedding with a white dress and everything, when everyone knew the truth of her business with Leroy; it disgusted her that she had the gall to continue bringing Leroy to sleep with her under her poor mother's nose, that lovely woman. For lesser things I would have ripped her to pieces, but this completely paralyzed me. In my shock and bewilderment, I even lost my ethical obligation that guided, as the compass guides the sailors, my outer and inner behavior in such cases; best to stay out of other people's affairs. If I had found it, I probably would have beaten her to death or bashed her with my shoe.

We had just crossed the bridge, I was overwhelmed, Blanca was self-righteous and inquisitorial. I stopped in the middle of the sidewalk and looked toward Cala Cala, carefully considering the silent mass of sleeping houses, the beauty of the sky, the vain and widespread pure sorrow of the night adjacent to the outskirts of the city. Blanca sometimes oppressed my heart like an alcoholic nightmare, and since she made my world quake, on the verge of letting out a scream worthy of entry into the insane asylum or making her howl by kicking her, I had to turn back to safe ground to seek energy. At other times of trembling, I watched my own fingernails, comforting myself with their hardness and precise design or I held my nose between my fingers to seek comfort in its bulbous form under oily skin; but being outdoors at night, it was best to look up, to the refreshingly solid and insignificant Milky Way. I said nothing. In order to distract her and remembering the story of Juno, I squeezed her breast somewhat violently and started to ask if she knew the names of the stars; I didn't know them very well but it's not too difficult to find the Southern Cross and Orion's Belt. Instead of replying to my astronomical interests, she wondered how I felt about Chica's wickedness. I again squeezed her breast disapprovingly and I could tell I was not nearly as tired as I thought I was. To my surprise I found the Southern Cross, sitting very low on the opposite hills. I pointed it out to her and she made me understand, with overt ill will, that it couldn't be, for she'd never seen it in that position. But anyway, she'd already entered the celestial topic. It occurred to me that a plausible explanation for seeing it so far south could be that we were now in the tropics. Here she completely forgot her moral judgements; she looked at me with delight and amazement, but didn't believe me. What did I mean we were in the tropics? It was only when I provided her with a lucid demonstration of my geographical knowledge that she was pleased with this new evidence. I noticed that she felt very important and adventurous now that she could say, in an even, natural tone: "When I was in the tropics . . ." I felt tenderness at the spontaneity with which she initially gushed:

"To think that I've been living in the tropics for weeks now and I had no idea."

But she ruined it all when she almost immediately added:

"Don't tell anyone that I didn't know."

Luckily the word *tropic* had acquired such a magical disproportion with respect to any other reality that she didn't insist. It didn't matter at all that the altitude of Cochabamba took away absolutely all its tropical character. However, it allowed her to enjoy the idea that we were now walking down a street in a city in the tropics, that she had first come to the tropics in an English mountain train, that we had loved each other in these tropics, that the man she loved was now living in the tropics. The palm trees and the heat and the warm seas that were missing hardly constituted a negligible accident in the middle of her madness for something exotic and legendary. We were the counterparts of the smiling and beautiful lovers of the islands of the South Pacific; the tropics conferred to our love a new, cinematic character of total paradisiacal innocence. We'd also grown to the stature of Burton and Livingstone and Dr. Schweitzer, because we had all set our feet down in the tropics. I appreciated and admired the silent stubbornness of her desire for greatness and was within inches of being moved by her definite poetic talent. But I saw her so full of respect for herself and for me, so grateful because thanks to my brilliant and confusing clarification of parallels and meridians we had reached such a legendary place, that I launched head first into a full description of the sky. First I put her into the required frame of mind by asking if she knew what azimuth and elevation were, and distance and even the colures. She listened to my explanations, straining to understand, her smiling eyes lost in the Milky Way. I continued, calling her attention to Alpha Orionis who shone like a diamond to our right, vibrating in infinity; then, toward Sirius the bright, glowing to our left over the sleeping mountain range (here she was especially excited by its invisible white dwarf companion—her eyes welled with tears trying to see it in the darkness that surrounded the star; it seemed to drive her mad this serious and dark presence accompanying such an extremely radiant sun; in a faint voice she told me that sometimes she thought of the two of us that way and then wanted to leave me). I had no idea where the hell the stars really were or if they were really stars or something else, but that didn't diminish at all the effectiveness of my description. Blanca walked on clouds feeling paralyzed by love, because we were having a traditional lovers' conversation. As I raved about astral names, I had totally lost my tiredness and promised myself a good reward, remembering that *The Art of Love* recommends that the prudent prince take his lady love to the terrace and to show her stars as preparation for bed. When I finished renaming stars with other names, seeing how many stars still remained anonymous I was tempted to bring the North Star with Great Bears and everything into the southern hemisphere, but last minute modesty stopped me. I, therefore, concluded the talk and kept walking slowly, with my eyes somewhat lowered, in the modest silence of the wise man.

XI

"AND HOW ARE we doing today?"

"Not too well. I've been thinking about things the way you suggested (interpersonal relationships and all that), and I think you're right, but not entirely."

I fall silent and look at the familiar wall tiles. His unlit pipe is in his mouth and he's supporting it with his left hand. From my point of view, I've said all that needed to be said. I'm extremely discouraged. I had the suspicion that this guy would not be able to cure me, now I'm certain. Otherwise, it's just as he says: I either get myself out of the hole, or I rot. It should be easier than that to go to hell.

"Don't you think that going to hell should be less complicated?"

"Why do you say that?"

"Because it's not easy."

"It seems to me a good thing that it isn't," he agrees wearily, as if he thought my reflection was utterly trivial, but the fact that I'd thought of it he found worthy of praise. The chimp is starting to try to put the key into the hole. "And what about sleeping and eating?"

"I'm still not eating solid foods, but I am sleeping a bit more."

"Good, excellent. That's better than nothing."

"But the nightmares are worse."

"Hmmm. You said that you've been looking at things from a point of view of interpersonal relationships and that you found the focus that we had come up with to be reasonable, but not entirely. Did I get that right?"

"Yes, sir, very right."

"Could you elaborate on that?"

Someone walks by outside, in the hallway. I imagine it's a nurse, a young woman, although it might be the old receptionist. Right, but not quite. My body still aches and I'm still bringing up my morning milk. Take the university, the famous academic career, the marriage. Take fear, take death. Everything becomes ridiculous inside a tiled doctor's office and a gentleman professionally lighting his pipe. How the hell can there be professionals about living? About living other people's lives?

"Look, I'm not very lucid today. It seems that I haven't been very lucid for years," I say, smiling, as if apologizing or looking for him to deny it. "But, do you remember that dog and the madman who defended me?"

"Of course."

"Well, do you know how I related that same story to my wife and the folks at the university, to my colleagues? Do you know?"

"No, I don't know."

"I said I had defended the madman. It occurred to me because I had some blood stains on the package of the revolver and on my clothes and hands. The dog attacked the madman; I felt extreme fear, but I overcame it and with my bare hands tore off the dog's testicles. If I hadn't, the poor crazy man would be dead right now."

"And what is the truth?"

"That I froze. That I didn't even insist that he come to my house, due to fear of being in trouble with the police. Do you see?"

"And do you know why you lied?"

"No. But it wasn't because of interpersonal relationships or anything like that."

"Let's see, let's see. Did you not get, or did you not believe you could get, your wife and your coworkers to believe that you are better than you think you are?"

"Of course, in part, that was the reason."

"Do you know what else you did it for?"

A sports car stops in front of me, right in front of the window. I hope the girl driving it doesn't see me here, almost under the ground, so that I can see her legs when she gets out. She doesn't appear to have seen me; she looks for something in the glove compartment and I would guess that when she closes it she still has not found it. Take the university career, the university, the marriage, fear, death. Which? Which career, which university, which marriage and fear and death? Mine. No wonder she wasn't more careful: She was wearing pants. Mine, those ones. My career, my university . . .

"No, the truth is that I don't. But let me tell you something else. Yesterday they offered me a full time research contract, good salary and everything, if I stay here. And I don't know if I should accept it or not; but every time I think about accepting it, I'm horrified. Of what? That automatically means more respect, it implies recognition, security, esteem, higher rank than those same colleagues who heard about my heroic behavior defending the madman."

"In other words, they have offered you a more important position and that seems to have heightened your stress level. Is that right?"

"Exactly."

"But that can have many causes. Don't you think?" he suggests and lights his pipe, throwing away the match with the usual swinging of the forearm hanging from his elbow. "What do you think is the real cause?"

"That is exactly what I was going to say. I lie about the dog so that those around me will respect me, but at the same time I seem to reject a proven way to acquire prestige and respect. Where does that leave me?"

"Would you like us to examine the issue more closely?"

"Very well."

I'm tired. I would like to not be here but somewhere else, somewhere I lost, where I could ditch this burden that is choking me. It's like walking with myself in tow, fearing for the one doing the carrying and for the one being carried, of not being able to carry him and not knowing where.

"Why are you smiling right now?" he asks me, interested and annoyed.

"Because I was thinking of a lost paradise again where I could magically stop being a person and become an angel or an American movie character or some other irresponsible shit like that."

"At least you are lucky to see that," he says indifferently.

"Of course I see that. I see this and a bunch of other things. And how does that help me? Can you tell me? The truth is that I fear even more than before, that I'm almost afraid to go to bed or to get out of bed or to sit at a table or to study or to go to the movies or whatever. When do you think I will get better from this?"

"I don't know. When were you hoping you'd get better?"

"I don't know either, but in less time at least."

"Look," he jumps, "I think it would be better if we're honest. These things don't get better in a day, or a month, or a year. There are two things at play here. One, you are who you are and as far as that is concerned, listen well, there is no cure. Have I made myself clear? You are what you are and you have to learn to live with that; the anguish and the fear and the senselessness and the lack of sleep are never going to leave you as they don't leave ninety-nine out of every one hundred people on the planet. What you do with that is up to you. Secondly: you have been and still are in a critical state of mind. You can get out of it, if you want to. If you don't want to, nobody, absolutely nobody, will be able to get you out. Lastly, I think we are both wasting our time. I can't do for you practically anything else but what I've done already. With people like you, my involvement can't go any further."

"You are right, absolutely right. But do you know something else? While it may be true that statistically ninety-nine percent of the planet's population lives dragging themselves along in nightmarish misery, my existence is not a statistic. It's true that I am completely shattered, but no one will convince me that man cannot be happy; moreover, I think man is more than anything a proposal for happiness and freedom and fulfillment. And I don't think you or anyone is tempted to or overjoyed to set your mind to a shitty statistical normality."

We said our goodbyes, courteously, but dryly. I walk along the long corridor toward the door with the impression that I didn't say all I should have said. I owe this guy much more than I admitted to. However, I feel better. Beyond the door, the clear and cold autumn air is waiting for me; I have to finish the last assignment of the semester to hand in tomorrow; I have to finally decide if I want the contract they offered me or not; if I have to remain within the confines of this prison, in the narrowness of this world of unnecessary studies, in a world of conforming with nonsense. But at least I depend on myself; it seems that this man, perhaps knowingly, put me on the way back to taking responsibility for my own life. I could almost say I'm happy, although I'm still overwhelmed by the certainty that what I'm thinking will continue to be meaningless if I don't overcome it.

12

I ARRIVED AT the hotel with my shirt slightly damp with sweat, but with a happy stride and in a light mood. Having to waste the afternoon accompanying the sister to pick out tiger skins bothered me a bit but it somehow also made me happy to have to leave work early. I almost felt like I was on vacation walking around town during the bright siesta hour, when the stores were still closed and only the movie theatres invited people in to relax in the cool dimness, people who, like me, could take the afternoon off at their leisure. Had I known which theatre Blanca and Eugenia had gone into, I would have left the sister to wither at the hotel while we saw an adventure movie.

The hotel porter lay sprawled out behind the counter, dozing. I went up to Luisa's suite immediately. The stairs and corridors were deserted. I quietly knocked on the door but no one answered; I repeated the call more aggressively; I had the knob in my hand to test if it was unlocked when the neighbor's door opened and a very small and very ugly child came out. He stared at me for a moment and I froze. My shyness made me laugh a little and I ostentatiously entered the room, carelessly. In the bedroom, a pleasant semi-darkness prevailed. Luisa had no doubt fallen asleep waiting for me, because I had to stay in the factory longer that I had estimated. I quietly walked to the bed, repeating her name with increasing intensity, but the lump would not budge. She had her back toward me and was covered up to the neck with the sheet and the rest of her clothes hung at the foot of the bed toward the floor. The curves of her body were very visible and I was happily certain that she was nude. I started to feel like a criminal; if I woke her up now, she had every right to get upset by my intrusion. I felt great going back again to the door on tiptoes to at least call out her name from a distance. I didn't dare leave for fear that the child was still out there and watching the furtiveness of my movements would mistake me for a thief or something. After several calls in a relatively respectable voice, I let out a "Luisa" like a trumpet, but the sister did not move. This was too much. Could she perhaps be telling me, through her stillness and her closed eyes how convenient it would be to not be so cautious and polite or so eager to go out and buy tiger skins? It was true that the sporty Lu had a well-deserved reputation of sleeping like a rock. But, that much so? I again approached the sleeping beauty and gently touched her shoulder; then I shook her more forcefully while calling her name. The bed creaked slightly from the movement. Without moving my hand from her shoulder, I stared at her hoping to see a sign of the truth. Her head was half turned the other way, her hands were at her sides, under the sheet; her breathing was deep, rhythmic and slow; however, on her sun kissed neck, I found a telltale artery, rapidly and violently pulsating. But more conclusive tests were needed. I reached under the sheet and stroked her breasts with some impudence; the immediate hardness of her nipples also seemed to support my belief, but still didn't seem conclusive; it could be a simple reflex. I had heard tell that when she was a child, her siblings would take her out of her bed sleeping and leave her sleeping wherever, and that the following day they would find her in that exact same spot. Although, now they told it as a happy family custom, one could assume that they had only done that atrocity once, but, could this be the second time? One more test. I lowered my hand toward her belly. She gently moaned, but did not open her eyes.

I took her many times, inspired by her wonderful passivity, but each time I called out her name or asked her to do something, she neither answered nor obeyed.

I lay beside her, enjoying the wonderful sunshine that lit up the room through the cracks of the closed windows. Luisa turned on her side, muttering something in a mumble akin to a sleeping woman as she swung her leg over mine and lay still once again. I got a bit annoyed. I shook her violently.

"Listen, Luisa," I said, irritated, "stop pretending to be asleep don't be silly. Hey, OK, stop pretending to be asleep, I'm telling you."

She mumbled in her sleep again, she complained, turned the other way and continued to breathe rhythmically. I suddenly remembered that Blanca could very well leave the theater and return directly to the hotel instead of going over to Chica's. It was true that Blanca herself had many times suggested the possibility of me getting into bed with her sister, but her wickedness or jealousy or whatever reason drove her would not have been enough to prevent her from making a Dantesque scene if she showed up now. I gathered my things and went into the bathroom to shower. Remorse lightly gnawed at me, yet it was hard not to sing for joy. While I was drying myself with great haste, the sister's voice reached me from the bedroom.

"Blanca," she called out, "Blanca, what time is it?"

"It's not Blanca, of course, it's me," I said, annoyed, sticking my head out the door.

"What?!" she exclaimed with surprise that could pass for genuine. "What are you doing here? How dare you? Why didn't you knock?"

"I was too hot," I answered in a tired and resigned voice, putting my head back in the bathroom and getting dressed. "Sorry. I didn't think you'd mind so much. I'll be done in two minutes and I'll come out so you can get dressed. Do you still want me to go with you to buy the fur?"

"Of course, why would I change my mind?"

"Because of how late it is. It's almost six."

"How awful. Why didn't you wake me up?"

"Because I was too hot, and besides, I've just arrived; it wouldn't have made a difference," I answered her, beginning to find our shamelessness charming. From the bedroom I could hear her happy laughter and the bed creaking. "What are you laughing at?"

"You are so nervy and ill-mannered that it makes you likeable. Nobody else I know would ever step over someone who's sleeping and take a shower in their bathroom because it's hot outside."

I went into the bedroom feeling surprised and happy. It made me laugh when she said: "step over someone who's sleeping;" but she was perfectly calm and innocent. I walked to the bed and gave her a kiss on the forehead; she made a defensive movement and pulled the sheet up to her neck, pulling it tight so as to erase her figure.

"You are becoming almost too nervy," she said in a light and natural tone.

"Hurry up and get dressed. I'll wait for you downstairs," I answered and left. I ran into the boy again, he was still guarding the corridor. As I walked away from him toward the stairs, I felt like he was pushing me with his gaze.

Luckily, sporty Lu did not make me wait more than five minutes. I was a little embarrassed by the mocking or conspiratorial expressions that I thought I noticed in the porter's face and also because Blanca could show up at any time and didn't want her to find me there. Luisa was especially nice and cheerful. We went down to the town square, talking naturally about nonsense. She asked me for advice on other things that she might take as souvenirs. She made some comments about how beautiful the afternoon was. And indeed it was stunning, clear, with a blue peace brightening the sky from one side to the other, while at the same time, cool and warm.

"Don't you think Cochabamba is a wonderful city?" I asked.

"Yes, it's quite beautiful," she replied, in a strangely profound voice. "But, can I tell you something? I'm glad that we're leaving on Monday. I've felt a little bit lonely here."

I didn't know if she was explaining away her afternoon slumber when she said that; but her words pierced me somewhere. I was about to affectionately grab her by the arm, but she turned her face toward me and said in a very different tone:

"Have you noticed how much Blanca has changed in these last few days?"

The observation startled me. We were arriving at the door of the first of the two bottle shops that I remembered, and I would have liked to have stopped her so that she could clarify want she meant. Had she noticed something? Had Blanca told her of my marriage proposal? It didn't seem probable. I had to wait until we left the store and she had checked out several jaguars, a number of wild hog, and two sloth skins that we didn't want to see, but that the salesman had strongly insisted on. Luisa had attributed to me a depth of knowledge about jungle hides and, in a very womanly fashion, insisted that I show off; she made me give her my opinion on each and every pelt the guy wanted to show us. Maybe her confidence in my knowledge diminished when, distracted by what she had said about Blanca, I was about to get her to buy one that was hideously big; it was so awful that the seller himself dissuaded her. Upon leaving I said:

"Hey, what do you say we go to the other place tomorrow instead? It is getting dark out and we won't be able to see them very well in artificial light."

"I'd love to. But, won't I be taking up too much of your time?"

"No, not at all; it doesn't matter at all."

"That's great. Thanks. We'll meet at the town square at whatever time you want."

"Perfect. Perfect. Hey, why were you saying that Blanca is acting weird?"

"There's something strange about her, I'm not sure what."

"What do you mean? Something bad?"

"No, on the contrary. She's more mature. I don't know. Haven't you noticed that she seems distracted most of the time?"

"Yes, a little, but that's not weird. You know her. She's always been that way when she's not interested in something."

"No. It's not that. I'm talking about something else. Her gestures, for example. She makes these weird gestures. Haven't you noticed? She even treats people weirdly. You see how close she has gotten to Pocho's fiancée, but it's different. It's not like it is with her other friends that I know."

Of course I had noticed everything. Lately she would place her beautiful hands on her belly with infinite tenderness as if to caress or protect it. But I was pretty sure that only I had been around to notice.

I again embarked on a series of previous calculations aimed at deducing if Blanca had told her sister about the pregnancy and the possibility of marriage. As a rule of thumb, I was inclined to think that if Luisa had actually slept with me while asleep, it was because she presumably knew nothing. But I couldn't ask . . . and yet it was almost foolish to imagine that she could have done and felt the things she did without waking up . . . I was telling myself that all that would get me nowhere when suddenly Blanca became clear to me. She certainly had changed a lot recently; right from the day of my proposal. She now had the look of the most legendary of matrons, her gestures, bearing, steps, and air, absolutely everything about her was worthy and slow. The word I found to describe her relationships with other people was "aloof"; with me, she was aloof and affectionate; with the sister, aloof and sororal; with Chica, aloof and slightly protective; with Leroy, just aloof. So it was no coincidence that we'd not slept together even once since then. It was from that night on that she had decided to be above sex, and her tropical madness was not anywhere near what I imagined. The thought of Blanca filled me with a terrified respect. It was hard to believe that such a fragile physical creature could be reconciled with her satanic will to dominate. Give me a fulcrum, a pregnancy, the possibility of demanding, of pressing and blaming with an undeniable right, and I will turn this demonized man into dust and plastic, and then, I believe, I will be able to love him in peace. What could one do with such a woman? Watch her, love her, pamper her, insult her, screw her . . .

"What side of the town square should I meet you at tomorrow?"

"Across from the police station. At eleven, OK?"

"Yup."

XII

THERE'S A DAMP smell emanating from the underground passage that runs alongside the city pool. The sounds of the swimmers above are diminished and muffled. I stop in front of one of the huge windows, like those of an aquarium, that allow me to see the vague bluish shadows of the swimmers, they look strange when seen from below, making bubbles in the water with their hands and feet. A boy dives in front of me, he approaches the glass and makes faces at me like that of an enthusiastic drowning man. He disgusts me intensely, but his fun doesn't last. His face contorts and becomes flushed, and he shoots up with a sort of hunger for air revealed around his nose. No one is swimming now near the window and in the distance there's nothing but what looks like an opalescent, heavy mass. Almost next to the glass, a long, twisted clump of hair descends slowly. I feel like throwing up. The other five I'm with are standing at the foot of the staircase leading to the outdoors and Speedy beckons me to hurry up.

And the great display of souvenirs. I meekly stand in line waiting to write my name down in the visitor log. The only thing that appeases me is that in front of my wife, Rosa Maria is talking to the Paraguayan doctor and it is a real treat to look at her and to listen to her voice. And from the visitor log, we immediately move on to the ticket counter; the show is about to start; the first of the exciting morning. We rush inside. We take our seats, because the waters of the springs are the clearest and most natural for many miles around; everyone is laughing and enjoying and squealing with delight. Now, now. The hatch closes amid mechanical and electronic sounds. Dr. Rodriguez has ended up next to us, and now raises an eyebrow toward his bright mop of hair, with a gesture of a man of the world. And, oh, delight, the entire platform is submerged into the water and then the seating arrangements facing the large windows make sense. We are now under water and a clown with a hose in his hand swims amusingly in front of our noses and, with what looks like breadcrumbs, attracts ducks that must have been swimming on the surface but now rush to get their spectacular treat. We all applaud. Then two girls appear and wake up my sleeping necrophiliac tendencies with their terrible blue appearance; and again the clown; and the women are carrying baskets, and they all have a picnic; they eat sandwiches, their hoses still in their hands from which they get air from time to time. And finally, the last wonder, they take Cokes out of their baskets and drink them; all underwater. The submerged theater starts to rise. They release the hatches. The slobbering Dr. Rodriguez cannot hide his joy. He approaches us and announces that there are glass-bottom boats that allow one to see the countless springs spouting water at the bottom of the pool. He adds that all this wonder was discovered by Spanish friars some centuries ago, but they didn't know what to do with it. "Except drink the water, probably," states Rosa Maria as she walks alongside us.

I put the earpiece into my ear and a very nice voice immediately begins to talk. As I reach the snake section, it warns me sweetly. Their glass cages keep them hot and highly active, even when the air outside is so thick with snow that one has trouble breathing. "You are currently facing the six boa constrictors kept by the zoo; the age of the specimens before you is estimated at between thirty and sixty-five years. In the wild, boas live in the rainforests of South America." I notice that my wife is looking at me with some apprehension. The snakes have tied themselves into knots behind the see-through walls, and one of them has one of its rings hideously flattened almost within reach of my hand. A very serious young man, who looks like a university student, ruins the show even more for me by explaining the poor snakes' behavior to his blond, young, sexy partner. The voice says that they are able to swallow a calf with ease. There they are, in the shade, while the soft voice describes, very scientifically, in my ear, the truth about the boas huddled in the partial shade of the cage. I remember, I remember that day how the reeds rippled and I almost think that it was the zoo official who spoke in my ear, ten years too late and with a delicious Camba accent. "It must be just a boa, coming down the little hill." The young college students stay still, close together, looking at the ferocious still bodies; it seems that he speaks in a loving hum about the shape of the scales.

My feet hurt. I feel the cold wind in my ears. I've been waiting for her for almost half an hour. Confined in their little box, the hour hand and the minute hand mark seven twenty. I stare at how the second hand races and feel as all the folks who are returning from work and have decided to walk on this corner walk past me. One of the sky trains stops briefly above my head and departs once again before the second hand has jumped (forty-five times five: two hundred and twenty-five) two hundred twenty-five times.

I hadn't planned on stopping at Jane's. She hesitates a bit after opening the door, but then she steps back and invites me in. The several books on her desk and her glasses within reach make me ask her if she was working. She replies that she was. Her mood lightens. She asks for my help. She puts her glasses on. While I explain the concept of structure to her, she listens intently. Her glasses are very distorting. For the first time I notice how faded the light blue of her irises is and figure that if I could get close enough I would perhaps be able to see in those blue circles what iridologists say they can see: her internal organs, her tiny blue and nude and disorderly members, the crack of her sex, all of it radially distributed around her pupil, behind butterfly-wing-like folds, that from here are merely a couple of dead spots on the cornea that eyelids open onto time and again, giving the impression of a febrile disease, of lethargic insomnia. All of her is stuck, at least for me, behind her glasses. And yet, when she

invited me in, startled perhaps because she was alone, she didn't
have them on and I could still see nothing, except for naked,
helpless eyes.

And I tell myself that here illusion is even worse, because one
cannot see the glass on the television screen; the images seem
accessible. "Nooo, I have never wanted to buy a television set,"
says Professor Ramachiotti, stretching out his soft frog mouth in
a demon-like gesture of contempt, "if one starts there, banality
befalls his life, everything becomes very ignoble." "This *petiso* is
so tightfisted, he doesn't buy anything, che," Otto almost blows
in my ear. "What? What was that, che? Adriana, tell me, please,
what was that all about?" In the center of the television set, a
beautiful girl has gone out to the field to call her father who is
working in the paddock adjacent to the house, but she has fallen
into a hole that her two younger brothers dug and disguised like
an Indian trap. Behind us I hear the comforting crackle of fried
meat that Marta is preparing. "She fell into the trap," Adriana
explains, holding back her laughter, not because of the fall, I
suppose, but because she had foreseen that poor Otto would not
understand the movie. "What trap, che?" Otto insists. With the
fall, the girl shows as much thigh as censorship will allow; she
gets up looking enraged like in a musical comedy and with a
tiny speck of mud on her cheek. The two brothers run away. "It
doesn't allow for conversation," Ramachiotti continues. "There
will come a day when spiritual life will become impossible; or
conversation, or anything; I remember that at my parents' house
we would read *Don Quixote* at this time of the day." A strong
smell of fried meat begins to pervade the confined air. "Why
can't this fool get diarrhea again, che, so that we can watch that
girl in peace," Otto wishes in a frantic whisper. Adriana shakes
her head as if examining the air in the room that really has
begun to darken slightly with a subtle mist of fat coming off of
Marta's frying. One of the younger brothers falls and the beautiful girl picks him up and comforts him, lovingly wiping snot
and tears, her own fall forgotten. "Che, Marta, where is the spray
air freshener?" Otto questions as he gets up; "You can't breathe

in here." Marta chokes with laughter, "but the air freshener will make it worse, Otto; it freshens nothing and ends up on the fried food." The mother comes out of the house in her obligatory apron and hits the steel triangle that hangs at the entrance; the camera focuses on distant and shimmering mountains; the father rises and begins to approach. Ramachiotti is bent over in his chair and about to put his hands on his belly; I look at him out of the corner of my eye without turning my head, because I do not want it to become public knowledge that I know he is about to shit himself. He stands up, but something makes him freeze and he stays hunched over for a few moments, even his eyes are paralyzed. It makes me want to tell Otto to hurry up and find the air freshener, but Ramachiotti recovers in time and rushes into the bathroom and the father, with his three children, approaches the house in a close and smiling family chain. Marta and Adriana burst out laughing when the poor so-and-so left the room. "Want a drink, che?" Otto asks as he turns off the television set. I say OK as I stare at the gray glass.

And people sit in their homes, at dusk, while I walk on the snow, wondering to myself if I will be able to get to Coralville. And the germs quietly imprisoned on the microscope slide, doing incomprehensible things. And the monsters, devoid of color in their embalming liquid, meditate eternally inside their jars. And the cities at night, from the windows of the tallest buildings, spread out amid the low darkness or indifferent to the moon. And the pilots of the huge atomic bombers that I saw from the road, in the hot night of the south, in the lit room, waiting restlessly, protected by the glass. And the dead in their shiny caskets with a split lid to view their impenetrable faces, wrapped in their exquisite white fabric lining.

13

"OK," SAID LEROY. "Luckily it all worked out. And it wasn't easy, let me tell you. If it weren't for those two guys, friends of my mother-in-law, the old man would be done for . . . don't you agree?"

It was obvious that my good friend wanted to bask in his own importance. To whom did one go when he wanted to get thieving old men out of jail, huh? To whom but to that noble fellow, the future son-in-law of his future and influential mother-in-law, huh? We were standing in the town square after crossing the street, almost right in front of the door of the jail, and Leroy seemed to be expecting me to burst into praise. You could see he needed an adoring public, discriminating and demanding individuals who were well aware of the feat so they could rave about it as he smiled modestly. The truth was that I was also quite happy and proud; I also wanted to discuss the situation and receive my share of pats on the back and pretend to be virtuous.

"Well," Leroy repeated. "I'm going into the Lucerna for a drink, old man, are you coming? We'll meet the poker guys there, before supper. Let's go," he insisted. When I hesitated, he added "five minutes . . ."

I was slightly tired. I thought longingly of my cold beer waiting for me on the coffee table; above all I really felt the need to have a good shower; I could feel my sweaty feet inside my shoes and my teeth furry in my mouth. I was also moved by Blanca's painfully imminent departure. But still, it was hard to give up on a long commentary on the release of don Joaquin. As for Blanca, the mere mention of the poor old man made her gag. To make matters worse, Blanca was still as pregnant as ever and seemed not to have the vaguest idea of whether to marry me or not.

"It's almost eight," I said, "Blanca must be waiting for me. Don't forget I didn't even go see her for lunch."

Leroy shook his head slowly and despondently. He scrutinized my face for a while as if the dim light of the evening did not allow him to capture the traces of catastrophe on my face. He waved his hands in the air gesturing his bewilderment.

"What is it about women's asses, for goodness' sake?" he clamored to the heavens while raising his arms. "What is it about them, I ask?! One day one meets a real man, who isn't scared of anything, not even mice, and the next day, some uppity chick shows up, goes coochie, coochie coo and . . . bang! Damn, you're whipped my brother! I hadn't realized. Listen bro, we've spent all day handling the release of that fucking old man suitcase thief, and you don't even have five minutes of freedom to celebrate it. It's just not right."

"That's absolutely right," I admitted, "it's just not right. Let's go to the Lucerna."

"That's better!" Leroy approved and we made a beeline to the lit doors of the soda fountain.

"Hey," I said, returning to the topic of the day. "I swear I was pleased with the old man's machismo. It's nice to see a seventy-year-old keep his composure. Did you notice his nerve when I offered to leave him my cigarettes? 'No sir, thank you very much, I don't smoke,' he said. And he had asked me for smokes twice before!"

Leroy made a doubting sound and disappeared through the door of the Lucerna, more concerned about finding out if one of our old friends was there than on elaborating on the moral character of don Joaquin. The place was almost full of wealthy and charming young men and women, flirting with each other; our buddies were nowhere to be seen.

"Let's take that big table by that column over there," Leroy proposed. Before taking his seat he warmly greeted two guys about six tables away that I couldn't see from the door. Finally, he motioned for them to join us. As we were in the process of sitting down, he informed me: "those are two of the guys from Perla Azul."

"The ones that beat us?"

"The very same ones. They're good guys, we've become good buddies," he commented, lowering his voice because the others were approaching, each of them with a glass in his hand.

I didn't recognize either one, which seemed weird at first, but under the circumstances of that night, it wasn't surprising. I liked them. The taller one of the two, whose name was Jaime Urquidi talked funny, with his mouth almost shut. They seemed like happy guys, sure of themselves.

"So you were the other one," the one who talked normally said. "We were looking forward to meeting you. Man, after one of those beatings, we have to become friends. Otherwise, well, there's the risk of fighting again. I'm still sore."

The guy was funny and we laughed. Osvaldo and Tu Padre showed up and came over to our table waving happily. Tu Padre still had the arm cast on and the sleeve of his jacket was carefully tucked inside his pocket.

"Sit, muchachos, sit," said the mumbler, making room for the new arrivals.

"As you can see, we got the raw end of the deal," I admitted. "Take a look, Tu Padre's wearing a cast. A huge bruise on my hip is just now beginning to disappear . . ."

"Ah," the mumbler interrupted me, full of glee, "I must've given you that kick. I am as fleet footed as a tiger, son. And consider yourself lucky that I didn't hit the target I was most likely aiming for, che, otherwise, the pitch of your voice would be getting higher and higher."

The arrival of the woman who was coming to take our order interrupted our fits of laughter. It was hard to complete our order, Osvaldo couldn't decide if he wanted coffee or beer. Tu Padre got us out of the predicament.

"Señorita, for this gentleman," he said, motioning to Osvaldo, "please bring a beer as well as a coffee. And don't pay attention to him, Señorita; he's been like this from birth."

"Just a moment, just a moment," requested the mumbler as soon as the woman had walked away, "We must inform the newcomers of what they don't know. My happy-go-lucky friend over here hits people and then complains about it, man. While it's true that Tu Padre still has his cast on and you have your bruise, for three weeks now I've had to eat porridge, che; mush, *tojorí* and raw eggs and bread crumbs; and I have another two weeks to go with my jaw wired shut, che. It's not the same thing, is it? And poor Rolo has to go and get his hair combed at the barber's to hide the eight stitches they had to put in his head."

After informing me, Jaime gallantly put the cup up to his lips and slid a sip of liquid into his mouth in a very refined fashion. At the same time, Rolo bowed and tilted his head so that I could see through a shell of slicked back hair the freshly healed wound.

"A work of art," I commented. "But don't pin the blame on me for that. I was carrying Tu Padre on my shoulder, minding my own business and trying to get to the door."

"Don't play innocent with us," Rolo advised. "On your way out you hit Humberto Blanco in the face with Tu Padre's head. His teeth are still loose. Man, it's too bad that he didn't come today. He definitely wants to meet you."

The waitress arrived with our order. She put Osvaldo's beer and coffee in front of him, smiling, gave me my ice cream without looking at me, and gave the others their beers.

"And besides, all this is old news," Rolo continued. "We all know who did what to whom. Musarana split my head open. Leroy broke Jaime's jaw. Jaime broke Leroy's nose. You loosened Humberto Blanco's teeth. As for Tu Padre . . . we all played our part."

"To Caesar what is Caesar's," Jaime stated, lifting a hand and turning toward me. "We have just determined that the kick you got was from me. Let's stick to the facts, che. The rest of the kicks and punches and head butts are all split and considered insignificant."

We laughed again, and each one of us took a sip of our drink. Tu Padre was red from laughing so hard. The other tables had begun to empty out; most of the women had left; nevertheless, to my right, I could make out the thighs of a rather pretty woman, engrossed in conversation with her companion. I remembered Blanca.

"And, are you single again?" Osvaldo asked me.

"No. On Monday," I replied, somewhat annoyed.

"And how is it that you are here at this hour, ascetic man? No doubt about it; God gives the most bread to those who have least teeth, and a beard to those with no chin, sorry Jaime," Tu Padre pondered.

"We wasted the whole day trying to get old man Joaquin out of jail," Leroy explained. "The miserable bastard couldn't find anything better to do than to steal a suitcase from a La Paz deputy chief of police."

"And did you get him out?" Osvaldo asked, uninterested.

"We got him out, thanks to my future mother-in-law. But on the condition that he return to Chile within forty-eight hours."

"A good guy, the deputy chief, he withdrew the charges."

"They're also saving the money they would have had to spend feeding that old piece of shit for his whole prison term," Leroy growled, "and they can get rid of him once and for all."

The climate wasn't suitable for commenting on the old man's manliness. I thought about how I would avoid bringing up the subject with Blanca and not tell anyone that the great don Joaquin had decided to give up the profession of thief precisely because he hadn't dared to help us out in the fight at Perla Azul; not because he was afraid of getting punched, but because he had a record in Sucre and La Paz. But, as he had said: "When one leaves a buddy in the lurch, he's too old. Time to retire. If you can't, you can't, and that's that."

"It will pain poor don Joaquin," I commented, "he loves this country very much. His wife was Bolivian . . ."

"He's a widower?" Osvaldo asked, still uninterested.

"Yes," I said, "Well, it's a quarter after nine. Time to go."

"Great pleasure meeting you," Jaime and Rolo said, almost in unison.

"As soon as you're a single again, we'll see you around these parts," Rolo added. "We have outings planned for the whole month."

"Thanks," I said. "Tu Padre you owe me your life, pay for my ice cream."

XIII

I'M FLYING THROUGH the night. All these people and I are traveling through storm clouds. Mushroom-like clouds, like atomic mushrooms, suspended above the Caribbean, are waiting in the shadows for us to pass by. Until not long ago, I could still see them in their entirety, despite the darkness, when the lightning bolts lit them from the inside like enormous grayish-yellow lightbulbs. The starry and serene sky was still within view, on the horizon, as distant lightning bolts ignited and faded at the edge of the night over the sea. Not anymore. We are right in the middle of it now. Luckily, the aircraft doesn't shake overly much; it glides quietly through the air and the roar of the engines has become almost abstract, as if it were heard inside my head; when I swallow my saliva, however, it seems as if I were briefly submerged in water; when the saliva is done passing through, the rumbling increases and comes out of the motors again only to wane again. Additionally, the dirty flame of the exhaust does not increase or decrease, nor does it change color or anything. And droplets of God-only-knows-what leave the motor gently, slide down the wings shivering, but never falling, as if they were frozen and trembling; they haven't become ablaze or smoky or anything. However, it all seems like a feverish nightmare. I would slide down something like inedible snow or limestone, gently, but knowing that the gentleness wouldn't last, and it didn't last; it was transformed into something like sandpaper where each grain became the size of a stone. Even with my eyes closed I could say exactly when we crossed the boundary between the cloudless air and the cloud that we pushed our way through,

because the sound changes when you are inside and it sounds
like the plane is struggling, trembling and howling, to get out
of its prison. Of course with my eyes open I also have the visual
cues of the threatening sky pressing against the double panes and
for moments I am unable to distinguish even the wing's profile.
This curious glow which bathes the womb of the aircraft inside
which we're imprisoned comes from huge spotlights that the
pilot turns on when he has trouble seeing anything, surely to
alert pilots of other planes that may have inadvertently changed
the altitude of their flight. Of course, since these devices are
directed by radar, it's very possible that at this time, in some
important airfield, they are warning those on our route that some
other plane has erred in its altitude. It's a good thing that those
lights exist; I don't think, however, that their yellow and white
lights hardly penetrate the fog. The clouds are too thick and
lightning is obstructing the view more than would be desirable;
the rough and arduous part of the flight is much longer than
the periods of calm. It would be nice to be able to sleep as she
is doing next to me, but I absolutely must not do it. Of course
I know that I will not prevent anything by simply being alert.
The powerful spotlights that the pilot has already turned on five
times in the last ten minutes exist for a reason, but how, I wonder, maneuverable is a heavy object—two heavy objects—hurling themselves through space at, say, five hundred kilometers an
hour? The light vanishes out there and that is not pleasant . . .
And another cloud, and another, and another. It's apparent that
the pilot makes every effort to avoid them. How does one not
notice the tiny void in one's ribs as well as the slight change
in the evenness of the sound that is triggered when the plane
swerves? When you see the wing, everything comes together;
the visual image of the wing rises or sinks in space, sometimes
in a discontinuous impulse which consists of two or three successive attempts. However, now I see nothing. Additionally, it
appears that the pilot has stopped swerving, probably because
it's no longer necessary. I can no longer see the milky glow of
the lights, especially because they are on incessantly. We have
now spent four and a half hours in the air; normally the flight

lasts five hours. In half an hour we will see the lights of Panama; the airplane will trace a light circle in the air and will place itself over the cement ribbon. They say that nothing is certain until it happens; when you travel, you can never take for granted that you will arrive at your destination. The lives of men are always open, exposed to every wind. By contrast, brief blue lights touch the window and reveal its frame; a border with a polished surface, screws, worn paint. An old airplane. Then, a violent, albeit brief, jolt. Some passengers have begun to wake up; she does not; huddled in the blanket brought by the flight attendant, she sleeps; her body curled up on the seat, her lips parted, and when the bolts of lightning are somewhat brighter, one can see a saliva stain on her travel pillow. The clock seems to have stopped. Five hours are indeed much longer than one might think.

Somewhere on the plane, a woman lets out a cry; the scream sounds much worse than the vivid light of the lightning bolt, than the plane going into the pocket of emptiness and even worse than the rustle of the wings when the air resettles. She lifts her head slowly, cleans the saliva off her face with her fingers, looks for me with her eyes full of sleep, and when they focus on me, she says:

"What happened? Did something happen? Something made a noise, I think."

I reply that no, that the plane moved a little, because it must have passed by a lightning bolt. Before I finish speaking, she has rested her head again and seems to have gone back to sleep. Her fearlessness makes me smile. She's now the only one in the whole plane who's sleeping. People talk quietly. Up ahead, on the door of the cockpit there is a little sign asking us to fasten our seatbelts; I feel for mine with my finger, because I've been wearing it since we took off; she also has been wearing it, but very loosely, to allow her to sleep. There is no rest now for our ears; the plane moves forward by leaps, not very violent ones, and with each jump the sound of the engine changes as if it were making a special effort. I wanted to believe that we were about to arrive in Panama, but since the neon sign doesn't prohibit smoking, it follows that we are not landing. Behind me, and above the panting of the engines, I hear the voice of the lady who cried out; every once in a while, when her words and a jolt coincide, her pitch slips into a kind of sob. I light a cigarette which they handed out to us at the start of the trip; she stirs in her seat, sits up and says, irritated:

"Why don't you try to sleep too? It's stifling hot in here. It's inconsiderate of you to smoke when there are people wanting to sleep."

I offer to try to fix the problem, shaking with rage, to center the fan on the window seat so that it disperses the smoke and it lands on me; she leans back and watches my manipulations, her eyes shining with annoyance. I have to loosen the seatbelt a little to move more freely. The jet of air coming out of the hole is very weak. Additionally I feel an unpleasant numbness and move with particular clumsiness; every adjustment of the fan is even worse than the previous. I give up and put out my cigarette.

"There," I reply. "Now go back to sleep."

She does not reply for a while. Then she sits up again violently. Turns on the light and takes out a magazine; opens it, puts it on her lap and says:

"Go ahead and smoke as much as you please. I can't sleep now."

"Alright, don't sleep then," I reply.

We have been flying for five hours and fifteen minutes. We should have arrived by now.

14

"It's weird that you're leaving tomorrow and we didn't see the storms over the Tunari even once. We didn't see the lights over the western hills, either," I uttered as I looked for the matches, first with my feet at the bottom of the bed and then behind Blanca's hips and back.

"That's not true," she replied, angrily. "You showed me the storms on two afternoons, and last week there was even one right here. And the other night we stared at the hills like dummies to see if we could see the blessed lights. Not just the other night, remember when I first got here; we missed about ten minutes of that movie because we were busy looking at the very same hills."

"What movie?" I asked, engrossed in the search for matches.

"What are you looking for?"

"Can you tell me woman, why it is that you like to ask stupid questions? I've had a cigarette in my mouth for the last hour and it's getting soaked in saliva. I'm looking for a train engine that I lost. Because I had it in my hand when I took off your panties, and now your panties are there, but the locomotive is lost."

"Idiot," she said, laughing and, taking care to ensure the bedsheet was under her armpit, leaned over between the bed and the wall; then emerged with matches between her fingers and her face taut with a mischievous smile. She looked downright ugly when she smiled like that, and now much more so, because she had two dark circles under her eyes. The gesture meant that she was in the mood again and preferred not to argue any further. She grabbed my cigarette with the same hand that held the matches and shut off the light with the other. My smoking paraphernalia flew across the darkness and bounced off the wall. No doubt about it now; Blanca was slightly drunk. I began to distinguish her tense features as she concentrated as I'd never seen her do before; then she experienced violent gratification, but inwardly, getting from it a muscular and powerful pleasure that made her body hard, almost like glass ready to explode into pieces by the waves it generated.

Then she made herself comfortable between the sheets and relaxed her body, but her eyes were still vibrant, fixed on the ceiling.

"I'd like for you to do all sorts of strange things to me," she said in an absurdly crystal clear voice, "but I am so, so tired that I think I would die from it."

She let her head roll sweetly on the pillow and fell asleep immediately, so deeply that I was able to get up and recover my cigarette and the matches and lie down beside her to smoke, bewildered, without waking her up. Everything Blanca had done that night was spontaneous, full of grace and completely directed toward herself. I considered and reconsidered my opinion of her in order to make sense out of what she'd just shown me, but it was getting me nowhere. The simplest thing to do was to chalk it up to a strange drunken phenomenon, but it seemed to be much more than that. I stared at her vague and beautiful form where I could barely make out the soft waves of her breathing and that the light of the cigarette modified every so often. One Blanca sleeping in the darkness; another under the reddish light of the ember; another one awake and happy; another one awake and desirous; another one irate; now another one that I was seeing drink for the first time in many years to the point that she was losing or gaining something that didn't fit the image. This woman was either wonderful or trashy. It was three-thirty in the morning and she was leaving the following day at nine; there was no time to find out. I could wake her up and talk to her at length; I could possess her until she cried out with pleasure or in pain; I could simply watch her sleep for a while, with my body foolishly stretched out on the bed and my two feet over there at the other end as if they didn't belong to me, while the other extremity up here inhaled smoke. A truck drove by down the street making everything shake. It was either headed toward the jungle or to the highlands or to another town in the same valley, or it came from there. At this very same moment, here lie a man and a woman, while others simply sleep and quartz grows on rocks and the jaguar walks across his hot and humid hunting ground and gold rests in its veins or in its sands, and everything is waiting for me to come and penetrate it, see it, kill it, pick it up. Tomorrow I will be here alone while she travels; and when the rainy season is over, this bed will remain empty in the darkness because I will have left for the jungle.

"Blanca," I called out softly, caressing her waist. "Blanca," I repeated. I kissed her ear, pushing her hair back with my tongue and called out to her again, "Blanca."

"What is it?" she groaned in a girly and whiny half asleep voice, and buried her face in the pillow, bending her neck.

"Blanca, it's almost four in the morning. Wake up."

"It doesn't matter," she whined again. "We leave tomorrow. We will get up really early. I want to sleep. I'm so sleepy. So sleepy."

"It's just that it's already really early," I told her very lovingly sliding my arm under her head.

"What time did you say it was?" she asked, opening her eyes wide. "Four?" she stared at me, her eyes shining. Then she sat up on her elbow. "Four?" she repeated.

"Almost four," I corrected her.

"Pfffff," she sighed and let herself fall back again.

"Hey, I'd forgotten to tell you. When we were coming back from Eugenia's house, I'd run out of matches. Remember?"

"When? What matches?" she asked and pouted her lips as if she were about to cry.

"After tonight's dinner, Blanca. Hey, didn't we have dinner at Chica's tonight? Remember that they gave you a going away party and Luisa refused to go again? Remember?"

"Yes, she couldn't go. She had a headache again."

"When we came back, I wanted to smoke, but I didn't have any matches. Hey, something must be happening to me."

Blanca got up on her elbow again and listened to me while staying perfectly still.

"It's weird. I felt all my pockets and I didn't have anything, and then, just as we were nearing Ballivián . . . Do you remember that it was really dark beneath the trees? There was a vagrant dog and he saw us; I hadn't seen him until I saw his eyes sparkle. And you know what occurred to me?"

During the pause I made to underline my amazing experience, she kept watching me, fascinated.

"It occurred to me to ask him for matches, just like that. As if one could simply ask a dog for matches. Like when someone at a theater lobby approaches you and says: 'Do you have a light, sir?' Don't you think that's weird?"

"No, I don't think it's weird at all. Those things always happen. What time did you say it was? Four, right? I'm going to get dressed."

"What's the matter, Blanca? Did you get upset because of the dog?" I accused my beloved's beautiful back as she looked for something among the clothes. "Would you please answer me woman? You know there's nothing that annoys me more than to be left talking to myself like a moron."

"Nothing's wrong. I'm looking for my slip because I want to go to the bathroom. That's what's wrong."

"Let's see Blanca, come here. Come."

"Leave me alone; I'm telling you. It's four in the morning and I have to get back to the hotel and sleep even if it's just a few winks. Besides, think about Luisa; I'm not going to do that to her again, honey. Let me go please."

"Blanca, beautiful, stay still; one more minute won't hurt anyone."

I wanted to add that after all it was the last night that we would spend together in who knows how long, but I couldn't, because she would accuse me of wasting precious moments talking about the dog that, incidentally, was not what had upset her. I was unable to guess the real reason; and I was completely sure that it was not due to unsatisfied desires. Experience had taught me that in those situations sometimes she also got angry, but if I sought her out, she would immediately submit. Instead, now she was as surprised at me as I was at her, and as tired. If time weren't pressing, we might possibly have realized that we would be separating forever, only after trying the most atrocious excesses to arrive at the most perfect failure. Although for sure if we'd had more time, we would not have lacked more desire. But now Blanca kissed me pleasantly and said:

"I know that I will regret this tomorrow, but right now, neither one of us wants to do anything. Let me have a shower, we'll get dressed and then walk until dawn. Besides, I want to have a serious conversation with you."

I was somewhat happy and somewhat resentful. That Blanca was able to circumvent the convention that required that she be crazy in love and desire on the last night with her beloved, even for a moment, was not something that, after several years in a relationship, I would have come to expect. Everything had an aspect of finality to it, and yet not. While the house filled with the sweet scent of some burning electric device spewing from the shower, I felt the presence of the woman over whose body the water in the bathroom ran. And she prepared to dress, to walk with me through the streets until the sun came up, to tell me God knows what nonsense that had no relevance either. It didn't matter that this was the same woman that ten thousand summers ago I waited for at night until she was undressed and in bed, because it embarrassed her for me to see her come to bed; and it also didn't matter that now my eyes were almost filled with tears as I remembered the smell of English leather and jasmine that always greeted me as I walked into her bedroom; or that I knew that she never wore elasticized panties, because she preferred the ones with the little button on the left hip and was always lying or confabulating. Because now we were parting and although we retained the love, we had lost the compass of love and other laws were now governing our paths. And still, this itself was a lie, because even without a compass there are still the postal system and telephones that modern society makes available to those who have lost each other so that they can be fooled. And also no, because I was fine and I couldn't care less if Blanca and her buttoned up panties went elsewhere, even if I shudder with love and desire every time I think about her. There are adventures of islands, and of crossroads, as Don Quixote used to say, and mine were always of crossroads; and roads, my dearest, are a function of time and are always open. Sometimes Blanca weighed like an unbearable burden on my conscience, in such a way that in those cases only the illusion of the slenderness of her waist afforded me the ability to love her despite the acute grief that she inflicted upon my spirit. But other times, such as now, any proof that she was not fully anesthetized was enough to send me spinning through the universe like an eagle with duck feathers and a head full of bubbles of happiness that she couldn't understand and sometimes made her angry, because she either guessed that I was at the tip of the runway, ready for takeoff, or simply because she did not understand. Why should I care? And meanwhile Blanca had a burdensome fetus growing in her womb or at the very least she was bound and determined to burden my heart with his ghost. This very room that tomorrow morning will be so precious to me, because it will have trembled with the rhythm of her body, did not matter at all. It was possible to pause one's life—like a fig that falls from its tree and is rejected even by the sparrows—or speed through time, take off toward the jungle, toward the woman, or up the mountain.

When Blanca returned, she was determined. She dressed expertly and hurriedly, distractedly smiling at me as she dressed. But, when she was about to ask me to do up the buttons of her dress, her terrible nose sniffed in search of recent traces; she must have smelled something fresh and ample because she furrowed her brow; and it was not simply the delicious air that runs through cities at dawn, and it was not like the sadness of a night that is ending. And her desire increased enormously, shaking with surrender or fear. And we loved each other again and were enormously happy. And now she didn't even care about missing the train, or even getting dressed again as she was before.

But while she combed her hair and I was bursting with joy, she started to shrink until I could see at the depths of her despair, the burdensome fetus.

When we left the house, the sun was climbing gloriously over the city and Blanca's eyes were wet with tears.

XIV

WHEN I RUN into him by chance in the middle of the cloudy and smog-filled morning, in the random enormity of gray figures that move about the sidewalks of downtown Santiago, I see his ugly face almost at the level of the average person's navel and notice at once that his head has become almost as bald as mine, that he has gained much weight in these little over ten years and that he wraps his flabby roundness in a somewhat threadbare black coat that seems incompatible with his great national importance and emerging international fame and I think he wants to appear as if he's in an all-encompassing hurry so that he can pretend that he hasn't seen me and walk past me, then, even if I cannot deny that it is, in fact, him, his figure becomes foreign to me, while at the same time the space around me becomes absurdly cubist and I feel an idiotic and terrifying need to ask him to confirm his identity. But it seems to me that I see a half smile on that face that is not looking at me, and my dull neurons arrange their circuitry to lower their voltage to a degree that allows objects, the street, people, vehicles, and him, to emit a tinge of positive emotion. And I smile. How can I forget, even in the indifference surrounding me that I have always felt that we belong to the same clan, even though in the last two decades I have never ceased to consider him a brilliant son-of-a-gun? How can I not, then, feel an out-of-control desire to give him a swift kick in the ass? How can I forget, at the same time, that image of his poor hide when his classmates, the scoundrels, would hang him from the hat racks that never even creaked from his weight or rust from his tears? How can I forget that the guy is truly a musical genius? And finally, there must be something we can still talk about, I think.

For all those reasons and also because I am foolishly walking from pharmacy to pharmacy searching for that salicylic acid soap that disappeared from pharmacies exactly one week after I started using it. Because I feel like my face is disfigured, my stomach is a bundle of knots and my chest is tight with distress, and because I feel like I've wasted the entire morning searching for that darned soap that, after all is said and done, will not cure my seborrhea anyway. I stop him. I greet him with all the affection I can muster and force him, in the name of our old schoolboy friendship to accept an invitation for a drink, or whatever, despite the countless pressing matters that await him at his office. I am convinced that he decided to believe my lie that I too must abandon urgent matters to speak with him. He is not wasting his time with just any loser, but even then, he looks at his watch twice before assenting.

But as soon as he accepts, I run out of things to say. We silently and awkwardly turn the corner onto the Plaza de Armas square. A couple of times we almost run into pedestrians, barely missing them, anxious to arrive quickly where it really doesn't matter to us if we arrive or not. And when we finally sit down at a table, we both rush to garner the attention of the waiter. Everything in the café is very German; round tiny dark wood tables, each one of them with a tiny nickel-plated flowerpot full of tiny flowers. It would all be very solitary if it weren't for an old woman devouring some *kuchen*, while at the other end of the restaurant, two waiters quietly purr as they're dozing off, their backs toward us, next to a glass cabinet where several types of pastries and cakes sleep in neat little rows trying to be appetizing. It was as if the two waiters were a couple of enormous two-toned sleepy cats, under a spell here for thirty years, since we were children, to care for and manage these timeless cakes that had been waiting for us since then. But this is not the time for the warm tea of our childhood aunties, but rather a winter morn, thick with smog; and my aunt is not here to offer me something sweet to satisfy my gluttony. Instead, my mouth feels rough from too much smoking the night before and my stomach, unstable from the alcohol, ready to lurch at the thought of eating anything.

One of the heavy, slow, and lethargic cats takes our order (tea and a double puff pastry chicken sandwich, hot for my friend and non-carbonated mineral water for me, please), and my regret at having assumed the hollow task of talking to this guy increases. This guy is becoming stranger and stranger to me by the minute, and I think about how great it would be for me to be outside, walking aimlessly by myself in search of my soap. Nevertheless, when Puss in Boots righteously walks away with our order in his left hand, out of pure fear and miserableness I don't do what I should do. I don't get up off my chair and exit peacefully and pensively, and leave this glutton to eat his double sandwich by himself with some mineral water to do with as he wanted, but rather, I stay sitting and shittily repressed. I smile and effortlessly ask him how things are going, with a stupid malevolence wrapped up in what I believe to be sophisticated language. At the same time I remember I used to be unable to talk about anything that wasn't intended to elicit laughter or that really mattered to me and committed me fully to something. That is who I was when this guy met me. Now I want to give him the opportunity to compare me to whom I was before and to notice the ease and ability for small talk that I have gained over the years. It's true that I now have a knot in my stomach, but my hands and tongue have loosened. How about that?

I tell myself over and over again that we have nothing in common, save for a very distant past that still matters to me because I haven't been faithful to it. In contrast, it doesn't seem to matter to him at all, because he is following his old path toward complete fulfilment. I have repeated the phrase "nothing in common" to myself several times; I cannot help but repeat it and I ask him if he ever gets stupid thoughts stuck in his head and I explain the mechanism of what is happening to me, but I change the example, to hide how empty our encounter seems to me while flattering him at the same time. I tell him that for a while now I have been unable to stop thinking about the music

he wrote when we were in high school entitled "Dead Comrade."
He is enthusiastically surprised that I still remember and con-
fesses that he had forgotten it. His mood changes, a little com-
municative window opens in him and he tells me that it happens to him often, but that the one who really is going through
some strange things is Guillermo. It seems that the mention of
Guillermo's mental state makes us bond. And he points out that
since he began painting only erotic subjects, he has been having prophetic dreams, paranormal phenomena, and a thousand
other strange oddities. He's so wrapped up in happiness and
friendship that he doesn't at all take into account the presence
of Puss in Boots, who has returned with our order and wants us
to let him set it down on the table and who undoubtedly gets
annoyed when my friend remembers that in the days of our old
conversations they called us "the geniuses." Then, with his voice
muffled by the remains of a huge mouthful of his sandwich,
he asks me what I think about Guillermo's oil paintings and
engravings; then he looks at me, happily blinking as he bites
into another piece of bread and chicken that must have taken
all thirty-two teeth to chew.

I reply that I have the same opinion that anyone looking at
them would: pure and holy sex. I allow myself to add quietly,
simply, and objectively that I don't know much about art, but
sex, you bet I do. And that I see the same thing as everyone: that
all shapes and all colors become vulvar or phallic; any subject he
tries turns into male or female. I say that the surfaces he works
on seem to be about to howl with arousal, orgasm, fertilization,
or pregnancy, and that I like his paintings very much.

"Hey," he says craning his neck toward me and waving in
surprise, "he is completely crazy and happy. I have returned to
caring about God, did you know? The other day I was in his
studio . . ."

"In God's studio?"

"One cannot have a serious conversation with you," he comments, really annoyed; but enthusiasm propels him and he continues, "I thought he would understand. But his weird experiences haven't helped him one bit. He couldn't stop laughing.

He was grabbing his belly with both hands when I told him and rolling around on that couch he has in his workshop, laughing his head off. And I don't understand anything. What I do know is that it's serious. You'll see when he suddenly lets go of his belly and puts his feet on the ground. One cannot do both at once. He either becomes grounded or he stops painting those things. You'll see. Seriously, you'll see. His fit of laughter started when I told him I was reading the *Book of Job*."

"Nice text," I comment, "I like it too. How is it coming along?"

"So-so. I still don't understand it. I understand it less each time . . ."

He suddenly interrupts his storytelling and his eating and looks at me with the same old ugly and friendly smile of years past. His hands clench in excitement on the edge of the table. The sinister, slimy patagium of an alarming premonition grazes my consciousness. Is he about to give me creative and liberating advice aimed at getting me out of the deep hole that everyone knows I'm in? For an instant, the acute regret of not being out there searching for my soap makes me despair. Even my head turns toward the door uncontrollably.

"Hey, miserable slob," he says, "let's do something. Are you up for it?"

"What?" I ask, trying to figure out his joy and his adventurous impulse.

"Let's forget all the office crap. Shall we? We'll go and find Guillermo and Matias and spend the day doing whatever we feel like, we can talk, and we can do anything we want. Are you with me?"

"Of course," I reply, starting to get excited, "the sky won't fall if we give ourselves a treat like we used to."

"That's it! First, we'll go get the car; then we'll go by Fats's workshop and the three of us will find that pussy Matias. Ok? I've got a new car, bastard; just got it yesterday; we'll try it out. It's over at the Bandera parking lot. Shall we?"

"Well, yeah, great; let's go."

"One minute, sir, one minute, first, my sandwich."

He sticks almost all the remaining bread and chicken in his mouth, and swallows it with a mouthful of tea, as if eating a giant wafer. I am momentarily infected by the speed of his swallowing and his happily rushed presence. But suddenly I'm turned off by everything and regret lodges in my gut. It's one thing to spend a while in civilized and controlled conversation, but a whole afternoon will cost another two hundred pesos. And that's only if they don't decide, for example, to continue partying in a whorehouse. I can see myself, with two nights of partying to my name, with dark circles under my eyes and oil dripping from every pore. With a cold discomfort that makes me see my friend and myself as sort of pitiful puppets, I signal to the waiter to come. My friend raises a hand to stop me.

"Mo, affhoe," he mumbles through what is left of his chicken sandwich, "I'll fay fo that."

He pats his clothes, frantically searching for his wallet, but I grab the check from Puss in Boots, who smiles for the first time as he bows briefly toward my friend's outstretched hand holding a huge bill.

We had just reached the sidewalk, when he stops and gives himself a furious slap on his forehead.

"What's the matter?"

"Damn it, we're screwed. I have a meeting with one of my assistants at noon. I screwed up."

"If you want, I'll walk with you to your office and then we'll go to Guillermo's workshop," I stupidly offer instead of taking advantage of the opportunity and saying goodbye.

He proposes a final decision that I accept so as not to remain standing in the middle of the sidewalk, obstructing people's way as they look at us with rage; El Enano will go and give instructions to his assistant while I go to Guillermo's workshop and then El Enano will come by and pick us up so we can go find Matías. It works out really well for him, because this way he can review an interview that will be coming out in the Sunday paper.

I walk away and turn in the vague direction of Guillermo's workshop. It occurs to me that it would be good to go to the library and approve the inventory of books that we are going to transfer to the municipality. Of course that can wait, my things are not as urgent as El Enano's. I cannot help but feel diminished and dominated by nonsense when I compare my reluctance to my friend's enthusiasm for giving instructions and reviewing interviews. As far as preparing tomorrow's lecture, never mind. I feel a helpless irritation, entirely idiotic, as I compare yesterday's situation with today's; it's as if the whole world were bent on hurling new things at me day after day, determined to not allow me to find one moment to devote fully to what is important to me. Luckily, I notice that things seem clearer at midday; things and people project a vague shadow on the pavement. It's intolerable to walk out here at this time of day. Men and women abound everywhere. I'm exasperated by the banality of the things on my mind.

"Taxi! Taxi! . . . Good morning. Straight to Alameda, please. I don't know where I'm going, but I know how to get there," I tell him.

"Yes, sir."

"It's so strange to run into friends that one met so long ago."

"That's just how it goes. People grow older. We also grow older. But you are still young," he says, looking at me in the rearview mirror.

"Left here please, and take a right at the corner."

"You know, I don't think that aging has anything to do with anything . . ."

"Halfway down the block, in front of that old house . . . This one."

I pay the fare and we part politely. Guillermo is looking out the window and greets me as warmly as ever. He yells out that he will be right down to let me in, and when he gets there, I'm wrapped in the abundance of his welcome.

"You finally decided to come and see me, old man. How's it going?"

"What's up, Fats? I did see your last show."

"What did you think of it?" he asks in a tone that sounds like he truly cares and he adds urgently: "Careful! There's a step missing on the stairs and there's a burnt out lightbulb too."

"I thought it's all about sex, my friend."

"True, about sex," he admits and bursts out laughing. "What else can one paint these days? Geez, I'm glad you came over. How long's it been?" he asks, opening the door to a huge workshop and inviting me in.

"Not that long," I reply, after mulling it over a bit, "about three or four years, just enough time for you to break the stairs and burn out a light bulb."

"Geez, I'm so glad you came. And you look happier now, are you?"

I see that he has a large canvas mounted on a huge easel; newly started. Everything else looks the same. Many paintings either completed or abandoned, turned toward the wall. They just might be the same ones as the last time I came. The same couch where he laughs at our friend's religious interests. The only significantly new thing is a stuffed hawk that has lost its head and hangs over the sofa.

"Hey, I have an invitation for you," I tell him as I settle into the sofa: he just stays there watching me at the foot of the easel, waiting for me to continue, "I've just seen Felix. We decided to drop everything and spend the day having fun, what do you think?"

"Wow, that's so odd! I'm almost scared about what's happening to me. Do you know that I woke up today wanting to see you and that I've been thinking about it all morning? And I didn't feel like doing anything but seeing you. But enough nonsense, what did you do with El Enano?"

"He's giving instructions to an assistant," I say, mockingly deepening my voice, "a trusted employee, who received the honor of replacing him in a rehearsal. He has to give him instructions, you know, otherwise, he'll mess everything up."

"That mouse has become real important," he says, with respect. "But he has not let it go to his head. He's a good guy. We could include Matias, too," he suggests and starts collecting brushes and spatulas that he then takes to a table where there are rags and several bottles.

"That was the idea," I inform him, getting nearer so I can

see how he cleans his utensils, "But he's kind of hard to track down . . ."

"What a coincidence. I'm supposed to pick him up before lunch. Hey, this is like sorcery. Maybe Felix is right and maybe there is a God or some other weird thing," he says, looking concerned, as he pours liquid from the bottle into a pot, he looks at me briefly and puts the brushes in, handling everything very carefully, but very quickly. "The trouble is that he has no telephone at his new house. But we can go and get him."

"It won't work," I state, watching him squeeze the brushes on the palette, one by one, after removing them from the bath. "It's already twelve thirty. If Felix gets here and finds no one, he'll think who knows what and he'll leave. You know him. It's best if I stay here and you bring the other guy."

"Much better. I'll get dressed in a minute. Do what you want, except paint. I'm sure there's something to drink in that cabinet. There's nothing to eat though."

Having finished with spatulas and brushes, he pours more liquid from the bottle onto a gigantic square trowel and rubs it vigorously with one of the rags. Then he smiles and walks into the house briskly. I get up and wander around the room, dancing and grimacing a little. Nevertheless, I still feel something heavy somewhere, in my soul, I suppose. Dear friends. Dear friends? The lively rhythm of Guillermo's steps returns. He must have forgotten something that he needs to get dressed. But no; he's ready to go. It almost seems like an illusion.

"I'm on my way, old man. Do you want anything? If you get cold, crank up the flame on the stove. Hey, please, if anyone calls, take a message. You want anything?"

"Nothing, thanks, just your liquor."

I hear him rattling down the stairs. I assume that he is taking the steps two by two, because otherwise I would have heard him jump over the broken step. I am surprised by his agility. He shuts the door firmly and immediately the silence of the great empty house actively rises from the farthest corners and thickens the air. I walk to the liquor cabinet and my footsteps make the floor cringe loudly, but the noise does not travel, it does not go into the rooms, it appears intrusively in the middle of the silence and then disappears. Before bending over to open the door of the cabinet, I freeze and turn my head like an antenna, because I am convinced that something has made a noise in another part of the house; the only thing I manage to sense is my breath inside my nose. I find an empty wine jug, several bottles of gin, also completely empty, and two half empty bottles of good moonshine, that together will get me about an ounce or two, maybe three. There are no glasses in sight. The only thing that can serve as an ashtray is an absurd stone mortar that I place next to the sofa. After removing my cigarettes I take off my jacket and hang it neatly on the back of one of the two old chairs that Guillermo always has side by side, as if they were a pair of shoes. Before I lie down to wait peacefully, I crank up the flames of the stove and watch the street through the dirty window; the day is overcast.

I lie on the sofa but have to get up to relocate the mortar-ashtray so that it will be right under my hand when I let it hang from the sofa holding my cigarette. But there's no rest. The comfort of the sofa becomes for me simply a place from which to observe. The silence of the house produces in me a childish fear and highlights the objects around me that are entirely alien to me: not just simply alien, but aggressive. They display the content and richness of a full life that isn't mine. Rows of paintings that turn their backs to me, a set of Guillermo's tools, two small easels folded against the back wall . . . A violent desire overcomes me as I yearn to possess a workshop like this one, old, dusty, inhospitable to others, where I could spend endless hours working quietly, alone. Alone? I lift one of the bottles and fill my mouth with a generous portion of moonshine, laughing a little at myself. Am I never going to stop being an imbecile? What I am is sleepy and, as it turns out, this place is perfect for sleeping.

Adriana believes that a serious illness could save me or perhaps falling in love with another woman so that I would have the opportunity to truly suffer; so that this soft, reasonable, and innocuous world that I have created for myself and where I can no longer breathe, will break apart. And maybe she's right, even if her saying it infuriates me. But women are not magical either, even if they are the possibility of magic. Because what is the point of making gestures of surrender, of assimilation, if there's nothing to surrender and nothing to assimilate but fear? Or perhaps, more precisely, if in order to give yourself fully to another you first had to free yourself from yourself? The terrible thing is that while one is living one has to keep on living . . . The Gods don't bother to speak to the deaf in complete sentences. Love is the natural state of man, but as it has the same indefinite nature as the mind and as existence, it's easy to degrade, to lose it in a tangle of legs and breasts and hair, to fall from love into fear.

A long and loud ringing breaks into the silence and takes me out of the semi-consciousness state that I had fallen into. I run to the window to let El Enano know that I will be downstairs right away. But what awaits me is the face of a woman that I find incredibly beautiful looking up at me.

"Mr. Góngora, please?" she asks in a somewhat deep, but feminine voice.

"He left, but will be back soon. I'll let you in right away."

"No, thank you very much. I have no time."

She lifts the sleeve of her coat slightly to let her watch confirm that she cannot wait. She is wearing gloves. Even in the gray afternoon light, her golden brown hair looks shiny. Similar to Adriana's, I think with distaste.

"Any message?" I ask in order to find out her name.

"No, thanks, I'll call him later."

She had retreated to the edge of the sidewalk, I guess so as not to get a stiff neck. When she is finished speaking, she turns gracefully and walks away quickly. I angrily regret being holed up here, and yet, I'm glad she didn't want to come up. The urge to lie down has gone. I walk around the workshop with a kind of excitement that she has left in me and that makes me smile because it is so idiotic. The space allows me to take ten long steps each way. I take them with the second bottle in my right hand and a cigarette in the other. As I recall Guillermo's well-deserved reputation as a tireless womanizer, I ask myself, alarmed like a schoolboy, if he has something going with her, but I immediately decide, also like a child, that *she* wouldn't. She looked rich.

She was probably coming by to pay for a painting she had commissioned, or to pick it up. The sound of the telephone ringing makes me jump. It's Felix. The phone must not be working properly. I can hardly hear it, but I can hear the anger making his voice quiver.

"I've broken down!" his mousy voice howls through the earpiece. "It looks like this piece of shit car either had a manufacturing defect or I've been taken for a fool."

"Speak up, I can barely hear you."

"I'm yelling! I'm going to find that asshole of a salesman. Wait for me for three quarters of an hour. Do you hear me? About for-ty fi-ve-mi-nu-tes. Did you hear me?"

El Enano's mishap makes me feel weirdly annoyed. Who knows how long we'll have to wait here, dying of hunger, because he doesn't know how to buy a piece of crap that'll run. And the others? It's almost two in the afternoon. I barely have enough moonshine for another two or three modest drinks. Luckily I have lots of cigarettes. I lie down again. The headless bird looks at me sadly through the hole in its neck. If no one has come or called by the time I finish the bottle, I'm leaving. Now I'm sort of paying attention to the phone and to the front door at the same time. First, the phone rings. I cannot hear anything but strange tapping sounds that almost hurt my eardrum. I shout "hello" repeatedly into the mouthpiece, but the sound remains unchanged. I hang it up violently. I launch a string of profanities into the air. Now I'm pissed! The piece of shit phone is broken; to get someone to come and fix it, I would need another phone; but if I go, Felix might arrive and think that we left him. Also, I have no house key. I would have to find a place that would allow me to see the front door as I phone. I go to the window to study the possibilities, and it starts to ring again. Again I hear the indifferent and infuriating tapping. I hang up. From the window I can see the empty street; there is no shop across the street, and there's no one walking on the sidewalk.

I'm thinking nonsense. My friends are adults. They will find a way to show up here as soon as possible. No doubt it has occurred to them to call the switchboard to correct the malfunction. It's not such a big deal to have lunch a little later. I can make the best of the delay and rest in this wonderful silence; at any rate, I've spent the past few weeks working on nonsense. We will soon have a chance to talk. It's idiotic to think that they couldn't come. It's simply a matter of waiting a bit and we'll have one of those beautiful conversations. There's something nice about getting ready to sleep and then waking up randomly.

As I awaken from a deep sleep, I realize that perhaps the incessant doorbell has awakened me. I remember a confusion of sounds that seemed nightmarish. My watch says it's ten after five. I am angered by the urgency, the insistence of the person downstairs. I become fully awake at the thought that it might be the girl again or my friends. But nothing is the same anymore. Although once again I run to the window, I know it's useless to do so. What did I feel before falling asleep? When I look down, I see the top of a head that doesn't belong to Felix.

"Yes? What do you need?" I yell out.

The top of the head turns from right to left. It must belong to a fool. Then, he moves back and his face comes into view.

"I would like to speak to Señor Góngora."

"He's not here."

"And do you know what time he's coming back?"

"Hey can you tell me what time it is?"

"It's ten after five. And at what time . . . ?"

"I haven't the slightest idea."

The abruptness of my awakening has left my heart in my throat. I feel my tongue rough, and metallic in my mouth. Again I throw myself on the couch. It's getting dark in the workshop. I would like to go back to sleep, but it's already too late. I light a cigarette, take a puff of smoke that tastes awful, and exhale in almost a whimper.

Alright. I want to talk. I am willing to put my misery into words. For lack of a better jury, my three friends would hear me out. Or I would listen to them and respond to them. Their comments would be for me, like a trial and a verdict. They knew me before I started this journey that has brought me to misadventure and fear. And although only I know how I have traveled it, it seemed right to me, for just once, to ask for their help or to allow them to graciously offer it.

I have just enough time to prepare tomorrow's seminar. I look for the bathroom in this huge, dusty, and gloomy house. The open doors of the empty rooms seem to wait until I pass by them, with some quiet purpose. As I wet my face leaning over the sink, the showerhead drips water onto the bottom of the tub; I turn to make sure that the noise is, in fact, coming from there. I finish getting ready to go out onto the street, and as I go down the stairs almost in the darkness, it suddenly occurs to me that the only possible answer was silence and absence. There is nothing more eloquent; nothing more accidental and true. Three friends who did not arrive. A beautiful woman who was not looking for me. Before closing the door, I see clearly again in my imagination, the shape of the headless bird, watching me through the hole in its neck. It does not mean anything, it doesn't symbolize anything, and it doesn't allude to anything or anyone. It makes me smile.

15

THE TRAIN LEFT extremely late, well after the noon hour. If I had been told twenty-four hours before that the *Altiplano* rainfall would produce a landslide on the railroad tracks and leave me the gift of Blanca for the entire morning, I would have walked with a more upright posture and at a brisker pace out of sheer delight. However, it was entirely different spending a whole morning with my eyes gritty because I had stayed up all night and with two women who, at the moment, had acquired the soul of express mail or of suitcases and had, for all intents and purposes, already left. And as a result there wasn't a chair in the entire city that could properly accommodate their beautiful buttocks, because the only thing that would do were train seats. They couldn't go back to the hotel room they had just left once we found out about the delay.

By now the beds were expecting new bodies and other private matters and diligent maids would have erased all traces of the passage of the two women. In the meantime, we had to find a place for them and for their packages and luggage, and in particular for a gigantic jaguar skin that Luisa had acquired and had become her most treasured possession. Traveling across the city with the enormous roll on the roof of the taxi, like a cigar on the back of a cockroach, was very odd. The possibility of leaving everything in storage and returning to town for a comfortable lunch was discussed exhaustively. But Luisa feared that the guards would not be as zealous and as honorable as her goods required and would not let herself be convinced by any argument. The first pretext was that there wouldn't be enough time. After a long tug of war, she grumbled:

"Fine, you go if you want. I'll stay. I'm not hungry."

And so we spent the entire time on a hard bench at the station, talking very little and reluctantly. I ended up falling into a state of very pleasant light sleep from which I must have entered into a heavy sleep, because Blanca woke me when the train finally arrived at the station and told me that my snoring had embarrassed them.

Chica and Leroy had come with us to say goodbye to the sisters. Knowing Leroy, I'm sure he must have been hiding somewhere, spying and waiting until we finished loading the suitcases, packages, and tiger pelt. Except for the pelt everything else was relatively easy. I worked hard to stuff it in the overhead bin, but it was so stiff that it seemed more like rhinoceros than feline. It was impossible to fit it into that compartment and have it stay there, and if it was behaving this way when the train was stopped . . . Furthermore, when I was beginning to feel my armpits and my back wet with sweat, the two sisters realized that they would have to change trains in Oruro and they preferred to handle the skin at ground level. Tucked transversely between the backs of two seats, it would have gone across the aisle and lost itself in between the two seats on the other side. It seemed to me, after all, an arrangement of medium decorum, but the sister objected because she feared passengers would step on it as they walked by. We couldn't arrange it lengthwise either, because although we could kick it under the seat, it would disturb the passengers traveling behind them and also those in front of them. As my original proposal had been to transfer it to the luggage car, I was thrilled to call the conductor to do just that. Not until I returned, sweaty and smelling of embalmed tiger, did Leroy appear on the platform, standing straight and fresh as a daisy, delicately leading Chica and waving at us with a jubilant air. He even dared to lament that it didn't occur to him to arrive earlier to help in the task. But the worst came later, when Chica and my beloved got sentimental and, their hearts trembling with grief, because who knew how long it would be before they saw each other again, they took out their hankies, with one leaning out the window and the other one on tiptoe below, and began patting at the corners of their eyes, taking care not to let their mascara run and then lifted their heads high in the air, after a brief jolt determined to stop the tears, but ended up crying even more. I longed for a moment alone with Blanca, but even when there was still a good half hour before the train left she didn't dare disobey her sister's harsh orders; in these cases she forgot sport and became very nervous and afraid to be alone, even for a moment, for who knows what reason.

The crying of the two women, Luisa's protests, Leroy's jokes, and my rage made the half hour go by sooner than I would have liked. I suddenly found myself standing on the platform, painfully following with my gaze the hand of my beloved as it disappeared around the bend as soon as it left the station. Now I had to return to a city that was entirely devoid of women and feminine sounds preparing meals for me. We walked in silence toward the exit. Chica was crying profusely, Leroy nearly broke my scapula with a slap as he suggested:

"Get over that fearful and feminine mood, my boy. The souls of Mucius Scaevola, Regulus, and Arturo Prat must now be pulling their spiritual hair out seeing how far men have fallen who only yesterday trod the sands of so many unimportant rivers in the treacherous jungle. Come have lunch with us now, what do you say?

"Go to hell," I said. "Sorry, Eugenia."

Chica looked at me with a shaky and teary smile. For the first time I found her really attractive. I couldn't take my eyes off her, enjoying the liquid smile she held for my benefit, either because she was very flirtatious or because she felt a deep, fleeting, and foolish fondness for me.

We had just parted when Leroy turned back to tell me that he would not be able to work all afternoon. I didn't want to ask him for explanations; I was tired of absolving or insulting him for the moral conflicts of a downright lazy man, and above all I didn't even feel I had the moral authority; I couldn't wait to get rid of them so that I could call a taxi with the little bit of cash

I had left and jump into bed and sleep until I got the hiccups; moreover in addition to the sadness I felt due to Blanca's departure, as she was moving away from me now toward the villages of the *Altiplano*, I couldn't ignore that my senses were working overtime: the sunlight was like a blinding ocean surrounding shaded islands on which, almost exactly at their core, trees and people rested or moved about. My senses enhanced the surprising midday air and, among other things, let me know that my body, sleepy and all, was moving with great agility and to their total satisfaction, ready for anything, happy with its tendons and muscles and bones and even with its skin overheated by the sun on its face. I truly adore her, I told myself, however, as much as I like having her with me, I also like it when she goes away and I can feel free again, because over there, on the other side of those mountains, is the jungle and behind me it is also noon over the *Altiplano* and over the desert and over the sea. Dearest, what a shame that your departure makes me as happy as your arrival! Or rather, how wonderful that my happiness doesn't depend on you and yet you are not alien to my happiness! I know that the heavy alligator that floats hidden in your soul would awaken and go mad if I told you all this, but what woman would not do the same thing if she were you? And also, my dear, what is there to do if things are as they are? If you were not horrified by the truth even in its most subtle forms, our common life would be, perhaps, easier, but it's also true that we are all in chains together and only the spirit, and only now and then, lifts its head in wonder, and amazed by its power it erases in a mere gesture all that is not freedom and joy. Freedom to love and to hate, to come and go, to die and to be alive, to be near and to be far, to be satiated and to be hungry. But the terrible thing is that one can never be sure of anything. So, my dear, if I could believe in God, I would do so now, in the midst of my joy, when I feel indeed thrown into the middle of existence and I have no one to turn to who can keep my treasure.

You have left me as poor as a church mouse and things will be grim until I have enough to eat regularly; within a few weeks I'm going to the jungle and Ramón says that things are really dangerous this time around; and it all gives me joy. But there is someone who, unknowingly, can take it all away: me.

I had stayed at the corner waiting for a taxi. But, to be honest, I was not at all sleepy. And the world was far too wide to go and watch over workers at the factory with a whip. Hunting. That was the answer. I would go hunting. I would walk along the shores of Lake Alalay, quietly, until I found ducks. I decided not to wait, because I remembered that cabbies had their *siesta* around this time under the shade of the trees of the square and I could easily turn into a mummy in the sun waiting at the corner and not one taxi would go by. I could almost feel that special air that lakes release, the pressure of the rifle against my shoulder, and the image through the sight aligned in front of my eye while my finger gently waits on the trigger. I also had no desire to eat lunch. Or perhaps it would be better not to go; it was too hot and there was not even one shitty tree on the shores for shelter. Of course, before anything else, I would need something to shoot at the ducks, and at that time everyone was sitting at the table, and dropping in on someone's home would be to crash their lunch. I also needed a float because the water was fiercely cold and I didn't know anyone in town who had a dog.

Another shortcoming of the lake: there were people living on the banks and there was a danger that the shot would ricochet . . . No, it was best to leave work behind for about three or four days and be cured by the Santa Cruz tropics. I was still a little embarrassed remembering when, on my last trip, a Santa Cruz girl had chilled my blood by slightly lifting her dress as she asked: "If you like me, why don't you jump me?" I had been told that there was this beautiful possibility if one walked along the river at sunset, but it didn't include the girl having a hairy mole on her thigh the size of a small black mouse. Be that as it may, looking up as if it were raining and asking her if there would be a moon that night was not justifiable. I was undoubtedly infamous among the girls of the village.

I could comfortably leave the factory for a few days in the care of the foreman. Nothing urgent required my presence in Cochabamba, except maybe selecting mahogany planks for an order that soon could mean an abundance of food for several weeks and some other items for my trip to the jungle. Of course, the foreman could make the selection much better than me, even though they say it's the master's eye that makes the mill go . . . Perhaps it's better to wait a while and then go hunting.

After wandering about under a sky that was beginning to cloud over, a rare event in Cochabamba at this time of year, I ended up going into a cinema. I carefully checked out the audience and after confirming, as per my usual routine, that all the young women were accompanied, I relaxed in my seat and waited for the lights to go out and for the movie to begin. I found the first scenes interesting, but soon, as I felt more and more sleepy, I began to recognize the characters, then finally the action and even the dialogue. The first time I saw it I probably arrived late. I must have gone with Blanca. With her no one ever arrived anywhere on time. At this very moment her hands are probably folded under her as she sleeps. And next to her, her sister, who reserved her stoicism for these situations would be green with motion sicknesses and feeling superior to the other, because the point was to feel sick and endure it, not to have an iron disposition as Blanca did without ever even exercising and who would become helpless only when I was around. I was almost sure that she was faking her pregnancy. Despite my insistence she refused a clinical examination. She argued that she had the incontestable evidence of her knowledge of her own body. She was even irritated that I would want to inject a little science into the matter. Suddenly, I realized that if she were actually pregnant, that wouldn't be a problem at all. Perhaps I would have to momentarily give up doing things my way. Blanca was not the type of person who would just like that bless an enterprise of dubious productivity, like going into the jungle to look for gold. Even her visit had turned out to be beneficial for her, although she would never admit it. She had, rather, a yearning for order, for savings, for a cautious and predictable life. Was she the only one? What I would have given to fulfill the blind desire of finding her at home after the movie, quietly doing her woman's work! Forever? Until we grew old and came to the inconceivable end?

Chances were that, if necessary, she would resort to an abortion and would send me a cable asking for money for the operation. We would be in a jam if she did, there wasn't even enough to have a tooth extracted. The room was suddenly dark and a thunderous roar shook us; I felt as if the walls of my skull had caved in; then came a moment of absurd silence. But then a storm of shrieks exploded in the dark, increasing the depth of the blackness; a river of screams, foolish running and silent collisions. A heavy and flabby mass tried to push through me to freedom and I had to defend myself by kicking, because otherwise it would have crushed me. I must have been successful judging by the whining, agonizing choking that accompanied me as I tried to get away. Someone opened a door and then immediately a wave of people formed a solid mass against the light, because although they were not many, they could not pass through the open door all at once. Even while immobilized they were beating each other with elbows and fists and hurling insults and screaming. When they finally emptied out the room, we noticed that it was raining unbelievably outside. There were only two injured: one was a woman whose husband had crushed her against a wall, and the other was a guy with a nosebleed. There was no fat man dying, so I calmed down. A skinny, ugly girl was standing in the middle of the foyer, gently urinating on herself, her legs shaking and spread out like a calf's.

Lightning had struck somewhere nearby and had melted the electric cables.

XV

Guillermo accompanies me to the second floor and opens the door to what will be my room.

"It's beautiful, Fats, just beautiful!

"For a great friend, a room that might not be large enough, but is welcoming," he says, with the same expression as that of our school years.

"Very nice," I repeat as I walk around. "It's nothing at all like Van Gogh's, except the brightness, but it seems like a place where, like the one he painted, all good things can occur," I say, feeling a little cheesy and academic.

"Hopefully Claudia will feel the same way and have, let's say, more concrete reasons," Fats answers laughingly and leaves the room.

Before I follow him, I'm drawn to a window opposite the foot of the bed. Through it, I am able to see the southern area of the beach, sunny and silent, interrupted by a large rock, against which waves crash leaving a gleaming hazy blur after the water rises happy and blue and then falls heavily; the distant flight of marine birds; the ocean shimmering in the sun and the white sand. I find it wonderful that so few of the houses are occupied. When vacationers fill them in the summer, I will already have left, hopefully with my work completed.

Downstairs I find Guillermo putting things away in a small room. He asks if I mind that he leave it locked, adding: "Remember that little children love painting and Claudia's two little angels . . ."

"If they come, leave me the key so I can lock myself in there, please. Claudia wouldn't pull such a stunt, I hope. A week of babysitting, imagine."

"Hey," he says looking like he is making plans, "did you have time for breakfast? I had two very thin pieces of buttered toast and a cup of black coffee." He looks at me still plottingly, "and the ocean air . . . you know. And what the hell am I going to do in Santiago in the morning? If I leave now, I will get there at eleven thirty, as hungry as a bear. Wouldn't it be better if we treated ourselves to a bellyful of seafood?"

I'm ready to reply that I would like nothing better, but he adds, "Hey. Do you remember when we used to hunt cows?" I nod happily. I hadn't thought of that for years, but I remember it very clearly. We hunted them for several weeks, every school day, after lunch; they were small, sleepy in their captivity, with iridescent wings and very affectionate.

"You know something, old man, I'm going to let you in on something: it's one of the few important things that I remember from back then, in that chain of silly hours when they were teaching us how to prepare sulfuric acid with and without water, the major premise and minor premise, the periodic table, what a way to learn crap! The most important thing: the cows."

"And you were lousy."

"What do you mean lousy?"

"Old man, remember that you barely caught two or three that were worthwhile, and they weren't that great either. Guillermo quit messing around; there must be a place where we can get a bellyful of seafood!"

"There is," he says, and stands up slowly, like he used to do in school when he was excited about something. "Lorenzo's house. He's a fisherman friend of mine. You'll see. The only person worth anything in this crappy resort town."

When he has the key in his hand and is ready to open the car door, a guy walks by leisurely and greets him with a nod and a "Good morning, don Guillermo," Fats replies disinterestedly, but with a smile and comments that this guy is also a good person, but not as good as the other. He lifts his head up to the sun and comments, over the roof of the car:

"What a beautiful day! I'm so hungry, my friend! We had to catch them after lunch," he recalls, smiling as if he'd just made a discovery, and then slides into the seat of the car and opens my door, "Most of them could be found in the shady corner of the yard."

"They didn't like the sun," I finish.

He silently nods a number of times and starts the engine. He heads out with the same leisureliness with which he does everything else.

"And they only lasted a day, for fuck's sake! We hid them under the bench, with the books, but by the next day there were none left. Maybe they flew away," he conjectures, with a happy, but indecipherable gesture. "Fuck, how outrageous! Lots of jerks laughed at us."

"And what did you expect? Remember that the one who was most interested in our hunting pursuits was Fermín Marín . . ."

"The only guy on the entire planet who was more stupid than Rudyard Kipling," we said, in unison, gravely, and burst out laughing.

The street is deserted. Guillermo drives without haste, reclining in his seat, his hands and body visibly relaxed, as if the car were driving itself.

"For fuck's sake!" he repeats, but doesn't add anything, so he must still be thinking about our hunting escapades.

He veers right and I stop paying attention to him because I'd rather look at the rocks and I especially like black rocks when the sun is shining on them. We drive toward some really large ones, right where the road ends.

"The house is back there. We have to walk about a block and a half. Lorenzo has two daughters."

"Pretty?"

"Don't be immoral, my friend, you're on a honeymoon," he replies as he looks at the trail. "The older one is really ugly, but has nice legs. The young one is a beauty. And the old woman, the mom, still looks pretty good."

We start descending toward the beach cutting across what seemed like luminous breaths of the sea, smelling of kelp, of rock, of salt crusts and bird droppings. Guillermo walks quickly ahead of me. He's carrying a box the size of a shoebox that doesn't look very light. I get a few gritty grains of sand in my shoe, which I remove by sticking my index finger between the leather and my sock after trying three times. I'm in the process of cleaning my dirty finger on my pants when I see the hut erected under the shelter of a great rock, and two dogs barking aggressively rush toward us. Guillermo tells me that they are friends. And he is right; they recognize him and start jumping around happily.

The family's loving and cheerful reception fills my heart with happy feelings. The affection they feel for Guillermo spills over onto me and I feel welcomed by the warm and loving smile of the two girls and their mother before their fond attention is diverted toward Guillermo again. Lorenzo is not in, but the señora says that he's at the cove; she immediately sends the eldest daughter to tell her father the wonderful news of our arrival. She then insists that we go into the house to shelter ourselves from the cold breeze, and only stops insisting when Guillermo smilingly reminds her that we are not weaklings and adds that on a morning like this no one could get him between four walls.

We sit outdoors around the table that they use when the weather is good. The señora doesn't take her eyes off the box Fats has brought with him. The weathered wood table, cracked and faded by the outdoors, increases the pleasure of the morning. The señora sits with us, watching us warmly and sends the pretty daughter, who cannot stop staring at Guillermo, to look for a tablecloth. Even the two dogs lie down near us occasionally wagging their tail.

"Listen, doña Consuelo," Guillermo complains, "don't send little Consuelo somewhere where I can't see her. The girl is too pretty to be kept hidden."

"Oh, of course," she laughs, "there you have it. The old woman of the house can quietly go and look for things, but not the girls. That's life. Consuelo," she calls out, turning toward the girl who had just left the house with the folded tablecloth in her hand, "come and sit here next to don Guillermo, he doesn't want to be alone with old women."

The girl blushes deeply and starts to open the tablecloth. She has big eyes, intensely green in the beautiful olive-skinned face and graceful waist; her breasts, whose weight pushes on the material of her dress when she bends over, are beautiful and I think she is not wearing a bra. After placing the linen on the table, she sits obediently near Guillermo, her eyes downcast.

The señora says to Fats that it seems like a miracle. They had been talking about him that very morning and thinking that he had perhaps been ill.

"Not at all sick, just stupid, doña Consuelo. Luckily the opportunity to introduce this friend to you came up. He'll be staying for a while at my house and I wanted to leave him in good hands. And another thing—he continues quickly so that the woman won't interrupt him—in addition to being like a brother, he's a big eater and of course, with this morning and the ocean air . . . So I said to him, who could do us the favor of preparing a little something for us at this hour? And here we are. What do you think?"

"Just grateful that you remembered us poor folk. And you are so lucky! We haven't had so much seafood come in since last month . . ."

"So what will you give us?"

"A good licking," says the señora, "and I will not leave Consuelo here for you, because I need her in the kitchen."

The women go into the house and we sit in silence watching the sea. Guillermo raises his hands over his head stretching so much that he reminds me of someone having a seizure.

"Shit, I'm an idiot for not coming to live here," he states, when he's done stretching.

The pretty girl steps out of the house without looking at us and heads in the same direction as her sister before her. She disappears among the rocks a few moments, then reappears and I stop following her with my eyes. Let her keep walking toward a cove that I am not familiar with; it's all the same to me in the happiness of the morning. She'll be back.

"What a beautiful woman! How old is she?"

"About seventeen, maybe eighteen."

The mother sticks her head out of the kitchen and says in a conspiratorial whisper:

"Don Guillermo, Consuelo has a gift for you. She finished it about a month ago. Ask her for it."

"What is it doña Consuelo?"

"A necklace made of seashells; she collected them at Penguin Island. But don't tell her I told you; she'll eat me alive if she finds out . . ."

"Hey," I wonder, "you don't think that doña Consuelo will deny us the seafood and give us acorns and goat cheese instead?"

"What!?" Fats asks.

"I mean . . . It would be natural. As it seems that we are back to the Golden Age and these girls must not be wearing any panties, defended only by their chasteness and honorable upbringing, and here malice has not yet found a contemptible breast on which to rest, and graceful young women are sweetly set up by their loving mothers, and the sweet fruits of the sea and the land are given to the innocent hand without any more work and effort than picking them up, what else can one do but expect cheeses and acorns . . ."

"Miserable, corrupt snake," he answers cheerfully. "Hey, man, it's so good that you are so well and so happy. It looks like something good is happening for you at last."

"Yes, it's happening, my friend, and thank you for lending me your summer house."

"Hell, brother, you look like you are happily on the mend."

"Hmmm," I utter, still looking at the path from which the beautiful girl will return.

"Hey, can I ask you something, man? If you don't want to answer, tell me to go to hell, but . . . do you have something in mind for the future? It sounds like an old woman's question, but tell me."

"Something like what? Do you mean work or what?"

"No, I'm not talking about that crap. I mean other stuff, stuff that matters. Like where things stand with Claudia, stuff like that."

"Glorious, Fats, just glorious," I reply, dodging the question.

But as I say it I remember her intensely and my mind fills with visions. I put her strong, vibrant, and cheerful image in different situations. She's at her door, sending the children off as they leave with her sister. She's in her bed still, lost in thought, dreaming of who knows what. She's taking a shower and the water runs down her body from her neck to her pubis and slides down her thighs, blissful because of the sun, because of the winter, because another day has started. There is nothing more wonderful than a cheerful woman. Tomorrow she will be swimming for kilometers in the sea, regardless of the fierce coldness of the water. I see her floating; I follow her pearly movement and appreciate having a friend like Guillermo. My eyes rise over the water and I can see, like a new discovery, the glory of mid-morning, now mine, high, sunny, clean and solitary.

"You know what I love best about Claudia, Fats?" I ask as I face the sea. "It has never occurred to her to ask me to live together. You know, most women have that compulsive phrase 'I'm so-and-so, pleased to meet you, are we going to live together?' Shortly before coming, it occurred to me to ask her why she had never brought that up. She stared at me and started to cry."

"That woman is crazy," Guillermo is startled.

"Don't speak nonsense, dear friend. She was absolutely right. She felt it was the last straw, that as soon as I got my nose out of the hell I lived in for years, I would tempt her without knowing what I want for myself."

"OK, OK. But, forgive me, my friend, she's still crazy. All normal women believe that they can make us happy."

"Right, exactly. That's what I'm saying. It's wonderful to find one that doesn't think she can do it all, and that will let me just unwind quietly and alone."

"Hmmm, could be, could be. Happy you anyway. I'm actually a little envious."

"Because of Claudia? Rightfully so, Guillermo. Rightfully so."

"Well, also because of her, but mostly for inventing the cow hunting game. Yes, yes," he repeats to himself, "there they are," he exclaims happily and points a finger at the three figures coming down the hillside, "I'll go meet them. Coming?"

"No, thanks."

I gratefully watch my friend's back as he moves away toward the father and the two girls. I am very grateful that he is lending me his summer house. It occurs to me that that was not what I wanted to tell him about Claudia. But I don't care. The morning air is wonderfully bright and blue. I light a cigarette; it tastes different with the fragrant sea air. I put my feet on one of the benches, relax all the muscles of my body, and realize that I am ferociously hungry despite the hour. I swallow a mouthful of saliva at the thought of the seafood that the woman is preparing behind me. It would be a good idea to get some wine. It would be great if they would accept Claudia and me as paying dinner guests. A wave crashes against the rocks in front of me. I have ahead a wonderful seafood binge, many hours of sunshine, many nights and days of contentment and quiet. And tomorrow, Claudia.

DR. JORGE GUZMÁN was born in Santiago, Chile in 1930. After completing his first degree from the Universidad de Chile, he received a Fulbright Scholarship for the University of Iowa to pursue a PhD in literary studies. He returned years later as Distinguished Visiting Professor and was visiting professor at University of Michigan at Ann Arbor, Indiana University, and University of Illinois at Chicago. From 1961 to 1995, he was a professor in the Faculty of Philosophy and Humanities at Universidad de Chile, where he also served as Director of its Centro de Estudios Humanísticos. He has published numerous scholarly works in addition to his works of fiction.

MONICA RUIZ ANDERSON was born in Chile in 1966. As a child, she was plucked from her extended family and exiled to Canada during the brutal Pinochet regime that terrorized her country with the murder, torture, imprisonment, and disappearing of thousands of Chileans. Her father, a supporter of Salvador Allende, was arrested, tortured, and jailed for two years prior to being exiled from his homeland. The family found refuge in Canada. Monica now lives with her husband and four sons in Winnipeg, Canada. She is a faculty member of the Department of Modern Languages and Literatures at the University of Winnipeg. *Job-Boj* marks her debut as a literary translator.

MICHAL AJVAZ, *The Golden Age.*
The Other City.
PIERRE ALBERT-BIROT, *Grabinoulor.*
YUZ ALESHKOVSKY, *Kangaroo.*
FELIPE ALFAU, *Chromos.*
Locos.
JOE AMATO, *Samuel Taylor's Last Night.*
IVAN ÂNGELO, *The Celebration.*
The Tower of Glass.
ANTÓNIO LOBO ANTUNES, *Knowledge of Hell.*
The Splendor of Portugal.
ALAIN ARIAS-MISSON, *Theatre of Incest.*
JOHN ASHBERY & JAMES SCHUYLER, *A Nest of Ninnies.*
ROBERT ASHLEY, *Perfect Lives.*
GABRIELA AVIGUR-ROTEM, *Heatwave and Crazy Birds.*
DJUNA BARNES, *Ladies Almanack.*
Ryder.
JOHN BARTH, *Letters.*
Sabbatical.
DONALD BARTHELME, *The King.*
Paradise.
SVETISLAV BASARA, *Chinese Letter.*
MIQUEL BAUÇÀ, *The Siege in the Room.*
RENÉ BELLETTO, *Dying.*
MAREK BIENCZYK, *Transparency.*
ANDREI BITOV, *Pushkin House.*
ANDREJ BLATNIK, *You Do Understand.*
Law of Desire.
LOUIS PAUL BOON, *Chapel Road.*
My Little War.
Summer in Termuren.
ROGER BOYLAN, *Killoyle.*
IGNÁCIO DE LOYOLA BRANDÃO, *Anonymous Celebrity.*
Zero.
BONNIE BREMSER, *Troia: Mexican Memoirs.*
CHRISTINE BROOKE-ROSE, *Amalgamemnon.*
BRIGID BROPHY, *In Transit.*
The Prancing Novelist.

GERALD L. BRUNS, *Modern Poetry and the Idea of Language.*
GABRIELLE BURTON, *Heartbreak Hotel.*
MICHEL BUTOR, *Degrees.*
Mobile.
G. CABRERA INFANTE, *Infante's Inferno.*
Three Trapped Tigers.
JULIETA CAMPOS, *The Fear of Losing Eurydice.*
ANNE CARSON, *Eros the Bittersweet.*
ORLY CASTEL-BLOOM, *Dolly City.*
LOUIS-FERDINAND CÉLINE, *North.*
Conversations with Professor Y.
London Bridge.
MARIE CHAIX, *The Laurels of Lake Constance.*
HUGO CHARTERIS, *The Tide Is Right.*
ERIC CHEVILLARD, *Demolishing Nisard.*
The Author and Me.
MARC CHOLODENKO, *Mordechai Schamz.*
JOSHUA COHEN, *Witz.*
EMILY HOLMES COLEMAN, *The Shutter of Snow.*
ERIC CHEVILLARD, *The Author and Me.*
ROBERT COOVER, *A Night at the Movies.*
STANLEY CRAWFORD, *Log of the S.S. The Mrs Unguentine.*
Some Instructions to My Wife.
RENÉ CREVEL, *Putting My Foot in It.*
RALPH CUSACK, *Cadenza.*
NICHOLAS DELBANCO, *Sherbrookes.*
The Count of Concord.
NIGEL DENNIS, *Cards of Identity.*
PETER DIMOCK, *A Short Rhetoric for Leaving the Family.*
ARIEL DORFMAN, *Konfidenz.*
COLEMAN DOWELL, *Island People.*
Too Much Flesh and Jabez.
ARKADII DRAGOMOSHCHENKO, *Dust.*
RIKKI DUCORNET, *Phosphor in Dreamland.*
The Complete Butcher's Tales.

RIKKI DUCORNET (cont.), *The Jade Cabinet*.
The Fountains of Neptune.
WILLIAM EASTLAKE, *The Bamboo Bed*.
Castle Keep.
Lyric of the Circle Heart.
JEAN ECHENOZ, *Chopin's Move*.
STANLEY ELKIN, *A Bad Man*.
Criers and Kibitzers, Kibitzers and Criers.
The Dick Gibson Show.
The Franchiser.
The Living End.
Mrs. Ted Bliss.
FRANÇOIS EMMANUEL, *Invitation to a Voyage*.
PAUL EMOND, *The Dance of a Sham*.
SALVADOR ESPRIU, *Ariadne in the Grotesque Labyrinth*.
LESLIE A. FIEDLER, *Love and Death in the American Novel*.
JUAN FILLOY, *Op Oloop*.
ANDY FITCH, *Pop Poetics*.
GUSTAVE FLAUBERT, *Bouvard and Pécuchet*.
KASS FLEISHER, *Talking out of School*.
JON FOSSE, *Aliss at the Fire*.
Melancholy.
FORD MADOX FORD, *The March of Literature*.
MAX FRISCH, *I'm Not Stiller*.
Man in the Holocene.
CARLOS FUENTES, *Christopher Unborn*.
Distant Relations.
Terra Nostra.
Where the Air Is Clear.
TAKEHIKO FUKUNAGA, *Flowers of Grass*.
WILLIAM GADDIS, JR., *The Recognitions*.
JANICE GALLOWAY, *Foreign Parts*.
The Trick Is to Keep Breathing.
WILLIAM H. GASS, *Life Sentences*.
The Tunnel.
The World Within the Word.
Willie Masters' Lonesome Wife.
GÉRARD GAVARRY, *Hoppla! 1 2 3*.

ETIENNE GILSON, *The Arts of the Beautiful*.
Forms and Substances in the Arts.
C. S. GISCOMBE, *Giscome Road*.
Here.
DOUGLAS GLOVER, *Bad News of the Heart*.
WITOLD GOMBROWICZ, *A Kind of Testament*.
PAULO EMÍLIO SALES GOMES, *P's Three Women*.
GEORGI GOSPODINOV, *Natural Novel*.
JUAN GOYTISOLO, *Count Julian*.
Juan the Landless.
Makbara.
Marks of Identity.
HENRY GREEN, *Blindness*.
Concluding.
Doting.
Nothing.
JACK GREEN, *Fire the Bastards!*
JIŘÍ GRUŠA, *The Questionnaire*.
MELA HARTWIG, *Am I a Redundant Human Being?*
JOHN HAWKES, *The Passion Artist*.
Whistlejacket.
ELIZABETH HEIGHWAY, ED., *Contemporary Georgian Fiction*.
AIDAN HIGGINS, *Balcony of Europe*.
Blind Man's Bluff.
Bornholm Night-Ferry.
Langrishe, Go Down.
Scenes from a Receding Past.
KEIZO HINO, *Isle of Dreams*.
KAZUSHI HOSAKA, *Plainsong*.
ALDOUS HUXLEY, *Antic Hay*.
Point Counter Point.
Those Barren Leaves.
Time Must Have a Stop.
NAOYUKI II, *The Shadow of a Blue Cat*.
DRAGO JANČAR, *The Tree with No Name*.
MIKHEIL JAVAKHISHVILI, *Kvachi*.
GERT JONKE, *The Distant Sound*.
Homage to Czerny.
The System of Vienna.

NICHOLAS MOSLEY, *Accident.*
Assassins.
Catastrophe Practice.
A Garden of Trees.
Hopeful Monsters.
Imago Bird.
Inventing God.
Look at the Dark.
Metamorphosis.
Natalie Natalia.
Serpent.

WARREN MOTTE, *Fables of the Novel: French Fiction since 1990.*
Fiction Now: The French Novel in the 21st Century.
Mirror Gazing.
Oulipo: A Primer of Potential Literature.

GERALD MURNANE, *Barley Patch.*
Inland.

YVES NAVARRE, *Our Share of Time.*
Sweet Tooth.

DOROTHY NELSON, *In Night's City.*
Tar and Feathers.

ESHKOL NEVO, *Homesick.*

WILFRIDO D. NOLLEDO, *But for the Lovers.*

BORIS A. NOVAK, *The Master of Insomnia.*

FLANN O'BRIEN, *At Swim-Two-Birds.*
The Best of Myles.
The Dalkey Archive.
The Hard Life.
The Poor Mouth.
The Third Policeman.

CLAUDE OLLIER, *The Mise-en-Scène.*
Wert and the Life Without End.

PATRIK OUŘEDNÍK, *Europeana.*
The Opportune Moment, 1855.

BORIS PAHOR, *Necropolis.*

FERNANDO DEL PASO, *News from the Empire.*
Palinuro of Mexico.

ROBERT PINGET, *The Inquisitory.*
Mahu or The Material.
Trio.

MANUEL PUIG, *Betrayed by Rita Hayworth.*

The Buenos Aires Affair.
Heartbreak Tango.

RAYMOND QUENEAU, *The Last Days.*
Odile.
Pierrot Mon Ami.
Saint Glinglin.

ANN QUIN, *Berg.*
Passages.
Three.
Tripticks.

ISHMAEL REED, *The Free-Lance Pallbearers.*
The Last Days of Louisiana Red.
Ishmael Reed: The Plays.
Juice!
The Terrible Threes.
The Terrible Twos.
Yellow Back Radio Broke-Down.

JASIA REICHARDT, *15 Journeys Warsaw to London.*

JOÃO UBALDO RIBEIRO, *House of the Fortunate Buddhas.*

JEAN RICARDOU, *Place Names.*

RAINER MARIA RILKE, *The Notebooks of Malte Laurids Brigge.*

JULIÁN RÍOS, *The House of Ulysses.*
Larva: A Midsummer Night's Babel.
Poundemonium.

ALAIN ROBBE-GRILLET, *Project for a Revolution in New York.*
A Sentimental Novel.

AUGUSTO ROA BASTOS, *I the Supreme.*

DANIËL ROBBERECHTS, *Arriving in Avignon.*

JEAN ROLIN, *The Explosion of the Radiator Hose.*

OLIVIER ROLIN, *Hotel Crystal.*

ALIX CLEO ROUBAUD, *Alix's Journal.*

JACQUES ROUBAUD, *The Form of a City Changes Faster, Alas, Than the Human Heart.*
The Great Fire of London.
Hortense in Exile.
Hortense Is Abducted.
Mathematics: The Plurality of Worlds of Lewis.
Some Thing Black.

FOR A FULL LIST OF PUBLICATIONS, VISIT: www.dalkeyarchive.com

RAYMOND ROUSSEL, *Impressions of Africa.*

VEDRANA RUDAN, *Night.*

PABLO M. RUIZ, *Four Cold Chapters on the Possibility of Literature.*

GERMAN SADULAEV, *The Maya Pill.*

TOMAŽ ŠALAMUN, *Soy Realidad.*

LYDIE SALVAYRE, *The Company of Ghosts.*
The Lecture.
The Power of Flies.

LUIS RAFAEL SÁNCHEZ, *Macho Camacho's Beat.*

SEVERO SARDUY, *Cobra & Maitreya.*

NATHALIE SARRAUTE, *Do You Hear Them?*
Martereau.
The Planetarium.

STIG SÆTERBAKKEN, *Siamese.*
Self-Control.
Through the Night.

ARNO SCHMIDT, *Collected Novellas.*
Collected Stories.
Nobodaddy's Children.
Two Novels.

ASAF SCHURR, *Motti.*

GAIL SCOTT, *My Paris.*

DAMION SEARLS, *What We Were Doing and Where We Were Going.*

JUNE AKERS SEESE,
Is This What Other Women Feel Too?

BERNARD SHARE, *Inish.*
Transit.

VIKTOR SHKLOVSKY, *Bowstring.*
Literature and Cinematography.
Theory of Prose.
Third Factory.
Zoo, or Letters Not about Love.

PIERRE SINIAC, *The Collaborators.*

KJERSTI A. SKOMSVOLD,
The Faster I Walk, the Smaller I Am.

JOSEF ŠKVORECKÝ, *The Engineer of Human Souls.*

GILBERT SORRENTINO, *Aberration of Starlight.*
Blue Pastoral.
Crystal Vision.

Imaginative Qualities of Actual Things.
Mulligan Stew. Red the Fiend.
Steelwork.
Under the Shadow.

MARKO SOSIČ, *Ballerina, Ballerina.*

ANDRZEJ STASIUK, *Dukla.*
Fado.

GERTRUDE STEIN, *The Making of Americans.*
A Novel of Thank You.

LARS SVENDSEN, *A Philosophy of Evil.*

PIOTR SZEWC, *Annihilation.*

GONÇALO M. TAVARES, *A Man: Klaus Klump.*
Jerusalem.
Learning to Pray in the Age of Technique.

LUCIAN DAN TEODOROVICI,
Our Circus Presents . . .

NIKANOR TERATOLOGEN, *Assisted Living.*

STEFAN THEMERSON, *Hobson's Island.*
The Mystery of the Sardine.
Tom Harris.

TAEKO TOMIOKA, *Building Waves.*

JOHN TOOMEY, *Sleepwalker.*

DUMITRU TSEPENEAG, *Hotel Europa.*
The Necessary Marriage.
Pigeon Post.
Vain Art of the Fugue.

ESTHER TUSQUETS, *Stranded.*

DUBRAVKA UGRESIC, *Lend Me Your Character.*
Thank You for Not Reading.

TOR ULVEN, *Replacement.*

MATI UNT, *Brecht at Night.*
Diary of a Blood Donor.
Things in the Night.

ÁLVARO URIBE & OLIVIA SEARS, EDS.,
Best of Contemporary Mexican Fiction.

ELOY URROZ, *Friction.*
The Obstacles.

LUISA VALENZUELA, *Dark Desires and the Others.*
He Who Searches.

PAUL VERHAEGHEN, *Omega Minor.*

BORIS VIAN, *Heartsnatcher.*

LLORENÇ VILLALONGA, *The Dolls' Room*.

TOOMAS VINT, *An Unending Landscape*.

ORNELA VORPSI, *The Country Where No One Ever Dies*.

AUSTRYN WAINHOUSE, *Hedyphagetica*.

CURTIS WHITE, *America's Magic Mountain*.
The Idea of Home.
Memories of My Father Watching TV.
Requiem.

DIANE WILLIAMS,
Excitability: Selected Stories.
Romancer Erector.

DOUGLAS WOOLF, *Wall to Wall*.
Ya! & John-Juan.

JAY WRIGHT, *Polynomials and Pollen*.
The Presentable Art of Reading Absence.

PHILIP WYLIE, *Generation of Vipers*.

MARGUERITE YOUNG, *Angel in the Forest*.
Miss MacIntosh, My Darling.

REYOUNG, *Unbabbling*.

VLADO ŽABOT, *The Succubus*.

ZORAN ŽIVKOVIĆ , *Hidden Camera*.

LOUIS ZUKOFSKY, *Collected Fiction*.

VITOMIL ZUPAN, *Minuet for Guitar*.

SCOTT ZWIREN, *God Head*.

AND MORE . . .